Waxing
Moon

Waxing Moon

H. S. Kim

WiDō Publishing

WiDō Publishing
Salt Lake City, Utah
www.widopublishing.com

This is a work of fiction. Any resemblances to actual people, living or dead,
is purely coincidental.

Cover Design by Steven Novak

Print ISBN: 978-1-937178-38-3
Library of Congress Control Number: 2013946684

Printed in the United States of America

"For Bernd"

"Our remedies oft in ourselves do lie,
Which we ascribe to heaven."
—Shakespeare

Part One

MRS. WANG, THE ONLY MIDWIFE IN THE VILLAGE, HAD been notified at the onset of Mistress Kim's labor, but she arrived a day and a half later in a leisurely fashion.

Nani, who received Mrs. Wang, had no chance to break the news to her, because the massive midwife in her late forties began to complain as soon as she stepped into the courtyard: the road condition was miserable, her back ached, and her eyeballs burned from lack of sleep. Besides, the baby she had just delivered was the size of a calf, she added, following Nani, who led the way with a lantern in her trembling hand.

It was a moonless night and quiet except for the occasional hooting of an owl perched on an old pine tree beyond the formidable stone walls that surrounded the property. Mrs. Wang cursed as she tripped over a stone, and she spat on the ground to cast away an evil spirit lurking in a corner, which she thought she almost saw. Her stomach growled, so she slapped her belly and said, "Keep quiet."

Nani stopped in front of the quarters where two pairs of shoes were arranged neatly, as if they were being displayed for sale. One was made of straw; the other was adorned with embroidery on the front and back.

Mrs. Wang exercised her stiff neck demonstratively. The maid, having not slept in many hours, yawned and began to announce the arrival of the midwife in a habitual manner, momentarily forgetting that only a few minutes before, Mistress Kim had given birth to a girl and then died with her eyes wide open. She started out matter-of-factly, but in the middle of the sentence her voice went hoarse as she remembered her mistress's final moments. The poor woman had held her and another maid named Soonyi by their wrists for hours until suddenly she let go of her grip, leaving purplish rings, and she had tried to say something, but her immobilized tongue choked her. During the labor her cry had sounded like the howling of a beast, and it still echoed in Nani's head.

No reply came from inside the room. Mrs. Wang took off her shoes impatiently and ascended to the antechamber, made of a century-old juniper tree. Nani remained behind, arranging Mrs. Wang's shoes on the stone next to the other shoes, and then lingered there. It was eerily quiet, and yet the air felt stuffy, as though an overcrowded party had just ended.

Mrs. Wang forcefully opened the latticed door. Two candles on a low table swerved in a synchronized motion as the breeze entered the room through the open door. At first, nothing was visible except the area around the low table, but the odor that met Mrs. Wang's nostrils quickly told her what had happened.

After a few moments, Nani entered with the lantern. Soonyi was sitting in the corner, seemingly as still and lifeless as a sack of grain, her eyes glittering with profound fear.

Mrs. Wang sat to feel the pulse of the woman on a cotton mat in a pool of her own blood. She dropped the still-warm hand of the unfortunate woman. Then suddenly, she shouted, "Bring the lantern close!" A creature between the dead woman's leg's squirmed. Mrs. Wang picked it up. She slapped the bottom of the baby, who immediately cried at the top of her lungs.

"Hot water, quickly!" Mrs. Wang shouted again. Soonyi sprang up from her corner and rushed out. Still holding the lantern, Nani trembled severely. Her mistress was still looking at her.

"Put that down and go bring linens or whatever you have," Mrs. Wang said sharply.

As she set the lantern down by the low table and left the room, Nani sobbed, her shoulders jerking.

The baby stopped crying when Mrs. Wang gave her a thumb to suck on. Mrs. Wang held the baby a little higher to show the dead woman.

Mrs. Wang felt utterly miserable. She had made a mistake, she thought to herself. Most of the well-to-do people she had dealt with fussed over the smallest signs of labor, so when a male servant, Min, from this house had handed her a letter the day before about his mistress's "excruciating pain," she didn't bother to look in his direction while she tossed millet in the air for her chickens in the yard. He urged her, using his hand gestures because he was mute, to please come with him, but she simply said that she would come when it was time for her to come.

It had happened in the past that, as a less experienced and more sympathetic midwife, she had rushed to the walled households only to find the pregnant mistress resting like a beached whale, hoping for contractions to begin. Mrs. Wang would be guided into a resting area and served meals and snacks and drinks for days on end, sometimes until cabin fever attacked her violently. As a result, she dreaded being summoned by the wealthy: they were predictably unpredictable.

But now, sitting in the room with the dead woman, she felt thoroughly regretful.

There was nothing she could do now, Mrs. Wang told herself. She then said it out loud to the face of the dead woman, as if to protest: "There is nothing I can do." She closed the dead woman's eyes. The tips of her fingers felt moist. She stopped then, not knowing what to do with the moisture on her fingers. The woman's oval face showed a certain pride, even in death. Mrs. Wang tried not to look at her. She didn't want to know her more than she already did.

The baby began to cry vehemently.

"I hate it when babies cry," Mrs. Wang muttered, and then looked about, lest anyone had heard her. She was ashamed, but the only others present were the dead woman and her baby.

The baby Mrs. Wang had delivered earlier was awfully large, and his mother had impressively sized breasts, already engorged, enough to feed twins. Triplets. Maybe she would take Mistress Kim's baby girl for milk for a while. But right at the moment, Mrs. Wang was too tired to think about the logistics of the arrangement.

The two maids reappeared, carrying a bucket of warm water and linens. Mrs. Wang clucked her tongue. She realized they were hardly older than the newborn they were going to bathe. Nevertheless, she told them what to do.

While the maids performed their duties, breathing rapidly, Mrs. Wang suddenly asked, "Do your people know what has happened?"

The two maids hesitated for a moment, glancing at each other uncomfortably.

"Have you swallowed a stone?" Mrs. Wang asked impatiently. "I don't mind tales, but I mind silence. Out with it. Now!"

Nani began to explain in an unsteady voice. Mistress Kim was the first wife of Mr. O, whose fortune and prosperity knew no bounds, except that he had no heir.

"Get to the point!" Mrs. Wang thundered.

So the story was that Mr. O was with his second wife at the moment, and when he was with her, he was not to be disturbed for any reason.

"What a pig," muttered Mrs. Wang.

☽ ○ ☾

Mrs. Wang arrived home at dawn. Her shins wobbled and her back was drenched and her head felt light from lack of sleep. As she opened her wooden gate with its missing hinge, it creaked, and her surprised rooster made an unplanned interjection of the loudest *ko-ki-yo-oo*. Her heart leaped and she almost fell on her buttocks. She was beside herself. Clenching her teeth, she strode toward the cage and took down the sickle hanging loosely. It was the tool used to trim bamboos that grew too tall and obstructed her view of the canyon.

It happened not so quickly as she would have liked. She grabbed the rooster who, intuiting the murderous instinct in his owner, struggled to escape. Mrs. Wang finally managed to chop off his head, which flew into the thicket of bamboo stems. The rooster flapped his wings as if he were winding up propellers to fly. The blood began to spurt out of his severed neck, dotting the ground in a chillingly beautiful pattern.

Mrs. Wang didn't stay to observe her rooster's last moments. Instead, she hurried to the kitchen to put a pot of water on the clay stove. Because she had been gone for so long, no fire was left. Lighting kindling, she murmured impatiently, "Come on. Get going. Good fire."

While the water was heating, she cleaned herself of the animal blood and went into her room to change. A piece of petrified rice cake was on a plate in her bedroom. God only knew how old it was. Overwhelmed with hunger, she devoured it, despite the few spots of greenish white mold that resembled certain winter flowers. Then she lay down on the warm part of the floor, under which ran a heating channel that was connected to the clay stove in the kitchen. Her bones melted on the heated floor and her spirit oozed out of her. While counting with her fingers how many hours she had stayed up, she fell into a deep sleep and woke up many hours later.

Smoke filled her room and the burned smell infuriated her. Cursing life and the gods, she ran to the kitchen, only to witness an empty, blackened pot on the kitchen stove.

Standing there in front of it, she was surprised to find herself strangely relieved. The rice cake she had eaten still felt lumpy in her stomach, and she wouldn't have felt like eating the animal she had killed so impulsively anyway. She hadn't meant to do that, actually. She had never done that before. In the past, she had always made sure that her animals died in such a way that they did not know about their own end. Why had she been so crass with her rooster? Was she going to cook the bird without depluming it? She took the pot off the stove and set it on the dirt floor to let it cool down.

She stepped outside. The sun was high in the sky, and her hens were cooing and flapping their wings, ready to get out of the cage. As soon as their door was unlatched, they rushed out into her yard. She hoped none of her creatures had seen what she had done to the rooster. A sickle wasn't the right tool to use to kill an animal in the first place. But then the brains of chickens were so small. What did they know, anyway? Now she regretted that she had no soup. It would have been good to have something hot. The thought prompted her to go to her vegetable garden in the backyard. She pulled out a few white radishes and shook the dirt off them.

While chopping the radishes, she felt her arms ache. She should make two entries in her journal about the deliveries she had just performed, but she decided to stay near the pot and keep vigil.

When the radish soup was ready, there was a knock on her gate. As she walked toward it, she could see the head of a young man above the gate, as if the head had grown out of the door while she slept.

"What is it?" Unlatching the gate, she asked, annoyed by his blank face.

He made no reply but motioned with his head toward the girl behind him. She was holding a little bundle in her arms. When she saw Mrs. Wang, she smiled broadly, as if seeing an old friend after a long time.

"What is it?" Mrs. Wang inquired once more, but then she realized that the girl was one of the two maids who had assisted her the night before, and the young man was the mute servant who had come to fetch her the other day. The baby must be the unfortunate offspring of the deceased woman. Mistress Kim. Was that her name?

"What now?" Mrs. Wang opened the gate and let them in.

Nani advanced and bragged that the baby hadn't cried at all, sounding like a proud mother.

Min stood in the front yard, gazing at the mountains on the other side of the valley. Nani brought out a letter written by Mr. O, the father of the baby.

The gist of the letter, apart from his excessive apologies for the inconvenience, was that because Mrs. Wang might know a wet nurse, he would let her decide what was to be done with her. He added a postscript: Nani is delivering the fee for the nursing mother.

There were two pouches, one for Mrs. Wang's services of the night before, and the other containing compensation for a wet nurse.

Mrs. Wang took both pouches in her hands. The one for the wet nurse was heavier than the one for herself. Maybe three times heavier. But she said nothing.

"Would you like some soup?"

Nani welcomed the idea. But Min made a gesture, which only Nani understood.

"He thinks we should get going for the sake of the baby," she interpreted for Mrs. Wang.

"I need to take care of my stomach first." The rice cake, she told herself, was hardly food: it was petrified and gave her only flatulence. She had worked hard and the chicken soup was what she deserved after all that work, except that it had vanished. So at least she would have radish soup before she did anything else for other people.

She invited the visitors to sit on the outdoor bench. The maid sat holding the baby, and the young man stood awkwardly, shooing away flies with his hands.

Mrs. Wang brought out three bowls of radish soup with

cold rice and kimchi. They ate ceremoniously, without words.

The meal put Mrs. Wang in a much better mood. So she asked, smiling, "What's his background? Who are his parents?"

"He is an orphan. Was found at the gate, bundled up in a basket when he was only a few months old."

"He is a good soul," Mrs. Wang said quietly. Good looking too, she said to herself.

Nani blushed and offered another piece of information about him. "Min wants to go live in a big city. But he will have to get permission. Actually, he wants compensation from our master for all his work before he goes."

"If he gets to leave with only Mr. O's blessing, he'll be lucky."

Nani said nothing but stared at her young man. Her eyeballs moved rapidly, as if she were dreaming, and then suddenly her eyes brimmed with tears.

Mrs. Wang wasn't a sentimental woman. So she said, "Are you all right? Do you want to lie down?"

Min put down his bowl by the well, sat down next to Nani, and clumsily rubbed her shoulder.

"Don't touch me, you idiot," Nani grumbled, her voice hardly audible.

"What's the use if he can't hear you?" Mrs. Wang didn't like this outpouring of emotion in her front yard. As if there weren't enough tragedies in this world!

"Oh, he can hear better than the creatures in the wild. That's for sure," Nani said.

The young man wiped Nani's eyes with his sleeve. And he moaned and groaned in his throat in an effort to soothe her. Abruptly, Nani stopped crying and spat out, "Idiot!"

"Let's go," Mrs. Wang commanded.

She poured the leftovers into a chipped ceramic bowl for her old dog. Mrs. Wang and Nani, with the baby, and Min began to walk down the narrow, dusty winding road into the valley.

"Oh, Big Sister! How could you do this to me? How could you close your eyes and abandon me?" Mistress Yee, the second wife of Mr. O, cried without shedding tears, frothing around her mouth. She drank water every few minutes and ate plums so that she wouldn't lose her voice and get too exhausted.

"I will not live without you! I *cannot* live without you!" she protested, flailing her arms in the air. Then she accidentally hit her dainty table, four dragons inlaid and lacquered, where she kept her writing brushes and papers. She was sure that she had fractured a finger. Cursing under her breath, she threw a millet-hull filled cushion toward the door. Mirae came in. She had been standing in the hallway, hoping her mistress would stop this nonsensical affair of mourning for Mistress Kim, whom, everyone knew, she had abhorred more than maggots. Mirae liked her mistress best when her mistress was being herself.

Just the other day, upon receiving the news that Mistress Kim had gone into labor, Mistress Yee had ordered Mirae to sew cotton cloth into a doll. Later in the evening, Mirae took the doll to her mistress. Mistress Yee smiled, transfixed, as if she had seen someone on the ceiling. She took a needle and pierced the doll between the legs, and then she handed it to Mirae. "Go bury this in the yard of my enemy." Mirae hesitated, unsure what it all meant. Mistress Yee dropped a bolt of silk on the ground and it rolled out to Mirae's feet. "It should be enough to make an outfit for you. You would look splendid in that color." Mirae took the silk and the doll and waited in her room until the owl hooted. She walked out in the jet black night with the doll and a wooden spatula to dig the earth. The task was harder than she had thought; she had to dig the dry earth without making any noise. She sweated, imagining herself in the silk, the color of an orange azalea. Such a thing was no use to a maid, for she would never have an occasion to wear it, but because her mistress entrusted her with a task so important and private, she felt hopeful. Someday, she thought, her mistress might be able to turn her into an elegant lady. That was a good enough reason to serve her mistress, no matter what she was asked to do. She covered the hole with the dirt and smoothed out the surface. Holding her breath, she tiptoed past Mistress Kim's quarters, from which faint groaning could be heard. When Mirae reported the successful accomplishment of her task, Mistress Yee said nothing, as if it no longer mattered.

Now, Mistress Yee moaned theatrically. "I must have broken my finger. Oh, gods, help me."

"Let me see it, Mistress," Mirae said, squatting down very close to examine her lady's finger.

"Don't touch me with your filthy hand!" Mistress Yee frowned.

Mirae knew that her mistress would menstruate any day now, but still she was taken by surprise. She had thought that they had become friends, even if in secret. She had devoted herself to her mistress even when it had meant risking her own life. For the first time, her blood boiled with hostility. She despised Mistress Yee for fussing so much over a minor scratch.

"Fetch me some potato meat to apply to my finger. It's swelling. Can't you see?" Mistress Yee cried, lifting her middle finger in the air.

Mirae sprang up and went to the kitchen where a huge cast iron pot was on the stove in which mugwort was being steeped to bathe the corpse. The aroma filled the kitchen. She took a deep breath and began to peel a potato. Then she raised a stone pestle and aimed at the potato in the stone mortar. At that moment, Nani entered the kitchen, out of breath and pink in the face. She had just returned from a trip with Mrs. Wang to drop off the newborn at Jaya's house.

Ignoring Mirae, Nani sat in the middle of the kitchen and sighed. In a minute she began to sob, thinking of Mistress Kim, her kind-hearted mistress. She felt exhausted. The situation had overwhelmed the young maid. Wiping her eyes, she got up and filled a gourd with water.

Mirae, almost done with crushing the raw potato, said, "My mistress broke her finger. She is in mourning."

"That's an interesting way of mourning," Nani commented and drank the water, dripping from both sides of her mouth onto her flat chest.

"Well, she was crying so hard. Wildly lamenting the death of your mistress. She was delirious and fell on her finger," Mirae said, wondering why in the world she was making up the story for the sake of her mistress. *What is the matter with me?*

"Heaven knows your mistress hated mine. As good as my dear lady was—she didn't speak harshly of anyone, including your mistress, in spite of all her ill intentions and deeds—I know that my mistress will not rest in peace. She will watch over her little one," Nani said and walked out of the kitchen. Beyond the threshold, she turned around and pointed out, "By the way, potato meat isn't for broken bones. It's for bee stings."

Mirae looked down at the crushed potato and wondered what remedy was for broken bones, but then she realized her mistress didn't have a broken bone. She snickered to herself. Her mistress just had a swollen finger, not even really swollen, so it didn't matter what she was crushing in the mortar.

She took a gob of potato paste and put it on a piece of gauze and carried it carefully to her mistress. On the way, she saw a group of people entering the gate. One of them was a professional wailer, another was carrying a bundle of bamboo sticks for the mourners, and another held an armful of white hemp clothing. Outside the gate, there was a banner made of cloth to indicate that the house was in mourning. But, oddly, the rice offering for the soul-escorting devils was missing.

"My lady, here is the potato paste for your finger," Mirae said, sitting down in a spot not too close to her mistress.

Furrowing between her eyebrows, Mistress Yee inspected the potato paste, which was already turning slightly brown. Then she said, "Put it on my wrist."

"Didn't you want this on your finger?"

"I changed my mind," she replied, and put her right hand out to be attended to.

Confused, Mirae put it on her wrist.

"That feels awful." Mistress Yee scowled.

"Soon it will get better," Mirae comforted her mistress.

"Now, go out and tell whomever you run into that I have a broken wrist, and that I have lost my voice from crying since this morning at the news of Mistress Kim's tragic death. You can cry, too, if you want. Go. What are you looking at? Do I have something on my face?"

"No, my lady, I am going," Mirae said and left.

What was on her mistress's mind? Mirae was still confused. In the yard, she saw Mr. O watching his cousin climb up the ladder to the tile roof with Mistress Kim's silk coat. When it was properly hung from the eaves, Mr. O shouted his first wife's name three times. Then his cousin carefully brought the coat back down and gave it to Mr. O, so that he could deliver it to dress Mistress Kim.

Mr. O looked a few years older than he had the day before. No residue of tears but he certainly looked shaken up.

In Mistress Kim's quarters, two maids were helping the hired undertaker bathe the corpse in steeped mugwort water. Her clipped nails and her hair from her comb were collected and put into five silk pouches. While the undertaker bound the feet and hands of the corpse tightly, the maids tidied up the room and waited for a male servant to bring the coat of Mistress Kim. Instead, Mr. O entered. The maids jumped up and stood by the sides of the corpse. He dropped Mistress Kim's coat on the floor and cleared his throat. He looked at his wife for a brief moment and left at once without a word.

The undertaker stuffed the mouth of the corpse with three spoonfuls of rice and put a coin in her sleeve to ease her journey to the next world. The hired mourner began to wail a sorrowful tune. Finally, both maids covered the corpse with her coat, dabbing at their eyes with a cotton cloth.

Walking around the yard, Mirae realized that no one was available to hear the tale of her mistress. Everyone was preoccupied with Mistress Kim. She went back to Mistress Yee and lied to her for the first time. She said that everyone knew how much she was suffering.

☽ ◯ ☾

To escape the sweltering afternoon heat, Mrs. Wang sat under a weeping willow by Sunset Lake on the way to a party at the home of the peasant family who had been taking care of Mistress Kim's infant girl.

She devoured a cucumber to quench her thirst and sang a song, the only song she knew by heart from her childhood.

A ri rang, A ri rang, A ra ri yo-o-o-o.

Her mother had sung this song to her as a lullaby, even though the lyrics were about unrequited love, until she was quite old—eight or nine. When she was ten, her mother married again, a traveling actor this time, and vanished from her life. So she was left with her grandmother, who was a midwife, not by training but by her experiences over the years. Her grandmother taught her how to read and write. She also taught her how to ease the pain of shrieking women and how to deliver babies. She told her to make an entry in a journal after each delivery. "You learn tremendously from reviewing and writing about your experiences," her grandmother emphasized.

When Mrs. Wang was sixteen, there was a flood in her village. She and her grandmother had to relocate themselves temporarily to a relative's house. On the way there, Mrs. Wang had to lift her long skirt so as not to get it wet. A young man witnessed the beautiful shape of her bare ankles from the corner of his house, and he fell instantly in love with her.

He wrote a poem about her anklebones resembling baby peaches and so on. He had his servant deliver it to Mrs. Wang, who read it and was unmoved. She tossed the poem into a chest where she kept some of her mother's things and never looked at it again. But the young man fell gravely ill, longing for her reply. He lost his appetite and developed a fever and talked to himself constantly. His parents thought he was possessed by some evil spirit, so they threw a bowlful of rock salt at him every morning and put a knife under his pillow every night. But he only grew worse. He looked out the window for hours every day and would not respond to simple questions.

His parents learned from a male servant what ailed their son. When they learned about Mrs. Wang's family background, they urged their son to forget about her. Of course, he couldn't. So his father locked him in the grain storage room and starved him from one full moon to the next. He came out unswayed and looking better than when he had entered, so the father said, "Maybe this is his fate."

The mother of the young man visited Mrs. Wang's grandmother, who eagerly agreed to the marriage proposal. Mrs. Wang, however, had no intention of marrying anyone, especially the young man who wrote the miserable poem that didn't rhyme. But her grandmother said that she wasn't going to live forever. So Mrs. Wang was forced into the marriage. But she was determined not to have a baby, for she knew what it was like to give birth. Whenever her young husband came near her, she beat him notoriously. Once, she dragged him to a young dogwood tree in the yard and tied him to it. He wrestled with the tree to free himself and finally uprooted it. Still tied to the dogwood, he walked around to find someone to untie the rope that bound his torso to the tree. The sight of this young husband made a scene, and the story had traveled all over the village by sunrise. His parents decided to lock their daughter-in-law in the grain storage room, but Mrs. Wang fled with her belongings in a sack.

She settled down in this village, where no one knew of her past. She had to pawn her mother's gold chrysanthemum hairpin to get a room. She worked hard and earned the reputation she now had. She was generous with the poor and proper with the rich. She was also a counselor for those in trouble. Fifteen years before, just once, she had made her way back to her hometown to see her grandmother. The old woman had gone mad and lost her teeth. She didn't remember her own granddaughter. Mrs. Wang asked her for forgiveness, and her grandmother said something, but without her teeth, what came out of her mouth sounded like "Go to hell." Mrs. Wang replied, "I am not afraid of hell, Granny. But I am afraid to see Mama in hell. She might very well be there for abandoning her only daughter, and I for abandoning my own grandmother." She placed her mother's gold hairpin, which she had retrieved from the pawnshop when she had earned enough money, in her grandmother's palm, and dragged her heavy feet away. That was the last time she had seen her grandmother.

Mrs. Wang felt the heat rise from the earth as the sun settled high in the sky as she remembered her grandmother. She thought she'd better get going before it got too hot. There was a good-sized carp swimming under the water. Taking a nearby stone, she threw it at the moving fish, but only water splashed on her. She laughed at her own ludicrousness. But the water cooled her down and made her feel much better.

The corn stalks on the way to the peasants' house were taller than Mrs. Wang. She could already smell food, probably fried scallion patties, as she neared the thatched-roof mud house.

"Here I am," Mrs. Wang thundered at the entrance.

"Please come in, Mrs. Wang. Thank you for coming to our humble home," said Dubak, a copper-faced farm worker with a simple smile as he bowed down.

"Ah, Mrs. Wang. You are here already and I am not half done with cooking. Please have a seat." Jaya came out into the yard from the kitchen with Mr. O's baby in her right arm and a spatula in her left hand.

"She is doing quite well, Mrs. Wang." Jaya smiled broadly, showing the baby to her. "I really thought she wouldn't make it. She was so small and weak in the beginning. But with my milk, look at her. She is thriving. Drinking more than my son. She sometimes leaves none for him...." She went on and on.

"How are you doing?" Mrs. Wang asked to divert her attention.

"I am doing fine, Mrs. Wang." Jaya smiled again.

"Are you carrying another?" Mrs. Wang asked bluntly, looking at her midriff.

"Yes, I am." Jaya's cabbage face turned purple. Naturally large, people often thought that she was pregnant when she was not.

Mrs. Wang cleared her throat. No children, no trouble had been the motto of her life, but there were people with a different outlook on life. So that was that. But right now, hunger pinched her stomach.

"Smells good here. I smelled fried scallion patties from the corn field," Mrs. Wang said. She was sitting on the raised floor at the entrance to the hut. Flies were buzzing around the food, which was covered with a hemp cloth.

"That's why I married her. She makes the best scallion patties in the village," Dubak said, dropping a bundle of potatoes in the middle of their yard. "Mrs. Wang, I would like you to take this. These potatoes taste like chestnuts. So flavorful they melt in your mouth," he said proudly.

"I appreciate your gift, but my aging legs are not as agile as they once were. I can't carry that sack back home. I will take a few," Mrs. Wang said, examining the cooked potatoes peeking out from under the hemp cloth on a low table.

"I will carry it for you."

"What did I do to deserve that?"

"You brought my son out to this world. He is such a good sleeper. He is sleeping right now by the way. But I must say, and forgive me for saying this, but Mr. O's daughter keeps my wife awake all night. Every night, she cries several times. My son and I sleep through thunder. But the baby girl's a very delicate sort," Dubak said, scratching his head vigorously.

Mrs. Wang quickly understood that the invitation to their son's one-hundredth-day birthday had a flip side. They were also wondering when another money pouch might find its way to them from Mr. O.

"Tomorrow is her hundredth day. We wonder if it will be all right to celebrate hers the way we do, or do they have something else in mind? Commoners like us don't know how to imitate the nobleman's way of life. Besides, we don't have the means to do it anyway," Dubak said, pulling his hair. "My wife says we should take her home for the occasion, so that they can see how well she has been fed and taken care of. But I say no, we can't go uninvited, even though we care for their offspring."

"I get your meaning. But I thought you were paid. I mean, your wife was paid for the entire period of nursing the baby up front. Is that not true?" Mrs. Wang asked, raising her caterpillar eyebrows.

"Yes, of course," Dubak answered. "But that's not—that's not what I am wondering. It's not the-the money," he stuttered.

"Of course it's the money," his wife interrupted. "Mrs. Wang, we are commoners. And I can only speak as a commoner. I was paid for nursing their baby. It's true they paid enough money for that. But is milk all that a baby needs? She needs clothes, she needs…" She couldn't think of what else a baby needed. "Personally, I am a little concerned that no one has ever come to see how the baby is doing. What if they don't take her back when she is done nursing? Are we stuck with her? I would like to know. What if another baby comes along? I can't care for this baby long unless—" She stopped her speech there.

"I will deliver your message. I just didn't know I was here for that mission." Mrs. Wang scowled.

"No, Mrs. Wang. That's not why we invited you. Please sit down," begged Jaya.

She brought more food to the table and then sat down across from Mrs. Wang, encouraging her to please take the chopsticks. When Mrs. Wang finally succumbed to tasting the food, Jaya pulled out her large breast to give to the whimpering baby girl.

"Do you like my scallion patties?" Jaya asked, a grin spreading across her face.

"Heavenly," Mrs. Wang replied as she picked up her third one. Right now, a bowl of mud would be delicious, she thought to herself.

After devouring half a dozen scallion patties, Mrs. Wang gulped down a large bowl of milky white rice wine. She was in an excellent mood. She burped and then she wanted to take a look at the babies. Jaya brought them close and Mrs. Wang examined them. Like his mother, the boy was double-chinned, twice the size of Mr. O's daughter. She was alert and staring at Mrs. Wang as if she understood what was being said.

"She sucks blood out of me all night long, and then when my baby boy wakes up, there is hardly any milk left for him." Jaya laughed superficially.

"When the mother of the poor thing finds her way to a good place, she will remember your effort. Even though I saw her only after she was dead, I knew she had been a good soul," Mrs. Wang said.

"Oh, we knew of her excellent reputation. A few years ago my husband was hired to escort her to her grandfather's funeral in her hometown. He said that Mistress Kim was more queenly than the queen of China," Jaya said.

Mrs. Wang got up, leaving a few coins on the table.

"What is this, Mrs. Wang?"

"Buy something for your son. What's his name?"

"Sungnam is his name. Star of the South," Jaya said self-consciously.

"A good name that is," Mrs. Wang said.

Dubak got up from the yard, where he had been mending his straw shoes. He put the sack of potatoes on his shoulder and a towel around his head.

"Are you sure you want to walk back with me with that on your shoulder?" Mrs. Wang asked.

"When you bite into one of my potatoes for dinner, you will be happy you let me carry this for you." He smiled, showing his horsey, square front teeth. He was already sweating. The blazing sun was still fastened in the middle of the sky.

Mrs. Wang led the way, thinking of the name of the boy, Sungnam. Southern star or northern star, he is a peasant. And a peasant is a peasant, she said to herself.

By the time she arrived home, the sun was heading west, and her animals were not excited to see her. The heat had been too much for them. She should have left more water, she thought, looking at the bone-dry bowls in the yard.

DR. CHOI ARRIVED AT MR. O'S HOUSE TO EXAMINE MIS-
tress Yee. She was sure she was pregnant. This wasn't the first
time she had thought she was pregnant. The other two times,
Dr. Choi's diagnoses had put the household in a somber mood
for a few days.

Mr. O was in his room, tapping his thin brass pipe on the
ashtray and fidgeting a little.

In the hallway outside Mistress Yee's room, the maid stood
behind the latticed door while the doctor felt Mistress Yee's
pulse. A few seconds later, the doctor nodded.

"What do you think?" Mistress Yee asked impatiently.

"Mistress Yee, you are indeed pregnant," the doctor
announced dryly.

"Of course I am," she said. I didn't need an old frog like you
to tell me that, she thought to herself. "Now you go and tell
my husband what you've discovered," she ordered him, without looking in his direction.

The doctor was amazed by her audacity. She looked half
contemptuous, half amused, and she gazed into thin air, as if
seeing something invisible, something only *she* had the power
to see. The doctor stood up, cleared his throat, and walked
out, looking grave.

A tray of plum wine was brought in for the doctor and
Mr. O, whose face was all mouth, from one ear to the other, at
the news. He was not getting younger and felt that this was a
divine gift, finally.

"Thank you, Dr. Choi, thank you," Mr. O said, as if it had
been the work of the doctor that his wife was pregnant.

"Mistress Yee is in good spirits, and by nature she is very strong. She will have no trouble carrying this through to the end," Dr. Choi said, remembering his first wife, Mistress Kim, whose sudden death confounded him, for her constitution had been in excellent harmony despite her delicate frame.

"I was sorry to hear the news about Mistress Kim," the doctor mentioned. He knew that it wasn't the right moment for condolences, but he couldn't stop his tongue once it got started.

"Poor woman. She was good through and through," Mr. O said. There was a tinge of melancholy in his voice. "Please," he said, recommending more plum wine to the doctor.

☽ ○ ☾

At that moment, Mrs. Wang was on her way to Mr. O's mansion. She thought her legs were going to break, the way she had recently walked miles and miles on low fuel. She sat under an old pine tree and listened to the silence of the earth. It was good to sit in the shade. She looked inside her pouch, where no more cucumbers or rice balls remained. She never carried enough food.

Out of nowhere, a deer appeared. Its innocent eyes stared at Mrs. Wang intently, making her feel rather uncomfortable. She pretended she was a statue, fearing she might frighten the little creature. She remembered she had bought deer meat from a hunter once and it was the best thing next to beef, but right now she wasn't in the mood to strangle this little creature. There was something about the deer or, perhaps in the atmosphere, that prevented her from acting hastily. She held her breath and stared back at the deer. *Those eyes.* She had seen them before. Lurid and sad and silent. A large pinecone dropped on Mrs. Wang's head, shocking her, and she jumped up. The deer ran away. Mrs. Wang sighed.

Her legs wobbled as she walked downhill toward her destination. The night before, she hadn't been able to sleep for some reason, and during those sleepless hours, she had thought of one wish: when she grew really old and it was time for her to go, she wanted to die instantaneously, in her sleep, without knowing it. That would be a blessing.

She approached Mr. O's vast land with its colossal grove of trees, and she listened to the loud and monotonous a cappella singing of summer insects. All of a sudden a young lad jumped out of a field screaming, with a leech on his leg. Mrs. Wang took a stick and removed the bloodsucking creature. She said, "Reserve your screaming for the end of the world. It's just a leech."

"I am sorry, Mrs. Wang. I was terribly scared," he apologized.

A woman shouted from the field, "Mrs. Wang, we are having some food. Why don't you join us?"

Mrs. Wang looked up into the sky to see what time it might be, and thought, people can wait but food can't. So she joined them for lunch. The farmers and Mrs. Wang passed the weathered *Jang Seung*, totem poles. Three offering bowls of rice, with incense planted among the grains, were lined up in front of the totem poles, whose grotesque expressions were varied but muted, with faded colors and chipped noses.

The farmers met up with two women carrying trays of food on their heads. Steamed barley and young pumpkin leaves and bean paste and green chilies were their lunch. The farmers ate and talked and laughed and shouted with their food in their mouths.

"Hope we will have enough rain this year," a woman said as she stuffed her mouth with steamed barley wrapped in a pumpkin leaf.

"Last year was terrible. The brittle surface of the field cracked at the end of the summer. How many lizards and snakes did the children find, all dried up on the rocks and paths? It was just awful. Do you remember?" a young lad said.

"What kind of crops the earth yields is up to the gods," said another woman.

"That's right," agreed a man.

"What brings you down here, Mrs. Wang?" the woman asked, her cheeks bulging with food.

"Some business with Mr. O," Mrs. Wang answered.

"Is Mistress Yee pregnant?" the second woman asked, grinning.

"So soon after the death of the first wife?" a voice asked.

"Who would have thought that Mistress Kim would die so young? What a pity. She was a good lady. What use are gold and silver and a nobleman's title? When the devil takes your life away, there is nothing left to boast about," another man said.

"She was not like the second mistress, for sure. But whose life does the devil take first? There is no such thing as fairness. Enjoy your life while it lasts. The dead know no pleasure," a sinewy farmer said caustically, staring intently at the woman on the opposite side.

"Mistress Kim had the eyes of an innocent doe," a woman said, pouring rice wine into the bowls.

☽　○　☾

It was Mistress Kim whom Mrs. Wang had seen under the pine tree. The doleful eyes even when her breath had left her. The thought chilled her bones. Uncharacteristically quiet, Mrs. Wang took one of the bowls brimming with rice wine, which was meant for the men, and drank it until the bottom of the bowl was exposed. Without thanking her hosts for the meal, she got up and walked away like a sleepwalker.

In no time, she arrived at Mr. O's southern gate, which seemed oppressively massive. She couldn't remember her impression of the place from her previous visit. Before she banged the gate with the circular brass piece that hung in the middle, she took a deep breath. But the gate was flung open suddenly. Mistress Yee was leaving with her maid in a spectacular palanquin. She was all covered up to protect herself from the harsh sunlight.

"Who is that?" Mistress Yee asked Mirae, looking directly at Mrs. Wang.

"Mrs. Wang, the midwife," Mirae answered.

"Did my husband send for you? What an impatient man! It takes a while for the baby to arrive," she said to no one in particular and laughed in a high-pitched voice. And then she left without saying another word to Mrs. Wang.

Stunned by both her striking beauty and her blunt arrogance, Mrs. Wang stood still for a moment and observed the palanquin ambling away. She mumbled to herself, "A rose has more thorns than any other flower." Before she entered through the gate, Mrs. Wang turned around suddenly to have a glimpse of the maid once more. She was dressed in orange silk, an unusual color and fabric for a maid. Perhaps she wasn't a maid. But she was treated like a maid. Mrs. Wang slipped into the gate, thinking the maid was also a thorny rose.

Mrs. Wang took another deep breath. Her left knee throbbed. Her mind was preoccupied with the thought of Mistress Yee. A gorgeous little thing, but with eyes full of malice.

"Oh, Mrs. Wang!" Nani, overexcited, greeted her.

"Here you are. I was hoping to find you. Go and let your master know I am here to see him. Tell him it is concerning his daughter," Mrs. Wang said.

"How is the baby, Mrs. Wang?" Nani asked.

"Couldn't be better," Mrs. Wang replied quickly.

"I am so glad to hear that. Your kindness will not pass unrewarded, Mrs. Wang. I know that Mistress Kim is watching over her baby," Nani said, her face suddenly turning sad, like an old apple.

"I have no time to lose. I have a long way to go back," Mrs. Wang said.

"Please follow me, Mrs. Wang. I will take you where you can sit and wait," the maid said, sniffling.

"Where is Mistress Yee going?" Mrs. Wang asked, following the maid. It was none of her business, but she couldn't stop herself from inquiring.

"She is going to the temple to pray for a healthy son. She is pregnant, Mrs. Wang," the maid whispered.

Feeling a little irritable, Mrs. Wang didn't respond.

The maid disappeared while Mrs. Wang observed the butterflies in the flower garden. Butterflies always fascinated her. The extraordinary designs on their wings seemed to have been printed with some unknown purpose. Without those black imprints, butterflies would not be quite butterflies. Quietly, she tried to catch a yellow butterfly with her two fingers. But the surprised butterfly fluttered away ever so slowly, teasing her. When she was a little girl, she had been equally fascinated but could never catch a single butterfly. She didn't know what she would do if she caught it. What does one do with butterflies anyway?

"Our master invites you to come and see him, Mrs. Wang," Nani said from behind her.

Mrs. Wang followed her, organizing her thoughts and thinking about what she was going to say.

"Mrs. Wang is here," the maid announced.

After a few moments of formal greetings and expressions of gratitude, Mrs. Wang settled down with Mr. O in his sparsely furnished salon. A painting of a phoenix on the wall with a handsome calligraphy read, *Silence Commits No Mistake.* Mr. O lit his pipe. Mrs. Wang stared at him. Something about him, the way he squinted his eyes as he sucked in the air frantically to get the pipe going, reminded her of someone else she had met recently. Tilting her head, she was recalling the manservant. Min, was that his name? Then she shook her head collecting herself.

"What should her name be?" Mrs. Wang asked in her straightforward way.

Mr. O was struck by the way Mrs. Wang spoke with such composed authority. She was surely a hen with no tamer.

"She is without a name. And she looks as though she is going to live for a long time. She needs a name to be called by," Mrs. Wang reiterated.

"Yes, I understand. I will consult the book of our genealogy and send the name by tomorrow," Mr. O said, puffing his pipe rapidly.

"One more thing before I leave," Mrs. Wang said.

"Yes?" Mr. O raised his eyebrows.

"How long would you have the peasant family take care of your daughter?"

"I shall consult my wife and get back to you."

"But she is not your daughter's mother," Mrs. Wang said boldly, looking straight into his eyes.

What Mrs. Wang pointed out seemed to be news to Mr. O, as if he had forgotten entirely about his first wife. One of his ears moved, involuntarily, and then his mouth fumed a white cloud.

Mrs. Wang watched him placidly. He reminded her of her former father-in-law, a chain-smoker. His teeth had been browner than a dog's, and he had coughed so deeply that the hollowness in his lungs resonated. She could have broken his legs, easily, when he wanted to put her in the storage room, but she preferred to run away. Her husband had cried when he learned of her plan. "I am not the only woman in the world," she had said to him to console his broken heart.

"Ah, Mrs. Wang, I know she didn't give birth to the child, but she is her mother now by law," Mr. O finally said.

"I suppose so," Mrs. Wang responded. She had no grudge against Mistress Yee, she told herself. Whatever suits them, she thought.

"The peasant woman, Jaya she is called, is hoping to be rid of any unnecessary burden before winter. But I know you will take care of the matter without my intervening further. I've come only because I arranged your daughter's stay at the peasant woman's so she could be nursed," Mrs. Wang elaborated.

"It hurts me to hear that my daughter has become a burden on the wet nurse and her family. I have rewarded them more than generously," Mr. O said, frowning. Actually, he had forgotten how he had rewarded them.

"Well, I have done my duty. I will go now," Mrs. Wang got up.

"Thank you for all your work, Mrs. Wang," Mr. O said, getting up, too, reluctantly, holding his skinny pipe.

Mrs. Wang walked out of the house, and it was already time for dinner. On the way back, Mrs. Wang sat under the old pine tree where she had seen the doe and waited for her to appear once again, but she only saw a bird defecate from a branch high above her.

AFTER MRS. WANG'S DEPARTURE, MR. O TOOK A NAP IN his bedroom, curled up on his side without a cover. He dreamed that he was watching himself as an ancient man with white hair and a long white beard. He had a cane in his hand, and he could feel the shortness of his breath as he was climbing a mountain. There seemed to be no end to his climbing. In the middle of the mountain, he stopped to look behind him, but, strangely, he was still at the foot of the mountain. He climbed again for a long time. He saw an old pine tree and decided to sit under it. But a woman was occupying the shady spot, so he hesitated to go near it. It was a young woman of bewitching beauty. He realized that it was his first wife, Mistress Kim, as young as when she had first arrived in his house after the wedding. He wanted to say something to her, but looking at his old self, he couldn't. He thought she wouldn't recognize him. He was frightened by the sheer youth of his wife, or rather by his withering self, so he walked backward away from her. But in his mind, he hoped his wife would recognize him, call him by his name tenderly. He fell, tripping over something. He couldn't make himself get up, so he screamed for help. His wife didn't come to help him, and the branches of the pine tree turned into snakes and slithered toward him. He got up quickly and yelled angrily at his wife for not helping him. His wife was nowhere to be found, but a beautiful flower bloomed under the pine tree. The snakes were coming closer and closer to him. He screamed even louder and woke himself up.

His back was drenched and his head was spinning. He was relieved to find himself in his own room. He cleared his throat and tried to say something, but he wasn't able to for a while.

It was still light outside but very quiet.

He sat up and reviewed his dream slowly. It made him angry for two reasons. His wife hadn't come to his rescue, and why had he been such an old man while his dead wife seemed intensely young? What could it possibly mean? And then he thought about the pine branches turning into snakes, the most ominous creatures one encountered in a dream. It chilled his bones just to think of them. But his wife had turned into a pretty white flower, looking magnificent under the pine tree. Mr. O slapped his knee and thought of Mrs. Wang's visit. What was it she had wanted from him? He had to think for a moment. The woman was like a man. Her voice was deeper than his, and her eyes glared like those of a general about to strike his enemy.

After a few moments, it came to his mind. She wanted a name for his late wife's daughter. His daughter. Their daughter. He couldn't recall having seen the baby.

Mistress Kim's funeral had lasted only three days, short-ened from a seven-day event, due to Mistress Yee's insuffer-able pain with her wrist or arm, he remembered now. By the time the funeral was over, the daughter of Mistress Kim had already been sent to a wet nurse.

"One ugly baby," Mistress Yee had reported to him in bed after having seen her. "Can't be a baby of a handsome man like you," she had said, squeezing him hard without warning, which paralyzed his jaw.

He cleared his throat and called out for some help. A male servant came in. Mr. O asked him to get water for his ink and to rub the black chalk onto the stone block to bleed. While waiting, Mr. O thought of the dream once again. It no longer frightened him. But he still didn't feel good that he had appeared such an old man in his dream and his dead wife so stunningly beautiful. She was not that beautiful, he said argumentatively to himself. She had been judicious, intelligent, and well-mannered to a point that was unnecessary between husband and wife.

Mr. O began to write slowly and precisely, *Meehua*, in Chinese characters. He looked at it scrupulously and let the rice paper dry. She might want her baby to be named Beautiful Flower, Meehua. That could be a name for a girl. Not very fashionable.

He smoked for a while, and there was an announcement that Mistress Yee had returned from the temple. She entered before he welcomed her, collapsed next to him, and complained about how hard it was to kowtow one hundred eight times for the health of his son. But she would be, of course, willing to cut her flesh off her body if it were for the sake of their son.

Mr. O massaged his wife's shoulder. She fit into his embrace like a spineless creature; his first wife had felt as stiff as a bamboo stick. He laughed, knowing that Mistress Yee wouldn't have kowtowed one hundred eight times for anything. But one never knew. She might have done it for her son, he thought. People changed. Yes, people did.

"Well done, my little lamb," he said.

"What is this?" She sat up. "What did you write? Is this for me?" A smile rippled around her lips.

Mr. O confessed what it was for. Mistress Yee laughed flightily, showing her white teeth. "You shouldn't do that to that creature. She was as ugly as a forgotten pumpkin in the winter field. This adds insult to injury." She laughed once again but this time indignantly.

Gently untangling himself from his wife's limbs, Mr. O tried to put his calligraphy aside. He was a bit self-conscious about his choice for the baby girl's name. It was definitely unfashionable.

"So what motivates you to do this?" Mistress Yee asked, with a strain in her voice. She would have bitten him if she could.

"The midwife came by this afternoon and demanded a name for the girl," he answered, still thinking about the dream in the back of his mind.

"So you waited until I left to do this!" she cried, raising her eyebrows suspiciously.

"Why are you so upset? I am doing my duty or else I will be mocked. The midwife criticized me already. I felt like an idiot in front of her," Mr. O grumbled.

Mistress Yee wondered if Mrs. Wang was in any way related to the dead whore. She had called Mistress Kim a whore on the nights when her husband had chosen to be with her and Mistress Yee lay alone, consumed with jealousy and a feeling of utter defeat.

"So who is this fatso called Mrs. Wang? Is someone else paying her? What does *she* gain in this game of getting a name for the ugly infant girl?" Mistress Yee asked coquettishly.

"The peasant woman wants another payment, which I will send promptly. I can't let the peasants gossip about me," Mr. O said.

"What do you mean? I sent the woman more than most peasants earn in a lifetime!"

Mr. O lit his pipe and puffed smoke with a blank expression. He wanted to send the name to Mrs. Wang as soon as possible, so that he could forget about it. He knew no other woman like Mrs. Wang. She had stared at him directly, as if he had done something wrong to her personally. In any case, he didn't want to see her again.

NANI WAS ON HER WAY TO SEE MRS. WANG. IT WAS after early breakfast, and the air was clean and so crisp she could almost touch it as she walked on the dirt road up the hill.

Her mother had come with Mistress Kim when she married into Mr. O's family. Nani was an infant when she arrived with her mother, who had worked as Mistress Kim's nanny since her birth. Some years before, Nani's mother had died of pneumonia, and Mistress Kim had promised that she would marry Nani off to a decent man. But unfortunately, Mistress Kim had also passed away. Nani hadn't known how lonely she would be without Mistress Kim, who had shown more gentleness and kindness than her mother sometimes; most of the time actually. Nani had been having dreams about her mistress lately, and she would wake up in the middle of the night, unable to breathe for a moment. Mistress Kim always appeared with so much blood on her face and clothes. "Mistress, why is there so much blood on you? Whatever happened? Speak, I beg you." But Mistress Kim would gaze far away without a word. Then she would collapse and sob heartrendingly, and Nani would scream and wake up. The other maids were irritated by her hysteria so early in the morning.

Birds with bright orange chests were chirping on the branches of trees as Nani passed by. She used to ask her mother how she could fly, and her mother had replied that she would fly if she was born again as a bird. Once, Nani had asked what her mother would like to be born as in her next life. Her mother thought for a moment and said that she would like to be born as Nani's mother again.

Tears bunched up in her throat as she thought of her mother. Her mother would never be born again as her mother, she thought. If she were born again now, her mother would be younger than she was. So how could her mother ever be her mother again?

Nani looked back again and again as she climbed up the hill, swallowing her tears. Then she spotted Min. He was coming, after all. She had told him the night before about her errand, and he had nodded in agreement, but in the morning he was not outside waiting for her. So she left without him. Now he was coming hurriedly, with his mouth slightly open, as if he would say something. Nani didn't look back anymore; she climbed up faster now.

Min caught up with her in no time. Now he was right behind her. She could hear him breathe. Without acknowledging each other they climbed for a while. Finally, she was out of breath. When she reached the middle point of the hill, she decided to sit under the old pine tree. Her chest was rising and falling rapidly, and the blood rushed to her cheeks and lips. Her mouth was completely dry. White flowers stood under the pine tree arrogantly, as if claiming the place as their own.

Min sat away from the tree and was looking down the hill. The sun was already blazing down on their village.

Nani observed Min, who plucked a pine needle from a branch and began to pick his teeth while looking at his dusty toe peeking out of a worn straw shoe. He watched Nani studying the flowers. He moaned, smiling stupidly, baring his front teeth. Tufts of his hair extended in all directions, manifesting how he had slept. He moaned again smiling broadly. Nani sighed involuntarily for something as small as a seed felt stuck in her chest. But her lips curled up.

He got up and Nani flushed, not knowing where to look. He came close—still smiling—picked one of the white flowers, and put it in her hair. *You look as pretty,* he groaned, waving his hand in the air. She shot a fierce glance at him and ran up the hill. Min walked, frowning pathetically with all his facial muscles.

Inseparable they had been in their childhood. But when Nani was no longer a child and Min had begun to develop strong arm muscles, Nani's mother pulled his ear, looked straight in his eyes, and said, "Stay away from my girl. I can't afford to have a son-in-law without a patch of land. You hear me?" All he wanted was to take care of Nani, but he stayed away from her until, serendipitously, her mother died in the middle of the harsh winter. For the first year after her death, Nani was in mourning, the second year she rejected him, the third year she was upset about everything, and now, in the fourth year, she seemed to be mad only at him. But once in a while, Min found a piece of meat tucked under rice or a boiled egg in his lunchbox and his raggedy shirt hemmed.

Min walked a little faster until he noticed that Nani lagged behind. There were thick bushes of mountain berries ahead of him. He picked up a fallen branch and bent the thorny bushes to make it easier for Nani to pass by. Suddenly, Nani screamed frantically. There was a cat snake in the middle of the dirt path, its head cocked but motionless. Min advanced carefully toward the venomous creature. He threw the branch at its head, but the snake was faster than him. It disappeared into the earth.

Nani burst out crying, her shoulders shuddering, but she marched forward. When her crying subsided, Min went ahead of her and opened his palm. It was full of mountain raspberries, some of which had been crushed and bled on his palm. Without meeting his eyes, she picked a few and dropped them in her mouth. They were tart. Min dropped a few in his mouth and gave the rest to Nani.

The last stretch to Mrs. Wang's house was the steepest. Min squatted in front of Nani, inviting her for a piggyback ride. He had done that so many times when she was a little girl, but this was the first time since they had gotten older. Nani hesitated for a moment but got on his back.

Min produced a hideous but familiar moan of happiness and raced up the hill.

Nani held on to his shoulders, which felt like rocks smoothed by the water on the seashore over the years. It was a hot day, but she didn't mind the extra warmth and the moisture on his back. She realized that this was the feeling she had craved for some time, but she didn't connect it with her recent unnamable frustrations. There was no one on earth she trusted more than Min. He was a parent, a brother, a friend, and a husband already, in her mind, though she knew there had to be more to it once Min really became her husband. Her mother had said, "Stay away from him. Once a servant, always a servant. He's got a good heart, but a good heart doesn't get you a roof over your head. You will understand what Mama means later. But don't you forget what Mama says." At that time, she wasn't interested in him, so what her mother said about Min didn't register in her mind. But now she vaguely understood what she might have meant. Once a maid, always a maid. After Mistress Kim's death, Nani had felt completely lost. She was demoted to kitchen maid and was doing errands of all kinds and getting orders even from that stupid maid of Mistress Yee's. She could run away and forget about everything and marry some stranger with a roof over his head, as her mother would have liked her to. But would life without Min be possible?

She slapped Min's shoulder violently and said, "Slow down. I am going to throw up if you go that fast."

Min moaned again with sheer pleasure and adjusted his pace. Nani was as light as a feather. He could run to the next village and not feel tired at all. His heart was burning with desire to do anything for Nani, and yet doing nothing seemed to be what she wanted him to do.

"I want to get down. Let me down," Nani kicked her feet in the air. Mrs. Wang's house was in sight.

Min let her down carefully and felt the chill on his back. She still had the white flower in her hair. No woman on earth could measure up to his girl's beauty.

Before they reached Mrs. Wang's gate, Nani turned around, pulling his sleeve toward her, and asked, "Do you want to run away with me?"

MIN LINGERED NEAR THE ENTRANCE WHILE NANI PRE-sented a piece of paper wrapped in a cloth to Mrs. Wang. It was the name for Mr. O's daughter.

Mrs. Wang unfolded the paper and placed it on the wooden bench. She looked at it for a moment. She guffawed suddenly and thundered, "Beautiful Flower! You can't live on a name like that. It gives you no base to live on. Beautiful flowers last only one season."

Nani sat in front of Mrs. Wang, looking at the writing upside down, and she followed Mrs. Wang's logic and understood it.

"Well, let me put this away for now. I'll get drinks for us." Mrs. Wang got up and went to the kitchen. Nani motioned to Min, who was patting the dog, to come over and sit. He came over reluctantly but didn't sit. He hadn't officially been sent to Mrs. Wang. He had just tagged along with Nani.

Mrs. Wang brought out three bowls of a seven-grain drink. She drank half of hers at once, and then she encouraged them to partake of theirs.

"Was this all you brought?" Mrs. Wang asked, wondering about the payment for Jaya.

"Oh, Mistress Yee said she would send the fee to the nursing mother soon, Mrs. Wang. This afternoon, in fact, Mrs. Wang," Nani said.

For some reason, Nani liked Mrs. Wang. She was fearless and loud and present.

"Sit down and drink," Mrs. Wang said to Min.

So he sat on the stone step where shoes were kept, and he drank, watching Nani intently.

"Tell me something," Mrs. Wang began. "When your mistress was dying—before I arrived, of course—I was with Jaya, whose son's enormous head was stuck and wouldn't come out. Anyway, what exactly happened that night?" Mrs. Wang gulped down her drink and stared at Nani.

"What do you mean, Mrs. Wang?" Nani asked looking puzzled.

"You don't need to say my name at the end of every sentence," Mrs. Wang said emphatically.

"I understand, Mrs. Wang," Nani said. "I am sorry, Mrs. Wang."

Mrs. Wang sucked on the roof of her mouth, but she realized that she wasn't going to change the maid's habit. She drank the last drop of her drink and encouraged them again to drink up theirs too.

"When your mistress was in labor and you thought she was dying, did you just watch her?" Mrs. Wang asked, looking at Nani critically.

"I didn't know she was dying, Mrs. Wa—, I mean, I thought she was in pain because the baby was coming. But Mistress Kim asked me in the evening, a couple of hours before you arrived, Mrs. Wa—, my mistress asked me to go and tell Mr. O to fetch the doctor, but Mr. O had just entered Mistress Yee's quarters. When I went to Mistress Yee's quarters, her maid stood like a guard dog, blocking me from advancing. I told her I needed to tell Mr. O that my mistress was in need of medical attention, but she said that she would tell him herself. I waited around. And then," Nani paused, looking uncomfortable and hesitant.

"And then what?" Mrs. Wang asked.

"And then," Nani began to shed tears, "I went back to my mistress. She was delirious. I kept telling her that the doctor was coming any minute. But it didn't seem she heard me anyway."

Standing by the wooden pole that was holding the front part of the thatched roof, Min observed Nani dry her eyes and blow her nose. He wanted to comfort her but stayed still, scratching his head, stealing a glimpse of Mrs. Wang occasionally.

"And I still see her in my dreams. She always dies with so much blood all over her." Nani sobbed now.

"It wasn't your fault. It was time for her soul to leave her body." Mrs. Wang turned to Min and asked, "Why don't you do me a favor while you are here? Can you split some firewood for me?"

Min grunted briefly in agreement and began to chop a bundle of logs with a maul.

"Mrs. Wang, will you please not tell anyone what I just said to you?" Nani pleaded.

"Why, I am going to shout what you said from the top of the hill." Mrs. Wang chuckled.

"I promised I wouldn't breathe a word about this, Mrs. Wang," Nani said, looking agitated.

"To whom did you promise what?"

"Mi-Mirae," Nani stuttered. "Mistress Yee's maid. She thinks she is a friend of Mistress Yee's. And now Mirae bosses us maids around," Nani grumbled.

"So did she ask you to promise something?"

"Well, not exactly. When Mr. O heard the news of Mistress Kim's death after breakfast the next morning, he must have wanted to know why he hadn't been informed earlier, and why the doctor hadn't been called in. Mistress Yee had told me that I should say, if asked, that Mistress Kim had died suddenly, before we even had a chance to call the doctor," she said, looking uncomfortable.

Mistress Yee hadn't spoken to Nani. It was her maid, Mirae, who had brought her a pair of new shoes and told her to keep her mouth shut or else she would not live to see the last day of her destiny. Nani had rolled her eyes, flabbergasted, at the way Mirae had employed the authority of her mistress. She did inspect the new shoes as soon as Mirae had left. They were beautiful, but they didn't fit her. Out of self-respect, she had to stop herself from running after Mirae and demanding a pair of shoes that fit her. In the end, Nani didn't have to lie about anything, for Mr. O had not asked her about Mistress Kim.

Now Mrs. Wang was asking about her mistress, and Nani realized that Mistress Kim might have been saved had the doctor been called promptly.

Mrs. Wang changed the subject abruptly. "Your boy has a wart on the back of his hand."

"He's got warts everywhere," Nani snapped, and then blushed deeply. She couldn't face Mrs. Wang. Min had another wart on the heel of his right foot. She hadn't meant to say "everywhere." There was no way to prove her innocence, but Mrs. Wang did not look shocked.

"Take a dandelion by the stem, and rub the milky juice directly onto the warts for a week or so. They will go away like snow melts in the spring," Mrs. Wang advised her.

Nani kept her glance away from Min, who was now stacking up the split wood by the chicken cage. There were fourteen new bright yellow chicks in the cage. Min widened his eyes like a child. With a corner of his mouth lopsided, he drooled because he forgot to swallow his saliva. Then a grin spread across his face.

Suddenly, Nani sprang up and said, "Oh, laundry! I need to boil the laundry. I must get back."

"Don't forget the dandelion. Warts spread. Even to other people," Mrs. Wang said as Nani got up.

Nani blushed again. Min bowed down to Mrs. Wang and groaned to thank her for the drink. Nani, still blushing furiously, left with him.

BEYOND THE MAIN GATE OF THE TEMPLE THERE WERE two more gates. Between the second and third gates stood four hideous wooden guardians, two on each side, looking down on visitors with their colorfully painted, bulging eyes. One of them held an iron sword in the air as if about to strike the visitors if they were proven to be unworthy.

This was the second time that Mirae had visited the temple with her mistress. There was something eerie about the place. Now she began to dread spending an entire day there.

Mistress Yee stepped onto the temple grounds. The deafening silence sank in her heart, and she felt powerless. She wanted to feel superior at all times, but in the temple she was made to feel small. It was like stepping into a painting: she became frozen, voiceless, an unnoticeable part of the whole.

The novice monks with shaved heads walked around with their glances low, absolutely unaffected by her incontestable elegance and beauty. Mistress Yee didn't matter. She was just another lump of moving flesh.

As she approached the main hall, she could no longer hear her own footsteps on the sandy path. Instead, the daily chanting of the Heart Sutra and the sound of the wooden hand bells rumbled steadily.

Mistress Yee passed the pagoda. Mirae followed slightly behind her. Mistress Yee took off her shoes and entered the main hall, where visitors were allowed to offer incense and meditate. A colossal brass Shakyamuni was seated in the middle, gesturing with graceful hands. Mirae arranged her mistress's shoes before she took off her own shoes and followed her in.

A young monk was tidying up the cushions on the hard-wood floor inside. The air, centuries old and well tamed, smelled different from the air outside. Mistress Yee didn't like the smell. This room was like a cauldron of wishes and prayers of unfortunate people.

Mistress Yee began to kowtow. After the seventh time, she whispered to Mirae, even though no one else was present, to fan her. Inside was much cooler than outside, but Mistress Yee was having a hard time because of the heat of her own pregnant body. Mirae took out a fan from her pouch and began to fan her mistress drenched in sweat. After the twentieth time of kowtowing, Mistress Yee sat back down on the cushion and didn't want to get up again.

"You do it for me," Mistress Yee whispered firmly.

"What do you mean, Mistress?" Mirae asked, sitting down close to her.

"This is too hard for me. If I keep doing this, I might have a miscarriage," Mistress Yee complained, pouting, and dragged her body toward the wall, so that she could lean against it. "Do it eighty-eight more times," she ordered. Her voice echoed in the hall. Amitabul, with his head slightly bent toward the worshipers, appeared to be smiling mysteriously. Mirae met his eyes and was glued to his benevolent countenance.

"Don't just stand there like a statue. Kowtow!" Mistress Yee shouted, disregarding the fact that she was in a sacred place.

Mirae held her palms together earnestly and went down and up, down and up. She prayed not for the son of Mistress Yee, but for her own sake. She looked up whenever she could to the smooth face of Buddha and cried out inside herself. She didn't want to be a maid; she wanted to be a lady; she wanted to have her own maid, who would fan her, who would kowtow instead of her if she got too tired. Tears and sweat mixed and dripped from her chin.

Mistress Yee, leaning against the wall, dozed off several times. Each time she awoke, she saw her faithful maid performing her duty. Some time later, at the sound of the dull gong that echoed through the valleys of the surrounding mountains, she awoke completely and found no one but Buddha himself, looking down at her sarcastically. His right hand seemed to point outside through the westerly entrance.

Making adjustments to her stiff limbs after having sat in the same position for a while, she got up slowly, furiously. The light outside was blinding. Someone was talking in a voice, deep and low and soothing. It was the head monk in his gray robe, with his wooden beads in his hand. Mistress Yee never liked any of the stupid monks, for they didn't discern her extraordinariness. Seeing her maid conversing with the head monk—with whom Mistress Kim had had a profound relationship and whom she had accused Mistress Kim of having an illegitimate relationship with (which her husband had refused to hear about, as if she had gone mad)—her blood churned. She almost fainted. Mirae was conversing with the monk as if she understood what the baldhead was saying to her. They were standing by Sari-tower, where the calcified remains of the great master from the sixteenth century were interred.

Mistress Yee walked gingerly toward them, feeling a little dizzy and nauseous under the direct sun. When she drew close, they didn't turn to acknowledge her presence. A few moments later, after Mirae bowed to the monk and he chanted a short prayer, they looked at her. Mistress Yee didn't greet them. She bit her tongue. She exhaled looking around at the five magnificent green mountains that enveloped the temple. A volcano was bubbling inside her, but it wasn't the right moment to erupt. Without the annual donation from her husband, this temple wouldn't sustain itself for very long. She could have slapped Mirae for having left her alone, but she was a little intimidated by the luminous atmosphere around the two, who behaved as if they understood a secret that was unavailable to her.

"May I inquire about the wellness of Mr. O?" the monk asked with his eyelids cast down.

Mistress Yee raised her eyebrows to stare at the monk. She could have strangled him for not asking after *her* health. The monk bowed slightly and began to walk away.

Turning crimson with internal fire, Mistress Yee decided to faint, and she fell on her maid to cushion her impact. Mirae uttered a cry of surprise. The monk turned around and didn't panic. He came over at the same pace as he had walked away, lifted Mistress Yee, and carried her easily in his two arms to the main hall. Mirae followed, realizing that her mistress was fully conscious.

The head monk, carrying Mistress Yee in his arms, was reciting something unintelligible. As he laid her on the floor, Mistress Yee felt his breath on her face. She could smell the man in the monk. She badly wanted to open her eyes and see how close this monk was to her face, but she decided not to. Mirae came in and assisted him by bringing a cushion for her mistress's head to rest on. He asked Mirae if she could bring a bowl of cold water for Mistress Yee from the water fountain.

While they were alone in the main hall, the head monk began to speak in his deep voice. But it wasn't clear whether he was speaking to Mistress Yee or to himself.

"There exist three poisons in life: desire, anger, and ignorance. One poison is the root of the other two. To attain enlightenment, you must swallow the root of your poisons, so that you die. You die many times to attain the enlightenment of Buddha."

Mistress Yee opened her eyes and looked up at the monk. He sat near her, with his eyes closed, and his palms met each other near his chest. Now, from below, she could see the packed muscle of his shoulders beneath the robes. His lips were reciting to keep his mind occupied, or unoccupied. Still lying down on the cool wooden floor, Mistress Yee said challengingly, "What is the root of *your* poisons?"

The monk opened his eyes but didn't look at Mistress Yee.

"Did you hear what I said? How many times have you had to swallow your poisons to be the way you are? And how many more times will you have to swallow them to get to where you want to be?"

For the first time, the monk met Mistress Yee's burning eyes. He saw her small feet extending out from under her long silk chiffon skirt. He clenched his teeth and began to chant something—anything—with his eyes closed.

"I wonder what you see when your eyes are closed," Mistress Yee said, getting up. She heard Mirae taking her shoes off outside.

"Please, give the water to the illustrious one. He must be so thirsty from carrying me," she ordered her maid.

Mirae carried the water carefully and placed it in front of the monk. He was still chanting with his eyes closed, his forehead beaded with perspiration.

Mistress Yee said, "Let us leave. I have learned so much from the master. I will practice dying every day, as he has set an example for me today." She bowed toward the monk in an exaggerated manner and then left the hall, smiling triumphantly.

As they descended the stone steps outside the temple gate, Mistress Yee said, "I love this place. I will have to return often."

"That's a wonderful idea, Mistress," Mirae said.

Without turning around, Mistress Yee addressed her maid. "I think the head monk is the handsomest man my eyes have ever beheld. Don't you agree, Mirae? Of course, this is just between you and me."

"Why, Mistress, he is very handsome," Mirae said. Her ears burned. Indeed, he was a handsome man.

"I saw you flirting with him," Mistress Yee stated firmly, raising her voice, still looking straight ahead of her.

Mirae stopped. "Mistress, what do you mean?" she asked, lowering her voice.

"You heard me, Mirae," Mistress Yee said cheerfully.

"No, Mistress, you must have hallucinated. The sun was so strong it must have blinded you. I was just talking with him." Mirae's voice was trembling.

"No, I saw him whisper into your ear."

"Mistress, you have misunderstood the situation," Mirae said. She passed Mistress Yee and stood in front of her, blocking her way.

"Don't panic. I can keep a secret," Mistress Yee teased, walking around her maid.

"Please! I don't mind if you think *I* am low and despicable, but the one we are speaking of possesses the purest heart," Mirae said pleadingly.

"Ha, you are in love," Mistress Yee remarked lightheartedly contemptuously.

"Mistress, I was kowtowing in the main hall, and I felt something strange. In the beginning, I found it tedious and felt tired, but I saw the smile on Buddha's lips. It was—there are no words to describe the smile. That smile was just for me. And then I heard the monks walk by after their daily chanting, so I rushed out and followed them. The head monk was the last in the group and he turned around. I bowed to him, and when the other monks disappeared into the dining hall, I asked if he could spare me his wisdom. He simply said that wisdom is within me. I raised my head and looked at him. I almost fainted because his smile was exactly the same as Buddha's smile. I told him how he resembled Buddha. He just repeated that wisdom is within me and that I should seek answers within, not outside. Mistress, I couldn't speak further. I felt light and happy. And that was when you approached us. There was nothing else," Mirae said. And she sighed noisily.

Mistress Yee turned around and shot a glance at her maid like a cat glares at a mouse in a cul-de-sac.

"Listen to me carefully, and don't you ever forget what I have to say now." Mistress Yee came a little closer and she continued, lowering her voice, "A monkey climbed trees, and hung upside down from branches, and leaped from one branch to another. She was much admired for her dexterity, although it was nothing for her. All the animals down below applauded and wished they could do what she did. Then a dog, losing her head momentarily, thought she could do what the monkey did. She began to climb the tree, despite the advice of her sensible fellow animals, and reached the top of the tree and leaped from there to another tree. Guess what happened to that bitch? She fell on the ground and crushed her head. Only the monkey felt sorry for her. When all the other animals left, murmuring about the stupidity of the poor animal, the monkey remained and buried the dog. She placed a tombstone on the dog's grave and wrote, *May this dog be born in the form of a monkey in her next life*. So in her next life, the dog was born as a monkey. The first thing she did was to climb a tree, but she couldn't because she was still a dog in the skin of a monkey. Once a dog, always a dog. So she died once again by falling from a tree, and as she died, she wished to be born as a dog. It took two lives for this dog to learn a lesson." Mistress Yee laughed and resumed descending.

Mirae followed her mistress quietly. The sun was fierce. Her legs felt tired from kowtowing repeatedly. It would take another hour to reach the point where they had left the carriage with the male servant. Mistress Yee had decided against the ride in the carriage for fear that its movements on the steep and uneven mountain road might imperil her pregnancy.

Mirae wished that her mistress had not told her the strange story. She wanted to shift her thoughts to the head monk and what he had said. *Within myself,* she said to herself again and again.

Mistress Yee stopped. "I cannot walk anymore. Carry me on your back."

Mirae squatted down in front of her mistress. Even though Mistress Yee wasn't terribly heavy, it was still a long way to go.

Once on Mirae's back, Mistress Yee pulled Mirae's hair for her own amusement. And she said a few nasty things about the odor from Mirae's sweaty back. And then suddenly, she reached down and felt Mirae's breast, which was bound tightly under her garment, as the traditional dress required its waistband to go around the upper chest of a woman.

Shocked, Mirae almost dropped her mistress.

Mistress Yee said, "My dear Mirae, if you drop me and I have a miscarriage, you know that would be the last day of your life, don't you?"

Indeed, it would be. Mirae flushed. Her disgust for her mistress's wriggling body on her back was growing by the moment.

"This is totally ready to be touched, Mirae. Next time we go to the temple, you need to bathe yourself before we go, though. Celibate or not, the head monk cares. In fact, celibates are more sensitive. When he carried me into the main hall, I felt the touch of his strong hands. They were firm and ready to be put to a better use. Just imagine what he will be thinking of tonight when he touches his hard, lifeless wooden beads!" Mistress Yee laughed. She continued, "I hope he seeks within to find some of the answers for his desire, for they are there, plain and clear."

"Mistress Yee, I must go and pee," Mirae begged.

"Let me down, you lazybones," Mistress Yee mocked her. "Now, look what you've done!" Mistress Yee cried. Her skirt was wrinkled.

Mirae went behind the bushes.

Mistress Yee walked down alone for a while. Mirae followed her soon enough. They could see Min beside the carriage, chewing on sour grass.

"That useless urchin," Mistress Yee muttered.

Min got up as the women approached and dusted the seat with his hand where Mistress Yee would sit. He tried to help Mistress Yee mount the carriage, but she dismissed him curtly with her hand.

Some time later, they could see Mr. O's land. After passing the grove of tall poplar trees, Mistress Yee ordered Min to stop.

"If I don't eat something right now, I think I will die," Mistress Yee said.

"Go and get some food for the mistress right now," Mirae ordered Min urgently.

"He can't talk. You go!" Mistress Yee shouted.

Mirae ran to the mud house by the cornfield. She was as hungry as her mistress. During their first visit, they had been nourished at the temple, even though her mistress hadn't liked the simple vegetarian food prepared by the novice monks. But today they had left abruptly, and her mistress had forgotten all about lunch.

Min pulled the carriage to the shade under a tree and observed an army of ants in single file going into a hole.

Mirae stepped into the yard and heard a woman laughing. Mrs. Wang sat with a plateful of boiled potatoes on the mud floor in front of the hut. Jaya was nursing a baby with her chest exposed.

"Listen. My lady, Mistress Yee, is outside, starving and exhausted. She is coming back from a trip to the temple. She needs nourishment," Mirae said urgently, frowning from the headache beginning to immobilize the upper right half of her head.

It took a moment for Mrs. Wang to recognize her. Mirae was out of breath. Then she sighed from her gut, mopping her forehead. Her face was a mess and under her armpit was stained with a brown half moon. She even stank a little.

Jaya, in the middle of telling a joke, was confused. "What do you mean?" she asked, inspecting Mirae from head to toe.

"Her mistress would like some potatoes," Mrs. Wang summarized.

"Oh, Mistress Yee is here? Where is she?" Jaya was excited.

"In her carriage. My mistress is exhausted from the heat and from her visit to the temple, where she kowtowed one hundred eight times. Just give me food. I will take care of the rest," Mirae said, feeling suddenly aloof. She was annoyed by the women so at ease and disheveled, one with breasts hanging out under her open shirt, and the other indulging in food with her legs stretched out, her waistband loosened. Flies buzzed round and round.

The peasant woman wrapped two potatoes and some salt on the side and handed them to Mirae.

"Give me a bowl of water too," Mirae demanded.

Jaya passed Mr. O's daughter to Mrs. Wang and went to the kitchen. She brought out a gourd of water and gave it to Mirae.

Mirae left without thanking her.

"That's the infamous maid of Mistress Yee. She thinks she can shit gold or something just because she is favored by Mistress Yee," Jaya said, rolling her eyes.

"She does look like someone who might shit gold or something." Mrs. Wang chuckled.

Mirae took the water and the potatoes with salt to her mistress. Mistress Yee drank the water hurriedly, but she examined the potatoes with suspicion. Abruptly, she shoved the food out of Mirae's hand. The potatoes fell and rolled into the ditch at the side of the road.

As the carriage moved on with dust billowing behind it, Jaya came out, her shirt still open, holding Mistress Kim's daughter in her arms, to find the potatoes in the ditch and her gourd cracked and abandoned. She spat toward the carriage, which was now turning around the potato field that she and her husband rented from Mr. O.

"MISTRESS KIM WAS NOTHING LIKE THAT," COMMENTED
Jaya as she returned and sat down on the open mud floor in
front of the hut.

Mrs. Wang didn't reply. She was peeling the last potato and
said, "Do you have some rice wine? Water doesn't go with
these excellent potatoes."

Jaya dawdled to the kitchen and poured a bowl of rice wine.
She drank a little and burped loudly. It tasted so great that she
had another sip and then took the bowl to Mrs. Wang.

"Mrs. Wang, this is all we've got to spare. We're saving the
rest for my husband's uncle, who will come to see his grand-
nephew, he hasn't seen him yet," she said and then smiled.

Mrs. Wang looked somewhat displeased at the half-full
bowl. But she drank it all at once.

"I saw Mr. O some time ago. He promised me he would send
another payment for your work," Mrs. Wang said.

"Well, in fact, yesterday Nani came to deliver gifts. A sack
of this, a sack of that, and some silk. But Mrs. Wang, we don't
need gifts. We need a payment," Jaya said grimly.

Mrs. Wang noticed a trace of a milky rice wine mustache
above Jaya's upper lip.

"My child, that's out of my hands. I can't force Mr. O to do
what you would like him to do. By the way, your potatoes are
sublime."

"Thank you, Mrs. Wang. Those potatoes go to Mr. O, along
with the rice and corn and beans every year. We pay our share
for their land. And here I am, sustaining their bloodline with
my milk, sacrificing my own son. What on earth am I to do
with a roll of silk anyway?" Jaya rolled her eyes.

"Sell the silk in the marketplace if you don't want to save it for your future daughter-in-law," Mrs. Wang advised her.

"Mrs. Wang, my husband's in the field the whole day. I take food three times daily to the field for the farmers, carrying Mr. O's daughter on my back, while my son takes his naps. When should I go to the marketplace to sell the silk? Who would buy the silk from me? People would think I had stolen it. And they would want a steal of a price! Last night, my husband and I were talking about how nice it would be if we got ourselves a patch of land, just enough to grow corn and potatoes. I would raise Mr. O's daughter as my social superior." Jaya's red face was covered with beads of sweat. Now that she had spilled the truth, she felt worse, because she so badly wanted a piece of land, and Mrs. Wang didn't seem interested in making her happy.

"She is your superior as long as you live on the property of the O family. About the land, as long as you live here and pay your dues, no one is taking it away from you. It is practically yours. Why does it matter to have your name written on a piece of paper? When you die, you don't take the deed with you," Mrs. Wang said weakly. She was also exhausted from the heat, and annoyed by the loud nonsense of the woman whose face was dripping sweat profusely. Most of all, she was hungry, still very hungry after three large potatoes. They were not that large, actually.

"Mrs. Wang, we are hard up these days. My mother-in-law, you know her, she's gone crazy, and my sister-in-law doesn't want to live with her any longer. She is hitting her mother sometimes, I hear. Anyway, to make a long story short, my mother-in-law might have to move in with us. When she moves in, she will be another baby to take care of, another mouth to feed. Of course, whom should I blame but myself? I was born with so few blessings. It's all my fault," Jaya said pathetically, inspecting Mrs. Wang with her apple seed eyes. But there was no reaction; actually, Mrs. Wang was dozing off.

Jaya got up, leaving the infant on the floor, and brought out the jug of rice wine and poured some into Mrs. Wang's bowl.

Mrs. Wang opened her eyes wide and sat up straight.

"His uncle doesn't drink all that much. If I keep it in the kitchen, too much will go to my husband, who shouldn't be drinking anyway. He's got this really evil habit of drinking and then wailing afterward. I can't stand it anymore," she said, forcing a smile.

Rubbing her stomach, Mrs. Wang said, "One should coat the stomach before alcohol. Don't you have a slab of fat or something?"

"Let me check. I think I have a little something here in the jar." Jaya disappeared into the kitchen and came out with a piece of pork fat and a few raw quail eggs.

Mrs. Wang ate the quail eggs and gobbled up the pork fat. She said it was very well seasoned, the pork fat. She drank the rice wine and said that she felt like a little nap, if that wasn't too much of an imposition. So the two women took a nap with their mouths open, the two babies in between them. Flies hovered about Mrs. Wang's unappeasable mouth, sometimes landing on her face, but she slept like a corpse. The afternoon slowly passed, and then the baby boy woke up and whimpered.

Jaya got up, rubbing her eyes and wiping drool off the corners of her mouth. Her hair was matted. She offered her breast to her baby boy. Mrs. Wang snored rhythmically.

Dubak entered then, filthy and sweaty and tired. The wife pointed to Mrs. Wang with her chin, but he, showing no acknowledgment, went straight to the kitchen and came out. He looked about, moving his eyes quickly. His wife said, "What are you looking for?"

He took the jug, which normally contained rice wine. Only a few drops came out.

"There is a little left in the kitchen in the cupboard," she said, lowering her voice.

He went back to the kitchen and didn't come out for a while. The wife, leaving their son on the floor, followed him in and found her husband sitting by the clay stove and drinking.

"Don't drink it all up. Your uncle's coming," Jaya pointed out.

The man pulled his wife close and tried to grab her by her thigh, but she shrilled and stiffened and pushed him away, grinning vulgarly.

"We have a guest," she said, raising her eyebrows. "She is being difficult, though."

Her husband fell into silence. She could see the concentration on his forehead. She didn't like the sudden shift of interest from her plump thigh to something else in his head. He went to a meeting every night with some of the other peasants and talked until late about silly things. "All the aristocrats, can they be aristocrats on their own? No, only because we exist as peasants are they aristocrats. There is no such thing as noble blood. Under the skin, we are all the same. Without us sweating in the field, they would not survive. There would be no rice for them. *We* are not the leeches, living off of *them,* as they would have us believe: it's *they* who live off of *our* lives."

Those were the words frequently uttered, reported Jaya's friend in the field when all the women got together to pluck the soybeans out of the pods. Her husband had hosted several of the meetings at their house.

Dubak gulped rice wine again and said, "I am going to Seoul to get a job." He furrowed his forehead.

"Oh, do shut up," Jaya snapped, snatching the jug out of his hand.

"Is this how you talk to your husband?" He went berserk, ready to throw something at his wife, except that he didn't see anything nearby to throw.

"I thought we are all the same under the skin, husband. *I* shall go to the capital city to get a job if you don't give me the credit I deserve. You should think about what would happen if I left you for the capital city!" she said and left the kitchen. Both babies were crying at the tops of their lungs.

"Heavens! Gods! What is the matter, my babies?" said Jaya theatrically. Her voice finally woke Mrs. Wang. She sat up and combed her hair with her fingers, feeling indifferent at finding herself at someone else's place.

"I need to go and check on Chilpal's wife. Her baby has breeched, and I need to turn it before it gets too late," Mrs. Wang said, standing up and looking around to make certain she wasn't forgetting anything.

"Mrs. Wang, please put in a word for us. My husband threatens to go to the capital city to look for a job," the woman said forlornly, nursing both babies.

Mrs. Wang looked at her and the babies and wondered what Jaya was talking about. She hadn't come out of her sleep completely yet. But she remembered why she had gone there in the first place.

"By the way, I want you to call the baby Mansong, Ten Thousand Pine Trees. Hopefully, with that name, she will live longer than her mother did," Mrs. Wang said.

Dubak came out of the kitchen. He opened a hemp sack and proudly showed Mrs. Wang the fat corn he had brought from the field. "Look here. These are sweeter than sweet potatoes. Take a few, please."

Mrs. Wang said, "Thank you very much, but I don't eat corn. It gets stuck between my teeth and that drives me crazy." And she left.

Without saying goodbye to Mrs. Wang, Jaya pouted and pried Mansong's mouth open to release her swelling purple nipple. The surprised baby didn't cry, but held her foot in her hand and gazed up at her wet nurse.

"I need to feed my son first," Jaya said, as if threatening her.

A patch of dark clouds was approaching rapidly. Dubak looked up to the sky, stopping his work of pulling the husks and hairs from the corncobs. He had expected another scorching summer, so he couldn't believe his eyes. A sudden gush of wind came, blowing away the pile of cornhusks and hairs. Large drops of rain hit the earth, and his wife rushed out to collect laundry from the clothesline. By the time she came in with a mountain of laundry, she was already wet on her shoulders. The rain possibly meant no uncle in the evening. This was the night she should sit with her husband and straighten out his thoughts on not wanting to farm and going to the capital city instead. These ideas only made him miserable. And if he left, the gods only knew when he would return!

MISTRESS YEE WAS IN BED, DELIRIOUS. THE TRIP TO
the temple had drained her. Mirae sat near her mistress and
fanned not her face but her feet: her mistress didn't want to
see Mirae's nostrils. Mistress Yee moaned at intervals. Nani
brought in a tray full of nourishments, including Mistress
Yee's favorites, candied lotus roots and poached pears in rice
liqueur. But Mistress Yee waved the food away.

Mr. O, after seeing off an old friend, arrived at Mistress
Yee's quarters. He cleared his throat outside the door, and
Mistress Yee began to moan more dramatically. Mirae sprang
up to open the door.

"How is everything?" Mr. O inquired, looking about the
room and at the tray of food.

Mirae just dropped her head, folding the fan she held.

"Leave us," Mr. O said. He never wanted the maids to be
around when he was with his wife. Mirae departed, leaving
the tray of food, for she knew that her mistress might ask for
food very soon. She didn't want to be summoned again.

Mr. O waited until Mirae had closed the door behind her
and scurried away before he sat near his wife.

"How is everything?" he asked again, taking a piece of snow
white rice cake. His mind was involuntarily pondering upon
the words of his friend from a neighboring village, who had
said that the peasants were out of control, some of them
demanding their share of the land. Mr. O's friend, also a land-
owner, had called them ungrateful bastards. They had lived off
of his land for generations but now what they wanted was to
bring him down to shame. His friend was completely wrought

up. Do any of my tenant peasants feel this way? No, impossible, Mr. O was convinced. His people would not want to see him bankrupt. That would mean their bankruptcy as well. His people weren't that stupid. They were family people, responsible people who put rice on their tables at every mealtime.

Mr. O took a bite of white rice cake, and Mistress Yee moaned louder.

Mr. O put his hand on her buttock. "How is everything?" he inquired once more, collecting himself.

"Send a messenger to my family. Let them know I am ill. I would like to say goodbye to them before I go," Mistress Yee said feebly, looking up at her husband sideways, who was still chewing on a piece of rice cake.

"Let me massage you," Mr. O said. He began to knead her thigh. But his wife pushed his hands away, sobbing.

"My little lamb, sit up and I will feed you something. I heard you haven't had dinner yet," Mr. O said, as if talking to a child.

"No one cares about me around here."

"The visitor had so much to say, and I just couldn't get rid of him quickly. He is my childhood friend. He feels quite at home here. By the way, he sends his best regards to you," he consoled her.

Mistress Yee just snorted and sat up and shot a fierce glance at her husband.

"Now, now, anger is the root of all miseries. Ease your mind," Mr. O said softly. He was tired and wanted to lie down with his wife, who often faked illness but was as strong as a horse.

"You don't understand. The head monk at the temple, he insulted me," she said resolutely.

"What do you mean?" Mr. O asked.

"When I was done with my kowtows, I realized Mirae was no longer with me. I was so preoccupied I didn't know she had left. She is such a busybody and pokes into everything. Anyhow, I went out to see where she was. And there she was, in front of Sari-tower, conversing with the head monk." Mistress Yee hesitated a few moments. "I can't tell you the rest, because if I did, you would stop the annual donation to the temple. And I don't want that to happen," she said in a saddened voice.

"Tell me, my dear. You can trust me."

"Well, it's obscene. Noble blood streams in your veins; you must not hear such talk."

"But it concerns you. I must know it," he urged with a strain in his voice.

Her eyes glared, reflecting the flame of the candle light on the low table. Mr. O felt that his wife was hiding something from him to protect him. He grabbed her small hand.

Slowly, quietly, she spoke, as if resigned, as if she were seeing the event once again: "The head monk was fumbling under Mirae's shirt. I didn't want to attract their attention because I was so ashamed to have witnessed such foul, abominable vice. I wanted to step back into the main hall so as to hide myself, but as I started walking backward, I fainted. I think the head monk picked me up and carried me because when I opened my eyes, I found myself lying on the floor in the main hall. The head monk was looking down on me, breathing hard. I was frightened, so I asked for Mirae. He assured me that I was in good hands. Mirae didn't come for a while. I didn't know where she was. I sat up, feeling sick. The head monk mentioned something about desire being one of the three poisons in life, obviously referring to his own contaminated mind, and perhaps he was pleading with me not to reveal any of the things I had seen. But you are so persistent. And I can't lie, as you know. So there you have it, the truth. But I don't want you to act upon it hastily. We all make mistakes, monk or not."

Mr. O considered the whole confession gravely.

Many years before, his father had taken him to the temple when the head monk was eleven years old. The father wanted to show his son what the unusually talented boy could do with stones. The boy was hard at work chiseling a piece of granite without looking up at the visitors. He was in the process of turning it into a statue of Buddha. He had started at the waist, which was smooth and curvaceous to perfection. It wasn't until he got older and married that Mr. O realized the sensual quality of the art. Mr. O's father praised the incontestable skill of the obvious genius, The Little Monk, as he was called then. That was the last time Mr. O had visited the temple.

At his deathbed, his father had Mr. O promise that he would make the annual tribute to the temple. So the son honored the wish of his father, and he would until his own death.

Mr. O was sure that the head monk at the temple was the same person that he was thinking of. Now that he knew what had happened to his wife and maid, he didn't quite know what to make of it. Once again he remembered the touch of the granite's cool surface. The waist of Buddha himself. If he were to pick out the single most unforgettable moment of his life, it would be that time when he had touched the unfinished statue of Buddha.

Mistress Yee sat there, holding her breath, thinking that at any moment her husband would explode, determined to murder the head monk. Then she would have to plead, she would have to visit the temple again to advise the head monk how to escape the wrath of her husband. She would have to punish Mirae properly and teach her to behave and to be loyal to her mistress forever.

"How does the head monk look?" Mr. O asked.

"Do you think I look at other men directly in the face? I fainted! I was ill. I almost died at the temple. They didn't serve me lunch when they knew well the distance I had to travel back! Can you just collect yourself and do something about it?" Mistress Yee said, baffled and irritated.

"What happened today is, if it's true, intolerable. It's an insult to me. And to my father," he said thoughtfully.

"*If* it's true?" Mistress Yee repeated. She knew very well that it was not the right moment to lose her temper. Her tale didn't seem to have disturbed him, as she had hoped.

"I don't mean it that way. I met that monk many years ago. My father revered him. He was the best sculptor alive. I saw part of his work when he was eleven. It was divine," he reminisced. "Perhaps next time you should go to the temple with another maid. You need to teach your maid—what's her name—proper behavior. If she could tempt a monk, she is unlimited in what she might do next," Mr. O said with a benign smile.

"I am not going there ever again!" she wailed.

"That's not a bad idea. As my father once said, one doesn't need a temple to see Buddha. And one doesn't need to see Buddha to learn what one already knows." He sighed, thinking of his father.

"Then, may I ask why you encouraged me to go to the temple?" Mistress Yee asked haughtily.

"My father went to the temple frequently. I asked him the same question that you are asking now. He simply replied that there are other things you learn by doing things you already know. But I encouraged you to go because you wanted to go. When an expectant mother wants to go to the temple to pray, to celebrate the future event, to practice focusing her mind—whatever it was that you intended to do—no husband would advise her not to go," he said, getting up slowly. "I am tired tonight. Mr. Chang drained me with his stories." He walked over to the inner quarters where their bed was prepared.

Mistress Yee sat there, feeling miserable and defeated. The rain subsided; only a few drops fell from the roof onto a puddle every now and then. Tears welled up in her eyes. She thought of her mother's words, *Don't ever give up on getting what you want. Life is a battle. But it's all in your mind. If you don't want to be trampled, you need to trample those who might trample you.*

She kept telling herself that there was no reason to worry. And there really was no reason to worry. But another voice, loud and persistent, kept whispering into her mind's ear.

She blew out the candle and wiped her eyes. She let her pitch-black satin hair drop from its twist and unbraided it and then slipped out of her clothes. Her husband was fast asleep. She lay next to him, awake, until deep into the night, sorting through her thoughts and calming her agitated mind. A few minutes before she fell asleep, she smiled, her eyes almost closed, remembering a scene from her childhood. A farrier had dipped a piece of metal into a furnace and a few minutes later he took it out to show how red, how hot, how powerful it was. "Don't you dare come near me, or you will be fatally hurt," he warned the children around him, smiling mischievously at the seven-year-old Mistress Yee.

BY THE TIME NANI WAS SO ITCHY THAT SHE WOKE UP, she already had six mosquito bites on her legs. They always bit her, no one else in the room. It was just before dawn. She lifted her left leg in midair and scratched until her skin bled.

She sat up. Even though it was midsummer, the heat had temporarily abated after the pounding rain.

The little maid, Soonyi, barely fourteen but appearing younger because of her small physique, lay diagonally with her limbs stretched out in four directions. She had joined the household only a year before to assist the kitchen maid. But since last spring the kitchen maid had taken time off to take care of her dying mother in the neighboring village.

In the corner was a lump of Mirae in a pathetic fetal position, bobbing up and down as she breathed rapidly. That was strange because she usually slept on her back, with her nose arrogantly tilted up and her long legs stretched straight out. Curious, Nani crawled on her knees over to Mirae. Even before she got close to her, she could feel the heat radiating from Mirae's body. She was hot. They were not on speaking terms, but Nani shook her shoulder, reluctantly. Mirae moaned and jerked.

"What's the matter?" Nani asked grimly. It was too early to start a new day.

"I think I am dying," Mirae barely managed to say.

Nani thought quickly. Her late mother had administered every domestic disaster. After she had passed away, Nani rushed to Mistress Kim with every little anomaly in the house. But now she was alone. She had to use her own head, and it wasn't always easy.

Fever. What did Mother do about a fever? What did Mistress Kim say about a fever?

Nani gaped at Mirae. She was drenched in sweat. Her hair was loose and a few strands were stuck on the side of her face. Even when she was sick, Nani thought, she was pretty.

Min never seemed to want to touch her. On the way back from Mrs. Wang's place the day before, he could have done whatever he pleased, but he hadn't. Was he simply a nincompoop? Or was she simply not attractive? Mirae moaned again, and Nani collected herself.

Her instinct told her that she needed to dry Mirae first and change her clothes. So she pulled out a new undergarment from the chest and began to undress her. It was almost impossible and she was also uncomfortable, considering the kind of relationship she had with Mirae: they were more or less enemies. But why? Nani rummaged through her memory to remember what event had turned them into hating each other. But there was really nothing. Mirae was just too pretty. She behaved like no maid. Supercilious she was. Mistress Yee's shadow. A shameless parasite. Nani began to untie the knot at her chest. She got nervous, noticing her fingers becoming clumsy.

Nudging at the little kitchen maid with her foot, Nani called out, "Soonyi!" She was sleeping with her mouth open. Nani hated to wake her up from her dream, but she needed someone else to assist her or at least witness what she was doing.

"Soonyi!" she called once again, in a louder voice.

To her surprise, Soonyi quickly sat up, gibbered for a few moments, and then rubbed the sleep from her eyes. Looking about, she whined, "What is it?"

"Light the candle, will you?" Nani asked, with annoyed urgency in her voice.

"What's going on?" Soonyi asked.

Nani didn't answer. She removed Mirae's top garment and began to pat her dry.

Soonyi rubbed her eyes, lit the candle, and gasped. "Gods! What on earth are you doing, Big Sister?"

"Get a bowl of water. She is sick. Can't you see?" Nani said, in an exaggerated tone of voice, just as her mother had used to speak to her when she was busy.

"All right. What happened?" Soonyi asked as she was leaving the room for the kitchen, knowing she wouldn't get an answer.

"Bring a spoon too," Nani commanded.

When Soonyi came back with a bowl of water, Nani held Mirae up and asked Soonyi to feed her water with the spoon.

"She is not swallowing it, Big Sister!" Soonyi cried.

Nani was sweating profusely now too. She thought hard, her teeth rattling from nervousness and her eyes focusing on the candlelight.

"Bring me a clean cloth," Nani said.

"Where is it?" Soonyi asked, moving her innocent eyes uncertainly.

"In the cupboard. In the kitchen. I don't know. Look for it!"

Soonyi frowned and sulked, pouting her lips. She went to the kitchen. The gray light from the east was emerging, and the roosters in the distance were announcing it. She looked about to find a clean cloth in the kitchen. She saw the low table on which she had served dried cuttlefish and sesame cookies to Mr. O's visitor the day before. The cookies were untouched. She ate one. It was even better than yesterday. A little less crunchy, but sweeter from the oozing honey. She ate another. She drank a little plum wine from the jug. That was the only wine she liked, because it was sweet.

Nani examined the skin of Mirae's chest. It was a whole new world. It resembled the flesh of a peeled peach. It gleamed, blinding her.

"Big Sister, is this good enough?" Soonyi came in and showed her a piece of white cloth that was used in the kitchen for making bean curd.

Nani sighed, and snatched it from Soonyi's hand. "We need to dress her in the dry clothes. You hold her from behind and I will put the clothes on," Nani said. Mirae did not put up a fight.

Nani dipped the cloth in the water and let the end of it hang in the hot mouth of Mirae, letting her suck the moisture.

"She needs to rest. Make sure she gets water constantly, even if it's one drop at a time. I am going to ask Mistress Yee what I should do about this. Stay right here," Nani ordered, pointing her finger at Soonyi.

"I am not going anywhere, Big Sister," said Soonyi, looking worried.

Nani left the room and walked up the steps to go across the yard to Mistress Yee's quarters. Her head felt light.

Min was walking toward the kitchen with split wood on his back for the stove. He was already sweating on his neck. As he disappeared into the rear entrance of the kitchen, Nani thought about Mirae's radiant skin. She walked faster and went to the outhouse, and when she came out, Min was coming toward her to go outside to do other chores. He passed Nani without acknowledging her presence. Nani picked up a pebble and hesitated for a moment, but before he went too far, she threw the pebble and hit him on his back. He turned around and shot a glance at her.

Nani sighed in frustration.

Min strode toward her and picked her up by the arms and put her back down on the ground. She slapped him hard because she felt frightened. His Adam's apple moved up and down. He stared at her for a moment, turned around reluctantly, and began to walk away. "Idiot!" Nani said to the back of his head.

Min turned around and looked down at his feet. A group of busy ants worked right by his foot. He moved carefully, so as not to step on them. He looked down once more, as if making sure the creatures were all right. He stared at Nani's skirt blankly and then his glance moved to her feet.

Her toes wiggled. Her fingers fidgeted. She wondered what Min was thinking. He came over to her slowly and grabbed her hand. His palm was moist and hot. They walked toward the storage room. She had the key to it. They entered in silence and closed the door behind them. In the dark they stood immobilized for a while, listening to each other's breathing and getting used to the dark. And then Min pulled her close to his chest and groaned like a beast. His arms compressed her organs in her rib cage so tightly that she felt they might explode. When he finally released her, the air temporarily trapped in her throat escaped violently through her mouth, producing a loud sound, the burp of a giant. He rubbed her head ever so gently and groaned again. Nani broke out sobbing, punching his chest. He groaned again. Nani said, "I hate you!" Min kept rubbing her head and groaned more loudly. His body was trembling ever so slightly. Nani stopped punching him. She relaxed in his arms for a while.

"Gods! What am I doing here? Mirae is sick as a dog. I have to go and ask Mistress Yee what I should do!" Nani sprang up and opened the door. Before she ran, she looked around and met Min's eyes. He was smiling down at her like Buddha. She pushed him away and ran like a little rabbit, looking back with a mischievous grin on her lips.

HALFWAY TO MISTRESS YEE'S QUARTERS, NANI suddenly turned around and went back to the maids' quarters. She
didn't think Mistress Yee would be up. Besides, she wouldn't
be interested in the welfare of her household members. She
would reprove her for making noise so early in the morning.

Nani slipped into the kitchen, out of breath. Her heart was
still pounding violently. She drank water in the kitchen, dripping it all over her chest. She stood there, lost in thought,
reviewing what had just happened in the storage room. Min's
body had felt like a perfect rock by a creek, smoothed over
eons, where everyone would want to sit and listen to the
sound of the cascading water or to lie down and find a million flecks of golden light dancing through the branches high
above which would make one's head spin as fast as the earth
rotated. For as long as she could remember, Min had loved her.
He cared about her as if there were nothing else in the world,
but why didn't he covet her like a normal man? She sucked
her cheek, puzzled, dissatisfied, but strangely happy too.

"Big Sister!" Soonyi said, coming into the kitchen.

Nani whirled around. "You startled me!"

"I am sorry, Big Sister. I was looking for you because I
needed your help to get started with breakfast," Soonyi said,
on the verge of tears. She was tired. While Nani was out, Mirae
had woken up and screamed about the cloth she found in her
mouth. "Are you trying to choke me?" she had asked.

"How is Mirae?" Nani asked.

"Oh, she is fine. After yelling at me, she fell back asleep as
soon as she put her head on the pillow," Soonyi explained.

"If she has the energy to yell, she will recover in no time," Nani said.

"What do I do with the soaked mung beans?" Soonyi asked.

"Go and rub them between your hands until they are hulled. And then you know what to do. I don't need to explain how to grind the beans, do I?"

"No, Big Sister. That's always been my chore," Soonyi assured Nani.

"When you are done, go to Mistress Yee and tell her that Mirae is sick. Very sick. Tell her she is as hot as an iron on the stove," Nani said, beginning to chop vegetables.

"I can't go see Mistress Yee," Soonyi whimpered.

"Child, what is the matter with you?" Nani asked, frowning. Half of her mind was elsewhere. Min had shoulders like … what?

"Mistress Yee doesn't like me," Soonyi said, turning pale.

"That's no news. She likes no one," Nani said, slicing summer zucchinis as thinly as she could.

"Should I talk to her when I take breakfast to her?" Soonyi asked.

"No," Nani replied, and placed her knife on the cutting board. "You don't bring up problems before breakfast. You do that when the mistress is done with breakfast, so that at least she won't have a table full of food to turn over. Besides, if she gets upset before breakfast and refuses to eat, you will be pleading with her to eat all day long."

Soonyi looked thoughtful. She definitely didn't want to spend all day begging Mistress Yee to take her meals.

"Of course, if we could get a chance to speak to the master, that would be the simplest way out of trouble. But we might have to talk to Mistress Yee. After all, Mirae is her favorite maid. And she is going to look for Mirae any minute anyway," Nani said. "Don't stand there like a scarecrow. Will you go get me some eggs? And wake up, will you?"

"Yes, Big Sister. How many?" Soonyi asked, widening her eyes.

"Please," Nani drawled. "Don't get my blood boiling so early in the morning. You go and get however many eggs you see in the basket. Don't you know that eggs are delivered every morning by the boy down by the creek?"

"Yes, of course," Soonyi said quietly and fled the kitchen.

Nani crushed garlic with the heavy wooden handle of the knife. After putting it aside in a little bowl, she began to chop onions, which made her sniffle. Suddenly, she turned around. Nani often thought that she caught a glimpse of her late mother. She sat down by the stove and cried a little, thinking of her. Sometimes at night, she would look at the door, thinking that at any moment her mother would come in and lie down next to her. And sometimes she would see her mother in her dreams; afterward, she would feel lonely and distracted all day long. Min made her feel good, but no one would ever be able to take her mother's place, she knew. She blew her nose. She tightened the string of her apron and began to cook zucchini in a pot, stirring the vegetable intermittently.

"Big Sister, here are three eggs," Soonyi said as she came in.

"Good," Nani replied.

"What is the matter?" she asked, seeing Nani's red eyes.

"Nothing. Now I want you to get a scoop of bean paste for the soup," she said.

"Sure," Soonyi replied, looking at Nani blankly.

"Get going. Don't stand around," Nani chided Soonyi.

A few minutes later, Soonyi came in with bean paste on a spatula.

"Get a strainer. And press the paste through it into the water," Nani ordered.

Soonyi did as she was told.

In the meantime, Nani broke the eggs into a bowl. She swirled them with a spoon, adding chopped scallion and gingko nuts and sea salt. She was going to poach them in a double boiler.

In an hour, there was a hot meal on a low table. Nani and Soonyi carried it to their master and mistress, who sat close to each other, smirking about something like kids. Nani was relieved to find her superiors in a good mood.

The maids wished them a very good appetite and left. On the way back to the kitchen, Nani lectured Soonyi about how she had put her face too close to the food as they took the low table in. This was what her mother had said to her some years before.

Soonyi denied having done so, just as Nani had vehemently argued against her mother's accusation.

They walked back to the kitchen. Nani was upset. She wanted Soonyi to acknowledge her own shortcoming and say that she wouldn't do it again.

In the kitchen, Soonyi took a gulp of water and dropped a piece of fried zucchini into her mouth.

"Soonyi, let me teach you something. Don't eat standing," Nani snapped. Her mother had also said this to her often. At the time, Nani hadn't understood. But now she did. It wasn't proper. It was something a maid would do. And a maid didn't have to live the life of a maid, her mother had emphasized.

Nani set the table for three in the middle of the hardwood floor in front of the maids' shared bedroom. Then she told Soonyi to go out and get the male servants for breakfast.

It was already getting hot.

Soonyi first went inside to see if Mirae was feeling any better and if she would like to eat a little.

"Big Sister!" Soonyi shouted from inside the room.

"Calm down, child," Nani said, employing her mother's tone of voice.

"Big Sister, Mirae is so sick!" Soonyi rushed out of the room.

Nani got up and hurried in. Mirae was indeed very sick. Her body was burning and her skin was erupting with a strange-looking rash. Nani thought for a moment and ran to Mistress Yee's quarters.

There was laughter from the room. Nani hesitated. No matter how serious the problem was with a maid, it seemed inappropriate to break up her superiors' happy moment.

She cleared her throat and smoothed her hair, feeling nervous, as if she had already done something wrong.

"What is it?" Mistress Yee asked, sensing movement behind the latticed door.

"It is Nani, Mistress Yee. I am here to let you know that Mirae is burning with a fever and her skin is developing a rash. She needs a doctor," Nani managed to say.

Mistress Yee rolled her eyes theatrically.

Nani stood in the hallway like a puppet with broken strings, frozen, expressionless.

"Should I buy the fish or not?" Mistress Yee asked. Obviously, she and Mr. O must have been in the middle of a conversation.

"It doesn't matter, my dear. What counts is not your deed, but your intention, your heart. If you have the intention to do good things, then you have done good things."

"You are my inspiration," Mistress Yee said brightly, laughing.

"Don't flatter me. It doesn't suit you," Mr. O replied.

"Are you still there?" Mistress Yee called out in her high-pitched voice, irritably.

"Yes, Mistress," Nani replied nervously. Her mistress might accuse her of eavesdropping.

"You should be taking care of Mirae if she is really sick," she said curtly.

"Yes, Mistress. She needs more than my care, it appears," Nani said timidly.

"If you can afford it, go get the doctor. You don't need my permission," Mistress Yee said, half amused, half tartly.

There was a pause. How long would Mistress Yee play out her little game before Mr. O stepped in to give his order?

"What are you thinking about?" Mistress Yee asked her husband.

"Oh, nothing," he replied.

"Of course, nothing. How could you think of anything else when I am in your presence?" Mistress Yee said, amused.

"Why don't you tell her to go fetch the doctor?" Mr. O grumbled.

"We can't get a doctor every time a maid gets sick. We will soon run out of money. We need to reserve some for the likes of me," Mistress Yee said in her nasal voice, laughing mischievously.

"Let her go. I need to talk to you," Mr. O said.

"Go and get that midwife, whatever her name is," Mistress Yee said sharply.

"What can a midwife do for a maid with a fever?" Mr. O complained.

"Maybe it is not just a fever," Mistress Yee muttered, giggling like a girl.

"Now, let her go and tend to the matter," Mr. O ordered gently.

"Leave us," Mistress Yee snapped.

Nani returned to the kitchen. She saw male servants leaving for their work. She stopped Min and explained the seriousness of Mirae's state. "We need to go and ask someone, a doctor, to find out what to do about the fever," she said, looking worried. "Let's go to the marketplace. I know an herbalist. He is as good as a doctor, I hear."

Min hesitated. He knew how awfully Mirae had treated his girl, and only the other day, Nani had said, "She drives me crazy." So he produced a groan of displeasure.

Nani retorted, "If we don't, we will have another funeral in this house. That would be two funerals within a year."

They hurried to the marketplace and found the herbalist perched with at least fifty huge standing hemp sacks displayed, their open mouths spilling out their contents.

Nani explained Mirae's symptoms. The herbalist said, "Sounds like chicken pox to me. If it is, it will run its course and go away. But you need something to help her with the fever." He picked a few roots and leaves from here and there. "Make sure to stay away from the sick one until the fever is reduced."

He divided the herbs into six portions, wrapped each in rice paper, and handed them to Nani. "Cook one for half a day. Divide the brew into three portions. Let her drink one with each meal. Do the same for the following five days. Remember to stay away from her while she has the fever. Especially anyone carrying a baby!" he advised her, winking at Min.

Nani blushed. Then she realized that she had to tell her mistress, not that Mistress Yee would go near Mirae while the maid was sick.

When she arrived back home, Mr. O was leaving with a part-time male servant whose hunting skill surpassed all. They would visit the gravesite of Mr. O's parents. The servant would trim the grass, and Mr. O would serve his parents rice liquor and some food and tell them his wife was pregnant.

In the kitchen, Nani emptied one packet of the herbs into a clay brew pot. She measured water and poured it into the pot and placed it on the stove.

While watching the pot simmer, she wondered if she should tell Mistress Yee what the herbalist had said about a pregnant woman needing to stay away from Mirae. She wasn't so worried about the cost of the herbs. She could take the small amount of money from the weekly grocery shopping money. But if Mirae's illness affected Mistress Yee's health in any way, then Nani would be in big trouble.

In the afternoon, while letting Soonyi tend the pot so that it wouldn't boil over, Nani went to Mistress Yee with a plate of fruit. Mistress Yee was reading a picture book and humming a familiar tune. She was in a good mood.

"Mistress Yee, Mirae is taking medicine for her fever. It looks as though she will recover in a few days, if not before," Nani said.

"Such a silly little thing. I didn't ask you a question. Didn't your mistress teach you not to speak unless you were spoken to?"

"I am sorry, Mistress Yee. Silly was my nickname by my mother, but I dare speak because Mirae suffers from chicken pox. Of course, we will keep her away from you until she is completely recovered," Nani said.

Mistress Yee dropped her book on the floor, turning pale and looking urgent, as if she had a fishbone caught in her throat. "Are you sure it's chicken pox?"

"Her skin is breaking out with blisters, and the herbalist in the marketplace thought so," Nani replied, kneeling in the far corner of the room without breathing.

"I should believe a dog? Go get the doctor!" she ordered.

"Yes, Mistress," Nani said. She got up with a tray and left. In the yard, she kicked a pebble and grumbled about Mistress Yee's temper.

Before sunset, the doctor came and took a look at Mirae. Then he reported to Mistress Yee that while it looked like chicken pox, it could very well be a combination of boils and a nasty cold. He turned around and asked Nani how Mirae had been lately. Nani said that she couldn't think of any anomaly; Mirae had behaved like her usual self. The doctor pondered for a moment and said that he couldn't rule out chicken pox entirely, but the rash was too severe for the usual case of chicken pox. And who in the world catches a cold in the summer?

Mistress Yee didn't want to hear another word from the doctor. She would stay at her father's house until Mirae was well.

Four days later, Mirae was feeling a world better. Her fever was gone, and she was eating again, but no one spoke about her dreadful skin. Her body was still covered with purplish rashes. A part-time maid simply commented, "Better to be alive than dead, though."

When Mirae took a bath after her illness, she saw herself in full view. She panicked and sobbed bitterly for the whole afternoon, and she stayed up late that evening. When she woke the next day, she refused to eat and stopped talking to all but herself. A month later, when Mistress Yee returned, larger and happier, Mirae was a different person.

Part Two

MOST OF THE VILLAGERS, INCLUDING THE CHILDREN, had bathed and came up to the hill all spiffed up in their clean and starched outfits. Soon the full moon would be in view. Some of the men and children played tug-of-war, and some of the women sat eating specialties they prepared only for Harvest Day. It wasn't a good year, they all knew, but no one complained about the drought or the bad crops or the high taxes they had to pay the government and their landlords. What everyone talked about was the news that had just come from the capital city: a foreign ship had arrived from a faraway land.

"There were nineteen people on the ship," one person said.

"No, eighteen," another voice said.

"What does it matter how many there were? They all got killed the instant they set foot on our soil," a man said.

"What did they do?" a woman asked, chewing on a rice cake.

"Nothing," another man said.

"Well, they did something. They entered our country without permission," someone said, sitting down to join the crowd.

"But that doesn't seem grave enough a crime to deserve death," said the woman with the rice cake. "And eighteen of them," she added, horrified.

"Nineteen," someone corrected her.

"Coming to our country without permission might be a crime. Who knows?" a man said.

"Well, that doesn't make any sense," a woman said. "If you come to my house uninvited, should I pull my dagger and kill you?" she asked, rolling her eyes.

"You would be behind bars," someone said and laughed.

"Surely, I would be for killing a neighbor," the woman said, nodding her head vehemently.

"Only one of them survived. When all were thought to have been killed, five of the best shamans were summoned from the southern provinces to expel the foreign spirits and the curse the ship had brought. In the meantime, soldiers inspected the contents of the vessel. They found the strangest thing. It was a piece of furniture, but neither chest nor table. As tall as a grownup, maybe even taller, it had a face, round as a pumpkin, and it ticked constantly, and once in a while it gonged all by itself. It had its own mind because sometimes it gonged once, sometimes twice, sometimes even twelve times. What was more interesting was that they found a man, the same kind as the dead, trembling for fear of death, and hiding, horribly diseased, in a barrel where they must have kept food. When he was dragged out, he saw the shamans dance in order to stop the ticking of the tall thing. So he simply touched something on the back of it and the ticking stopped. And so this man escaped his death. The king himself ordered him to stay in the palace," a man explained, excitedly, foaming around his mouth and waving his hands.

"So he lives?" a woman asked.

"So he does," someone answered.

Everyone laughed.

"So what did they come here for?" another woman asked.

"That seems unclear," a man answered.

The enormous moon was coming up from behind the hill, and the children were playing tag in the wooded area. Under the old pine tree, a few women were clicking their tongues about the poor maid at the big house whose skin had erupted in an unsightly rash.

Mrs. Wang arrived and wanted to know where the left-over food was. She was about to collapse, she warned them. The women under the pine tree quickly got up and served the midwife some of the very best food. Sitting on a mat, Mrs. Wang devoured everything. Then she wondered if there was rice wine.

After she had finished a large bowl of rice wine, she said, "Look over there at the moon. How beautiful it is! Everyone is so busy talking that no one's looking at the moon!"

Everyone turned and looked at the moon. They fell into a brief silence because the moon was so close that they felt they could reach out their hands and touch it. It was translucent, and it almost seemed that *it* had come to see *them*. Mrs. Wang felt briefly levitated. This was why she had come: to see the moon. Of course, there was the food too.

"It looks like a large pearl!" a child exclaimed.

"What is a pearl?" a younger child asked.

"It *does* look like a pearl!" another child said.

"I see a bunny up on the moon," a girl said.

"There are two of them," a boy said.

Jaya stood up and bowed to the moon several times solemnly. She was praying for Sungnam. She prayed that he would not be a peasant like his father but someone better, someone with no boss or landlord whose invisible hands would strangle him. She prayed for Dubak, that he would focus on farming and stop going to peasant meetings where they talked about their rights and high taxes and other nonsense. She prayed that she would give birth to a healthy child.

Then she collapsed near Mrs. Wang, who leaned against a tree, humming along with the people who were singing and dancing.

"Mrs. Wang, people over there are talking about the news from the capital city. Have you heard it? About the surviving yellow man, who's now a friend of the king?" Jaya asked. She held Mansong in her arms without knowing that her nipple had escaped Mansong's mouth. Mansong was staring at Mrs. Wang with curiosity. She was no longer an infant.

"It's about time for you to wean the babies. You need to reserve yourself for the coming one," Mrs. Wang advised.

"It's hard to wean Mansong. Unlike my Sungnam, she doesn't take solid food," Jaya said. In the moonlight, she looked pretty. Everyone looked pretty. It was a beautiful night.

"Look at her teeth. She is behind the schedule. Give her porridge and steamed vegetables. Or else you will not have enough milk for the next one," Mrs. Wang urged, getting up to go and listen to the group of young men and women talking about the current news from the capital city.

They were discussing the yellow man's religion and how self-sacrificing those who believed in this religion were. They shared what they owned with others, especially those in need. And they believed everyone was equal. Some of the peasants listened intently, their faces illuminated by the moonlight.

"Dream on," Mrs. Wang snapped. Everyone turned to look at her. Unintimidated, she continued: "True. We were born equal. But look around. Some are rich, some are poor, some are peasants, some are aristocrats, and some are like Mr. O with no worries about what to eat the next day for the rest of his life."

People sat, thinking hard. Somehow it seemed Mr. O was to blame for their miserable lives. The hostility toward their landlord was palpable.

"Before you become slaves of some religion, remember that you have been slaves to your landlords. You don't need another master. That's my point," Mrs. Wang said heatedly.

Everyone fell silent. What Mrs. Wang had just pointed out made sense. They were slaves, basically, to the landlords.

"They feed you lunch on Sundays, Mrs. Wang. They give you medicine when you are sick," a young man protested, licking his lips.

"Well, what was it they gave you last Sunday?" Mrs. Wang challenged him jokingly.

They all laughed and quieted down to hear the answer.

"I was late. When I got there, the food was gone," the young man said ruefully.

More laughter broke out.

Some of the women were getting ready to descend. Their children were getting fussy, and, actually, they were also getting tired. There were loads to carry, besides their sleepy children. It had been a long, exciting day.

The radiant moon seemed mounted above them, gently brightening the whole world. They collected their belongings, while some of the men drank the last drops of rice wine, babbling on about the rights of the peasants. Mrs. Wang collected leftovers for her dog.

Groups of people began to descend the hill, warning each other to mind their steps.

Mrs. Wang made a sharp turn to go up the hill to her house. She bade farewell to the villagers and they bowed to her goodbye. Her old bones ached as she climbed the steep path. Fireflies accompanied her. Despite the familiarity of the sight, she was still moved by the little creatures, glowing at intervals in midair as if they existed just to amuse her. The air was filled with the pleasant smells of tall grass and wild flowers and ripe fruits. She took the air into her lungs with deep gratitude. Suddenly, she heard footsteps. A fox? A wolf? She stopped, concentrating with every nerve. She didn't want to attract an animal's attention right then. It would be a hassle to have to deal with it. But the sounds kept coming nearer and nearer. Then she heard a human voice, singing or crying.

"Who is it?" Mrs. Wang demanded.

A young woman came into view. She was singing in a sad voice, but the words were hard to understand.

"A young woman wandering about in the night. What a pitiful sight! Where do you belong?" Mrs. Wang thundered.

"Where do I belong?" she asked herself in an undertone, nervously. "Oh, why do you ask? I belong nowhere." She tittered and then cried. Her unkempt hair partially covered her face.

Mrs. Wang grabbed the young woman's wrist and pulled her close to her. "Let me look at you. You are the maid that belongs at Mr. O's household. Aren't you?" Mrs. Wang pulled her a little closer.

"I don't belong there. I belong in the mountains, where the beasts are and where the ghouls roam about," she cried, trying to pry her hand from Mrs. Wang's grip.

"What's your problem?" Mrs. Wang asked, looking at her fiercely. Without waiting for her answer, she continued, "Do you think roaming about in the mountains, at the graveyard, will lesson your sorrow? Alter your tragedy? Change your life? You are mistaken, my child," she said and laughed exaggeratedly. "You had beauty no one could surpass before the illness struck you. But beauty is fragile, unreliable. It's seasonal, like that of an annual flower. An annual flower is pretty because of its appearance, but a perennial is worthy because of its nature. It comes back. It endures. It is persistent." Mrs. Wang stopped here and thought about what her point was. She had to admit that she was shocked to run into this young maid, whose beauty had once been stunning. Now her face, even in the moonlight, was visibly bumpy from chicken pox.

"What do you know about me? You know nothing about me. You don't know what I had. Who says I am a maid? I was about to fly. I was even prettier than my mistress. She herself said that to me. Do you understand?" Mirae shrieked and fell on her knees.

"Go back to the graveyard and dig up the corpses and find out who was the best looking when they were alive. Ask if that makes any difference in the coffin beneath the earth. You imbecile! You are not worth speaking to." Mrs. Wang passed around the maid and walked on briskly. But still, she looked back, concerned. She was relieved when she didn't see Mirae anymore.

As she pushed her squeaky gate open, she felt good and tired. There was no place like her little place. Her dog, at seeing her, went amok, jumping around and whining. She fed the creature with the leftovers from the festival. It was getting chilly. She emptied the remaining charcoal from a metal pail into the furnace and lit a fire. She should, she thought, go to the market soon to prepare for her winter hibernation. First of all, she wanted to buy a load of dried fish and some garlic. She had enough wild greens, all dried and bunched up, dangling in straw ropes from her eaves, to last the winter.

ON THE SAME DAY AT MR. O's—EVEN BEFORE THE
annual memorial service for the ancestors, which normally
took place right after dawn—Min took a bundle in a basket
to Nani, who was busying herself in the kitchen with Soonyi.

"What've you got there?" Nani asked, casting her glance to
the dates and nuts she was arranging on wooden plates used
only for the memorial service.

Before he revealed what was in the basket, the baby inside
whimpered like a puppy. Nani raised her eyebrows in surprise,
although this wasn't the first time that he had brought in a baby
from the front gate, abandoned by some wretched soul on a day
of celebration or a dead one from the field ditched by an unfortunate woman out of wedlock. Now that Nani's mother had
passed away, and also Mistress Kim, there was no chance that
this baby would get to stay in the house. Mistress Yee would
throw a tantrum when she found out that the baby was there,
and everyone in the household would be walking on eggshells
for days. Nani wasn't afraid of that. She was used to Mistress Yee.
But it wasn't always trouble-free to relocate the baby. Min must
have felt extra sorry for these abandoned babies because he
had once been a baby in a basket. Nani remember her mother
talking with other maids about Min almost a decade before,
summarizing in whisper the reasons why people abandoned
their own children. "Scarcity of food after drought and birth
out of wedlock are the common causes of such a terrible act.
But sometimes, well, rarely, the master of the house planted
his seed somewhere illegitimate. And doesn't one have to reap
what'd been sewn one way or another?"

Min stood there like a totem pole. Without saying anything Nani sliced off the top parts of apples and pears, as was the custom when preparing offerings for the memorial service.

"What are we going to do about this?" Soonyi asked, but her concern was superficial.

Nani stripped the smoked beef as if she heard nothing. The baby moaned pitifully, with the last bit of energy left in its system. Min looked grim but still stood there, planted. Nani arranged chestnuts on a plate. They were raw. She couldn't remember whether chestnuts were supposed to be cooked or arranged raw on the table for the memorial service, and she was sure that Mistress Yee had no clue either. Her remarkable ignorance about housekeeping was advantageous to her inferiors, except that when Nani wanted to know something there was no one to learn from.

She wiped her hands on her apron, thinking intently about what to feed the infant if she should end up having to do so. Unexpectedly, Min picked up the basket and left the kitchen. Soonyi stood up and opened her mouth to say something, but she didn't, she just looked at Nani sheepishly. After a few moments, Nani ran after Min. Near the well she pulled his arm and said, "Where're you going?"

Min yanked his arm back and walked on. Nani grabbed his arm again and asked, "What are you trying to do?"

Min stared at her briefly and walked away again. Nani remained behind and muttered, "What's he going to do with the baby? Is he going to starve it to death?" She realized that she had hurt his feelings. She walked slowly back to the kitchen.

"What on earth do you think you're doing?" Nani shouted hysterically when she saw Soonyi take a bite of mugwort-flavored rice cake. "That's for the memorial service. You know very well you can't taste food before the service!" Her voice turned metallic. "Get out. You are no help. Go get Mirae. What's she up to? Wake her up!"

Soonyi sprang up and left the kitchen, pouting and stomping. She climbed up onto the raised entrance and walked gingerly toward the bedroom. Holding the ancient door-pull, she took a deep breath before she entered. She was afraid of Mirae. Her appearance scared her. She dreaded confronting her because she didn't know what to expect each time. "Don't drop your jaw and stare at her. And don't scream," Nani had advised her. When Mistress Yee first saw her own maid after she returned from her extended stay away, she did exactly that: she dropped her jaw and couldn't speak for a long moment, and then she heaved a sigh as if she were in great pain and finally said, "Get that out of my sight!" It was typical of Mistress Yee, but it was cruel nonetheless. No one called her bosom buddy, nevertheless everyone felt sorry for her when her own mistress called her "that" just because her skin was now disfigured. It was unjust, unfair, heartless, everyone had grumbled quietly, frowning.

"Are you up?" Soonyi asked feebly, knowing very well that there would be no reply either way.

Mirae's upper body was in the sunlight coming through the window, and her eyelashes fluttered as Soonyi spoke. Soonyi didn't know that Mirae had gone to bed not long before. Nowadays she disappeared in the middle of the night and slipped in quietly before dawn. And she slept like a log until after breakfast. People got used to what they thought of as temporary madness. They were expecting her to get better sooner or later. In the meantime, Nani had to take over her job as well.

"Are you still sleeping?" Soonyi made another attempt, weakly. "Nani wants you."

Mirae opened her eyes ever so slightly and then closed them again. Soonyi slid toward Mirae on her knees. Mirae's face, unlike when she was fully awake, appeared to be peaceful, expressionless, and undisturbed. Her skin didn't look too bad. Soonyi inspected her face indiscreetly, holding her breath, puckering her mouth, and narrowing her eyes.

"So what do you think?" Mirae asked, opening her eyes, looking up directly at Soonyi. Her tone was neutral.

Surprised, Soonyi pulled herself back and turned red. Mirae didn't scream, nor did she look upset.

"I have two eyes, one nose, and one mouth, just like anyone else," Mirae said calmly.

Soonyi felt mortified. Not knowing how to respond, she kept her mouth zipped.

"What does Nani want?" Mirae asked, cocking her head.

"She wants you to help out, I guess," she said, her voice weakening at the end. She couldn't remember exactly what kind of help Nani wanted of Mirae.

Mirae flung her covers aside, went to clean her teeth with sea salt, and then marched to the kitchen. Soonyi followed her. She felt tense, interested in what Mirae was up to. She hadn't been in her right mind, let alone cooperative or working, since she had recovered from her illness.

In the kitchen, there was nothing much more to be done. Nani was cleaning up and getting ready to deliver the wooden vessels for the memorial service. When she saw Mirae, however, she stopped her hands and waited for Mirae to say something. But Mirae said nothing. She simply picked up one of the trays and walked toward the master's quarters.

"What is she up to?" Nani said in an undertone, standing with her arms akimbo, just as her mother would have done. "Don't just stand there. You carry a tray too," Nani reproached Soonyi.

"What are you so mad at me about?" Soonyi sulked, furrowing her forehead.

"I'll be right back," Nani said and left the kitchen. She walked briskly to the storage room, hoping to find Min with the baby in the basket. She felt bad that she had dismissed him earlier. So compassionate and softhearted, he couldn't ignore the abandoned baby. But Nani was so busy with no extra hands to help her. The kitchen maid hadn't yet returned from her mother's. All she heard from her was that her mother would be dying any minute now. In any case, she was glad that Mirae had finally collected herself and gotten up. Hopefully, she would go back and tend to Mistress Yee.

Pausing in front of the storage room, Nani looked about before she opened the door. Min couldn't be in there, for she was the only one among the maids and the servants entrusted with the key. Her mother had given her the keys to various places before she died, and Mistress Kim had entrusted her with them. Still, she went in. The smell of the fabric and the paper and the wooden boxes made her sneeze. She looked up and down. There were bolts of silks and cottons stacked up. She took down one particular roll of silk and touched it aimlessly, thinking about something totally unrelated. Mrs. Wang's house was what stirred her mind. She would have liked to have a house—a cottage with a thatched roof—and her own animals, and her own little patch of vegetable garden, away from everyone, maybe with Min. "Crazy," she said aloud, thinking of Min and how he had run away from her with the baby earlier. "Crazy," she said once more.

"Crazy is right!" thundered a voice.

Stupefied, Nani dropped the bolt of silk, which fell on the ground and rolled, unfolding itself until it reached the shoe of Mistress Yee who seemed to have been transported into the storage room magically. Nani wanted to pick up the silk, but her body was unwilling to move as quickly as she would like. When she finally bent down, Mistress Yee barked, "Get your filthy hands off my silk!"

Nani flinched, her lips quivering. She didn't know where to fix her glance. She was supposed to be in the kitchen. What would Mistress Yee do now? Her stomach knotted.

"I didn't know I was breeding a thief under my own roof. How did you get hold of those keys?" Mistress Yee asked, narrowing her eyes. She walked on the bed of silk toward Nani, whose eyes were brimming with tears. She wanted to say that she wasn't a thief. But she felt so small, powerless, overwhelmed. The storage room seemed to have darkened. It was hard to see what expression was on Mistress Yee's face. She could only hear Mistress Yee's heavy breathing and the rustle of her dress as she approached.

Many months pregnant, Mistress Yee ballooned in the middle. So when she stepped on Nani's foot, Nani thought that it was an accident. Except she didn't remove her foot. Mistress Yee pressed until Nani cried.

"Where did you get the keys?" Mistress Yee pressed harder on Nani's foot. Her crimson lips parted, fuming fiery air, right above Nani's nose.

"Mistress Yee, I didn't take them. They were given to me. Mistress Kim gave them to me. She used to send me here to fetch papers and brushes and other things," Nani quickly said.

Mistress Yee slapped her and shrieked, "Don't you ever mention the dead woman's name. It will bring bad luck to my baby." She released her foot and said, "I am taking your wage for this month since you ruined my silk."

Nani cried all the way to the kitchen.

"What is the matter, Big Sister?" Soonyi asked.

Nani sat by the stove in the kitchen and cried more. Mirae entered and said, "We need the rice liquor. They are about to start the ceremony."

"The hell with their ceremony!" Nani shrieked. She took off her shoes and cotton footwear. The top of her left foot was bluish yellow.

"What happened to your foot? Big Sister, it's blue!" Soonyi shouted excitedly.

"Shut up," Mirae uttered quietly. "Where is the liquor?" she asked, unperturbed.

Nani ignored her and tended her foot as if it were a baby.

"Your foot will get better in a little while, but the liquor is needed right now or else she will turn your other foot blue to match," Mirae said.

Soonyi quickly got the jug of rice liquor from the cupboard. Mirae snatched it, poured a bit into a small ceramic cup, and looked at Nani. "Drink it," she said to Nani, and left the kitchen.

"Don't mind her. She is out of her mind," Soonyi comforted her. "And she shouldn't pour the liquor before the ceremony."

Unexpectedly, Nani took the ceramic cup and drank the liquor all at once. She screwed up her face as the heat of the alcohol rushed down her chest. The heat immediately spread into her shoulders and stomach.

Never having seen Nani drink, Soonyi whispered, "Big Sister."

"Don't speak to me right now," Nani said and turned her head toward the wall. Her eyes were brimming with tears.

MISTRESS YEE WAS IN HER ROOM, SCRATCHING HER enormous tummy. For some reason, she felt terribly itchy. She hated being pregnant. Things were happening to her body without her consent, it seemed, and this state of affairs often put her in a foul mood. She was waiting for Mirae to arrive. The doctor had informed Mistress Yee that her maid was no longer contagious. In truth, Mistress Yee was glad to have Mirae attend to her because she was the only maid with the ability to anticipate and accommodate her needs. The others were clueless and subservient, and they repeatedly required detailed instructions. When Mistress Yee's subordinates were stupid, she needed to be wise and careful; this tired and frustrated her.

"Here I am, Mistress Yee," Mirae announced.

"Open the door," Mistress Yee ordered from inside her room, leaning against the cushion with her legs stretched out. Her dainty feet in her white silk footwear wriggled in boredom.

"Sit down," Mistress Yee ordered cheerfully.

Mirae sat and cast her glance down. Mistress Yee examined her face, amused and surprised. Then she said, "Cheer up, Mirae. It doesn't look as bad as you might think. You are still the prettiest among all the maids." She laughed in approval of her own sarcastic phrase.

Mirae sat silently.

"You've changed," Mistress Yee suggested. She took a moment to study Mirae's reaction. "I don't just mean your appearance. Your attitude too."

"I am sorry, Mistress Yee. I don't mean to be rude to you. And I am here to serve you," Mirae confessed.

"I don't mean your attitude toward *me*. I am talking about your attitude toward *yourself*," Mistress Yee said, grinning maliciously.

Mirae said nothing.

"Do my hair, Mirae," Mistress Yee ordered, turning around to face the folding screen which she had brought as part of her dowry. Embroidered meticulously in colorful silk and gold threads, it depicted the beginning of spring with cherry blossoms, blackbirds, and a girl on a swing by a stream. "You know, Mirae, that is me." Mistress Yee pointed at the girl on the swing.

"I know, my lady," Mirae said.

"You see what I am saying? In the past, you would have said, 'Oh, my lady, you must have been the prettiest girl ever lived.' But now, you say, 'I see, my lady.' That is not you, Mirae. You've changed. That's not a good sign," Mistress Yee said, smiling.

"I am sorry, my lady," Mirae said, taking a comb and perfumed oil.

"No apologies between you and me. You've been very good to me." She laughed. Her pitch-black hair fell on her back. Mirae began to comb it. "Do you know what has changed?" Mistress Yee asked mockingly. "A maid with a pretty face thinks she can marry up. In the end, she becomes a concubine to an aristocrat and has an illegitimate child. As soon as there is another girl with a prettier face, the man leaves her and her child. And that's the end of her glory. A maid with a homely face, on the other hand, marries a servant in the household, or even better, if she brought a male servant from outside into the household she would be given a place of her own, and she would live as a wife and mother in her own place. That's the only difference between a pretty maid and a not-so-pretty maid. I had always wondered what might become of you with your pretty face. But now, it's my opinion that chicken pox might not be a villain after all," she said, observing Mirae's reaction as she gazed at the sliver-framed looking glass in her hand.

Biting her lip, Mirae kept combing her mistress's hair.

"Hurry, Mirae. I have to dine with my husband when he is done with the memorial service. I couldn't attend with my belly this large; it's impossible to kowtow to the ancestors. That reminds me of something. I need you to deliver a packet to the temple tomorrow. My due date is approaching, and your master wants to make a special offering so that I will have a smooth delivery," she said, looking intently at herself in the looking glass.

Still, Mirae said nothing.

"Look here," Mistress Yee turned around suddenly, pulling her hair away from Mirae's hands. "I don't enjoy chattering alone. I am not your entertainer. Do you understand that?"

"I do, my lady. I will try my best not to be an annoyance," Mirae said.

"You will have to." Mistress Yee turned around and faced the folding screen again. Now Mirae had to braid her hair all over again because the braid had come loose.

When her hair was done, Mistress Yee sat up, supporting her belly with her hands, and said, "I can't wait until this is over. It's so hard to move about. I feel like I have swallowed a watermelon whole. Anyway, I was thinking that you would be the perfect nanny for the baby."

"It would be my pleasure, Mistress," Mirae replied, gloomily.

"But when I come to think of it," Mistress Yee said quickly, "well, I will have to hire someone else. No offense, but it'd be cruel if the first thing my baby had to see was you with your skin condition. Don't you think?" Mistress Yee said, pouting. She lay back against the cushion with her eyes closed so that Mirae could shape her eyebrows. Mirae clenched her teeth with shame. No tears, she told herself. She took the tweezers and began to pluck Mistress Yee's eyebrows into the shape of a seagull's wing.

"Easy!" Mistress Yee shrilled irritably, her eyes still closed. A teardrop oozed out from under her eyelid.

"I will be careful, my lady," Mirae said, holding her breath.

Mistress Yee was tempted to tell the story of her own mother, who had once been a maid, a very pretty one. Mistress Yee's father, General Bin Yee, a descendent of a famous general and, later, a member of council in the government office, had two wives already and had an affair with her mother. The first wife died of tuberculosis, and the second one was accused of indecency and removed from the house and lived elsewhere in solitude. Her mother had to face opposition from General Yee's relatives and friends and the vicious accusations that she had caused the second wife's misfortune. "Is it true?" Mistress Yee had asked her mother one day. She didn't answer then. But some days later she said, "I did it for you." When all that had happened, Mistress Yee wasn't even born. As a child, Mistress Yee held a grudge against her mother. General Yee wasn't a loving man. Mistress Yee didn't get along with him, who played the role of a general even at home. As Mistress Yee grew older, she realized that, as much as she resented her mother, she was, slowly but surely, becoming her mother's daughter.

Applying a wet cotton pad to soothe Mistress Yee's raw skin, Mirae announced that her job was done. Mistress Yee opened her eyes and said, "Mirae, please don't pull your face long. Will you stay depressed forever? It's funny. What would you have done differently that you can't do now because of your skin? You were my maid, and you are my maid, and you will be my maid unless I dismiss you. It's remarkably annoying to see you act as if you'd had a different life before the chicken pox, or whatever it was."

Mirae remembered very well how Mistress Yee had promised, or seemed to have promised, something grand, although intangible, when she was in need of help. Mirae had participated in the affairs of her mistress as if they had been scheming for a shared purpose. She sighed deeply as she was tidying up the room after her mistress had left for breakfast. She was not grieving over her disfigured skin. No, her heart sank because she had wasted her life for nothing and that she had been gravely mistaken when she thought she had a friend in Mistress Yee. "How foolish," she said aloud to herself. She laughed and laughed until she sounded like a madwoman and tears trickled down her cheeks.

EVERY YEAR, BEFORE MISTRESS KIM HAD PASSED AWAY, on holidays, especially on Harvest Day, Mr. O's servants were busy delivering packages of food to the peasants on his land as a token of gratitude and friendship. But this year, there was no such order from the master. A day after Harvest Day, Nani realized that there was an abundance of leftover food. She knew that some of the peasants expected to taste the food served on the altar in memory of Mistress Kim.

Early in the morning, Nani decided to send some food to at least a few people, thinking that Mistress Kim would have liked her to do so. She was looking for Min to make the delivery, but he was nowhere to be found. She should have been more sensitive when he had brought in the baby in the basket. But then, who had the time and the means to mother an orphan even for a day?

After a while, Nani gave up looking for Min. In the end, Bok, the errand boy for Mr. O, delivered food to a few homes, including Jaya's.

Grumbling, and feeling still a little guilty for having been heartless, Nani staggered with a mountainous load of laundry to the creek. She was the only one there doing laundry. Everyone else was probably sleeping in after the gluttonous holiday. She began to beat the sheets and clothes with a wooden bat on a flat rock. She saw Bok race by like a puppy. Nani stopped her work and shouted to him, "Have you seen Min?"

"No! He didn't sleep in the room last night," the boy shouted back, still racing across the rice field.

"Where on earth has he gone?" Nani said under her breath, beating the blanket cover harder. She hadn't meant to hurt his feelings. She would tell him that. But where was he?

The tree branches on the surface of the water danced dizzily. Suddenly, Nani raised her head to look at the surrounding mountains and was amazed by the change in the colors. It was definitely fall now. Summer was the time she had to be patient with the scorching heat and the long, stubborn afternoons that didn't want to surrender. But then the fall would ambush her, and just when she was savoring the best season of the year, it would flee without warning. Nani could feel the crispness in the air. Soon it would be too cold to do laundry in the creek.

By the time she was done with the laundry, a couple of women showed up with their laundry on their heads. They exchanged greetings, but Nani didn't feel like chatting. There were things to be done. Realistically speaking, she felt that she was the only functioning maid at the moment, and the workload was getting to her. She hurried back to the house, and as she entered the gate, Mirae was leaving, all dressed up, just as she had often done before the infamous chicken pox. Widening her eyes, she surveyed Mirae from head to toe and was impressed. Whatever had happened to her? She was back to herself. This was good, but immediately the familiar hostility she had always felt toward her churned her stomach. "A lady is born," Nani said, clucking her tongue sarcastically.

"I am going to the temple," Mirae said coolly. "Mistress Yee wants you." Mirae walked away briskly.

Nani clucked her tongue again, lingering for a while to watch Mirae sashay. She was swaying her rear end just as lasciviously as before. "Good old Mirae," Nani remarked resentfully.

The first thing Nani did was to inquire after Min when she saw Soonyi. He had not been sighted since the day before, but no one seemed to think it strange. She hung the laundry behind the maids' quarters. Then she sat down by the tool shed and pensively ate an unpeeled radish, long, white, and juicy. She was thinking about Mirae; she had seemed pretty in spite of her uneven skin. When her mother was alive, she had called Mirae a mountain fox. Legend told that a mountain fox had turned into a pretty woman at night to seduce a man so that she could eat him whole in the morning. Nani was only nine years old so the story went over her head. But now that she was older, she knew vaguely what her mother might have meant. Mirae was a different sort. There was no one to compare to her.

All of a sudden, Nani sprang up, tossing the tail of the radish in the air. She ran to Mistress Yee's quarters as fast as she could. Still panting as she was taking her shoes off, she announced her arrival. There was no reply from inside. Her heart pounded. She announced herself again, more quietly.

"What's the fuss?" said Mistress Yee irritably.

"Mistress Yee, I was told that you wanted me to come," Nani said feebly.

"I am glad you are still alive," she replied. "Come in."

Nani opened the door and said, "Mistress, I was doing the laundry. I am sorry I am late."

"Come close," Mistress Yee said, smiling unexpectedly.

Anticipating calamity, Nani approached. She was sure that Mistress Yee was about to fire her, considering what she had accused her of in the storage room.

"My blood circulation is really bad, and it makes my legs fall asleep all the time. I need a good massage on my legs," Mistress Yee said as she pulled her long skirt up. Then she pulled up her long, silky white underdress and then her long white under-pants, baring her legs. Nani began to massage her legs carefully, rotating her thumbs with just the right amount of pressure.

"Ah, that feels so good. You have the touch. Did you do this for the dead woman?" Mistress Yee asked, her face completely relaxed and her eyes closed.

"No. I did it for my mother," Nani replied. Her forehead was slightly sweating.

"Well, you are doing a good job," Mistress Yee said.

A little while later, just as Nani thought that Mistress Yee was asleep, she suddenly spoke: "Nani, how old are you?"

Startled, Nani quickly answered.

"I hear you are engaged to the dumb boy. What's his name? Min. Is that correct?" Mistress Yee said with a mysterious smile.

Nani, speeding up with her massaging, was at a loss. She didn't know what to say.

"Now, that is not something to be embarrassed about. Did he ever give you an assurance he would marry you?"

"We haven't really talked about it, Mistress Yee," Nani replied.

Mistress Yee opened her eyes and burst out laughing. "You couldn't have. He can't speak!" She laughed some more. "Of course, I understand that there are other ways to communicate. And I am sure that you have mastered that language by now. But I want to know if he intends to marry you."

Nani turned apple red and focused her glance on the floor.

"Do you know that he's been disappearing at night regularly?" Mistress Yee asked in an all-knowing tone of voice. "Does he come to you?"

"I beg your pardon, Mistress Yee?"

"You heard me," Mistress Yee said, her eyes closed.

Nani was speechless.

"Does your silence mean yes?" Mistress Yee asked, fixing her glance on Nani.

"Mistress Yee, my mother taught me to behave." She stopped, unsure about what else to say.

"I don't really care what you do at night," Mistress Yee said curtly, still smiling.

Nani bit her lip and lowered her glance.

"If what you say is true—if Min doesn't come to you at night—then we need to find out where he does go every night," Mistress Yee said. Her tone was uncharacteristically serious and quiet. She raised her eyebrows questioningly and stared at Nani.

Mistress Yee seemed to expect Nani to come up with a scheme to find out where Min went at night. But she didn't really believe what Mistress Yee was saying. Min had no place to go, she was convinced, except that he had disappeared the day before because they had a little argument over the abandoned baby. Should she confess the event from the day before? That would demystify his absence. But then she would need to explain why she hadn't mentioned the incident earlier, so she sat there, listening to her own breathing.

"Will you go look for him?" Mistress Yee asked.

"Yes, Mistress Yee," Nani quickly answered.

"Where will you go to look for him?" Mistress Yee asked, her eyes sparkling.

"Well, first I will go to the field and see if he is helping out the farmers with the hay or something because he's always wanted to lend a hand. He is very strong, you see, Mistress Yee. Then I will go to Dubak's house to ask if he has seen him. They are friends," Nani rattled on until she realized that Mistress Yee was not listening to her.

"No need to go look for him. We know where he is. We are going to marry him off. I just wanted to let you know that. It seems as though he hasn't done anything to be obliged to take you as his bride. We would like to arrange a marriage between him and a village girl with a baby, out of wedlock," Mistress Yee said casually.

Nani opened her mouth. But her tongue was frozen, and her limbs were dissolving into nothingness.

"Massage my feet." Mistress Yee wriggled her toes impatiently.

Nani grabbed her left foot and began to massage it. Mistress Yee giggled, pulling it away from Nani. Nani could no longer hear or feel anything. She wanted so desperately to see Min and ask him if he loved her. Mistress Yee, still giggling, stretched her legs toward Nani, suggesting that she should go on with the massage. But Nani got up slowly and walked toward the door, as if sleepwalking.

"What are you doing?" Mistress Yee cawed to the back of Nani's head. By the time she grabbed a teacup to throw at her, it was too late: Nani was out of sight.

MIRAE ARRIVED AT NOON, WHEN THE MONKS WERE having their lunch in solemn silence in a small, dark room adjacent to the kitchen.

As she made her way down the freshly swept path toward the main hall, time frozen in the air, she could hear only her own uneven steps against gravel filled ground.

In the main hall, she sat against the far end wall and beheld the Buddha. Failing to conjure up the enlightened state she had experienced the most recent time there, she sighed, wrinkling her forehead. Her heart was a hollow place. The Buddha had no smile, the air was acrid, and all the objects in the room appeared deplorably worn out and filthy. There was a huge spider in the corner of the ceiling, suspended like a lonely acrobat. She pondered what she would like to be in her next life. Maybe a lady with many maids. Or perhaps the queen of China. No, a spider in a temple. Actually, she didn't believe in future lives. Or past lives. Only stupid people did, she thought, and smiled bitterly.

Her legs felt wobbly from the long walk. Slowly, she slid down to the floor, making a Chinese character, "Big," with her body, her arms stretched out horizontally, her legs slightly parted, and her eyes closed.

The dull and sorrowful sound of the bronze gong seeped in, filling the room. Afternoon meditation. A group of monks in their heavy drapes took careful steps to the altar room, above the stairs behind the main hall. She could imagine thirty or so bald heads in their huge robes, silently mounting the stairs. In a few moments, silence was restored. Mirae opened her eyes.

The spider plunged and miraculously landed on an invisible place in midair. It knew exactly where it was going. Mirae sat up and surveyed the Buddha, whose glance, last time, had fixated on her from wherever she looked at him. Now, no matter how hard she tried, she couldn't make eye contact with him. It didn't matter. She no longer felt reverence for him.

What comforted her, though, was that she was anonymous there. That no one would pay attention to her was small serendipity. She hoped to stay there as long as she could. She suddenly felt curious to see what else was there in the temple. She knew only the main hall and the kitchen. She could explore the place without attracting anyone's attention. She got up and slipped out and walked away from the main hall. She passed the enormous stone water tub which collected water from the hill through a bamboo pipe. A child novice arrived to fetch a pot of water. He glanced at Mirae as he walked back to the kitchen. Mirae kept walking without knowing where she was going. Passing the overgrown bamboo, she stepped into a clearing where she could see the surrounding mountains and the valley. The earth seemed to be on fire with fall colors. Her heart throbbed. She lingered there for a while, soaking in the scenery, until she heard the rumbling of a nearby voice. She turned and looked about to locate the source of the voice. Involuntarily, she walked toward the original part of the temple which had not been renovated since its construction centuries before.

Listening to the soft, soothing chanting from within, she sat on the stone steps and leaned her head against the wooden pillar. She had no doubt that it was the head monk inside. What was the question she had asked him? She couldn't recall now. He had answered her with sincerity, as if she were a lady, an important person. He had treated her with respect. No one had ever treated her that way.

Down below the dirt path there was a small vegetable garden in which a few pumpkins were hiding under their leaves.

She stared at them placidly, counting them. She paused, struck by an idea. She wanted to live there, among the monks. She wasn't sure what she would do, but she wanted to live there. She could make pumpkin soup for the monks. She could garden, although she had no experience with gardening. She could do the laundry. But then, why should she wash the stinking laundry of the bald heads?

A drop of water hit her forehead. Immediately, large drops of rain began to fall, loudly, everywhere. Surprised, she looked about. The only place where she could stay dry was inside. She pulled off her shoes quickly and stood in front of the wood-frame door. She ran her fingers through her hair, feeling self-conscious about her skin. At least the scabs were gone. Slowly, she opened the door and went in. The head monk, undisturbed, sat there, as if dead.

Closing the door, she stood, not knowing if she should sit. And if she did, where? She had expected the head monk to be surprised, or at least to acknowledge her, and to inquire after Mr. O's health as a formality. But he didn't even seem to have heard her come in. She wet her lips.

The room was small. Her breathing was the only sound. The head monk seemed to have drifted into a different world, where there was no entrance on her side, only an exit on his side. He was there but he was not there. She relaxed and immediately felt bored.

Inspecting his profile, she let the time pass. The best part of his face was his nose, and then she changed her mind. It was his lips. They were expressive even when they were still.

All of a sudden, she hiccupped. Covering her mouth and clenching her teeth, she tried unsuccessfully to stop hiccupping.

The head monk opened his eyes as if he had come alive from a dream. He said something, not to Mirae, but to the world he had just left.

Clearing her throat, Mirae began to speak, only to end with a loud hiccup.

The head monk rose, clasped his palms, and bowed obliquely to Mirae. She rose, too, and said, "I am sorry to have disturbed you."

His eyelids slowly peeled back, baring his eyes. Mirae dropped her head because she didn't want to surprise him with her disfigured skin. Heat suffused her cheeks. "I have been struck by chicken pox," she confessed.

The head monk acknowledged this by dropping his eyelids briefly, and then he made his way out.

Mirae stepped in his path. She was not sure what she was doing. But she mumbled, "I need to talk to you, if that's all right."

He stopped and she sat down in front of his feet.

He sat, too, and looked at her, his eyes full of calm compassion.

"I would like to live here. I will do anything. I will cook and clean," she said rapidly.

There was silence. The monk seemed not to have heard the urgency in her voice.

Staring at his face, lean and smooth, she could feel the age of what was holding his body, the core of him, the unreachable realm. A thousand years. She thought of the house snake who was supposed to live in between a roof and a ceiling, generation after generation, looking down on the life cycles of the inhabitants. Finally, one day when it shed its skin for the millionth time, it would become human and take over the house.

"What about your duties at Mr. O's?" the head monk asked.

Mirae's eyebrows shot up. She almost laughed. She had expected him to say something different, something profound. But what he had said was mundane, boring, stupid.

"I am not a slave. My post as a maid can be terminated. I am there because I have nowhere to go, but if you let me live and work here, I will be very happy," Mirae said, imagining herself standing triumphantly in front of Mistress Yee, asking to be released forever.

"How old is this idea?" the head monk asked gently.

"I beg your pardon?" But as soon as she spoke, she understood his question. "I was sitting outside, listening to your chanting. It occurred to me that I would really like to come and live here," she confessed, lowering her head.

The head monk smiled and said, "Do you remember the rain a few minutes ago?"

Mirae, puzzled, raised her head.

"It is gone now. If you go outside and look up at the sky, you wouldn't know that it had just poured. What comes so suddenly often goes away in the same manner. Living in a temple is not difficult, but living away from the world is not easy. One must not make a quick decision, for the mind doesn't always know what is best for one," he said. He got up to leave the room.

Mirae was unhappy. He was so stubborn. She had meant what she said. It wasn't one of her whims. Couldn't he see her face? Everyone was whispering about her skin behind her back. How could she live on like that?

She pulled his robe and cried, "Please, Illustrious! I am torn inside. I am on the verge of going mad. I hate my life. I hate my mistress. I hate the way I look now!" She wanted to shake him to make him pity her and embrace her.

He stood there like a tree, planted deep, its roots gripping into the earth, strong and immovable. This wasn't the first time that a woman had come to unburden herself to him. Surprisingly many women had opened up to him, with various agonizing problems, all overwhelming to them. Mistress Kim also had spoken her mind to him. He still remembered her clearly. She had come often, once a month, to meditate, to be away from her daily life. Her demeanor, unhesitating and precise, yet gentle and feminine, had struck him. When she sat in the meditation hall, his desire to go and catch a glimpse of her was intoxicating, but instead he fidgeted in the altar room and then took a long stroll to miss her departure. One day, he entered the meditation hall like a shadow, and she heard him come in. She didn't turn around but spoke to him resolutely. She wanted to know if it was easy to live away from the world. He hesitated, his forehead perspiring with cold sweat, not knowing whether the question was directed to him or to herself. "I am glad you don't answer me," she said. "I will not trouble you again," she added. And she had never come back. That was some years before. The last thing he had heard was that she had died while giving birth. He had burned incense and prayed for her afterlife for forty-nine days, as requested by Mr. O. But the thought of her didn't leave him, even after the forty-ninth day. She would appear in his dreams. And he would say that it was not hard to live away from the world, now that she was no longer in it. He would wake up and lament his shortcomings.

The chilled air wafted in as the head monk opened the door. Mirae stood helplessly watching him leave. His feet slithered into his wet slippery shoes. She called out to him feebly, but he walked away vigorously, his wet feet squeaking. As soon as he arrived at the kitchen, he devoured a luscious and juicy persimmon. He stood in the dark kitchen and looked at the small rectangular window. The world outside was burning orange. Placing a few persimmon seeds into a vessel where the kitchen monk saved the seeds of fruits, he sighed regretfully. It wasn't Mirae or Mistress Kim who disturbed him. It was his mind that was doing the disturbing. He left the kitchen and walked back to where he had left Mirae.

Only a missive in Mr. O's handwriting awaited him. He sat on the stone steps and looked up at the sky with his eyes closed. The light penetrated his eyelids. He saw orange and black dots swarming in a vast ocean in his eyes, making him feel warm and buoyant. A pair of fluttering lips met his. He kept his eyes closed and his body still, lest everything fall apart like a puffball in the wind. But the lips didn't linger. He opened his eyes and there was no one. All he saw were fat pumpkins haphazardly spread out in the vegetable garden, scrutinizing him with their invisible eyes.

He opened the letter from Mr. O, but it was actually from Mistress Yee, asking him to pray for blessings on her future baby and her health, and she also mentioned that she would come and see him soon.

MIRAE CAME DOWN THE MOUNTAIN HURRIEDLY. HER legs wobbled by the time she reached the market place. She no longer thought about her visit at the temple or the head monk or how she begged him to allow her to live at the temple. Mistress Yee entered her mind. And Mirae realized she had no one she'd call a friend in the entire world.

A few shoppers and peddlers meandered. A blind man, dressed in rags, began to sing poignantly. A crowd of people gathered around him. Mirae joined them. She observed the daughter of the blind man, young and pretty and filthy.

From the opposite side of the crowd, a brawny man, probably a farm worker from his dark complexion, stared at Mirae intently. She blushed deeply, feeling dry in her throat. An old woman, drunk and cheerful, stepped out in the middle and danced to the tune of the blind man's song. People clapped and cheered. The dark-skinned man on the opposite side was inching toward Mirae. In a moment he was not too far from her. The crowd momentarily applauded at the end of a song. The blind man took a bow, and his daughter picked up the coins from the cloth spread in front of her father. The crowd dispersed immediately, and the man lingered, his devouring gaze still fixed on Mirae. She suddenly turned around and walked toward the restaurant district. It was too late for lunch and too early for dinner. She found herself in an alley. From behind he grabbed her shoulder. For a while they stood, facing each other with ravenous stares. Then, he pulled the knot at her bosom to untie her upper garment. She slapped the back of his hand lightly. He pressed against the mud wall. Her breathing became heavy, and his became a groan. He touched her face, and she was wondering what he was thinking. He smirked, and all of a sudden, Mirae was sure he despised her for her scarred skin, and she felt ashamed of her appearance. She pushed him away angrily. Unprepared, he flew and landed on the ground, slightly scraping one of his fingers. He grinned, licked the blood on his finger, and shot her a glance. His neck was flushed.

"Don't come near me," Mirae warned him.

"That's not what you want to say," he said, quietly.

"Stay away from me or else," Mirae squealed, extending her arm like a shield.

"Whoa," he said, and snorted. "You led me to this alley, and you let me untie your knot, and now you say, don't come near me? That's not going to make you a lady, is it?"

He was filthy, Mirae realized, and he stank too. She was disgusted. Quickly retying the knot of her upper garment, she tried to walk away from him. But he grabbed her skirt and chortled.

"Let go!" Mirae shrieked.

He scowled and pulled at her skirt, which came off easily. She stood in her long white underskirt, baffled.

"You see, you planned this. I know all about girls like you," he said, grinning broadly.

"Give that back to me!"

"I will. Only after we settle our business here," he said, looking obviously pleased to see her at a loss and worked up.

"I am going to scream. Give that back right now!" she demanded.

"Go ahead and shout. The crowd will gather and wonder how in the world you and I ended up here. I will tell them you led me here and offered your skirt. We will be bound together and dragged to the court. You know what the sentence is for a maid who seduces a decent man? You will be flogged in public, if not worse. If that's what you want, go ahead and scream. Scream away!" He approached slowly.

Retreating, Mirae tripped over a stone and fell on her buttocks. She looked up at him fiercely with the instinct of a murderer. She picked up the stone, which was really too small to kill anyone with, and she got up, holding it tightly in her palm with all her strength.

"By the way, whatever happened to your skin?" he asked derisively, coming closer, burping up the fermented smell of rice wine.

Swallowing her saliva, Mirae hurled the stone at him, which landed on his forehead, producing a sound like an acorn falling on hard ground.

He growled and covered his forehead with his hand. At seeing his palm smeared with blood he narrowed his eyes. His upper lip twitched. Then he spat. "This is a bad day for you and me," he declared, grabbing her by the wrist.

Mirae shrilled and kicked him in his groin. One of her shoes slipped off and flew away. He grabbed between his legs, groaning. She ran as fast as she could. It was dusk and there was no one in the market place.

The earth was restless, Mirae could feel, as she heard the rustling of the tall grass by the field under the immense and darkening sky. She made her way down the steps that led to the creek and sat on the flat rock where women beat their laundry. She dipped her hands into the water and splashed it on her burning face. It had been a long day. She cleaned her neck and her shoulders and wet her hair to keep it down. A large lump was settling in her chest, and it wasn't a very good feeling. Cursing the gods, she got up and walked up the steps. She realized how late it was. Mistress Yee might slap her, but then she was going to tell her that she had gotten lost, and the rain had come which had prevented her from descending the mountain promptly. She could make up some other stories,

which would let Mistress Yee know that she had nearly lost
her life carrying out Mistress Yee's errand.

A figure drew near her when she got up to the grassy area.
It was a man, tall, broad-shouldered, and walking stealthily.

"Who's there?" she uttered, stopping, holding her breath.

It was Min, the dumb boy. Mirae sighed with relief and said,
"You frightened me! Should have said something." Then she
remembered that he was mute. She laughed hysterically. It
was just the dumb boy. There was nothing to fear.

Min stood there, staring at her, unmoved.

"Doesn't she ever laugh at you like this? Nani, I mean. How
are you?"

She observed his shoulders, and his log-like arms. Until
then, she had never really noticed him, even though they had
lived in the same household serving the same master. He spat
and motioned with his hand that Mirae should hurry home.

"Did you come looking for me?" she asked, taking a confi-
dent step toward him. His whole body exuded a pungent odor
of alcohol. Mirae frowned, holding her nose with one hand
and fanning with the other in an exaggerated manner. She
laughed ridiculously.

Min lowered his head, as if to examine his straw shoes. His
large toe on the right side was peeking out. It wiggled in an
attempt to go back inside. Abruptly, he turned around and
walked toward the house where they both belonged.

Mirae sprinted after him, whispering something to herself,
her white teeth glinting. When she caught up with him, she
grabbed his shirt from behind and pulled him toward her.
Unexpectedly, he fell backward and landed on the grass, and
he didn't move. Mirae tapped him on his side with her foot
to see if he was conscious. He groaned. She collapsed next to
him and lay down. He didn't move. She sprang up suddenly
and complained that the ground was cold. She sat on him like
a horseback rider and boldly touched his chin. He felt hard.

She giggled. She examined his face, feeling amused. Nani would kill her if she found out about this, she thought. She giggled again. Just because he couldn't talk it didn't mean that *she* needed to be silent. "Hey, dumbo," she said, and then she didn't know what else to say. How did one talk with a man who couldn't talk? She tittered. Impulsively, she untied his shirt, laughing uncontrollably. She didn't know what she was really trying to do. She fell on his chest, burying her head under his chin, still laughing. He shook her and grabbed her buttocks in his hands. Sitting on top of him, she rocked like a little boat in a tempest, docked between piers. Clutching at his shoulders, she looked up at the sky, where millions of gems sparkled. The sight was fantastically entrancing. All of a sudden the stars were falling and then the field in front of her shimmered in wet silvery sequins.

Min heaved and groaned like an animal in pain. Mirae looked down and saw his face as if for the first time. Then she laughed like a mad woman and he pushed her aside and got up. He walked away without looking back. Mirae grabbed her last shoe and threw it at him, but he had already walked too far. She watched her legs, as if they weren't part of her own body. Ignoring the dripping blood on her thighs, she stood up, fixing her clothes roughly and straightening her hair. Then she realized she had cried; her cheeks were wet. She sat again on the grass and thought about what in the world she had just done. She was a little ashamed because it was Min the dumb boy she had shared this experience with. He wouldn't be able to talk about it. It made her feel slightly better. She got up and walked home.

Everyone was caught by surprise when the first frost came, because it was still the middle of the fall. No one had yet started pickling.

Enough samples of kimchi from her past clientele would arrive for her, which would last until spring, Mrs. Wang knew, but she hadn't stuffed her blanket with new cotton or pasted new wallpaper to keep the draft out. She would have to order a new quilted coat this year, for her old one was unraveling at the hem. And her shoes! She definitely needed better shoes for winter.

Mrs. Wang dreaded snow. She was beginning to fear slipping on the ice when she descended to deliver babies on short notice. She was thinking about posting an announcement that one should try to have a baby only in certain seasons. It was too much for her to go around on frozen hills and fields. She was getting old.

Sitting in front of her portable stove in the middle of the room, she was waiting for the sweet potatoes to be roasted. She kept stabbing into them impatiently with her chopstick.

Suddenly, she realized that someone was kneeling, as if being punished, before the room. It was Mirae. Her eyes darted about, and she jerked at the slightest noise from the dog or the chickens.

"Come inside! It's chilly out there," Mrs. Wang advised her.

She placed two small potatoes in a bowl. Mirae came in sheepishly. Peeling a steamy sweet potato, Mrs. Wang exercised the muscles around her mouth. "These are the best kind," Mrs. Wang said to herself, smiling contentedly. She ate it with her eyes almost closed, appreciating the taste and the warmth and the comfort that it brought to her stomach. Then she asked Mirae if she would like one, stabbing a large one in the copper stove.

"I am not hungry, Mrs. Wang," Mirae said despondently.

"Did your mistress send you here? Did she yell at you? If she was able to yell at you, she is not having a baby today. Trust me," Mrs. Wang said reassuringly. "Have a sweet potato. It just melts in your mouth," she said, taking another one out of the stove.

"It's not that," Mirae said, wiping her eyes.

"Oh, oh. Don't you shed tears in *my* house. If you are worried about your mistress, you can go now and tell her that I said I would be coming for lunch," Mrs. Wang said.

"She doesn't even know I am here," Mirae began. "I am ashamed, Mrs. Wang. I don't know how to say this, but I need your help." Mirae paused, sighing from the depths of her chest. "I am pregnant," Mirae confessed, looking miserable.

Mrs. Wang peeled another sweet potato and didn't hesitate to devour it, thinking, why are women so often surprised to find out that they are pregnant? Is it that hard to remember how you get pregnant?

Aloud, she said, "All the more reason to eat something." Mrs. Wang pushed the plate with a large, hot sweet potato toward Mirae. She covered her mouth in an effort to stifle a cry.

There was nothing like steamy sweet potatoes on a chilly day, thought Mrs. Wang, taking another one, but her appetite had diminished with the two sweet potatoes in her stomach and her troubled visitor.

"What kind of help do you need from me?" Mrs. Wang asked, nonchalantly.

Finally, Mirae broke down and sobbed. She hated herself for being in a position where she had to beg for help. Above all, she abhorred the change in her body, even though only she could notice it so far.

Mrs. Wang got up and said that she was going to do the dishes. In the meantime, she hoped Mirae would decide what kind of help she needed.

Her chickens went crazy when she went out to the yard. They thought that food was forthcoming. Her dog jumped up and down, slobbering messily. Mrs. Wang sat by the well and didn't do the dishes. Instead, she washed herself up and cleaned her teeth with a spoonful of sea salt. She then fed her chickens and swept the yard and drank a huge bowl of water. She appreciated that Mirae hadn't followed her out, crying and begging for help. She was a proud girl, all right, but then why in the world was she so stupid as to get herself pregnant? Mrs. Wang was still puzzled. Normally, those who got themselves pregnant and wailed about it afterward were missing something in the head or so dreadfully naive that Mrs. Wang didn't even bother to react to them.

"Mrs. Wang, don't you have some honey?" Mirae called from behind her. She was standing on the extended entrance of her room. "I am craving something sweet."

"Not to spare. But I have rice malt you can dip your sweet potato in," Mrs. Wang replied and went to the kitchen to fetch some. "What an insolent girl," Mrs. Wang grumbled to herself.

She brought out the rice malt in a small bowl, and in a wink Mirae had eaten the sweet potato with the syrup.

"Thank you for your kindness." Mirae rattled on, ignoring Mrs. Wang's grin. "I have been repelled by any kind of food smell, but then suddenly I felt so ravenous. I guess it's normal. I saw Mistress Yee act the same way in the early phase of her pregnancy."

"So have you decided what kind of help you need from me?" Mrs. Wang asked insouciantly.

"Don't press me. I know you have no sympathy for me. But I have no one to turn to. If Mistress Yee found out about my state, she would kick me out of the house, and I have no place to go. I need to be rid of this growth in my body," Mirae articulated with composure.

Mrs. Wang disliked the supercilious maids as much as subservient ones. "That's not a good enough reason for terminating your pregnancy," she replied.

Mirae pursed her lips determinedly and then said defiantly, "Well, Mrs. Wang. Let me then tell you the truth. This is going to be the worst reason you've ever heard. But I don't care what anyone says about it. I don't want to have a baby. That's all there is to it. I don't care whether Mistress Yee would kick me out of her house or not. I just cannot imagine myself breast-feeding a baby. I know I will kill the baby." Mirae's shoulders quivered and she bowed her head. "I never wanted to be born. Never," she whispered almost inaudibly.

A black crow cawed at that moment, crossing the sky above Mrs. Wang's thatched roof, splashing its silver-gray shit directly in her yard.

Mrs. Wang suppressed her habit of laying down her principles regarding this matter.

"Your calamity is beyond my ability. What you need to do is see an herbalist or an acupuncturist. Go to the market and see Mr. Jo behind the fabric store. He might have an answer for you," Mrs. Wang said, surveying Mirae's face.

Mirae looked up distrustfully and asked, "What can he do?"

"Many things," Mrs. Wang said and chuckled. "He can concoct a brew that will erase the growth. It takes a while to bring about the result: one cycle of the moon at least. Tell him you talked with me already," Mrs. Wang advised her.

"Thank you, Mrs. Wang. I will not forget your kindness," Mirae said, tears spilling from her large eyes.

In her younger days, Mrs. Wang would interrogate the girl about the man, urge her to go and talk it over with the pig, and so on. But her experience had taught her not to waste her breath.

Mirae got up, bowed politely, and awkwardly thanked her again before she put her shoes on.

"By the way, he might have some remedy for your skin too," Mrs. Wang said. "Not that you need to correct it, but if you still feel depressed about it, I'd ask."

Struck by the power of new hope, Mirae momentarily forgot all about her pregnancy. If only she could look the way she had used to look! She would do almost anything, she thought. "Is it true?" Mirae asked half doubtfully. "I heard that chicken pox scars can't be cured."

"Those aren't chicken pox scars," said Mrs. Wang simply.

"What was it then?" Mirae asked.

"No idea. Go and ask yourself," Mrs. Wang replied. "You will have more trouble when your scars go away. Nothing comes without a price. Just keep in mind that you will not be Mistress Yee even if you serve her a hundred years."

"I don't want to be Mistress Yee. She is the nastiest woman I know," Mirae said fearlessly.

"You need to watch your mouth and stay out of trouble. Now go. I can't idle away all day," Mrs. Wang said.

"May I take another sweet potato?"

"Take the little one."

Mirae took a medium-sized one and got up. She walked down the hill, feeling much lighter than just an hour before.

After Mirae left, Mrs. Wang mixed rice flour in water and simmered it to make glue for pasting new wallpaper. She skewered persimmons with strips of bamboo and hung them to dry in the sun. She pulled out her old coat and examined it to see if she could wear it for another year.

THE RICE FIELD, LUSCIOUS AND GREEN ALL SUMMER, WAS turning frigid gray and austere. Even the wild animals had disappeared. In good years, it was a peaceful period for farmers. But in bad years, as this year was due to the drought, it was a restless period for them even though there wasn't much else to do besides making straw shoes and straw sacks, working as roofers, or hanging out around Mr. O's mansion to pick up odd jobs.

One day early in the morning, when a farmer named Jaegon was on his way to the open marketplace to sell thimbles and knickknacks, he ran into a dog, brownish white and scrawny, by the rice field. What attracted his attention was the thing it was carrying in its mouth. The lump was bloody and, to his surprise, it appeared to be a human fetus. He tried to stop the dog to have a closer look, but it walked in circles around him, distrustfully. He didn't want to investigate the matter further, for his mind was rushing to the market. He wanted to be the first one to occupy an opportune spot. So he hurried off to his destination, looking back at intervals until the dog was no longer in sight.

Later that afternoon as the merchants were discussing the meaning of life, Mrs. Wang stopped to buy a thimble. She wanted to stuff her blanket with the new cotton. She was wondering what was being talked about so intensely.

"Oh, a horrible thing I saw this morning," Jaegon began. He told her about the bloody fetus and how he regretted not having pursued the case further.

"A lot of things look like a fetus," Mrs. Wang commented. "Especially at dawn. It could have been a dead chipmunk," she suggested, raising her eyebrows.

"Oh no, Mrs. Wang, it wasn't a chipmunk for sure. I saw it with my own eyes," Jaegon retorted.

"Do you have a large needle for sewing blankets?" Mrs. Wang said, diverting his attention.

"Sure I do," Jaegon replied quickly and opened his box to show Mrs. Wang needles of all sizes.

"That one looks just right," Mrs. Wang said and pointed to the thickest one in the box.

"Ah, that's for sewing up knitted stuff. The next one down is what you want," he said confidently.

"Give that to me then," Mrs. Wang said, and paid for the thimble and the needle.

"What else?" he asked, widening his eyes and shoving the money into his sack.

"That will do for now."

"Thank you, Mrs. Wang," he said, smiling broadly. "Have you eaten?" he asked out of politeness, even though he had nothing left to offer.

"Oh, I have. But what have you got? I can always eat more," Mrs. Wang said and chuckled good-humoredly.

At that moment, someone from a distance was calling Mrs. Wang desperately. Jaegon and the other peddlers looked in the direction of the high-pitched voice, but Mrs. Wang packed her needle and her thimble carefully into her sleeve without looking around. She was used to this sort of urgent voice wanting her attention immediately, and most of the time it was a false alarm.

Soonyi from Mr. O's household wanted Mrs. Wang. Stopping behind her, Soonyi panted loudly, with her cheeks rosy and forehead beaded with perspiration. "Mrs. Wang, my lady needs you. Mr. O sent me to fetch you right away. The wagon is waiting at the entrance of the market. Please come with me quickly or else," Soonyi said without breathing until Mrs. Wang interrupted.

"Or else what?" Mrs. Wang asked, stepping away from the crowd leisurely.

Soonyi rattled on excitedly. "Mrs. Wang, my lady is in such pain. She can't even speak."

Mrs. Wang walked on toward the entrance of the market, counting how many days had passed since her most recent visit with Mistress Yee and recalling her due date. It was early, and yet this little monkey was making a scene in the marketplace as if Mrs. Wang lived only to be summoned from wherever she was and whatever she was doing. Mrs. Wang had planned to have a drink at the pub, but now it looked as though she wasn't going to.

Twin midgets were performing circus tricks at the entrance of the market. One was standing on the soles of the other, who was lying on her back, holding a bowl of water on a stick clenched between her teeth. The one on the top was bending down carefully to drink the water from the bowl through a straw. Mesmerized by the breathtaking sight, Soonyi halted and dropped her jaw.

"Well, should we stay and have some fun?" Mrs. Wang asked, chewing on a dried squid leg.

Soonyi collected herself and led the way to the wagon, where Bok was taking a nap, leaning against one of the wheels.

Soonyi hit him on the head. He got up and bowed toward the wagon. Mrs. Wang was behind him. She offered him a dried persimmon. He bowed again and took it at once.

"Never eat dried fruit in a hurry. Or rice cake. You will choke on it, and there is no remedy for choking," Mrs. Wang said, getting on the wagon with the help of the errand boy, whose cheeks were bulging with the persimmon he was about to swallow. He nodded solemnly.

Soonyi pulled his ear. "What a piglet you are! You just had lunch."

"Big Sister, I am a growing boy," he grumbled.

"Here, children. I've got some dried squid." Mrs. Wang shared her squid with them, anticipating that there would be lots of food soon at Mr. O's. She also thought that her visit would last a while.

The mule-drawn wagon began to rattle on the stony road, and Mrs. Wang wondered if she had fed her chickens that morning, if she had closed her gate properly, and if she had hung laundry out.

The sun felt good, even though the air was chilly. Mrs. Wang closed her eyes, leaning against the haystack, and Soonyi kept talking about the recent incidents and affairs in the grand house of Mr. O. Mrs. Wang was the last person to mind good gossip.

NANI RECEIVED MRS. WANG, LOOKING GRIM. SHE lacked her usual childish lightness. Her voice low and hoarse, she said, "Oh, Mrs. Wang, so kind of you to come promptly. Our lady is waiting for you."

"Give me some water," Mrs. Wang demanded.

"Surely. Please follow me," Nani said and walked on.

Mrs. Wang, following behind, could see that Nani's figure had fully matured.

"Soonyi, stay in the kitchen. Keep an eye on the fire in the oven. When the water boils, reduce the heat and add the chopped onions in the bowl. Mistress Yee wants beef stew for dinner. So beef stew it is, until she changes her mind," Nani whispered the last sentence in a strained voice.

"How old are you?" Mrs. Wang asked Nani.

"Too old for marriage, too young for the grave. I just don't know what to do with my life, Mrs. Wang," she replied with a sigh.

Mrs. Wang narrowed her eyes at the maid. She herself had said so once a long time before.

Mr. O was lingering outside his wife's chamber, looking lost and impatient. As soon as he saw Mrs. Wang, he visibly relaxed. Skipping any formalities, he said, "What a relief to see you, Mrs. Wang. Please, hurry in."

Nani arranged Mrs. Wang's shoes and quickly stepped ahead of her in the anteroom and announced Mrs. Wang's arrival, but only low groans came from inside.

Then Mirae answered from inside, "Please come in."

Nani opened the door before Mirae finished her sentence.

Stepping into the room, Mrs. Wang looked in the ceramic chamber pot with a lovely blue magnolia blossom design. Frowning slightly, she sniffed the urine. Mistress Yee was lying with her legs raised on several pillows and her eyes half closed. Mrs. Wang sat and asked Nani when Mistress Yee had most recently eaten and urinated.

"She has no appetite, Mrs. Wang," Nani said.

Mistress Yee opened her eyes, threw a bronze bowl in her maid's direction, and barked, "That wasn't the question! Why do I have to put up with a pack of stupid maids?"

Mrs. Wang advised her, "You need to calm down. The color of your urine indicates you are not well."

"I want the baby out! I have a small frame. There is too much pressure on my hip. I can no longer sit or walk. What am I to do?"

"Let me have your hand, please." Mrs. Wang put her hand out.

Taking Mistress Yee's petite hand, Mrs. Wang closed her eyes and held her breath. After a moment, she released her hand with a deep breath.

"Please undress."

"We did that the last time you were here. Why do you need to do that again? The baby isn't coming out now, is it? I am so frightened. How in the world will a baby pass through me? I will die before that happens!" Mistress Yee complained in a high and fragile voice.

Mrs. Wang didn't respond. She just motioned for the maids to help their mistress undress. Mirae was lost in thought. Mrs. Wang snapped her fingers right next to Mirae's ear. She jerked.

"What is the matter with you, Mirae?" Mistress Yee scowled.

Mrs. Wang could see that the maid was unwell. She seemed extremely fatigued.

"I think that you might be coming down with something. You'd better leave your mistress at once so that she doesn't catch anything," Mrs. Wang said firmly.

"Oh, heavens! Is that chicken pox again?" Mistress Yee shrieked.

"No, I don't believe anyone can have chicken pox twice in a lifetime," Mrs. Wang reassured her.

"Don't get near me if you are sick. This is a bad omen. And it also means you don't care what happens to me! I will have a word with you later." Mistress Yee narrowed her eyes.

Mirae got up and bowed, looking bleary-eyed and chalk-pale like a ghost.

"She looks bad," Mrs. Wang pointed out to Nani.

Mrs. Wang examined Mistress Yee with dexterous hands. There was nothing so exquisitely created in the entire world as this woman's vagina, she decided, just as she had each time she had examined Mistress Yee. Her charcoal hair against her porcelain skin was a work of art, like the calligraphy by virtuoso Han, known for his dynamic strokes and even tone. Of course, she would not reveal her thoughts to anyone; nevertheless, she thought it unfair that she was the only one besides Mr. O to have the privilege of viewing Mistress Yee's private parts.

Mistress Yee's belly was moving up and down, and Mrs. Wang gently massaged her, asking the usual but necessary questions.

Mistress Yee giggled and said, "You are tickling me."

"Turn to your side, please," Mrs. Wang requested.

"Oh, gods, Mrs. Wang, you know how hard it is for me to move," Mistress Yee complained.

Nani, perched in the corner, came over to aid her mistress. Mrs. Wang rubbed Mistress Yee's side warily.

"That hurts." Mistress Yee winced.

Ignoring her complaint, Mrs. Wang kept massaging her belly carefully.

"I had a shooting pain in my lower abdomen the other day. Mr. O's been preoccupied with the politics recently, and he doesn't realize my due date is approaching. Please tell him he will have to pay attention to me every second from now on."

Mrs. Wang said, "You must rest but move about a little. Energy begets energy. Take plenty of fluid." There was a tinge of gloom in her voice. Mrs. Wang moved toward the door.

"Mr. O won't let you leave the house," Mistress Yee said, while Nani dressed her mistress promptly. "Nani, show Mrs. Wang where she will stay."

"Yes, Mistress Yee," Nani said quickly and led Mrs. Wang out.

Standing in the yard, Mrs. Wang said, "I need to see Mr. O right away."

Nani's face was a question mark.

"No," Mrs. Wang corrected herself.

"What is the matter, Mrs. Wang?" Nani asked.

"Let me write a letter to Dr. Choi. No. Go quickly and tell Dr. Choi to come as soon as possible," Mrs. Wang said.

"What's the matter, Mrs. Wang? Is there something wrong with Mistress Yee?" Nani asked with a grave curiosity.

"Go quickly. No. Get the boy. Your boy. What's his name? Send him to fetch Dr. Choi," Mrs. Wang said.

"Mrs. Wang, Min is not here." Nani dropped her head and explained that he had disappeared again. The first time he had disappeared, the maids and servants had kept it secret, but now he'd been gone more than three days. Mr. O had found out this morning, when he was looking for him to go fetch Mrs. Wang. Soonyi had slipped and complained that Min had not been seen for many days.

"Many days!" repeated Nani, tears swelling in her eyes. "This is the third day. But Soonyi said 'many days.' Mr. O was furious. I am sure that Mr. O will have his legs maimed when he returns."

"You need to go fetch Dr. Choi. Get someone who can run fast, or you go if you can afford to be absent for a while," Mrs. Wang said.

"Yes, Mrs. Wang. I will get Bok. He moves as speedily as a mouse," Nani said, and rushed to the backyard, where Bok was probably trimming the branches of the fruit trees and sweeping.

Mrs. Wang sat by the well near the maids' quarters and pondered the news of Min with renewed interest. He was a good-looking young man, she remembered. His eyes were lively and he carried himself seriously, in spite of his lowly state. A servant with a disability was like a chipped bowl, a disposable item, but he didn't behave like one.

Feeling wretched, she paced back and forth, and then around the well. If she could, she would have liked to have a sudden attack of stomachache so that she could go home and leave everything up to Dr. Choi. The baby inside Mistress Yee didn't seem to be active. This was the last news she wanted to break to the would-be parents. The poor would blame fate, the wealthy the doctor or the midwife or the pregnant woman or all of the above.

From inside the maids' quarters, Mirae called her through a slit in the door. "Would you like to come in and have a seat?" she asked in a feeble voice.

Mrs. Wang went inside. She wanted to lie down for a short while before the doctor arrived.

"You need some red ginseng to recover," Mrs. Wang said, surveying Mirae whose eyes were encircled with dark rings.

"Thank you, Mrs. Wang, for saving me earlier. I could not sit there any longer with Mistress Yee. When I see a pregnant woman, I feel like throwing up. I don't know why," Mirae confessed, looking miserable.

"Simmer a few roots of red ginseng and a handful of dates overnight in a clay pot. Drink the brew several times a day for a while. You will feel better. You should also eat some pork," Mrs. Wang suggested.

"I can't get hold of regular ginseng, let alone red ginseng. You know that, Mrs. Wang. I am a maid. Everything good goes to Mistress Yee first. My mistress doesn't care what happens to me anymore," Mirae said, hopelessly. She produced a cushion for Mrs. Wang.

"Even a dog needs attending when it's sick," Mrs. Wang said. "You will not recover speedily if you don't take a remedy and, above all, good nourishment. If you don't have an appetite, take licorice," Mrs. Wang said, lying down and placing the cushion under her head.

"I want to leave this house before Mistress Yee has her baby. I can't be a nanny. I just don't want to take care of a baby after what I've done." She bit her lip and couldn't continue, but she didn't cry.

"Whatever happened to Min?" Mrs. Wang asked abruptly.

Mirae widened her eyes and wondered how in the world Mrs. Wang had penetrated her thoughts. "What makes you think I would know anything about him?" she asked awkwardly.

"I just heard that he had disappeared," Mrs. Wang said.

"Oh, that. He is involved with those crazy peasants who meet at night. I'll bet they drink, mainly, and gamble a little too," Mirae said.

"Where is he now?" Mrs. Wang asked, looking into Mirae's eyes.

"The gods only know. But when he returns, he will have to face the consequences. Mr. O said we should report to him the moment that Min is sighted," Mirae said thoughtfully. Her mind drifted back to the time when she had lain with him in the field, some months earlier. It was crazy, she thought, but the more she tried to dismiss the incident, the stronger it flashed back. She had been possessed, she decided: otherwise, she would never have felt anything for a handicapped man. She was now ashamed for having been with him. And she hoped that her secret would remain a secret until she died.

"Is he the one?" Mrs. Wang asked, her eyes barely open.

Mirae was stunned. Somehow, she managed to maintain her cool. "The one what, Mrs. Wang?"

From outside, Nani called, "Mrs. Wang, are you there?" Nani opened the door and informed her that Bok had run to fetch Dr. Choi. She sat, panting, examining the two inside with a friendly but suspecting smile. "Is there anything wrong with Mistress Yee?" she asked matter-of-factly, although inside she was extremely curious about what might be wrong with her pregnant mistress.

"I almost fell asleep," Mrs. Wang said, sitting up, "And I would sleep if you could just leave me alone for a minute."

"Sorry, Mrs. Wang. It's just because our previous mistress, you know what happened to her, and I am worried," Nani said in a monotone.

Mirae burst out laughing until tears welled up. When she gathered herself, she said, "You are such a fake!"

"*You* are the one who is a fake, always getting sick at your convenience. How dare you call me a fake? You get sick every day just when there's much to do. You think no one notices that? A long tail will be stepped on, sooner or later. I see your scheme!" Nani said vehemently.

Mrs. Wang cleared her throat and sat up straight, frowning contemptuously. She thundered, "You two, who taught you to behave that way in front of your senior? Don't you have any manners? Take me to the visitors' quarters so I can rest."

"I am sorry, Mrs. Wang," Nani said. Then she explained sheepishly that a servant had just started a fire in the heating chamber in the visitors' quarters; it would take a while to get the floor warm.

"Prefer to be in a cold room to a coop with squabbling chicks," Mrs. Wang said.

"Please forgive me, Mrs. Wang. Dr. Choi will arrive soon. I was just going to bring sweet rice drink. May I give you a back massage?" Nani asked.

"Do you have anything to say?" Mrs. Wang turned to Mirae.

Mirae lowered her head and whispered, "Sorry."

Mrs. Wang cleared her throat.

Nani approached Mrs. Wang and began to massage her back. "My mother used to say I was the best masseuse," she said cautiously.

"Well, I will go get the rice drink." Mirae got up.

But Mrs. Wang said, "I don't feel like anything sweet right now."

"I will bring something else then," Mirae said and left. "Bitch," she muttered on the way to the kitchen.

"So I hear that Min has joined the revolutionists," Mrs. Wang said.

"He doesn't know what he is doing, Mrs. Wang. He is a loner. How could he join any group? He is passing around pamphlets without knowing what they really mean. I read the pamphlet and asked him if he really believed what it said. He just shrugged. He is so ... so naive!" Nani pressed sharply on Mrs. Wang's spine. She continued, in a hushed voice, "Do you know what it says in the pamphlets? We are all born equal, and we deserve what the aristocrats deserve. They stole not only what belongs to us but also our right to live like human beings." She continued to massage and held her breath, waiting for Mrs. Wang's response.

"There is time for everything," Mrs. Wang said quietly.

An eerie silence hung between them. Nani stopped massaging Mrs. Wang and sat down behind her. "Mrs. Wang, some of them are in jail. Have you heard the news?" Nani asked in a restrained voice.

"Don't stop. No, right under my left shoulder. There. That feels good. I have to say, your mother was right when she said you were the best masseuse," Mrs. Wang said sleepily.

"Mrs. Wang, do you support this whole thing?" Nani asked, looking at the door.

"What thing?" Mrs. Wang asked.

"You know what I am talking about, Mrs. Wang," Nani said exasperatedly.

"I never said I don't," Mrs. Wang replied.

"Mrs. Wang, I need your help. May I confide in you?" Nani asked desperately, massaging fast.

"Slow down, child," she said.

At that moment, Mirae came in with a tray holding a few dishes, one of which was leftover yam noodles sauteed with beef strips and vegetables. The nutty aroma of the sesame oil from the dish permeated the air and whetted Mrs. Wang's already aroused appetite.

"Please," Mirae set the tray in front of Mrs. Wang, who, raising her eyebrows, examined the food. "Please help yourself," Mirae encouraged her.

Mrs. Wang took a bite of yam noodles. "Don't just look at me. You have some too," Mrs. Wang suggested weakly.

After the snack, Mrs. Wang said that she would need a little rest. Mirae and Nani left the room, and once out of Mrs. Wang's earshot, Mirae lashed out, "She must breed a bear in her stomach!"

"She has a great appetite," Nani said dismissively.

"She eats more than a cow! Didn't you see how she licked the whole tray clean?" Mirae shook her head disapprovingly.

Nani didn't want to talk behind Mrs. Wang's back, especially with Mirae. As they arrived at the kitchen, Bok was running toward them. Dr. Choi, he said, had arrived.

DR. CHOI ANNOUNCED THE WORST POSSIBLE SCENARIO in a monotone. It was even worse than Mrs. Wang had anticipated. He ruled out a stillbirth, but because Mistress's description of shooting pain in her abdomen and other symptoms he didn't think the baby would be normal. He believed the longer it stayed in the womb, the worse it would get.

Heartbroken, Mr. O didn't even ask what Dr. Choi meant by normal. He simply dropped his head, as if stabbed in his heart and whispered in a choking voice that the heavens had plotted the cruelest curse against him, and that he was the most wretched soul on earth, and he should go out in the field and hang himself and let the vultures peck on him. With his shoulders dropped, he walked to his room and locked himself in, refusing to drink or eat or be spoken to.

Mistress Yee also shut herself in her room, but only after having thrown a fierce tantrum. She didn't say, though, to leave her alone, so the maids hovered near her door like bees swarming around a beehive, having to listen to her every moan and groan. She was asking herself out loud what had gone wrong, why it had to be her, and, above all, how all this would affect her health. She was frustrated that her husband wasn't making himself available to comfort and console her.

In the kitchen, Soonyi was brewing the concoction that Dr. Choi had prescribed for Mistress Yee. It would induce contractions. As it was a delicate matter, Mrs. Wang kept coming back to the kitchen to check on the consistency and the color of the brew. "Don't let it burn," Mrs. Wang warned firmly. If the brew got too concentrated, then it would work as a tumor-dissolving remedy, and it would eradicate any growth in the body, malignant or benign.

In the visitor's quarters, Dr. Choi puffed smoke as Mrs. Wang entered. "It should be done in an hour or so," she informed him.

"Thank you, Mrs. Wang. Your service to the whole community is praiseworthy," he complimented her.

"I do what I can," she said shortly.

There was silence for a brief moment while they both thought about the same thing. And Dr. Choi asked judiciously, "What is your opinion?"

"The ground is fertile, but the seed is frail," Mrs. Wang stated boldly.

His jaw dropped. Mrs. Wang shot him an inquiring glance. He blushed and puffed smoke vigorously, and then he rubbed his temple until it turned red. Finally, he managed to say, "But then the late Mistress Kim proved that he wasn't the only problem."

"She proved nothing as far as I am concerned," Mrs. Wang said, bristling. "Poor woman. It was partly my fault she died."

"How so, Mrs. Wang? You mustn't say such a thing!" he said emphatically.

"She was dead when I arrived the night she gave birth to her little girl," Mrs. Wang admitted regretfully.

"Then it wasn't your fault she died," he said.

Mrs. Wang didn't bother to respond. She was distracted. She wondered about Mansong, Mistress Kim's daughter, who must still be in Jaya's care. The most recent time she had seen Mansong was at the Harvest Day Festival, up on the hill. How could she have forgotten all about the little girl! She had told herself to keep an eye on Mansong for the sake of Mistress Kim, whose eyes glistened in the dark with immeasurable sorrows, as she had to depart the minute her daughter arrived.

"Oh, eat your own shit!" she whispered, condemning herself.

Dr. Choi's eyes widened and his skin turned white, contrasting with his tobacco-brown teeth. "I beg your pardon?" he asked, almost timidly.

"Oh, nothing," she replied, getting up. "I need some fresh air."

Outside in the yard, the air was chilly and crisp, but it felt good in her lungs. She strolled through the gate that opened to another walled yard. As soon as she stepped into the yard, she felt the tension in the air. The waxing moon was caught between the naked branches of the persimmon tree on the other side of the yard. Something moved, but Mrs. Wang didn't know what it was. She approached the stacks of roof tiles near the persimmon tree. Something moved again. She stopped, and the thing behind the roof tiles that had moved also froze. Mrs. Wang cleared her throat and said, "Who's there?" But no reply came forth. She observed. The shadow against the wall revealed the shape of a person, hunched and bunched up with something, but maybe not just one person. It was none of her business, Mrs. Wang concluded. She turned around to go back to the visitors' quarters, but a stifled sob broke out feebly. Nani came out and begged, "Please, Mrs. Wang, don't tell anyone."

Mrs. Wang at once realized that Min was there too.

"He just now arrived, all beaten up. He can hardly walk. But he won't reveal anything. Please don't tell anyone that he is here," Nani pleaded again.

"If you don't want anyone to know about it, keep your mouth tightly shut. Now, what is going on in the kitchen?" Mrs. Wang asked.

"Oh." Nani thought for a second, and then remembered what was supposed to be happening in the kitchen. "Oh yes. Soonyi is there, keeping an eye on the pot. And Mirae is attending Mistress Yee. Everything is under control."

Mrs. Wang stared thoughtfully at the moon and then walked to the kitchen. When she saw Soonyi dozing off in front of the stove, she picked up a wooden spatula to nudge her, but then she changed her mind. Instead, she silently appropriated a half-full jug of quince wine from the tray, of which Mr. O had partaken earlier, and she left the kitchen, walking back to the persimmon tree. She placed the jug by the roof tiles and said, "Let him drink this. It might help alleviate the pain. Sleep is the best remedy when you are in pain with bruises and must not be seen."

As Mrs. Wang walked away, she heard Nani whisper "Thank you, thank you, thank you!" She went back to the kitchen and bellowed, "What on earth are you doing!" Soonyi sprang up, calling out the names of people she had seen in her dream. Mrs. Wang clucked her tongue and stirred the potion in the earthenware pot on the stove. "Bring me a hemp cloth," she said.

Soonyi opened the drawer in the kitchen and produced a brown cloth. "Is this what you want?" she asked hesitantly. Without replying, Mrs. Wang snatched the cloth and placed it on top of an empty ceramic bowl to strain the potion. She poured the scalding tarlike potion onto the loosely woven cloth with the utmost care so that she wouldn't spill it. Soonyi gagged.

Mrs. Wang chuckled. "Hand me the wooden spoon," she ordered her. Soonyi sniffled. "Concentrate," Mrs. Wang said, firmly.

"Sorry," Soonyi said and handed her a wooden spoon.

"Where is Nani?" Mrs. Wang asked, wringing the cloth out with the wooden spoon.

"I think she went to the outhouse."

"Must have eaten something wrong. It's taking her a while," Mrs. Wang commented, giving a last push with the spoon. "There," she said, exhaling deeply. "Take this to Mistress Yee," she said, tasting the potion from the earthenware pot with her finger. Soonyi gagged again. "What tastes bitter is good for you," Mrs. Wang explained.

Soonyi placed the bowl on a tray and put a rainbow color quilted cover on it.

"Put the lid on the bowl," Mrs. Wang said sharply.

"Sorry," Soonyi said. She put the lid on and walked out.

Mrs. Wang followed her. "Mind your steps," Mrs. Wang grumbled from behind her.

Nani was coming toward them.

"You sure take your time in the outhouse," Mrs. Wang said. "You take the tray and go with me to Mistress Yee. And you," she said to Soonyi, "Go back to the kitchen and spread out the remains of the potion on a flat basket to air out. We might have to brew it once more if it doesn't work by tonight."

Nani took the tray. When Soonyi was gone, Nani thanked Mrs. Wang. She informed her that Min was in the storage room.

Mrs. Wang said nothing.

When they arrived at the door, Mirae announced, "Mistress Yee is sleeping."

"Wake her up," Mrs. Wang said.

Mirae went inside. A minute later, Mistress Yee screeched, "What do you want?"

The door opened.

"Mistress Yee, you will have to drink the potion before it gets cold," Mrs. Wang said.

Mirae helped her mistress sit up. "You smell, Mirae," Mistress Yee complained.

"It's probably the potion. Please drink it all at once, and let one of your girls know at the slightest sign of pain or nausea," Mrs. Wang said.

Mistress Yee held her nose as Nani neared her with the tray. "Oh, gods. Do I have to drink this?" Mistress Yee asked, screwing up her face. Mrs. Wang ignored her. "Oh, Mother, Father, this stuff stinks like a rotting corpse!" Mistress Yee cried.

Reluctantly, she drank it. Mrs. Wang left Mistress Yee's quarters with Nani. In the yard, Bok came and informed Mrs. Wang that Dr. Choi had to leave suddenly because his daughter had contracted food poisoning.

Mrs. Wang expressed her sympathy, and she told the errand boy to go and tell Mr. O that Mistress Yee had just taken her potion, and that Mrs. Wang was waiting for her contractions to begin.

"Yes, I will," the boy replied and trotted away.

Nani led Mrs. Wang to the visitors' quarters, but Mrs. Wang said, "I need to go home briefly and take care of my animals."

"Mrs. Wang," Nani began cautiously, "what if Min went to your place early in the morning to feed them. If he could hide at your place for a couple of days…"

Mrs. Wang said nothing at first. Only after they entered the visitors' quarters did she ask if Min really had a reason to hide.

"It's my hunch, Mrs. Wang, that he has done something. He's been beaten badly. I think he escaped from jail."

"Then you shouldn't wait until morning. Go tell him before dawn to leave the house. If he is being searched for, this is the first place that will be visited."

"No one dares disturb Mr. O's household, especially while the mistress is in this condition. But Min has to hide from Mr. O as well. Mistress Yee says that Min eloped with some girl, and Mr. O says that he will break his legs when he is sighted again in the house," Nani said quickly and nervously.

Mrs. Wang thought for a moment and sighed. "Listen carefully. Your boy, I think, is deeply involved with the peasant revolutionary group that talk ceaselessly. But now they are taking action, it seems. In other provinces, some of the peasants have been hanged for their unsuccessful riots. Now the peasants are acting up in the neighboring villages."

"But Mrs. Wang, that can't be. He is deaf and mute. He is ignorant. He isn't cut out to do things like that. He does only what he is told to do. He is a mule," Nani protested defensively.

"He is told to do what he's been doing. If he is a mule, he isn't going to change his mind overnight. He can go and hide at my place."

"Mrs. Wang, what are we going to do?" Nani cried.

"I don't know about you, but I need to rest my eyes for a moment," Mrs. Wang said, sitting down. Her stomach growled, but for some reason she didn't feel like eating.

"May I stay with you, Mrs. Wang?" Nani asked, looking distressed.

"I'd like to rest if you don't mind." Mrs. Wang lay on the mat and closed her eyes.

Nani dragged her feet out of the room and closed the door. When she tried to put on her shoes, her feet didn't fit. They were swollen and felt like logs when she finally forced them into her shoes. On the way to her room, she suddenly looked up at the night sky and wished for her mother.

From the kitchen, giggles leaked out. Nani stood beside the door and peeked in. Bok and Soonyi were playing pick-up-stone. Nani stepped inside the kitchen and yelled, raising her eyebrows, "What on earth are you doing? Don't you know our lady is in critical condition? And you are here giggling away, playing like a couple of children?"

"Big Sister, I was waiting for you. Bok kept me company because I was scared," Soonyi explained and rolled her eyes.

"Bok, go now. It's late. You need to go and sleep," Nani said.

Bok left, yawning. Soonyi picked up the stones and dropped them in a box. Nani and Soonyi washed up and scrubbed their teeth with salt.

Lying side by side on their mats, Nani advised Soonyi, "Among aristocrats, seven is the age you stop being alone with the other sex until marriage. Being a maid doesn't mean you can roll about like a common stone in whichever direction you get kicked. Reserve yourself until you know what you are doing." Soonyi was already fast asleep when Nani was done with her lecture. Sometime later, Nani fell asleep only to be woken up again when Mirae rushed in to look for Mrs. Wang, for Mistress Yee was having a contraction.

BEFORE SHE REACHED HOME AT NOON, MRS. WANG
heard her dog howl. She stopped on the path, treaded mostly
by her alone for many years. Her dog never cried like that.
Mrs. Wang hurried home and pushed the gate open forcefully.

Her wimpy dog, Tiger, stood in the middle of the yard,
howling worriedly as he watched the unexpected stranger on
the wooden bench.

Mrs. Wang patted Tiger. Min sat there, staring at his feet.

Mrs. Wang tapped him on the shoulder, and he raised his
head wearily. He looked drowned in exhaustion. "Go feed my
stove with the logs behind the house." She unlatched the cage
and let the chickens out as she walked to the kitchen to find
some food for Tiger. In a minute, Min carried a bundle of split
wood to the stove in the kitchen. Mrs. Wang left the kitchen
with a day-old barley soup in a bowl. As soon as she poured it
into his bowl, Tiger gulped it down noisily.

Mrs. Wang went back to the kitchen and put water in a pot.
She dropped a few cornhusks into the water and let it boil.
She also soaked rice in water for lunch.

"When you are done, wash your hands and come on in,"
Mrs. Wang said.

She went into her room and pulled her journal out of a
drawer.

Twice blown by fate, Mr. O howled like a dog, she began. She
wrote the details of the birth, and she finished with a sentence,
I hope I need never return to Mr. O's.

When she put her brush down, she realized that Min
was lingering behind the latticed door on the open wooden
floor. Mrs. Wang clucked her tongue, pitying him for being

utterly inadequate. Opening the door, she motioned to him to come in.

Min came in like a cautious, shy cat and sat near the door.

"Find a warmer spot to sit or, even better, lie down so that the heat will soothe your aching muscles," Mrs. Wang said, getting up to go back to the kitchen.

She brought in the food and the cornhusk tea on a tray. When she entered, Min was asleep. She decided that sleep was a better remedy for him than food at the moment. She covered one bowl of rice for Min, and she began to eat the other bowl of rice.

As she was eating, she couldn't help but examine Min's face, his long legs, and his ragged outfit. Something about him reminded her of someone she knew. She held her chopsticks in midair and thought for a moment. The shape of his chin, angular and awkward; there is another person who has that chin. The lips, full and shapely.

But when she was done eating, she had to go to her drawer and pull out her old journals. Once in a while, she reread them. She had to dig deeply. The pages of those books at the bottom were brownish yellow and frayed. She was thinking, eighteen years perhaps, appraising Min.

The book was bound with bamboo sticks and waxed cotton threads used for kite fighting. She had done it herself. Nowadays, there were blank books she could buy at the marketplace, but back then she had to cut the papers and starch them to give the pages stiffness and longevity. She flipped through the pages, recognizing some names. Some of the babies from that time were having their own babies now. Dubak was one of them.

She couldn't find the journal entry with Min's name at first, but then there was a record of a baby boy, born in a hut by the Snake River in the neighboring village, which she had no recollection of. But it said a woman named Hong, pregnant out of wedlock, apparently had tried to kill herself (it didn't say how), but she survived. Mrs. Wang looked closely.

She appeared to be no more than seventeen and was extremely shy. During her labor, she made no peep, enduring her pain like a cow. In fact, her eyes resembled those of a cow. A handsome baby boy was born, and I knew I wouldn't see her again. So I asked her what she intended to call her son. She didn't seem to have thought of a name for him yet. She just wrote O on my palm, which I presumed was his last name. Then I realized she couldn't talk. She was mute. How silly I was, not to have recognized that from the beginning! Had I been a little more sensitive, I wouldn't have interrogated her with all my questions. As I was leaving her hut, she tried to offer me a few copper coins, but I didn't have the heart to take them. I pulled a silver coin from my pocket and left it before the entrance. I didn't have a good feeling about this woman. She carried a smell of loneliness. In fact, no one showed up to cook kelp soup for her. But I had to tell myself that her private life was none of my business. I wish her all the best.

Mrs. Wang read the journal entry once more and sighed. Min groaned in his sleep, twitching his lips. She looked at him once again. She shook her head.

Her floor was getting warm now and it felt good. She lay down and closed her eyes, trying to recall the woman in question, but she could not remember anything about her. Her eyelids were getting heavy and her limbs were softening. The previous night she had hardly slept, and she could feel the effect of it in her joints. She fell deeply asleep and had various dreams, none of which she could recall when she awoke to her dog's wild barking.

She sat up, feeling dazed. She was also extremely thirsty. But first she had to check on why her dog was barking so fiercely. She stepped out of her room. Beyond her bamboos spread a crimson sheet of the sunset. Her lungs expanded as she breathed in the fresh air. Each time she saw the sunset, she was happy that she had settled up on the hill, remote from anyone else. Down in the valley, where the land was more expensive because of conveniences, such as the proximity to water and the market, it was now getting overpopulated. Unlike other people, Mrs. Wang often needed time alone.

Her dog was barking toward the wooden gate and jumped around happily to see Mrs. Wang. Then he went to the gate to bark again.

"What's behind the gate?" she asked Tiger, examining her wooden gate, loosely put together and the upper hinge still out of order.

He stared at her innocently.

Mrs. Wang gathered her chickens and coaxed them into the cage. Suddenly, she remembered that Min had slept in the room with her. She turned around to check for his shoes, but they were gone. She hurried to her room and realized that she had been reading her old journal before going to bed. A few books were out on the low table, and the one she was reading was placed now near the latticed door. Obviously, Min had removed it from the low table to read it by the light near the door. Mrs. Wang lit her candle and sat to check on the open book. It was the page about a baby boy of Hong being born in a hut by the Snake River. But he couldn't have deduced anything from that page—unless, of course, he had other relevant information about his birth.

Her stomach growled. She put her journals back into a drawer and went to the kitchen. The cornhusk brew had been removed from the stove. She had planned to give it to Min for the swelling. A few things were missing, she realized. Dried meat that had been hanging from the ceiling, along with the garlic, was gone. A bottle of ginseng wine, which she had received as a gift, was also gone. She went to her room and checked her money jar. Untouched.

MANSONG TURNED ONE. SO DID JAYA'S FIRSTBORN. BUT the winter was a bad time to celebrate a birthday because food was scarce, and the cold, dreary weather kept people inside, all bundled up. Jaya had waited for the occasion to strike a deal with Mr. O: she wanted a piece of land for being Mansong's permanent caregiver. She was practically the mother in every sense of the term, everyone professed. But the funereal atmosphere at their landlord's suspended her ingenious plan. In the meantime, she went around grumbling to her fellow peasants about how much it cost her to have another mouth—not just a mouth, but an upper-class mouth—to feed. The sheets of ice on the road, however, kept her inside because her belly began to obstruct the view of her steps when walking. Behind her back, village women gossiped about how enormous she had gotten; she seemed about to give birth to triplets. Mr. O must have provided generously for Dubak's family when everyone else was feeding on cabbage soup with barley. That was the conclusion they drew in the end, and they felt resentful.

Indeed, that winter Mr. O's household was in a somber mood. No laughter broke out; no word was spoken without restraint; everyone whispered or gestured. When the ice in the creek melted, even though the water was still flesh-cutting cold, the maids from Mr. O's household rushed to it with the laundry. They met up with two other village women, part-time employees for Mr. O from time to time. The water gushed down the creek impressively, accompanied by a pleasantly deafening sound, and they had to shout to one another to be heard, and it felt really good to shout after the long, silent, repressive winter at Mr. O's house.

"So cold!" Nani said, dipping her hands in the water cautiously.

"It is!" a woman nicknamed Quince—literally, Ugly Fruit—said.

"Hand me the sheets," the other woman, nicknamed Cliff due to her flat chest, said.

"It was the coldest winter that I can remember," Soonyi said.

"As long as you remember?" Quince guffawed.

"How many winters have you lived?" Cliff teased her.

Soonyi blushed. "I hear that this has been the coldest winter in a decade," she said, pulling back the loose strands of her hair.

"Soonyi, stomp on the laundry. This is too bulky," Nani said.

"She weighs as much as a feather. What's the point of Soonyi stomping on it?" Cliff laughed, getting up to do the job herself. She slapped Soonyi's buttocks and said, "You need to put on some meat there if you ever want to be eligible." Her plump behind swayed as she stomped rhythmically on the pile of sheets.

"There's a new maid at Mr. O's, I hear," Quince said. "Good looking, I hear," she added. And she winked at Cliff. The two village women laughed until tears squeezed out, but Nani scowled. She never understood why some of the women talked that way when marriage hadn't brought *them* a better life. In fact, the husbands of both of these women were scumbags, lazybones, good-for-nothing drunken bums. That was why they had to come out early in the morning to wash someone else's laundry: to feed their husbands, who had not earned decent wages in years!

"Tell us about the new maid," Quince said, smirking.

Nani ignored them, pretending that she couldn't hear anything, and she kept beating the laundry with a bat, splashing water in all directions.

Quince pinched Nani on her bottom from behind which made her jump. The other three burst out laughing, and Nani said, "Stop it! You are acting like children." And she shot a warning glance at Soonyi. The other two laughed, crying, panting, and sniffling.

"I am going to have you both fired," Nani threatened, but realized immediately that was not the right thing to say. She had no authority over these women.

There was a brief moment of sulking silence. Quince broke out belligerently, "What makes you think you can talk to us like that?"

Nani said nothing.

"You could be my daughter," Quince said, and Cliff nodded hard in condemning Nani for disrespect.

"Thank the gods I'm *not* your daughter. What gives you the right to pinch me on my bottom? My own mother would have never done that," Nani said sharply, surprising herself.

"Listen to you! Is that how your mother taught you to speak to your elders?" Quince roared.

"No, she didn't teach me that. She taught me to respect the elders who deserve respect!" Nani cried.

"You little smartass!" Quince got up as if to strike her.

"Calm down." Cliff also got up. "Look, Nani, you owe her an apology. Say you're sorry and that'll be the end of this," she said.

"She owes *me* an apology," Nani said.

"Listen to her. That's what happens when you eat rice from the same pot as the aristocrats. They despise their own kind. They think they are floating on the clouds, way above us," Quince said sarcastically. She was actually a little afraid that Nani might report the incident to Mr. O, and she might end up with no employment. She couldn't afford to hang around at home all day until the farming season started.

Nani did her laundry. Tears trickled down her cheeks. On the contrary, she felt she was at the bottom of a pit, not knowing how to escape. There was no way to divorce herself from her servile status: born a maid she was going to die one. Just like her mother.

"No need to cry. It's all a joke," Cliff said.

Nani wiped her eyes. She didn't want to deal with the women anymore. She beat the laundry as hard as she could.

Quince began to complain about her husband, who stayed out late at night, drinking, and the gods only knew what else he was doing. The other night, she had to carry him home when he was found passed out on the street. She found out about it because her dog barked like crazy. She went out to find him lying unconscious. Once on her back, he threw up all over her. Oh, the foul smell! She said she wasn't going to fetch him again; she was going to let him freeze and die on the road.

Only Cliff was listening with her ears pricked up, for she had spent that night with Quince's husband. He had fed her sweet words she had never heard before. He pouted, saying his wife was no fun. He would do anything, he said, to go back in time so that he could marry Cliff, not Quince. Every time he came to visit her, he flattered her not only with words but also with little gifts.

Nani's purple hands were becoming numb from cold, and the tip of her nose felt frozen. After the arrival of Buwon, Mr. O's son, the amount of laundry seemed to have quadrupled. Some days, she felt all she did was laundry. The baby produced at least twenty diapers a day, among other things, and those weren't just to be washed. She had to boil them to really clean them, and then they also needed to be ironed. Mistress Yee also produced a lot more laundry than ever before: whatever her son drooled on had to be washed immediately, be it her cushion or her skirt or her pillow.

The women wrung out, folded, and packed the cleaned laundry into four bamboo baskets to carry it back. Quince and Cliff followed Nani and Soonyi; each had a basket on her head. At the back entrance to Mr. O's, Quince wanted to know if she and Cliff should follow in and help with hanging the laundry. Nani said no, she and Soonyi could take care of it easily.

In the backyard, Nani told Soonyi to hang the laundry. She needed to go to the kitchen to prepare lunch. The kitchen maid who had been on leave because of her dying mother had finally been dismissed. After her mother's death, her father fell senile and she had eleven siblings to take care of. Naturally, Nani took over her job.

There was now another maid, even though she was only taking care of Buwon. When he was born prematurely, he could not latch onto his mother's nipple. Mistress Yee noticed part of his upper lip was missing, and she dropped him on the floor, screaming, "Take him away!" That wasn't the only thing about his appearance that scared her. He had a rather large, misshapen head, and one leg was slightly longer than the other. She and Mr. O argued about that. She insisted that one was longer and Mr. O denied it. And this argument went on for some time, until Dr. Choi confirmed Mistress Yee's view.

When Nani arrived in the kitchen, she found Chunshim drinking water like a thirsty horse. Mistress Yee had wanted Min to marry Chunshim, but he wasn't around to be married off. Chunshim greeted Nani, wiping her mouth on her sleeve. Nani ignored her and took out the chopping board and began to slice dried green peppers. Chunshim stood there thoughtfully and then she exited the kitchen. Nani lifted her head and clenched her teeth. But a second later, Chunshim poked her head into the kitchen and said, "I know you're angry at me. But it's just a misunderstanding."

Nani dropped her knife on the chopping board and got up. She didn't know what she was going to say.

"Look, I know you think I am engaged to your guy. But I am not," Chunshim said, quietly.

"I am not concerned about that at all." Nani flushed.

"Oh," Chunshim said, genuinely surprised. "That's not what I hear."

"Whatever you hear, it doesn't concern me," Nani replied sharply.

"I am grateful that Min introduced me to this household because ... after my husband died, I didn't know what to do to feed my baby," Chunshim said.

No husband was in the picture, but she fibbed on anyway.

"Look, I don't really care," Nani said.

"Well, I just don't want you to think I am going to do anything you wouldn't like. Min has helped me lots, but he is not in love with me. He's never done anything dishonorable. You can trust me on that," Chunshim said.

Nani sighed after Chunshim had left. "He is not in love with me. Huh, *he* is not in love with *me?*" she imitated Chunshim sarcastically. "But maybe *she* is in love with *him?*" Nani yowled. She sprinkled sesame seeds in a pan and put the pan on the fire to toast them. "Huh, he is not in love with me, she says. I don't give a damn if he is in love with her or with a dog!" she said and scowled.

The last time she had seen Min was the night Buwon was born. She cleaned and fed him. She drenched him with wine to ease the pain and dragged him to the storage room. In the middle of the night, when Mistress Yee screamed and awoke everyone in the house, Nani ran to Min to tell him he needed to go and hide at Mrs. Wang's, but he had already disappeared. All he left was his vomit at the entrance of the storage room, which Nani had to clean up, then and there.

"He is not in love? He's been in love with *me* all his life!" Nani said, suddenly feeling incredibly jealous.

"What are you talking about, Big Sister?" Soonyi asked, standing at the entrance of the kitchen.

Nani blushed, wondering how long she might have been standing there.

"What should I do now?" Soonyi asked.

"Once and for all, Soonyi, I want you to use your head and figure out what you should do instead of asking me constantly what you should do!" she barked.

Soonyi pouted. And then she said, "I can't."

Nani stared at Soonyi for a brief moment, and then they both burst out laughing.

"Go and find out if braised chicken sounds good to Mistress Yee," Nani said, raising her eyebrows.

MISTRESS YEE TOOK A LONG TIME OVER LUNCH. SHE
examined the taste of each bite on her tongue suspiciously,
asking what the ingredients were and sometimes spitting it
out, demanding to know if everything had been thoroughly
washed. Finally, Buwon was brought in. He had just taken a
nap and had a bowel movement, reported Chunshim, placing
him on a yellow silk mat to be viewed.

With his partially missing upper lip, he looked hideous
when he smiled. Even though Chunshim was just a nanny, she
felt strangely responsible for his appearance and tried to make
nothing of it by smiling and clapping when Buwon stretched
his mouth to smile.

Mistress Yee lowered her glance and observed her son as if
an exotic fruit had been brought in from a faraway land. She
showed, however, no curiosity or interest, but contempt.
Buwon smiled, producing sweet baby sounds.

"What a good boy! He is such a good boy. He hardly ever
cries," Chunshim complimented him.

His head was still enormous. Dr. Choi had said that it was
large because it was distressed during the birth, and he had
assured her that it would shrink, by and by. But that son of
a bitch had lied! Mistress Yee could see plainly that Buwon's
head was growing by the day; in fact, that was the only part of
his body that seemed to grow. Mistress Yee winced.

"What's that on his forehead?" Mistress Yee asked, frowning.

"Ah, that, Mistress, he scratched himself with his fingernails.
That happens with babies. My son scratched himself at this
age all the time," Chunshim explained frantically.

"Don't you ever bring up your son in my presence!" Mistress Yee squawked.

"Forgive me, Mistress. I will never make that mistake again," Chunshim said, lowering her head.

"Out!" Mistress Yee waved her arm dismissively.

Chunshim wrapped Buwon in a silk layette and withdrew. Mirae took the silk mat and folded it away.

"Bring me the box," Mistress Yee ordered, half lying on her cushion.

Mirae brought out a lacquered box in which Mistress Yee kept her secret. Dried dark green leaves were wrapped in a parchment. Mirae knew exactly what her part was. She crushed the leaves and rolled them in a paper. She licked one side of the paper to glue it to the other. She lit it and handed it to Mistress Yee, who sucked it, deliciously, with her eyes closed. Her delicate blue veins rose on her temple. "Ah," she said and exhaled deeply, untying the ribbon on her upper garment.

Sometime later, Mistress Yee passed out, or looked passed out. Mirae collected the articles quietly and put them back in the box. She removed the remains of the rolled-up parchment from her mistress's hand and puffed just once before she discarded it. She sat there, thinking what would happen if Mr. O stepped in right then. Of course, Mistress Yee wouldn't have smoked had Mr. O been home. At the moment, he was away at the temple. He had left suddenly the other day, and only when he arrived at the temple did he send a servant to bring what he needed for a stay longer than a couple of days. Mistress Yee had told the servant to report that she was ill, very ill. So far, no message from Mr. O had come. Surprisingly, Mistress Yee hadn't shown any signs of desperation, but Mirae knew it bothered her mistress. The only thing that prevented Mistress Yee from throwing one of her fits was Buwon, a daily reminder of her downfall. Whenever she saw him right after her lunch, she felt aghast and went hurriedly out for a walk or smoked in her room and passed out. When she woke up, her wan face looking confused, she talked funny, she called out a name no one recognized, or she acted like a little girl, and it always took a few moments for her to come to grips with reality.

Something worse might happen, Mirae's intuition told her, but she didn't know what or which side she would take. Suddenly, she found herself wondering what Nani was up to. She slipped out and sprinted to the kitchen where she found Nani and Soonyi laughing about the way Quince had swayed her buttocks. They couldn't stop laughing, even when Mirae appeared at the entrance. Soonyi, covering her mouth, wiggled her tiny bottom in an effort to imitate Quince, and Nani kept laughing, ignoring Mirae.

A moment later, Mirae asked, forcing a smile, "What's so funny?"

"Oh, one of our laundresses, she shook her buttocks in front of us, and she farted loud. Then she—" Soonyi couldn't continue. She began to giggle, bobbing her head. She wetted her lips with her tongue. Nani giggled, too, as she dried the dishes with a muslin dishtowel.

"I didn't hear the fart!" Nani said, gathering herself.

"Well, I did," Soonyi said. "It was as loud as a cannonball. You-you couldn't—oh, my—you couldn't hear—oh, my tummy, oh, it hurts—you couldn't hear because of the running water," Soonyi managed to say and laughed, a teardrop oozing out of the corner of her eye.

Mirae didn't ever find their jokes or tales funny. But she smiled, sitting on the stool, taking a dried persimmon stuffed with walnut. Nani snatched the plate and said, "There are no more persimmons after this. Mr. O is going to ask for the walnut-stuffed persimmons as soon as we run out of them. He did that last year. I had to go around the village, hunting for whatever was left. I had to barter with a chunk of dried beef for a few persimmons!"

"Does Mistress Yee want something?" Nani asked.

"No," Mirae replied, chewing the persimmon.

Nani surveyed Mirae, who normally didn't come to the kitchen unless Mistress Yee sent her.

Mirae wondered if she should tell them about Mistress Yee, what a degenerate she had become. But what was in it for her if she gave away the secret?

"Is she all right?" Nani asked, looking concerned.

"She is far from being all right. I don't know what's going to become of her," Mirae said aloofly.

But neither Nani nor Soonyi asked any questions. Nani sighed, polishing the wooden trays. Soonyi was sharpening the knife on a whetstone, waiting for Nani to say something. But Nani stacked up the trays and began to fold up the dish-towels, saying that the winter seemed to take a long time to say its farewell.

"She passed out," Mirae finally said. She wanted their undivided attention.

"What do you mean?" Nani asked, alarmed.

"She passed out," Mirae repeated.

"How?" Nani asked urgently.

"She smokes the bad stuff," Mirae explained.

"What's the bad stuff?" Soonyi asked, widening her eyes.

"Mirae, you need to explain in plain language," Nani commanded her because she now saw that Mirae might be toying with them.

"Don't you breathe a word of what I have to say," Mirae began.

"Hold it!" Nani exclaimed. "If you shouldn't share what you know, you can just stop right there. We are not the only ones with ears." She was surprised to have said exactly what her mother had said once to another maid.

"What do you mean?" Mirae asked.

Nani's mom had warned her that birds and mice eavesdropped on secrets, and that they chirped and squeaked, so the whole village would know them within a day. Thinking of her mother, Nani said, "Mistress Yee would kill you if she found out what you are doing."

"So don't tell her what I am about to say. I am not trying to gossip behind my mistress's back. I am worried about her. She is smoking the leaves, and sometimes the Chinese powder. When she sees her son, her spirit sinks low and she smokes. Mr. O should know about this, so that he can do something about it," Mirae babbled. "I came in here to make some tea for her. When she wakes up after smoking, she is always so thirsty."

Nani was dismayed. Her mother had said that addiction to opium would ruin even the emperor of China.

"Well, please don't tell anyone. Although we might have to tell Dr. Choi about this when he comes to check on Buwon," Mirae said. "Or maybe it's just a phase," Mirae added authoritatively.

Nani put a pot on the stove and said, "This is not good."

"No, it's not," Mirae said.

"Is it really bad?" Soonyi asked.

"Really bad," Nani responded, sighing theatrically.

"I know," Mirae said.

Chunshim poked her head in and asked, "Can someone help me?"

"What is it?" Mirae asked.

"Don't be afraid to come in. No one's going to bite you. You always just poke your head in as if the kitchen were not worthy of your feet," Nani said sarcastically.

"No, it's not that. I want to be able to hear the boys. What are you all doing here?" she asked, smiling broadly.

"What is the help you need?" Mirae asked.

"Oh, Buwon has diaper rash, and I am going to need warm water to bathe him. Can you prepare water and bring it in?" Chunshim asked.

"At your service," Nani replied.

"Thank you. I can always rely on you," she said gratefully and ran back to the room.

"She has it real easy," Nani said, going out with a large pot to fetch water.

"Is she always this grumpy?" Mirae asked Soonyi quietly.

"What?" Soonyi asked.

"Nothing," Mirae replied, and left the kitchen, forgetting the tea, for she had never intended to make it in the first place.

AFTER DRIFTING MANY DAYS, SLEEPING IN BARNS, sustaining himself with the dried meat he had taken from
Mrs. Wang, and stealing eggs from chicken cages, Min managed to arrive at the confluence of the Snake River and
another river whose name he didn't know. And there it was:
Sowok Island, where the lepers were now being shipped to,
for leprosy was believed to be contagious. He offered the ginseng wine as the boat fare to the rowing man in his sixties. The
old man took Min gladly. He asked Min if he would pour the
wine for him. They drank together in silence. The boat glided
on the water smoothly. Three hawks were flying around and
around in the middle of the sky that was heartbreakingly blue.
Min looked up and counted the three hawks, again and again,
until he got dizzy.

"Why are you going there? You look fine," the rowing man
inquired tactlessly. "It's not a contagious disease, as far as I can
tell, though. I have been transporting the lepers for a decade
now. Nothing has happened to me. Their limbs fall off, like
leaves in the autumn. But they don't complain. It's interesting: they are all quite content. There is a yellow man who lives
among them. Have you heard of him? He was the only survi-
vor of the ship that arrived this past summer from a faraway
land. He was in the palace for a while, but the important members of the government council voted against him influencing
the king so he has been exiled to this place."

The boat arrived at the dock. Min bowed to the chatty old
man and walked up the hill.

It was a small island. Once he climbed up the steep path to the ridge, he could see the whole island, and the silvery water on the other side blinded him as he savored the vastness of the water and the calm of the island. He descended slowly, feeling the shock of the weight of his body against the ground each time he took a step. When he reached the bottom of the hill, he saw scattered huts, and some people by the shore, fishing with their spears. He stood behind a tree, observing them from a distance. Later on, they roasted fish on a fire, and the aroma made his stomach twist with hunger. He chewed on acorns and fell asleep behind a large rock.

Min opened his eyes to find a crowd of people standing near him, looking down, examining him. They were happily surprised. One said he was mute. Another said he was also deaf. Min almost fell back at seeing the foreign man, hardly yellow actually except for his hair. He was ashen white, as if he hadn't seen the sun in years. What haunted Min even more were his large blue fish eyes, which moved just like normal eyes but seemed to conceal his feelings.

Min panicked when they took hold of him, remembering the time of his apprehension for having helped the head of the peasants' revolutionary group. He had delivered the pamphlets explaining the condition of the peasants and the unfair tax system and the minimal wages. He had posted warning announcements for the government officials to reconsider. But all had failed, and the leader had been decapitated soon after the arrest. Min was beaten up, but he had been released when they found out he was deaf and dumb. He wished to have been a martyr, too, but his disabilities prevented even that wish from coming true. The officers had assumed he knew nothing about what was going on. After his arrest, he had been dragged, just like now; many hands grabbed him and they were looking down, studying him, except that these people were not cursing and slapping him to speak. All were silent. He was taken to a hut and fed fish and boiled radish. He ate hurriedly in front of them, bearing their stares. No one made any comment.

He spent the night there in the hut with the yellow man, or white man, whichever—it didn't matter really.

In the evening, the man scribbled fiercely for a long time in his leather-bound book. It was not in any language that Min recognized. He closed his eyes and thought of Mrs. Wang's diary. Hong was her name. The other day, when he had reached the start of the Snake River, an elderly woman informed him that the woman named Hong had moved away to the island called Sowok, where lepers were quarantined. Min had never been curious about his birth or his birth mother, who had abandoned him. What had driven him all the way to the island was his curiosity about his father.

After his release from the police, he received a new assignment from the peasant revolutionary group. He was supposed to set Mr. O's house on fire. He couldn't possibly do it as long as Nani lived there, and besides, when he had snuck into the house, Mistress Yee was having a baby. He couldn't bring himself to carry out the order. Seeing Nani also affected him. She had sobbed when she saw him bruised all over.

When he read the page that Mrs. Wang had left open, he couldn't breathe. Did she know his intention to set the house on fire? Was that why she was revealing the secret of his birth?

In the early dawn, the blue-eyed man was cooking in the kitchen. He made porridge with salt and sliced a piece of fish, not cooked but marinated in salt and vinegar. He brought it in on a tray with two spoons and one pair of chopsticks. Min and he ate together. The porridge tasted bad and the fish worse, but Min was grateful that the man didn't speak. Judging by the way his eyeballs moved, he wasn't mute; he was a normal man.

When the meal was over, Min grabbed the tray, for he wanted to do the dishes.

Later in the morning, the lepers were lining up outside his hut. And the foreign man took one person at a time. He examined the person's tongue and eyes and gave the person some white powder to put on his or her wounds. Min went out the door and gagged when he saw a person missing three fingers and half of a nose. And he was wondering what that white powder did to the patients.

Sometime past noon, after the last person had been treated, the foreign man and Min sat together by the fire, roasting their hands, observing each other's faces.

There was something repugnant about the colors of the man, Min had to admit. Tinted yellow hair and the carp eyes, but the most poignant part was his bloodless skin color. It was like death itself. And it saddened Min. He was probably dying like the lepers but with a different disease.

The man went fishing. Min went up the hill, caught two snakes, and skinned them. Outside the hut, he seared them on wooden skewers and offered them to the foreign man when he came back without catching any fish. The man looked at the meat and ate it with Min, cautiously. Min missed eating rice and kimchi and hot soup.

In the evening, the foreign man scribbled again in his book. Sitting in the corner, it dawned on Min that his profession might be along the lines of Mrs. Wang's. Perhaps he was writing about his patients. A little later, the man pulled out a map and spread it on the floor. He pointed with his pen to where they were, and then he pointed to another place far away, indicating where he came from. The man's eyes immediately reddened, and Min's chest knotted with sympathy. The map of the world was a beautiful thing to look at. But the words were written in another tongue. Min hadn't known that there were so many different places all over the map. There must be people in all those places, living and dying, with stories as painful and strange as his and this man's.

Min suddenly realized that it was impossible to guess the man's age. He could be anywhere between twenty and fifty. What had made him leave his country? It was odd. With his finger, the man traced the route he had taken.

They lay next to each other, candlelight still flickering on the low table. Min saw the man cry. Min groaned to tell him that everything was going to be all right. But his unexpected groan sounded wild and must have scared the man out of his wits. He wiped his eyes and stopped crying.

27

BEFORE DAWN, THE SOUND OF THE GONG AT THE TEM-
ple rippled gently into the hollowness of one's soul.

Mr. O was sitting in front of the wall in the guest room at the
recommendation of the head monk. His mind was intensely
focused on the sound of the gong.

Let your mind be open, and let it be part of everything that
surrounds you. Don't let any of your senses exert effort to recognize one particular phenomenon, whether it is a sound or
a pain or a thought the head monk had said. Mr. O was frustrated because that was not possible. He didn't know how to
do it. The first day he had said, "Damn it, I can't!" And the
head monk, sitting next to him in the hall with the Buddha of
the Universal Light, ignored his complaint.

Now, alone in his room, Mr. O sat facing the wall, trying
to immerse himself in the low, vibrating sound of the gong,
but his attention was directed to only one thing. His stomach
was the center of the universe at the moment. Ever since he
had come to spend time at the temple, he'd been feeling his
stomach painfully shrink. Meals were served only twice a day,
and the portions were meager. He stared at the wall and tried
to let the sound of the gong seep into his mind. He was counting automatically, and then he was distracted and lost track of
his counting. He opened his eyes, stopping his counting, and
looked about. He was staying in one of the cubicles near the
old part of the temple, behind the main hall. The cold room
was minimally furnished.

When he had arrived six days earlier and announced that he
was going to stay indefinitely, the head monk had accepted his

proposal with a bow. Mr. O had expected his sudden appearance would disturb the entire schedule of life in the temple.
But things went on or, rather, nothing happened.

That first day, the head monk had silently showed him the
guest room and then left. Mr. O called him back, so he could
blurt out the whole story.

"My son was born. But he was born disabled. The doctor
thinks he won't be normal. He will be slow in learning, or he
may not be able to learn anything at all. There is something
wrong with his head. I felt like jumping into the well in my
yard with him. There was no place I could think of to come to
hide, except this place. My father used to come here with me.
Do you remember? I need to stay here for a while. I need to
think about things."

The head monk listened, unperturbed, with his eyes cast on
his feet, his lips slightly apart, and his palms meeting tightly
under his chin. When Mr. O finished pouring out his heart to
him, the other man paused for a moment and then asked if he
would like some tea. Mr. O was upset because he saw that the
head monk was not affected by his tragedy, which was gnawing
at him. Mr. O replied angrily that he hadn't come to drink tea.
The head monk bowed slightly and wished a good stay for Mr. O.
He chanted something from the Heart Sutra and then left.

In a few moments, breakfast would be ready. Mr. O couldn't
wait. No one would bring him food, or come to fetch him, so
Mr. O got himself ready while other monks rose to go to the
main hall for morning chanting and whatever else they had to
do before breakfast.

It was still dark outside when Mr. O stepped out the door
and walked briskly to the kitchen. A group of monks were
walking in single file, the head monk following at the end.
Mr. O watched the bald heads from behind, amused, and suddenly felt an urge to fling a stone with a sling at their heads,
one by one. And then he remembered that he had done

exactly that to an elderly servant a long time before. Sitting on a branch of a pine tree, he flung a stone using a homemade sling, which hit the servant on his forehead. He fell and bled. Mr. O laughed hysterically then. Suddenly, his own laugher echoed in his head now.

Mr. O paused by the main hall and watched the monks walk into the kitchen. No one had scolded him for injuring the servant. He couldn't even recall what had happened to the servant.

Slowly, he dragged his feet to the kitchen and entered the room where all the monks sat in silence. They passed the rice bowls to the right and around the table until everyone had a bowl of rice and a bowl of clear soup with a few green leaves. There was also pickled radish on the table. Mr. O sat next to the head monk and ate, conjuring up the image of a roasted duck. When they were done with their meals, they poured hot water into the rice bowls and with their spoons they cleaned the bowls and drank the water with whatever was floating in it. Mr. O was the first to get up and leave, in order to avoid cleaning the table and doing his own dishes. He could lower himself to do many things, but doing the dishes wasn't one of them.

He went for a walk. There was a path that led to the peak of the mountain. He was climbing steadily up and when he paused to breathe, he turned around and saw the head monk following him from a distance. He waited. The head monk came close and passed him. He followed, and from behind he asked, "Don't you all kowtow at this hour in the main hall?"

"Yes, we do," the head monk replied, and he stopped. He picked a leaf from the ground and handed it to Mr. O. "Would you like to?" he asked, pointing to the ground, handing the leaf to Mr. O.

"What?" Mr. O asked.

"There is a caterpillar crossing the road. Someone might step on it," the head monk said.

Mr. O picked up the caterpillar with the leaf and asked, "Where shall I put this?"

"Wherever you think it might want to be," he replied quietly.

"How do I know where it would like to be?" Mr. O wondered, slightly annoyed.

"Well, it was going that way, and perhaps we should put it over there," the head monk suggested.

Mr. O put it down and walked on, ahead of the monk.

They climbed to the top. The valley was blanketed with thick fog, but they could see the temple, situated deep in the middle of the mountain, in the brilliant morning light.

The head monk sat on a rock, and Mr. O sat on another rock. For a while they said nothing, but finally Mr. O broke out, "I have been kowtowing one hundred and eight times a day, and meditating—at least trying to meditate—but nothing is really happening to me. I can't really forget anything. My mind is crowded with thoughts, and they all rush to me as soon as I close my eyes to meditate, facing the wall."

The head monk sat still, observing a small bug on his robe.

Mr. O looked about and cut a leaf from a plant and handed it to the head monk, saying, "Do you want a leaf for the bug?"

The head monk looked at the freshly cut leaf with regret. And he said, "No, this bug has a pair of wings. It can go wherever it wants to."

Mr. O frowned deeply.

"So what's the point of all this? Mr. O demanded. "Why do you kowtow to the Buddha? Why do you chant? Why do you meditate? Why do you eat only twice a day? Why do you not do what you want to do? What's the point?"

The head monk smiled like a baby, fluttering his eyelashes in the sunlight. And he answered, "There is no point."

"Oh." Mr. O paused, dumbfounded and slightly piqued.

"There is no point," the head monk repeated quietly. "You call yourself 'I,' and I call myself 'I.' The novice monk also calls himself 'I.' And yet, I call you 'you.' You call me 'you.' We call the novice monk 'he.' Because we think that 'you' are not 'I,' and 'he' is not 'I.' But everyone on earth is 'I.' I am borrowing this body to live this life. You are borrowing yours to live this life. The fact that you are in your body, and are called Mr. O, is a coincidence. Nothing more. All Mr. O possesses or doesn't possess is also a coincidence. But 'I' is troubled with the 'me' that wants, desires, wishes, loves, hates, feels unhappy about, and is dissatisfied with. If you let your 'I' think this way, every 'I' feels troubled."

"I don't get it," Mr. O said, shaking his head.

"Your son was born. You expected him to be a certain way. But he arrived differently, in a disabled body. You are disappointed. You feel cursed. You are suffering because you want him to be not who he is. But remember, he is also 'I.' He is you. He is 'I.' This is what I wanted to tell you. That's why I followed you up here." The head monk got up and descended.

Mr. O didn't move. He sat still and watched the head monk become smaller down on the path to the temple. His mind was in a violent state, and he could hardly breathe.

The other day, at home in bed, when his wife had whispered, "Should we get rid of him?" his spine had curled with immeasurable fear for the naive wickedness in his wife. But he couldn't enthusiastically reprimand her, for the same thought had crossed his mind. Every morning, he woke up hoping his son was just a nightmare. But he wasn't. He was there, everywhere, tainting the smell of the air in Mr. O's world. The whole village was talking about him. Even the peasants pitied him. Or so he believed. For the first time in his life, he cried in bed alone. Whenever he looked into his wife's eyes, he shrank with harrowing loneliness. And he grew wordless. His wife found him boring now. He wanted to find solace. So he had come to the temple, hoping to find a remedy for his deepening sickness. But even the head monk had proved to be of no help.

Mr. O came down to his cubicle behind the main hall. He vowed that he would not give another penny to the temple from then on. He got up and walked out. The novice monk, not older than eight, followed him, wondering where he was going. Mr. O turned around and said, "Tell the head monk that I am gone. I will send my errand boy to fetch my belongings." Mr. O stopped at the stone tub where the spring water gathered. He took a gourd to scoop it up. He turned around and asked the novice monk, "Would you like to live in my house?"

The boy raised his eyebrows.

"Do you want to be a servant in my house?" Mr. O asked. He drank some cool water.

"A migrating bird flies to the south, but in spring, it ends up here again," the boy said timidly, blinking his eyes involuntarily.

"Is that what your master told you?" Mr. O asked, throwing the gourd back into the stone tub of water.

The boy nodded.

Mr. O retorted, "Some never return from the south because they die during the winter." He walked on. He turned around a few moments later and said, "Tell the head monk I left."

"He knows," the boy replied.

"Doesn't he teach you not to fib?" Mr. O yelled and walked on.

28

Right around dinnertime, a voice shrilled like a crow's caw. Several people stopped working and listened from their yards. A woman screamed and then a man shouted, "I'm going to kill you!"

Neighbors came out with wide eyes to see what was going on. For sure, the noise came from Dubak's household.

A few people hurried to his house. Dubak's wife came out in the yard and shrieked for help. With her large belly, she could not run. When she saw the group of people approaching, she shrieked, "My husband is killing me!"

Dubak was following his wife with a raised rake in his hand, about to strike her.

A neighbor man hugged Dubak from behind to prevent him from attacking his wife. Another man grabbed Dubak's arm, saying, "Give that to me."

"This woman, I am killing her today! I am killing her!" Dubak foamed around his mouth.

"Please help me! Take that rake away from him," Jaya wailed wildly. Her hair was tousled, and her face was so swollen from the pregnancy that it was hard to see her eyes.

"Shame on you," said the neighbor, shaking Dubak.

"She killed my mother!" Dubak shouted, his voice breaking. He collapsed on the ground, sobbing.

People gasped and looked at one another and then looked at Jaya.

"Jaya, what happened?" asked a neighbor woman.

"Mother!" Dubak cried.

"Where is she?" asked another voice.

A baby cried from inside.

"My son! My little boy!" Jaya got up and rushed to their one-bedroom mud house.

The crowd followed. And Dubak shouted, "Murderer!"

The elderly mother was lying on the floor in their bedroom, and Sungnam was crying and Mansong whimpering.

Jaya picked up her son and comforted him. Several women came in and examined the elderly lady, and when they realized she was really dead, they all turned to Jaya again.

"I didn't kill her!" she howled, holding her son tightly to her bosom.

"How did she die?" a neighbor man asked.

"She was eating rice cake. She was eating too fast, too much at a time. She choked on it. What could I have done? I was in the kitchen when all this was happening. She cackled, or so I thought, and I came in to find out what was going on. She fell and died before I could do anything," Jaya said, trembling.

"No! That's not true," yelled Dubak. "Jaya sent me out to get firewood. We hadn't run out of it yet, but she said I should get some more. So I went up the hill without suspecting anything. She was roasting petrified rice cake to make it soft to feed my mother."

Jaya cried, "She only has a few teeth. Of *course* I had to roast it to make it soft!"

"Why would my mother want to eat rice cake right before dinner? In recent years, she's been eating food in broth or water because she couldn't chew well. Jaya stuffed rice cake into my mother's mouth. When I left, my mother was sleeping. When I came back, the whole plate of rice cake was gone and my mother dead!" he shouted deliriously.

The neighbors stood in the room, murmuring among themselves and not knowing whom to believe. Jaya had always complained about her mother-in-law being a nuisance because, having lost her mind, the old woman wandered off to unlikely places at least once a day. Someone always brought her back home by the evening, but never once had Jaya gone out to look for her mother-in-law. Everyone suddenly remembered that. How could a daughter-in-law stay home when her elderly mother-in-law, senile and frail, had disappeared for half a day? What if she had never returned? Was that what she secretly hoped for? On the other hand, wasn't Dubak the one who said, annoyed, "Mother, if you want to get lost, get lost someplace where we can't find you!" But a son could say that because he wouldn't have really meant it. He was her own blood.

Mansong looked up with interest at the seething crowd. She had a runny nose and chapped lips and unkempt hair. But she was smiling. The pitiful sight of Mr. O's daughter, which hadn't aroused compassion in the past, provoked outrage in people's minds now.

Suddenly, Dubak came over and snatched his wife's hair. Surprised, she fell, dropping her son on the floor. Another woman picked him up and comforted him. Dubak dragged Jaya out of the room. People followed. The men tried to untangle the couple, but not forcefully enough. The women followed, telling Dubak to stop, but not so condemningly.

Jaya shouted defiantly, "Kill me, then. *Kill me!*"

"I will! You deserve to die," her husband said, glaring and spitting on her. There was a small ax nearby which he had used to split logs to make kindling.

Holding their collective breath, the villagers watched.

Suddenly, Mrs. Wang appeared in the yard and said, "Do you have something to eat?" She looked about awkwardly and said, "Oh, I thought there was a party. Everyone was rushing to this house, so I just followed to have a bite." She laughed wholeheartedly.

"Well, Mrs. Wang, Dubak's mother passed away," a man announced in a loud voice from the crowd.

"My condolences," Mrs. Wang said, looking for Dubak.

"Well, that's hardly the end of the story!" a woman screeched.

"Death is never the end of the story."

"Mrs. Wang, this woman of mine has murdered my mother," Dubak declared, his chest heaving, his saliva splattering. Some observers were sobbing already. "And I am going to kill this one to bring justice to my mother!" He picked up the ax vindictively, and the crowd gasped.

"Well, well," Mrs. Wang spoke quickly with faked cheerfulness. "Let's have a seat. Let us witness the justice done to your mother. In fact, bring your son out to the yard so that he can see how a son brings justice to his mother so someday he will bring justice to his own mother. Ah, don't strike your wife in her belly. Your other child lives there." Mrs. Wang raised her eyebrows and stared at Dubak unflinchingly.

The crowd was hushed. Mrs. Wang stood still, without blinking. Dubak clenched his teeth. Mrs. Wang said under her breath, "You fool!"

Dubak dropped the ax and wailed pitifully, kneeling on the ground. A man took the ax away. Jaya took her baby and cried. The crowd murmured, avoiding Mrs. Wang, who got up and went into the room and picked up Mansong. She carried her out and said to Jaya, "From now on, I will take care of her."

It was dark outside and Mrs. Wang really didn't have enough energy to climb the hill carrying a child.

After a while, near the old pine tree, she stopped, breathing hard. Something glinted under the tree. It was a man's embroidered blue silk coat under the radiant moonlight.

"Ah, Mrs. Wang!" the man shouted, surprised.

"What brings you here, Mr. O?" Mrs. Wang approached. In the dark she couldn't see the details of his face but only his shapely lips and his angular jaw line. She was thinking he must have been exceptionally handsome in his youth.

"I am on my way home," he said. He didn't want to admit that he was coming from the temple.

"All alone?" Mrs. Wang asked.

"Yes, yes. My business came to a close earlier than I had expected. My servant was supposed to fetch me the day after tomorrow, but I decided to return home today. I have been away for too long," he explained, still sitting. Mrs. Wang sat, too, to take a little break.

"Whose baby is that?" Mr. O asked.

"She is hardly a baby now," she replied.

"I played around here when I was little. I climbed this tree like a monkey," he reminisced.

"I need to go," Mrs. Wang said, getting up. She had no time to hear about Mr. O's childhood. She was starving.

"Yes, I need to be going too," he said and got up. But he felt strangely hesitant to get on the path to go back to his house.

Mrs. Wang abruptly asked, "Mr. O, would you mind carrying this child for me? My old body is going to collapse before I arrive at my door."

Mr. O was taken aback at this odd request. No one had ever asked him to do anything like that. And he wasn't even sure if he could do it. He had never held a baby in his life. And yet, he couldn't refuse. Mrs. Wang's arms were already extended to him, and the child was looking at him intently. He took her in his arms awkwardly and followed Mrs. Wang.

"Oh, that feels so much better. Your kindness will not be forgotten," Mrs. Wang said.

Along the way, a large doe appeared behind the shrubs. It followed them.

Near her house, Mrs. Wang suddenly said, "I adopted her today."

"Is she an orphan?" Mr. O asked.

"No. Her father lives but isn't ready to take her at the moment."

"How villainous!" he exclaimed. He honestly couldn't believe that a parent would refuse to take care of his own child, especially when the child was healthy and perfectly normal.

"Blessings are for those who embrace them," Mrs. Wang remarked meaningfully. "And I thank you a thousand times," she said, taking Mansong back from Mr. O's numbed arms. He descended and she ascended. The doe made her way hesitantly into Mrs. Wang's front yard and lingered there. When Mrs. Wang turned around to say something to her, she jumped back into the shrubs and disappeared into the night.

ALL MORNING, NANI AND MIRAE PULLED THE LOOSE
threads out of the winter blanket covers and sewed up the
lighter covers for spring. Now they were ironing the pillow
covers. Nani sipped water, squirted it through her teeth onto
the fabric, and pressed it with a hot iron.

Mirae, her skin almost recovered, blossomed again. With
her naturally crimson lips and her shiny pitch-black hair, she
stood out from everyone around her.

"What's your favorite work?" Nani asked.

Mirae replied, "None. Ask me what's my least favorite work."

"What's your least favorite work?"

"Emptying Mistress Yee's pisspot," Mirae said, frowning.

"What's the next?" Nani asked.

"Giving her a massage," Mirae said.

"What's the next?" Nani pestered her.

"Everything else," she replied.

"Is there really nothing you like doing here?" Nani asked.

"Nope," Mirae said with a blank expression.

Steam escaped from the cloth as the hot iron pressed on
it. Nani looked at Mirae and saw how pretty she was. And she
thought, not for the first time, that Mirae wasn't cut out to
be a maid. "In your next life, don't be born a maid," Nani said
with a tinge of sarcasm.

"So what is it that you like so much about being a maid?"
Mirae asked, snickering.

"Oh, shut up," Nani said, feeling ashamed of her nonexistent
ambition to rise above her lowly state. She must have been a
maid for eons, one life after another. She knew no other life.

She liked ironing. When the wrinkles on a pillowcase were smoothed out, she felt happy. She liked cooking, especially sweets. Sweets arranged on a plate, such as walnut-stuffed dried persimmons or pressed honeyed puffed rice dotted with black sesame seeds, simply delighted her. Oh, and the smell of freshly dried stiff laundry just off the clothesline: such a simple thing but so precious and familiar.

"Watch out!" screamed Mirae, smelling the burn from the iron that the daydreaming Nani held.

Nani jerked and rescued the pillowcase under her iron. She examined it and found just a bit of yellow. "Oh, gods of the mountain, help me," Nani sighed as she pressed the last pillowcase.

"So tell me," Mirae urged her. "What's *your* favorite work?"

"I am not going to tell you," Nani said, sulking.

"Whatever you say," Mirae said, folding up the pressed pillowcases.

From outside, Soonyi called, "Big Sister!"

"Big *Sister!*" imitated Mirae, drawling.

"Hello?" Soonyi said, opening the door.

"Can you not shout?" Nani scolded her, venting her frustration.

"Sorry, Big Sister. The group of women has arrived," Soonyi said.

"Oh ... them," said Nani.

"Who?" asked Mirae.

"The shamans from Yellow Horn Mountain," Nani replied, getting up. "Finish folding the pillowcases and put them aside, will you?" she asked, leaving the room. A group of shamans, five of them, were carrying their paraphernalia into the yard.

"Weren't you instructed to enter from the back door?" Nani asked.

"We were. But we had to come through the front gate. From a distance, we saw the dark spirit hovering over the rooftop.

We had to announce our arrival to the spirit defiantly. If we had snuck in from the back door, the spirit would think we were cowards. We wouldn't be able to cast out the spirit then," said the oldest of the five shamans. They wore hats in the shape of cockscombs, made of brilliant orange-and-yellow paper. They brought gongs, cymbals, bow chimes, and a drum that looked like an hourglass painted blood red.

"Please follow me," Nani said. She led them to Mistress Yee's quarters.

As she stepped into Mistress Yee's courtyard with the shamans, Chunshim was leaving with Buwon in her arms.

"Is Mistress Yee in?" asked Nani, knowing very well that she was.

Chunshim nodded, looking distressed from her short visit with Mistress Yee.

Nani cleared her throat and announced the arrival of the shamans. Mistress Yee told her to come in with them. They walked in, their bulky outfits swishing and their articles clanging. The room, filled with seven women, changed its scent. Mistress Yee told Nani to go out and fetch Mirae.

When Mirae arrived, Mistress Yee told her to have Chunshim bring in Buwon. If they were to perform Kut, the shamanic ritual, Buwon had to be present so that they could unearth the source of the curse that had possessed his body. There was some discussion about where Kut should be performed. In the end, it was decided to hold it in Mistress Yee's courtyard because she was the one who wanted it.

The shamans were setting up their altar on a straw carpet in Mistress Yee's courtyard, tuning their musical instruments and trying out their voices.

Nani quietly took her shoes off and stood, holding a stack of blankets, huge against her small body, at Mistress Yee's entrance. She heard nothing from inside although she figured that Mirae must be inside with Mistress Yee.

"I brought some spring blankets," Nani announced, trying to peep around the heap of blankets.

Mirae came out and closed the door behind her. "Mistress Yee is resting at the moment. Give them to me," Mirae said.

"In the middle of Kut?" Nani whispered doubtfully.

"It hasn't even started yet," she said, taking the blankets from Nani.

"They are starting any minute," Nani said, pointing to the courtyard with her chin.

Mirae paused for a brief moment and then whispered into Nani's ear, "She's doing it again."

"It? Oh, that," she said.

"Can you open the door for me?" Mirae asked, turning around with the blankets in her arms. Nani opened the door to Mistress Yee's room. The lady was lying on her silk mat with her upper garment loosened and her eyes closed.

Mirae picked up the red lacquered box and put it aside. She came out quietly and said, "She will wake up in an hour or so. You have to see how she looks when she wakes up."

Out in the courtyard, Chunshim brought Buwon bundled up in a silk blanket. He was dressed in a blue-green jacket and a black headdress.

One of the shamans said that Buwon should be propped up to watch Kut. But he was too young to sit still for a long time, so Chunshim would either have to sit holding him up or put him in a harnessed basket and tie it on one of the pillars of the house. "Whichever," said the shaman, straightening her hat and looking at the thin air as if she were looking at a mirror and seeing her reflection.

Chunshim sat on the straw carpet and held Buwon on her lap. Four of the shamans began to play their instruments. One of them sang too. There was no prelude. From the beginning, it was climactic, loud, and harrowing. They howled and whined and hissed. And suddenly the fifth shaman jumped high and landed in the middle of the straw carpet and began to dance, whirling forcefully.

The music played like torrential waves, unrestrained and raging. The dance went on relentlessly all afternoon and all evening until the waxing moon shot up in the middle of the ominous sky. After dinner, Mistress Yee was fed up with the noise. She was getting a headache. She asked Mirae if there was any way to have Kut come to an end. "Do they know it's a fixed price? They don't get paid more just because they prolong it," she said, scowling. Mirae tried to interrupt Kut, but the shamans were in ecstasy.

The errand boy, Bok, ran into the kitchen where Nani was cooking red beans for the next day. "Don't run," Nani scolded Bok when he came in breathlessly.

"Big Sister, Master has arrived. He just stepped in the gate," he said.

"Oh no! Oh, heavens. Oh no!" Nani jumped up and ran to Mistress Yee's quarters. Mr. O hadn't been expected to arrive at that time. Or was she mistaken? But Mistress Yee wouldn't have invited the shamans to perform Kut had she known he was arriving now.

Nani grabbed Mirae. "Look, Master has arrived," she informed her.

Mirae didn't look alarmed.

"He just stepped in the house! Do you hear me? He is approaching. What are we to do?" Nani had to shout to be heard in the midst of the gongs and cymbals.

"What can *we* do? I've already tried to stop them because Mistress Yee is having a headache from the noise," she said.

Nani was confused. She saw poor Chunshim still sitting on the straw carpet, yawning from ear to ear, and Buwon was fast asleep despite the deafening noise.

At that moment, Mr. O appeared. Nani's heart sank. He neared and froze for a moment. Chunshim got up reflexively.

Nani stepped down from the ante-floor outside Mistress Yee's room and ran to Mr. O without putting her shoes on to welcome him. But her voice blended in with the noise, and Mirae just bowed from where she was.

Mr. O was tired. He hadn't sent for his horse. Instead, he had walked the whole day alone, on an empty stomach, getting lost a couple of times in the forest, and then he had to climb up the path to Mrs. Wang's house, carrying the child. It had been a long day. When he approached his own house, he only thought of going straight to bed. But the noise from behind the gate alerted him. He asked Bok what the noise was. The boy reluctantly released the information.

All of a sudden, Kut came to a halt, and silence fell heavily. Mirae announced that the master had arrived. But the shamans were oblivious to their surroundings. One of them began to speak with a spirit. Finally, it seemed they had managed to invoke the right spirit, the one that had been trapped in the household. Mistress Yee emerged, covering her forehead with her hand. Mirae stood behind her.

"Who are you?" the shaman asked the spirit.

"I live here," the dancing shaman replied in a trembling, ethereal voice.

Nani stared at her, noticing that her voice had completely changed.

"Are you dead?" the shaman asked.

"I am in between the dead and the living," the voice said.

"What makes you linger among the living?" the shaman asked.

"My body is pierced and staked to the earth. I can't move freely," the voice said, gnawing at Nani's heart.

"Is that why you are borrowing the body of the little boy here?" the shaman asked.

"Sometimes," the voice said.

Mistress Yee stepped down on a stone next to her shoes and shouted, "Who is this spirit?"

Ignoring her, the shaman asked, "What do you want?"

"Pull the needle out of my body. Bury me properly," the voice said.

Nani pronounced her late mistress's name as if sighing and collapsed near Mr. O. She recognized her mistress. It wasn't her voice, but the way she spoke; it was her.

Bok tried to pull her upright but he couldn't.

Mr. O didn't know why the maid had mentioned his first wife's name, but his hair stood on end.

"Where can we find you?" the shaman asked.

"Behind my quarters," the voice said.

"Leave the baby at once, and I will bury you properly," the shaman said.

The spirit groaned in a way that was at once terrifying and heartrending. Nani jerked, stifling her cry. Mistress Yee grabbed one of her shoes and came toward Nani. She lifted her shoe, aiming it at Nani's head. Bok let out a piercing cry, vicariously expecting the pain. Mistress Yee struck Nani's head with her shoe, and the beads from the shoe scattered on the ground, glittering under the torchlight. Mr. O turned around and went to his quarters. Bok followed him.

At that moment, Buwon began to jerk with a seizure, and Chunshim screamed. Mistress Yee watched her son with terror, and Mirae stood still, feeling the chill in her spine.

The shamans packed up their belongings and waited for Mistress Yee to produce the payment. But she said that she would send them the money when the baby's condition improved.

"That wasn't what we were promised, Mistress," the eldest shaman said calmly.

"That was what I asked for," Mistress Yee snarled.

"We unearthed the source of the calamity that has befallen your son. Mistress's job is to hear the spirit out and do what needs to be done to undo the curse, according to your judgment. Beyond that, we have no say in Mistress's business," the shaman said.

"According to my judgment? You don't think I believe the dancer's gibberish, do you? What spirit? Her body is pierced? Generations of people have died in this household. How should I know whose body was pierced with a needle? What nee—" Mistress Yee stopped abruptly. Needle. She suddenly remembered the needle. The needle. She looked at Nani, who was obviously quite affected by the ritual. Was it really Mistress Kim? She ascended the stone step and retreated to her room. A moment later, from inside, she called for Mirae who, upon hearing her name, jerked and rushed to her mistress. Then Mirae brought out an envelope for the shamans. They cleaned the courtyard and left without saying goodbye.

THE WAXING MOON WAS THINLY VEILED WITH DARK, 30
rapidly moving clouds. An old owl in the pine tree behind
Mr. O's house stared down on the roof. Bok's cat sat on the roof,
snarling. Bok threw a stone at the cat and urged it to come down,
but the cat seemed unimpressed by either the stone or Bok's
pleading. The stone he threw up fell back down and hit his own
head. "How did you get up there?" Bok asked. The cat looked
down at him and screeched again, looking up at the moon.

Bok gave up and went to the bathing place, where Mr. O
had left a tub full of water and his clothes. He emptied the
water and cleaned the wooden tub with a straw ball, applying ashes for the scrub. When he had tidied up everything, he
picked up Mr. O's laundry and took it to the hamper behind
the kitchen. Mr. O's laundry was not to be mixed with anyone
else's. Not even with Mistress Yee's. And it was supposed to be
folded and placed in the hamper neatly. So Bok took the time
to do it. He heard whimpering from the corner of the laundry
room. Frightened, he spoke softly, "Who's there?"

Nani got up and said, "Separate the undergarments from
the outer ones."

"Big Sister, what were you doing there?" Bok asked.

"I was talking to myself," Nani answered.

"Why?"

"Why what?"

"Why were you talking to yourself?" Bok asked curiously.

"Bok, someday you will understand. Women sometimes
have conversations with themselves. Don't ask why. All right?"
Nani said. She had actually been looking at an outfit that had

belonged to Mistress Kim. After her funeral, Mistress Yee had ordered Mirae to incinerate all Mistress Kim's belongings. The part-time workers and the maids hunted madly for things to keep for themselves. Nani guarded her mistress's things fiercely, but in the end, most of them were taken, and Nani resigned herself to thinking that it was good that some of Mistress Kim's things had survived. She kept one of Mistress Kim's outfits, not to pawn or to wear, but for the sake of the memory. It was a pine-nut-colored outfit that Mistress Kim had loved. Nani had stroked it fondly tonight. Was it really she who had spoken through the dancer? Now some doubts rose in her mind.

"Why are you looking at me like that?" Nani asked.

"Were you really having a conversation with yourself, Big Sister?" Bok asked, looking innocent.

"Go to bed," Nani said.

"Big Sister," Bok began, smiling shyly.

"Don't pester me now," Nani scolded him.

"I am still hungry," Bok said, rubbing his little belly.

Nani stepped out of the laundry room, and Bok followed her to the kitchen. She scooped out a bowl of rice and poured vegetable broth over it. He began to devour it happily.

"Don't eat fast. You are going to have a stomachache," Nani advised him. She stood up and got a quail egg marinated in seasoned soy sauce. She put it in his mouth and licked her fingers. "It didn't turn out good this time," she commented.

"Well, it's the best thing I've ever had," Bok said, grinning, wanting one more.

"It's for your master's breakfast," Nani said.

Mirae came in, surprising them.

"What a piglet you are!" Mirae said, raising her eyebrows. "You eat all day long," she said.

"I am a growing boy," Bok replied, pouting, but still chewing the food.

"What is it?" Nani asked anxiously.

"Nothing. I am going to make some tea for Mistress Yee," Mirae said.

"Tea, at this hour?" Nani asked.

"Yes, tea. At this hour," Mirae said.

"She will pee all night long," Nani said contemptuously.

"I will tell her about your concern," Mirae said sarcastically.

"I was concerned about you," Nani said, thinking of the chamber pot that Mirae would have to clean the next morning.

Mirae didn't get the meaning and put the teapot on the stove and prepared the tea leaves.

"Go to bed," Nani urged Bok.

"All right, Big Sister," Bok said and left the kitchen.

"I picked up the beads," Mirae said, grinning.

It took a moment for Nani to realize what she was talking about. And she left abruptly, slamming the kitchen door behind her.

Mirae carried the tea on a tray. The moon was out, but strangely, it didn't shine where she walked. After passing through the gate that led to Mistress Yee's quarters, the ambushed cat jumped out from nowhere and shocked her. She dropped everything and broke the teapot. She cursed the cat, or was it a cat? She looked behind her but saw nothing. She picked up the broken ceramic pieces and went back to the kitchen and placed the tray by the stove for someone else to take care of. And she left again to go see Mistress Yee. She had not asked for tea. Mirae had made it as an excuse to go see her.

She announced her arrival and wondered if Mistress Yee would need anything.

"Come in, child," Mistress Yee said from inside. She hadn't called her "child" in years. Mirae stepped into her room and closed the door behind her. Mistress Yee was lying on her silk mat. She didn't open her eyes.

"Sit down. I thought you might come," Mistress Yee said, her eyes still closed.

Mirae waited impatiently for her mistress to verbally permit her to speak. Finally, Mistress Yee asked in her fuzzy, dreamy voice, "What is it? I am tired."

"Mistress, I am frightened," Mirae confessed.

"Of what?" Mistress Yee asked, opening her eyes.

"The doll. Do you remember?" Mirae said, trembling.

"What doll?" Mistress Yee asked, slightly grinning.

"The doll you asked me to make," Mirae replied.

"For what? I don't play with dolls anymore," Mistress Yee said. She snorted.

"No, Mistress. On the night when Mistress Kim was having a baby."

"Did you make a doll?" Mistress Yee asked.

"Yes, Mistress," Mirae said softly.

"What for?" Mistress Yee asked, raising her eyebrows.

"Well, Mistress, do you really not remember the doll?" Mirae asked, baffled.

"No, but if you do, fill me in," she said.

"Mistress Yee, you asked me to make a doll on the day that Mistress Kim began to have contractions," Mirae said, finding it difficult to regurgitate the details of the crime.

"You are being convoluted, Mirae," Mistress Yee pointed out, closing her eyes again.

"I brought the doll to you. And you pierced it with a needle. And I buried it by her quarters in the middle of the night," Mirae said in her unsteady voice.

"Mirae, are you sure you are not making this up?" Mistress Yee asked.

"No, Mistress," Mirae said.

"Why is it I have absolutely no recollection of this incident?" Mistress Yee asked, sitting up.

"I can take you to the place where I buried the doll," Mirae suggested. "If you saw it, you would remember it," she assured her. A certain nostalgia flooded Mirae's chest. She was having an intimate conversation with her mistress again. Once, she had adored Mistress Yee and had done whatever it was she wanted.

Mistress Yee got up and said, unexpectedly, "Take me."

Surprised, Mirae got up and led the way. This might be a chance to become friends again with her mistress. She would prove her loyalty. Mistress Yee would love her once again. A gem she was among the maids. Mistress Yee herself had said that once.

The moon was suspended in the middle of the sky, weeping. It didn't shine. Mirae went without a lantern so as not to draw attention to Mistress Yee and herself. Mistress Kim's quarters had been out of use since her death. Mirae led her mistress behind the building and looked about.

"It was around here," Mirae said.

"Think carefully," Mistress Yee said.

"Mistress, I need to get a hoe to dig. May I?"

"Sure, I will stay right here," Mistress Yee said.

After Mirae left, a voice spoke from inside Mistress Kim's quarters, giving Mistress Yee a deadly fright. The door opened from the inside and there stood Mr. O with his stern face.

"What on earth are you doing here?" Mr. O questioned her.

"Husband, I am confused and most embarrassed to be found here in the middle of the night. I know it's not proper for me to wander about like this, but I am here under dire circumstances to be shown something that would solve the mystery that baffled me this evening. I will explain everything later. Would you please close the door and listen from within? I don't think you need an explanation if you listen carefully," Mistress Yee said most sincerely.

Mirae went to the tool shed and tried to find a hoe. When she grabbed one, the same cat sprang out again so that she felt like her heart stopped momentarily. She threw the hoe after the cat, cursing. But the animal disappeared. She picked up the hoe again and ran to Mistress Yee.

"Let me see. I am sure it was here," Mirae hit several places on the ground with the hoe. She dug here and there unsuccessfully for a while.

"I don't believe you have done such a thing," Mistress Yee remarked.

"I would bet my life that I did, Mistress Yee," Mirae said.

"There seems to be nothing," Mistress Yee said.

"Ah, here, my lady," Mirae said gladly, digging rapidly. "It's right here." Mirae took it out of the hole, shaking the dirt off the doll.

"My gods, Mistress!" Mirae gasped, dropping the doll on the ground.

"What is it?" Mistress Yee asked.

"It's bleeding," Mirae said, her voice trembling.

"What is that?" Mistress Yee asked innocently.

"It's the needle-pierced doll I buried the night Mistress Kim was having a baby," Mirae exclaimed, breaking down with fear. She sobbed.

"My gods, Mirae, how could you have done this?" Mistress Yee gasped, really surprised that her own scheme to ensnare her maid was remarkably ingenious. And she fainted, falling carefully on the ground.

Clenching his teeth, Mr. O closed his eyes as he listened. When he heard his wife fall, he came out of Mistress Kim's front door quickly and hurried around the building to strangle the maid. The moon was now bright enough to see all that was going on in the backyard of the deceased Mistress Kim's quarters.

Part Three

MIN STARED AT HIS COMPANION'S TOES BETWEEN
which blood and oozing puss coagulated. The soles of his
shoes completely worn out, his fungus-infested feet visibly
suffered. Despite that, he had kept a steady pace behind Min
for the past two days, but now he began to lag. Min picked up
a stick and handed it to him.

He was feeling lightheaded and fatigued, Min could tell.
Sweat broke out on his forehead and he started whispering.
Min just waited patiently until Blane stopped babbling. Then
they would resume their journey.

His eyes bloodshot, Blane suddenly let out a mournful
squall. Min put his hand on his friend's arm. Blane wanted to
go home. Min understood.

The map of the world Blane had was fascinating. Min imagined a country full of people like Blane. He knew very well
how hard it had to be to be singled out. For the past two days,
children burst into tears at the sight of Blane or threw stones
at him with such intense hostility. All his life, people had
mocked Min for having a disability. It had become a part of
his life. But when he saw how even children, well, especially
children, reacted to Blane, he realized that it wasn't him, possibly, that was wrong. Without rhyme or reason people had
tortured him all his life for being different.

Min was the supplier of their meals as they traveled together:
edible roots with fresh dirt still on them or raw eggs or acorn
mush. When they were lucky, they got to roast a snake or
grasshoppers. Blane frowned when Min skinned a snake. Min
smiled, which he did sparingly. But in the end he convinced
his companion to eat.

At night they lay several yards away from each other while a bonfire crackled in between them. There was nothing Min loved more than the night sky full of stars. Behind each star lay a story so complex and yet plain as his life. Before falling asleep, Nani came to his mind. Her childlike smile, her small feet that carried her everywhere so fast, her lips so endearing especially when she pouted in an exaggerated manner. Then he would fall asleep hoping for a dream of his sweetheart.

When a rooster yodeled, Min opened his eyes and smelled the cool earth that he so loved. Fresh air tainted with faint cow dung smell from the field. Inhaling deeply, he got up and in no time he was off to look for things to eat. He moved like a reptile. In a little while he returned to his friend, ashen-faced, fearful, and a heart full of loneliness. Min handed him mountain berries, one egg, and a pair of old straw shoes. The shoes fit him snuggly. Min grinned satisfied. No longer did Blane snatch from Min's hand for he knew now he wouldn't starve as long as he was with Min. But once he tasted the berries, he ate the rest hurriedly, making a mess all over his mouth. He refused to eat the egg. The texture of raw egg in his mouth repelled him. Min cracked it and dumped the whole thing into his mouth.

When the sun on the east resembled the color of someone's throat, they got up and marched on. Min chose hilly paths, away from residential areas, to avoid people with ill feelings. Half a day later the two young travelers arrived at the belly of an ancient mountain, which was thickly dressed in luscious green and the atmosphere impregnated with unperturbed calm.

A temple was in sight. Min stopped at the entrance where the name of the temple was carved on a huge wooden board. He turned around and waited for Blane, who was at least thirty steps behind. He dried his forehead with his bare hand. He was hungry. Wan and fatigued, Blane let out a sigh as he approached.

After passing the humongous wooden statues of guardians painted in bright red, blue, white, and green, Min turned around to check on his friend. Blane's jaw dropped staring at the guardians in awe.

When Mr. O's father had passed away, Min had accompanied Mr. O and Mistress Kim seven times over forty-nine days to the ritual to send off the spirit to a good place. Min, a young lad then, played in the yard or wandered off in the mountains until the ritual was over by noon. He was there with Nani's mom to aid their master and the mistress. He carried things.

Now they were passing the pagoda and a tree and an impressively old building, from which low rumbles flowed like ripples on an enormous lake. Min led Blane to a large stone tub where fresh water gushed down through a bamboo pipe, erasing all other sounds. Both Min and Blane gulped down water, washed their hands and filthy feet, and then drank more water. Min came close to his companion and pointed at his beard, dyed purple from the berries he had eaten that morning. Using Min as his virtual mirror, he cleaned his face carefully.

Min felt comfortable in the temple. It was his second home in a way although he had visited it fewer than two dozen times. He took his friend to the kitchen. It was empty, but as soon as they sat on the floor, a few monks entered followed by the head monk. Min got up rather frantically and bowed. The monks knew Min was a servant from Mr. O's household and that he was born with numbed tongue, but who was this amazing-looking creature whose stare gave them goose bumps? His appearance shocked the monks, the head monk could see plainly, although no one gasped. He had heard about the new religion that missionaries had brought, promising salvation without effort and everlasting life in heaven, and that the most converts were peasants for it promoted equality of the classes.

As was the custom at the temples, no questions were asked, and all present were fed. Min made eye contact with Blane to make sure he didn't worry about anything.

In the middle of the meal, Blane fainted. The head monk picked him up like a feather and carried him to a room behind the main hall and laid him on a cotton mat. The head monk peeled Blane's eyes open and inspected them. Then noticing his feet, he went out with a novice monk who immediately heated the room with split wood. The head monk came back with a concoction of oil and juice from the stems of common plants to put onto Blane's feet.

Min slipped into the main hall by stealth, vaguely remembering how he had fallen asleep behind the statue of the Buddha at the age of seven or eight. Mistress Kim had kowtowed without a break all that afternoon.

The Buddha he remembered seemed to have shrunken. But the smell, he had to close his eyes to fish out the scene that it evoked. But he couldn't. He sat in the middle of the floor and observed the visage of the Buddha. His mind gradually drifted to Nani and her frown that made him think she was concerned about him. And then to Mirae and her hideous laughter. It had tortured him to say the least. She had ignored him whenever they had run into each other. Then recently she was sitting by the well. Watching her from behind, Min could tell she was crying. He went close and tapped on her shoulder. She turned around and got up. He was ready to hug her. Her eyes were brimming with tears, but then she laughed like she was mad. Suddenly she spat on him saying, "Don't you ever come near me!" Min turned around and left her. He realized he had absolutely no feelings for her. It was Nani he had loved and would always love. Would she forgive him for having been with Mirae? He wasn't entirely sure. Someday he would have to tell her about his misconduct.

Someone tapped on him. It was a novice monk. He said it was dinnertime. Wouldn't he want to come with his friend? Min was dazed. He must have dozed off. It was the sweetest sleep he'd had in months. He got up and went to see Blane who was sound asleep. Thinking that his friend needed sleep more than anything, he didn't bother to wake him. Instead he lay next to him and fell asleep so deeply that he couldn't remember anything he dreamed the next morning when he awoke.

After breakfast, the head monk gave Min a pouch full of money. On the way down he handed it to Blane who wept before he took it. The only thing he had that was worth something was his gold ring from his grandmother. And frankly he didn't know if that would pay for his fare back to his homeland.

Both young men were full of energy. They walked down fast, humming. The sun felt good on their shoulders. The world issued a new morning like a present, and the noisy chirping of the birds rendered giddiness in the young men's throbbing hearts.

IT WAS ALL HER FAULT, MISTRESS YEE SAID REGRETFULLY, blowing her nose in her handkerchief. "As the saying goes, the darkest spot resides in the shadow right under the lamp. I didn't know I was breeding an enemy in my own home," she sobbed, referring to her negligence in overseeing her maid. After Mirae had been expelled with a restraining order, Mistress Yee promised Mr. O that she would be more careful in the future.

She had interviewed a few dozen applicants for the position in the past several months. But no one so far was good enough. Young ones were too young, old women were too old, some were too ugly, some were too fat, some were too skinny, some seemed too lazy, and so on. Mistress Yee didn't realize it, but she was looking for someone like Mirae.

The rumors about Mirae varied. Some said she had died in the mountains. Some said she had married a merchant and left for the North.

Amid all the rumors about her, Mirae had gone home, if she could call it home. Her father had not been known, and her mother had died when she was little, but she had an aunt. They had lived together until the aunt placed Mirae with Mistress Yee and married a widower twice as old as she was. He was an oil presser and owned a shop in the capital city.

When Mirae found her aunt's house behind the oil shop, she collapsed on the wooden sidewalk in front of it. A shopper with her baby on her back gasped. Another shopper asked, horrified, "Is she dead?" The oil presser immediately said, "No! She is alive." And he carried Mirae inside his house behind the shop.

"Come on out!" he shouted.

Mirae's aunt, Gomsun, came out of the sliding door, frowning. "Stop yelling. The twins are sleeping!" she squealed, pulling up and tying her skirt around her chest. "What on earth is that?" she asked, looking at her husband, who was carrying a young woman on his back.

"I have no idea. She just fell in front of our shop. Do something about it," he said, unloading Mirae in the yard. Then he hurried back to the shop, where now more people gathered to hear about the woman who had collapsed and died right there, moments earlier.

Gomsun came close, unconcerned, and examined Mirae. She didn't recognize her niece. They hadn't seen each other for some years. Gomsun tapped on her and said, "Open your eyes and speak."

Feebly, Mirae said, "Aunt Gomsun." And she lost consciousness again.

"Oh, my little Mirae!" Gomsun shouted. "What has happened to you?" she wailed. She shook her niece and poured a gourd of cold water on her face. And Mirae twitched her lips, but she didn't wake. Gomsun dragged her up to the entrance floor and cried, "My little Mirae! What's happened to you?"

Her twin boys woke up and cried. Ignoring them, Gomsun rushed to the shop, turned around to come back to fetch her twins, and then ran to the local doctor.

"Oh, Dr. Chun, please. Please, you must come with me," Gomsun said noisily.

"Calm down and explain what's going on," the old doctor said, twiddling with his long white beard.

"My niece, you see, I have a niece," she said. "I haven't seen her for so long. Anyhow, she is sick. She has just arrived in the heat. She collapsed and doesn't seem to want to wake up," Gomsun cried.

Dr. Chun got up slowly and said, "Go ahead and go. I will come soon. Make her drink water."

"Please hurry," Gomsun said, reluctantly stepping out of the house.

Gomsun walked, looking back every now and then to see if the doctor was following. When she spotted the ancient doctor with his errand boy as she turned around at the East Gate Marketplace, she felt relieved. So she cursed all the way home. Business hadn't been good lately, and a funeral would mean no business for a few days. She and her husband couldn't afford that.

When she arrived home, she found Mirae still lying on the floor, but she was now conscious.

"What happened? Is this my little Mirae?" Gomsun sat down and laid her twins on the floor. She rubbed Mirae's cheeks and cried. "Why, you are a woman now!"

Mirae closed her eyes.

"Poor thing," Gomsun said. "What happened?" Gomsun asked curiously. "How's your mistress?"

Mirae opened her eyes and turned her head around to face the wall. Her eyes were burning at the mention of "your mistress."

Dr. Chun arrived with his errand boy. He closed his eyes and felt Mirae's pulse. He finally said, "She is exhausted. Her kidneys are very weak. Recently, she has experienced a stressful event. She needs rest and good food. Above all, though, she needs to feel better about things in general."

"Whatever happened to her skin?" Gomsun asked. That was the first thing she had noticed.

"Recently I suffered from a skin disease. Some said it was chicken pox. But the herbalist who concocted brew for me said it wasn't. His remedy didn't work very well, though," Mirae said.

"You had chicken pox when you were a baby!" her aunt said.

"Did I?" Mirae felt relieved. Then obviously it was nothing permanent. Her scars would go away. She closed her eyes and sighed.

"Too much heat in her system. Cold cucumber soup. Kelp soup, radish, black sesame seeds, watermelon, and berries. These are all good things for her. Apply black sesame oil to her skin. The scars will disappear gradually. I will send my boy back with some herbs. Brew them and let her take it three times a day for the next forty days," Dr. Chun said.

Gomsun converted forty days of herbal brew into currency in her mind. And she said, "Forty days! She is just exhausted from the long trip in the heat. She is young. I am sure she will recover soon."

"If she had been old like me, she would have died. Her kidneys are very weak. Her condition will affect her liver if it's not taken care of immediately," the doctor warned her. He left with his errand boy.

Gomsun ran after them to say something about the cost of the medicine. But she only ended up saying, "Thank you, Dr. Chun. Thank you for coming."

That evening, Gomsun and her husband had a fight under their blanket. How in the world are we to feed another mouth? That was her husband's point. And Gomsun was frustrated. She agreed with him, but still she felt offended. None of the visitors from his side of the family had ever caused a conflict so serious as this between them. So she turned around and stopped speaking to her husband altogether.

Mirae drank the brew and ate some rice with steamed radish. She couldn't sleep that night; she listened to her aunt argue with her husband. There were seven children in the house, aged between zero and eight, and five of them were sleeping with Mirae in the same room. Some of them snored, some of them ground their teeth, one talked in her dreams, and another sleepwalked.

"How long are you staying, my darling Mirae?" Gomsun asked the next morning at breakfast. Her husband was roasting sesame seeds in a huge cylindrical container on the stove in the preparation room.

Mirae didn't reply.

After the argument with her husband the previous night, Gomsun had thought that Mirae could work to pay for her room and board.

"It's not that you are unwelcome here. I just thought you might want to keep busy. Energy begets energy, if you know what I'm saying. And we always need helping hands here," Gomsun said, stuffing her mouth with rice.

Mirae didn't speak for a few days, which baffled Gomsun and her husband. But she did work. She got up early in the morning to help roast the seeds and nuts. Taking a gigantic wooden spatula, she stirred them occasionally, staring at the fire burning tempestuously in the stove. She also helped with packaging the various oils. She cleaned the preparation room at the end of the day. In the evening when she cleaned, she applied leftover black sesame oil to her skin and thought about what to do with her life. Surely she wouldn't be an apprentice at the oil shop for too long.

When she was finished with the herbal medicine, Mirae looked refreshed and healthy again. Gomsun sent her out to the shop to be the shop assistant, and sales doubled within a few days. Some customers came just to look at her. Gomsun was ecstatic. She and her husband counted their money under the blanket every night now, giggling and clapping instead of arguing about their unexpected long-term visitor. One day, Gomsun's husband brought home a pair of new shoes and some blue fabric for Mirae. He said, "For all your work." And he grinned self-consciously.

Stupefied, Gomsun stood there with her jawbone unfastened. She wanted to yell at someone, but she couldn't decide whom she was angry with. Her husband was the kind who didn't remember her birthday, let alone buy presents for her. But she just said, smiling, to her niece, "The blue suits you well, sweetheart." But on the way to the seamstress's, not far from the oil shop, Gomsun asked coldly what Mirae's plan was for the future.

"There is someone waiting for me back in the country," Mirae said.

Gomsun turned around and said, "Oh, really?"

"It was a joke, Auntie. Go in. I want you to get yourself measured for an outfit. Blue isn't really my color. You have it," Mirae said, smiling.

"Oh, how kind of you. But are you sure?" Gomsun said.

"I am dead sure. Your husband bought it for you, really. But then, to be polite, he offered it to me," Mirae said.

Gomsun decided to believe that. She was measured for a skirt.

On the way back, Mirae confessed, "I am thinking about leaving."

"Oh no! Why?"

"Would you like me to stay?" Mirae asked.

Gomsun didn't quite know what to say. Did she want her pretty niece to stay or to leave?

"Why, of course! You are the only blood relative I've got. I want you to live with us the rest of my life," Gomsun declared, surprising herself.

"How nice of you, Auntie. Then I need to go back and fetch my stuff at Mistress Yee's house. But I need some money for the travel," Mirae said. "I will pay you back later by working in the shop."

"I will pay for your travel expenses, naturally," Gomsun said, imagining herself in the blue outfit.

"But your husband would be angry," Mirae said cautiously.

"I won't tell him then," she assured her niece.

Back in the shop, Mirae thanked Gomsun's husband for his generosity.

"Whatever you need," he said, smiling.

"I just told Auntie I was going back to my previous employer to collect what I left there. May I borrow some money for my travels? I will come back and work harder than before," Mirae said.

"Of course I will. No need to pay it back. Just don't tell your aunt. She is obsessed with money. She loves money more than she loves me," he said and laughed.

"I won't tell her anything," Mirae said, smiling brightly.

SOMETHING INTERESTING NEEDED TO HAPPEN OR ELSE
Mistress Yee was going to die of the doldrums. Every day was
the same. Her husband was preoccupied with the housekeeping business all of a sudden. Her maids were stupid. Mirae, she
now realized, was irreplaceable. Many interviews with can-
didates from all over the province had convinced her of that.
And the weather was gorgeous, making her extra fidgety.

She and her husband sat together, drinking tea and eating
a red bean snack.

"I think I need to do a good deed so Buwon will recover
speedily," Mistress Yee said.

Mr. O reluctantly accepted her proposal.

So the next day Mistress Yee set off in a carriage to the largest
harbor city on the west coast of the peninsula. She was accompanied by Nani and two male armed servants. Cherry trees blossomed as far as her eye could see. She couldn't remember the
last time she had traveled. It was good to be away from home
and to see new places. Life at home had recently been dreadfully tedious, with one shaman ritual after another to make the
trapped spirit leave for the place where it belonged, and the end-
less visits from renowned doctors for her disabled son.

Buwon was able to crawl now and responsive with a smile
to every sound. The size of his head had shrunk, but his upper
lip was still deformed, and one of his legs was now obviously
shorter than the other. Mistress Yee could not bring herself to
feel connected to her son. She had begun to dread the afternoon
visits with him. Often she made excuses not to see him at all.

Spring was her favorite season, every living thing compet-
ing for life and showing off its colors. Against her husband's

warning of possible taunting or an attack by angry peasants, she took off her veil to let the pedestrians admire her beauty. People paid respect as they passed because she was dressed exquisitely and accompanied by a maid and servants.

After seeing what had happened to Mirae, Nani tensed up around Mistress Yee. She never knew when her mistress would erupt, accusing her of something she might or might not have done. But today Mistress Yee was in a good mood. She frequently asked Nani to pluck a certain flower and bring it to her. She would smell it and toss it away on the path.

When they finally arrived in the harbor city, where a large ship from China was docked, Mistress Yee waited at the pier while one of the male servants was making a deal with a fisherman.

"Nani, look at the men over there. Look at their hats." Mistress Yee giggled. "Is it true that Chinese men don't change their clothes until they wear out?" She looked at them with a curious expression.

"Go and smell them. Come back and tell me what they smell like," she ordered Nani.

Flabbergasted, Nani blushed at her mistress's ridiculous request.

"Go and smell them, I said!" Mistress Yee snapped, fanning herself vigorously.

"Yes, Mistress," Nani said and slowly made her way toward the seamen buying their lunch at an open grill.

The vendor spoke fluent Chinese. Nani was mesmerized by the intonations of the language. One of the men asked her something, which she couldn't comprehend, and she ran back to her mistress, a little frightened. Mistress Yee watched her maid, amused.

"So?" she asked.

"They smelled like fish," Nani managed to say.

"*Everything* smells like fish here, you idiot!" Mistress Yee said. But she didn't go on scolding her, for a bearded vendor, trying to sell a pearl, distracted her.

☽ ○ ☾

"Yes, three thousand fish," the male servant said.

Shocked, the fisherman repeated, "Three thousand fish?"

"Yes, my lady wants three thousand fish to be freed," he emphasized.

"I've got ten buckets of sardines here. Could be a thousand fish altogether. I will go and catch some more," the copper-faced fisherman said. The most recent time this had happened to him it was a childless woman, but she wanted to buy only one hundred fish to free. People who believe in an afterlife should do this a little more often, he thought. Some people believed that the fish could have been people in past lives. That meant if they freed the fish, then they would receive blessing from saving lives and their own wishes would come true in return.

"Let me ask my lady if she agrees to that," the servant said and returned to Mistress Yee.

"No, we don't have time for him to go and catch more fish. Get another man with three thousand fish," Mistress Yee snapped.

The male servant went back to the crowd of fishermen. The rumor had spread now, so everyone wanted to talk to the rich lady's servant, offering his deal. Finally, three fishermen put their fish together, claiming that the total was three thousand. Mistress Yee demanded that they count them. They dutifully counted out three thousand fish.

One of the fishermen took Mistress Yee and Nani on his boat. He rowed some distance away from the pier and said, "This is a good spot, my lady."

"Let them out," Mistress Yee ordered.

The fisherman poured two buckets into the deep green water, saying, "Long live the sardines!"

The sun was brilliant and the fish were swimming around the boat in a frenzy.

"Save that one," Mistress Yee said, pointing to one of the sardines in the third and last bucket.

"What for, my lady?" the fisherman asked, puzzled.

"So I can have it for lunch," she said, grinning mischievously.

"But—" he said and stopped. Didn't she want to save the lives of these fish for her own blessing?

Suddenly, Mistress Yee looked up and saw a figure intently looking down from the ship that was about to depart. It was Blane.

The sun blinded her. She looked down to balance herself. She looked up again, but now there was no one. She looked at the sardine that she planned to eat. It flipped helplessly in the slippery tin bucket. She looked up once again and thought for a moment. And then she freed the last sardine on a nameless impulse.

"That was good, my lady," the fisherman said, pleased.

"Nani, do you see someone up there?" Mistress Yee asked.

"No, mistress," Nani said, squinting her eyes. But she saw someone else on the pier as she spoke.

The fisherman poured out the contents of the third bucket. Then he rowed Mistress Yee and Nani back to shore. The small boat docked, and Mistress Yee got off the boat with the help of the fisherman. He smelled bad.

"Take me to a good place to eat. I am starving," Mistress Yee said to her male servants, who were waiting for her at the pier. The Chinese men were boarding, and there was an announcement, accompanied by a drum, that the ship was departing in a short while.

Nani, meanwhile, had her eyes trained on Min. He was still standing on the deck, his head lowered.

The male servants took Mistress Yee and Nani to a small restaurant with a fine reputation. It was a part of a rather small but fancy inn. Mistress Yee was served poached bass, and Nani made an excuse to leave her for a moment. Outside, the male servants were having steamed mussels.

Nani knew that Min would be watching for her from some-place around there, so she walked rapidly to a less crowded area. Min caught up with her in no time. His clothes in tatters, he reeked of stale sweat and who knew what.

"What on earth are you doing here?" she asked.

Min groaned and explained briefly with hand gestures, but he had no way to describe Blane's appearance. So he skipped that part, but Nani got the gist of his message.

"You are going around helping other people when *you* are in great need of help? Do you know what happened to Mirae?" Nani frowned. "She got eighty lashes of the whip. That was some time ago, right after you disappeared. She's been kicked out of the house. All we know is that she might be dead," Nani said, without telling him about the nature of Mirae's punishment.

Tears welled up in Nani's eyes. Min looked at her, con-cerned. He thought that she feared what might happen to her in the future. But Nani was remembering something that Mirae had said. After the beating, Mirae was locked in the storage room with her wrists and feet tied up. Nani brought her ointment for her bruises and something to drink. She dug a pebble out of Mirae's mouth with her fingers. The smooth stone had been forced into it before the beating to prevent her from screaming or biting her tongue to commit suicide. She fed her the broth. Mirae drank it and then said, "I ate your boy." At first, Nani thought that Mirae was delirious. But Mirae's look of malicious glee quickly changed Nani's mind. Humiliated and most notoriously abused, Mirae wanted to pass the pain on to someone else. "Dig your own grave," Nani spat coldly. As she got up, Mirae began to laugh hysterically. She taunted Nani with details of her dalliance with Min. Even after Nani had left the storage room, Mirae went on telling the story, knowing that Nani was behind the door, listening with heart-piercing pain.

Nani wanted to say many things but couldn't say a word. Min stood there, wiggling his big toe, which peeped out of his straw shoe. His state was no better than that of a beggar. He was looking over at the man who whetted knives and tools for the fishermen. The blade he was honing on the whetstone glinted in the sun.

"I am going," Nani warned him.

Min didn't turn to look at her.

She pulled his sleeve to get his attention. "I am leaving," Nani said, placing a coin in his sleeve. But Min refused to take it. He had money left after he had paid the ship fare for Blane. He pulled out a pouch from inside his trousers and showed the money to her.

"Where did you get it?" she asked suspiciously. But she couldn't linger any longer. Mistress Yee might be looking for her.

"What are you going to do now?" Nani asked, thinking that she didn't care what he did with his life. But she choked on her words and tears rolled down her cheeks.

Min shook her shoulder and looked into her eyes. He wanted to live there with her.

"I can't stay here with you," Nani said. If only he had asked her the year before! She would have gladly gone with him to the ends of the earth. But now she felt differently.

"Don't let Mistress Yee see you. Her servants can catch you instantly. You know how she is. She's gotten worse. Go! And don't follow me," Nani said.

Min went over to a vendor who sold rice malt pumpkin candy, and bought a few candies. He offered them to Nani.

"Go," Nani said again, taking only one. If they were meant to be together, they would meet again like two rivers at a confluence. She turned toward the restaurant. Min didn't follow her.

Mistress Yee was taking a short nap in the private room where she had dined. The low table had been removed. Nani sat on the attached bench before the entrance to the private room, staring at her mistress's shoes. Suddenly, she conjured up the sharp pain that she had felt when Mistress Yee whacked her head with a shoe on the night of the first shamanic ritual. Nani had become Mistress Yee's favorite dartboard.

Thinking of Min in rags, filthy from head to toe, Nani felt a pang in the middle of her chest, but she didn't feel like chasing after him. When Mirae had revealed their frivolous affair, Nani had cursed him to hell. She realized now, though, that she didn't hate him. On the contrary, she thought that she would always love him. For the first time, she realized that she didn't have to live in the same nest with a person in order to love him.

Mistress Yee woke up with a sharp pain in her abdomen. A doctor was summoned to the inn to check on her, and a messenger on a horse was sent to deliver a message to Mr. O that his wife was staying another day in the harbor city due to her illness.

After a treatment of acupuncture and herbal medicine, Mistress Yee fell asleep rather early that evening, and the male servants snuck out to an open pub by the water where squid catchers were getting ready for night fishing.

☽ ○ ☾

Nani went out to see if by chance Min was still around. And there he was, standing under the eave of a large store that sold souvenirs for foreign seamen and travelers. The store still had its lights on. When he spotted Nani, Min was so glad that his face turned tragic.

"Did you have dinner?" Nani asked him.

Rubbing his tummy, he nodded. Earlier he had grilled sardines and a bowl of rice.

They strolled on the pier, but there were too many drunkards, so they walked down to the shore where mussels covered the rocks and seaweed gathered thickly around their feet.

Min pulled something from his pouch. It was a jade necklace. Nani looked at it. She had never owned such finery.

"What good is a jade necklace to a maid!" she said sarcastically, her eyes still fixed on the pretty stone.

He put it around her neck, and Nani didn't protest. They sat down on a dry spot among many empty shells.

Nani wanted to ask him whether what Mirae had said about a passionate fling was true.

Min wanted to hold Nani. When Min joined the subversive peasant group to fight against the aristocrats, he had given up his future with Nani. He had purposefully stayed away from her, but now that he had defected from the movement, he wanted her again. When he was ordered to set Mr. O's house on fire, he couldn't bring himself to do it because Nani was there. He didn't want to be a hero. His dream turned out to be small: he wanted to be happy. And he couldn't imagine happiness without Nani.

Mirae couldn't have made up the story about Min. Nani mentally reviewed all the things that Mirae had said to her. Every word had pierced her heart, and all of those words were still there. They had taken up residence in her heart.

After he had put Blane on the ship, he had been planning to return to Mr. O's house and elope with Nani. Meeting her in this harbor city had served to show him, once more, that Nani was his fate.

There was now no noise but the soothing waves, spreading their foamy blanket again and again. The air felt cool and calm. Nani was tired. Min stretched his arm around her shoulder. Nani allowed it, but she realized that she was no longer desperate for his touch.

Min groaned, pulling her closer to him. But Nani untangled herself from his arms. She said, "I am not going to be your wife."

Min stared at her, overcome with desire. When he had been with Mirae, he had felt disgusted and good at the same time. He pulled Nani close to him and tried to kiss her. Nani slapped him and said, "Idiot, it's too late!" She ran away as fast as she could, but she didn't go back to the restaurant right away. She saw squid catchers unloading their boats at the pier. Thousands of squid spilled out from the net onto a large mat. She asked one of the fishermen how many squid she could free with a silver coin. "Thirty," he said. So she freed thirty squid while making a wish.

WHEN THE MESSENGER ON HORSEBACK FROM THE WEST coast set out to Mistress Yee's house to inform her husband, Mr. O had already left for a meeting. All the landlords in the region, with several military officers from the capital city, gathered in a private house to discuss important matters over a late luncheon.

Good-looking maids brought in exquisitely arranged food and drinks and placed them on the low tables. Musicians played ancient instruments from a pavilion in the middle of a pond filled with colorful carp and lotuses bursting into full bloom. It was a closed courtyard, providing perfect acoustics, and from all four sides one could see the musicians and the other visitors. The banquet was sumptuous. Kisengs, professional entertainers who covered their faces with fans, were there to serve the drinks, to tell tales, and to get pinched by the naughty powerful men.

One of the officers gestured to the musicians to lower the volume, so only the flutist was now playing; his tune was as ethereal as the sudden blooms of flowers in the spring season.

"His Highness is concerned about the riots of the so-called peasant revolutionary group here in our region. Most of the members have been captured and beheaded, but some are still around, indoctrinating innocent people. And this is what brings us here together," the officer began.

"In the capital city, we have implemented a new rule that the immediate family of these criminal peasants be stripped of their possessions, and be ineligible for employment," another officer said.

"And how may we strip them of their possessions? Do we need to do this by ourselves or do we hire government officers?" a landlord from a neighboring village asked. It brought some laughter around the table.

"We will be providing one officer per one hundred inhabitants. This village, exceeding one thousand inhabitants, will receive ten officers before the moon begins to wax," the same officer announced.

"In the capital city, we hang the heads of the dead peasants at the entrance of the village as a deterrent," another officer said.

By this time, not many landlords were listening. Most of them were getting red in the face, and their limbs were relaxed; some of them were making clandestine eye contact with the fan-covered kisengs.

Small conversations broke out in layers while the officer talked loudly at the prominent landlords about various schemes for preventing further riots.

"Who is that girl over in the corner?" asked a landlord with a beard.

In the society of kisengs, there was a strict rule that newcomers were not permitted to engage in conversations with men at a party, unless, of course, the men they were serving initiated the conversation.

"She is a newcomer. Needs much training," a middle-aged kiseng, named Dimple, replied quickly and poured another bowl of ginseng wine to distract Lord Ahn.

"What is her name?" he persisted.

"She is called Pumpkin," replied Dimple, smiling.

It was also customary that one didn't go by one's real name in the world of kisengs. Each girl had a pseudonym, which she picked when she joined the society. The pretty girl's pseudonym wasn't Pumpkin, but Dimple was playing with the landlords. As expected, the men laughed, examining Pumpkin's hand, which held her fan, and her shoulders, which were encased in silk the color of an orange azalea.

"Exceptional looking!" Lord Ahn exclaimed.

Some kisengs giggled.

"Amuse us with a story," he suggested to no one in particular.

Dimple began quickly, "Once upon a time, there was a woman hauling water at a well. A general came her way and asked her for some water. He was returning from a battlefield, weary and spent. The woman took a gourd and filled it only half full, and then took a few leaves from a willow branch to drop on the water. The general, very thirsty and impatient, was incensed. He threw the gourd to the ground and chided the woman severely for her odd behavior. He asked once again for water. She did exactly the same, leaves afloat in a half-full gourd. She explained that there was no remedy for choking on water. So she wanted him to drink slowly, blowing the leaves away from his mouth which would slow down his gulping. The general was impressed and grateful for her wisdom. He took her to be his wife."

They all clapped.

Lord Ahn pursued his quarry: "How about you, Pumpkin?"

Pumpkin thought for a moment and said, "I heard this story quite recently."

Caught by the familiar voice, Mr. O, who sat near Lord Ahn, turned around to hear the story.

"Once there was an evil concubine whose jealousy soared up above the sky, for the mistress of the house was having a baby," Pumpkin began. The gentlemen gave her their undivided attention. "She asked her faithful maid to go and make a voodoo doll. The maid didn't know what it was for, but her mistress wanted her to make one, so she did. The concubine pierced the doll with a needle between its legs and gave it to the maid to bury behind the quarters of the mistress of the house. The maid then realized what her mistress was up to, but she did as she was told, for a maid has no choice. The mistress of the house died after she gave birth. Sometime later, a dog unearthed the doll. The master of the house wanted to know what it all meant. The concubine accused her faithful maid of the crime. But the wise master of the house said, 'She is your maid and does what you tell her to do. She might have buried the doll, but the idea must have come from you. So you are the guilty one.' The master ordered eighty lashes for the wicked concubine and sent her away." Pumpkin trembled slightly as she ended the story.

The men applauded.

"That was a great story," said Lord Ahn. "Don't you think so?" he asked Mr. O, who was unable to utter a word for his heart was pounding so loudly.

Mr. O was aghast. He was at once ashamed, and all he hoped was to leave the place as soon as the meeting was over.

"How about you, Mr. O?" said Lord Ahn. He was asking for a story.

"Oh, I will pass. I am not much of a storyteller," he replied uncomfortably, his face reddening.

"What's Pumpkin's real name?" asked Lord Ahn.

Dimple raised her eyebrows in alarm and sulked, "Master, don't you like Dimple anymore? I am going to cry if you let me down."

He laughed, pleased.

Mr. O watched Mirae behind her fan and was impressed with how similar she was to his wife. They had the same body shape and crimson lips and shiny, pitch-black hair. They both carried themselves with aloofness. But he had to say that Mirae—for now he was convinced that the woman was indeed his former maid—was even prettier. Why hadn't he noticed that while they had inhabited under the same roof?

At the end of the party, Lord Ahn got up and reluctantly walked out, turning back once or twice to see Mirae again. But Dimple took his arm and saw him off. Other kisengs were also seeing off the visitors. Mirae sat in the room while the maids came in to clear the tables.

Mr. O got up and went close to Mirae, dropped the pouch he had on his waist, and said, "I want to compensate you for my misjudgment."

Mirae looked down at the gold coins that spilled out of the blue silk pouch and then looked up without hesitation. Her eyes were fiery. She smiled suddenly and said, "If Master would like to soothe my scarred heart, he should grant me the ring on his finger for me to live by."

"The gold coins in the pouch amount to more in value than the ring," he said. But Mirae didn't reply. Mr. O was moved. This maid, who could have had Lord Ahn, the richest man in the province, was in love with him! He blushed. Mirae smiled coquettishly, taking his hand to gently wriggle the ring off his finger. At her electrifying touch, he parted his lips involuntarily. As he caressed her hair clumsily, his lungs expanded, making him feel that he was above the floor.

Dimple came in abruptly to have warning words with Mirae, but upon finding her flirting with Mr. O, she was jubilant.

"Ah, Lord O, you are one step ahead of everyone!" she exclaimed excitedly. "This is Cherry Blossom. Her beauty could melt the heart of the toughest samurai on the neighboring island," she babbled.

Mr. O stood like a broomstick, not knowing what to say. The situation was unfamiliar to him.

"Please, Lord O. Let me know what you would like. If you would like to have a meeting with Cherry Blossom, I can arrange it. Just name the time and the date," she said, twisting the end of his sleeve.

He forced an awkward laugh because he thought it was the right moment to laugh, but it did not make him feel more comfortable. He hurried out, still laughing awkwardly. As he got on his horse, he had a hunch he wasn't going to be able to sleep that night.

When he got home, the news awaited him from the west coast that his wife would be delayed by a day, due to a violent stomachache. He was relieved.

35

DUBAK'S WIFE, JAYA, CAME HOME FROM THE OPEN MAR-
ket feeling furious. A vendor had refused to sell to her, accusing her of having killed her mother-in-law. "You stuffed the old
woman with sticky rice cake," he shouted, attracting attention
from the shoppers and other venders. And it hadn't been the
first time she was humiliated in public by a stranger. She cried,
screwing up her face, when she got home. Her neighbor was
babysitting her son, but Jaya didn't feel like picking him up
right away. Instead, she sat on the floor where red peppers
were drying on a straw mat. She had been going out of her
way to make interesting dinners for Dubak after the funeral
of his mother. He hadn't really forgiven her for who knew
what, and he still had his doubts which he could use against
her should an occasion arise. But for now, his wife was feeding him well—the gods only knew how she managed to, with
their meager household budget—and she cooperated in bed
pretty much every time he was stiff before dawn. She used to
push him away, hitting him between the legs with a pillow and
complaining that it was an insane hour for such activity.

Today, Jaya had visited the market because she heard the
news of the squid arriving from the west coast. Dubak loved
seafood, but it was hard to get it, except in the spring, when
the road from the west coast was no longer frozen and the
weather was not too hot to make everything go bad immediately. Jaya had meant to stuff squid with ground-up soybeans,
greens, and chopped carrots, and steam them on the cooking
rice. She would have sliced the colorful dish and arranged it
artfully. The taste would have cheered up any sulking heart.

But now she saw her stupidity plain and clear. It didn't matter how hard she worked to make sure her husband wouldn't try to stab her again. The whole village was bloodthirsty.

"You can have my innocent blood," she said and took a rope made of straw.

She walked over to the totem poles at the entrance to the village. She lowered her head and proclaimed that she was innocent. She had fed her mother-in-law rice cake, true, but who could have predicted that the old woman would choke and die like that? Jaya cried mournfully, telling the totem poles once again that she was innocent. It was true that her senile mother-in-law, who had wanted to be served a meal every time she turned around because she had forgotten she had just eaten, was a nuisance. Whenever Dubak came home, the mother complained that Jaya starved her. And sometimes she did starve her, but just a little. Who could have withstood such a mother-in-law? She had done a decent job taking care of her. When her mother-in-law choked on the rice cake, she didn't know what to do but watch her die. She tried to pour water into her mother-in-law's mouth, but it was no use. She turned blue and ceased breathing.

Jaya wiped her eyes and said accusingly, "I am going to kill myself to teach the villagers a lesson. *They* will be the murderers!" She prayed that she would be reborn a bird, never again a woman, a poor woman. And then she turned around and walked to the twin pine trees. She threw the rope over a branch of one. She tied a knot and stuck her head in so the rope went around her neck. Holding the other end of the rope, she began to pull. She jumped and pulled the rope at the same time, and she felt it suddenly tightening on her neck. She was just slightly above the ground, but it was enough to choke anyone to death.

Mistress Yee's carriage was just passing the totem poles, and the servants stopped when they heard the sudden thud coming from over by the twin pine trees. The branch couldn't endure the weight of a pregnant woman: it broke and Jaya fell on the ground. She was moaning. Nani ran over and found what had happened.

"Have you lost your mind!" she exclaimed.

☽ ○ ☾

From the carriage, Mistress Yee inquired after the noise and why the servants were stopping. One of them said that there was a woman crying under the twin pine trees. The other said it might be Dubak's wife.

"That's not a reason to stop!" Mistress Yee cried from inside. Her legs had been cramped for so long. She wanted to get home as soon as possible.

The male servants hollered to Nani to come back as they were walking away.

"My water broke!" screamed Jaya.

"Oh no!" Nani didn't know what that meant, but it seemed like an emergency.

Nani ran to the male servants and announced that she had to look after Jaya.

Nani was frightened and asked Jaya if she should run and get Mrs. Wang.

Jaya said that she would be dead by the time Mrs. Wang arrived. And then she began to scream from the extraordinary pain. Her contractions began and her labor proceeded rapidly.

Nani trembled for a minute and then calmed down as the contraction momentarily subsided. She had witnessed two births. And she remembered what Mrs. Wang had done with Mistress Yee. Nani pulled a handkerchief out of her sack, folded it into a ball, and stuffed it into Jaya's mouth.

Jaya spat it out and said, "What the hell! I am no Mrs. Kim. I will scream as much as I want!" Tears oozed out of the corners of her eyes. "Look, I want you to tie the other end of this rope around the pine tree, will you?"

Nani did as told, instinctively understanding what it was for. Much sooner than she had anticipated, the pain returned to torture Jaya. Nani offered Jaya her wrist to hold, as she had done for Mistress Kim, but Jaya held onto the rope and pulled it with enough strength to uproot the tree. She screamed like an animal, tormented by an invisible enemy. Nani clenched her teeth and wiped the sweat off Jaya's forehead and chest.

"Nani, here it comes! Pull!" Jaya screamed.

Jaya pushed. The baby's head emerged. Jaya pushed again. At the third push, the whole bloody boy came out, and Nani caught him. She held the squirming body in her hands. She couldn't help but shed tears as she carefully wrapped the wet, wrinkled newborn in her handkerchief.

"Nani, give me the baby and run to my home. Get a pair of scissors and bring them to me," she said.

Nani ran. Then she stopped. She didn't have to go to Jaya's house. She should just run to the closest house.

She ran into Quince's house and yelled, "Anyone home?"

Quince looked out from her kitchen, unimpressed. "What's the fuss?" She got up when she saw Nani's bloody hands and shirt.

"Jaya had her baby by the twin pine trees. I need a pair of scissors, quick!" Nani said frantically.

At the mention of Jaya's name, Quince snorted and said, "I'd be a dog if I helped her."

"A dog knows when to bark and when to whimper. If you don't help a woman who's just had a baby, you are no better than a dog. Give me a pair of scissors right now or else you won't be working for Mr. O anymore. And your husband: he just returned from the west coast, escorting Mistress Yee. I will go over now and tell Mistress Yee that he no longer wants to be employed. Should I do that?" Nani shot her an indignant glare.

Quince laughed. But there was no need to cross Nani. Her large buttocks jiggled as she stepped up on the stone step to her room to see if her sewing box was there. She pulled out a pair of scissors from a woven basket and handed them to Nani. "Calm down, child. Nothing bad is going to happen. Once the baby's out, the baby's fine."

"Give me a sheet or something to wrap the baby with," Nani demanded. "I had only a handkerchief."

"Sure." Quince pulled a dry sheet from a clothesline and folded it into a small square. "What did she have?" Quince asked. Her tone was suddenly intimate and interested.

"It's a boy," Nani said, showing mild annoyance.

Remembering what Mrs. Wang had done, Nani went to the kitchen and dipped the scissors in water briefly. Then she put them in the fire for a few moments until they stopped sizzling. And then she dashed out.

She cut the umbilical cord, feeling extremely anxious. She didn't know if it caused the baby or the mother any pain.

Jaya thanked Nani profusely and cried, remembering how she had tried to kill herself. She thought she would name her son Soseng, Rising from Death.

Nani walked home feeling proud. Her chest was wet with the sweat of exertion. But there was something that made her chest cold besides her own sweat. She touched it mindlessly and found the jade necklace. She held it in her palm for a moment and said out loud, "My dear boy, I wish you the best of luck."

36

MISTRESS YEE TOOK A LONG BATH. SOONYI SOAPED HER
and washed her hair. The little maid wasn't up to her standard.
She was a delicate sort for a maid, and Mistress Yee had to tell
her what to do too many times. No one was like Mirae. She had
given up on finding a maid like her. She was history now. But
she couldn't help thinking about her now and then. Leaning
back in the wooden tub, she closed her eyes and inhaled the
fragrance from the dried iris petals floating in the water.

"Tell me, Soonyi, where did Master go yesterday?" she asked,
her eyes still closed.

Soonyi, wondering why Mistress Yee didn't ask him herself,
replied, "He went to a meeting at Lord Ryu's house. A messenger came after breakfast, and Master left when the sun was high."

"Tell me, when did he come home?" Mistress Yee asked.

"Sometime before dinner, Mistress," she replied timidly.

"You are such a bore," Mistress Yee said, opening her eyes.
Mirae would have told her all that and much more without her
asking. But she didn't have enough strength at the moment to
whack Soonyi.

After the bath, Mistress Yee returned to her room. She was
still very tired. She told Soonyi to go and tell Nani to make
beef soup with mung bean sprouts and scallion. "Tell her not
to make it too spicy this time," Mistress Yee said.

Soonyi lowered her head and dashed out. While walking
toward the kitchen, she chanted, "Beef soup with mung bean
sprouts and scallion. Don't make it too spicy." But when she
arrived in the kitchen, she saw Nani in her bloody clothes.
"Big Sister! What's happened to you?"

Nani smiled and said, "You silly, don't get excited about every bloody blouse you see. Some blood is a sign of a midwife. I just delivered a baby, Jaya's baby!" she announced proudly, stretching her chin up and out.

"Really?" Soonyi gasped.

"Yep," Nani said.

"How was it?"

"Scary. Interesting," Nani said. "It wasn't like the night when Mistress Kim had her baby. Jaya's baby burst out like . . . chestnuts in the fire. Just like that. I even cut the umbilical cord for her," she bragged.

Soonyi stared at Nani, a little awestruck. Then she remembered Mistress Yee's message. "Oh, Big Sister, Mistress Yee wants beef soup for dinner," she said, wondering what it was that Mistress Yee had specified about the beef soup.

"I need to wash up and change," said Nani and rushed out of the kitchen.

Nani undressed in her room, and once again she touched the jade necklace. She took it off. She wrapped it in a cloth and placed it deep in a chest of drawers, among the things that had belonged to her mother. Suddenly, her legs wobbled. She collapsed on the floor and cried silently, missing Min. She couldn't swallow her own saliva, for her throat ached as if a fishbone had gotten stuck there. Finally, Min wanted her, but she didn't want him anymore. How did one change one's mind? If she could only change hers, she would do it and marry him and live happily. But she could not make herself do something she didn't want to do.

"Big Sister!" called Soonyi, opening the door. "Sorry," she said, seeing Nani still half naked and sitting on the floor.

"Close the door!" yelled Nani. She got up, washed, and got dressed quickly. She fixed her hair, looking at herself in Mistress Kim's palm-sized mirror. Mirae had taken it from Mistress Kim's room after she had passed away, and when she was kicked out of the house, she had forgotten to pack it in her bundle.

"Should I put the water on the stove?" Soonyi asked.

"No, peel a radish and cut it into small cubes. Peel a few cloves of garlic and crush them too," said Nani.

Soonyi was still chopping the radish when Nani arrived in the kitchen. She wanted to make sure that the cubes of radish were identical in size.

Rolling her eyes, Nani snatched the knife and attacked the radish. She said, "When I'm thirsty, I'm better off if I go and get water instead of lying down on the ground with my mouth open, hoping it will rain. That's how slow you are."

Soonyi peeled the garlic cloves, pouting.

Nani tasted the first cube of radish and said, "Mmm, this is so sweet. Here, taste it, child."

Soonyi opened her mouth and took the radish. "It's good."

"Soonyi, I am sorry I was harsh, but if you want to survive as a maid and be respected you have to know what you are doing. If you wait until your superiors tell you what to do, they get tired of you. My mother used to tell me that you shouldn't *ask* the mistress what she would like for dinner; you should *tell* her what is for dinner. Of course, you have to come up with a dish she will like. But you need to train your superiors to appreciate what you cook and do. Do you understand?"

Soonyi nodded miserably.

"By the way, where is Quince? She is supposed to be here by now," Nani said, frowning. Ever since Mirae had left the house, Quince came in to help with cooking in addition to the laundry she had been doing every other day.

Nani was now making soybeans in a marinade of rice malt syrup, soy sauce, and sesame seeds.

"Slice the lotus root paper thin, and when you get a chance, pierce the pine nuts with the pine needles," Nani ordered her.

"How many pine nuts?" Soonyi asked blankly.

Nani looked at Soonyi and sighed.

"All right, all right," Soonyi said.

Quince came in then, and the first thing she said was, "I heard you actually managed to deliver Jaya's baby!"

Nani was proud, remembering the moment she had caught the baby. She forgot how frightened she had felt when she first held the slimy creature in her hands.

"Boy, Jaya was telling us all about how great you were!" Quince said. "I'm late because I took soup to her, and she was raving about you."

Nani blushed.

When the dinner was ready, the three of them carried various dishes on trays to Mistress Yee's quarters and arranged the dishes on a low table.

"Soonyi, soup to the right of the rice!" Nani whispered in a restrained voice, setting seven different kinds of sauces right in front of the soup bowls.

"When are you going to learn, Soonyi? Huh?" said Quince, guffawing like a man.

"Lower your voice!" Nani admonished her.

"Nani, do you know what we call you?" Quince asked. Soonyi turned red and fidgeted because everyone, herself included, referred to Nani by her nickname behind her back.

"Mother-in-law!" Quince said and laughed again boisterously.

Nani raised her eyebrows fiercely. At any moment, Mr. O would enter with his wife. So Nani bit her lip, suppressed her anger, and focused on the arrangement of the food on the table.

As they finished arranging the dishes, Mr. O entered. Nani dismissed Quince and Soonyi, who would go back to the kitchen, tidy up, and prepare the night snack. Nani remained to pour drinks and to listen to them fuss about the food and to provide explanations about why some things tasted a certain way and so on. A few moments later, Mistress Yee also entered. She sat with her husband. Nani took the covers from the rice bowls, poured the wine, and moved to the corner where she awaited instruction.

"So how was the trip?" Mr. O asked Mistress Yee.

"It was not easy. I thought you would run to me when you got the message that I was sick and therefore delayed," Mistress Yee said sulkily.

"When I was a boy, Dr. Choi said that if you had a stomachache from meat it would take a day to recover, but with seafood, if you didn't die immediately, it would take only one burp. So I was not worried," Mr. O replied.

As Mistress Yee lifted her spoon to take a bite of rice, she noticed what was in the beef soup. She placed her spoon back down on the table, and said, "What is this?"

"What's wrong?" Mr. O asked, looking over at the dishes on his wife's side.

"Come over here, Nani," ordered Mistress Yee. Her voice was cold and metallic.

"Yes, Mistress," Nani said, her neck perspiring.

"I asked for beef soup with scallion and mung bean sprouts!" Mistress Yee shouted.

"Mistress, we made a mistake. May I go and make beef soup with scallion and mung bean sprouts now?"

"And what am I supposed to do in the meantime?" Mistress Yee said scornfully. "One is a buffoon and the other a mental case. I really need a new maid," Mistress Yee complained. "Mirae always did exactly what I told her to do. She never failed to carry out my orders. What is the matter with all three of you? Not one of you girls has a head on her shoulders. I am going to start interviewing some more girls again and pick out a maid myself in a few days," Mistress Yee said.

For a while it had seemed taboo to mention Mirae's name in the house. But lately, Mistress Yee seemed to have forgotten all about why she had let Mirae go. She brought her up occasionally, as though what Mirae had done was not worth holding a grudge about.

"Leave us alone," Mr. O ordered Nani.

Nani got up gladly and left the room, closing the door behind her. But she stayed in the hallway between the room and the anteroom, in case she got called in again. She thought about what Quince had called her. That had come out of nowhere, considering that Nani was very kind and helpful to the other maids and the male servants. She frowned, thinking of Soonyi's lapse of memory about the beef soup. She was going to pinch Soonyi as soon as she saw her.

Mr. O rubbed his chin and said, "I am curious. You say that your previous maid always carried out your orders."

"She did. She even knew what I was thinking before I opened my mouth," Mistress Yee said and immediately flushed. "What are you trying to say?" she challenged Mr. O.

"If she did everything you asked her to do, she must have committed the evil deed according to your will," Mr. O said calmly, as if he had rehearsed his speech.

"What do you mean?" A blue river rose on one side of Mistress Yee's temple.

"I am just-just asking," Mr. O said awkwardly. He hadn't meant to argue with her about Mirae the maid. His mind raced to Mirae the kiseng. His heart quivered and his mouth dried up at the thought of her touch. The memory was so strong that it felt as though it had just happened.

"I see what you are getting at." Mistress Yee snorted. "I didn't mean to tell you this, but Mirae was in love with you. She wanted to get rid of Mistress Kim, and then me so that she could have you. I tried to awaken her from this impossible dream and lead her to goodness, but she was not made of honest material. She was already knee-deep in the swamp of her vanity. You saw what she had done with your own eyes the night when you were hiding in the room of your beloved first wife! By the way, I've been meaning to ask, why were you there in the dead woman's room?" Mistress Yee asked.

Mr. O didn't hear anything but "Mirae was in love with you."

"What are you thinking about?" Mistress Yee asked, frustrated at seeing her husband lost in his own thoughts while she was talking.

"No, no," he said distractedly.

"I asked why you were in her room," she said.

"Oh," he said, remembering. "Whatever the shaman said that evening made no sense to me, but I heard her voice. I heard her. Or at least I thought so. And my feet carried me there. I went inside. I sat where she used to sit. I felt the air curdle around my body. Soon I felt suffocated. I thought it was the old, moldy air in the room. But I know it was her. I was scared. I thought she was going to strangle me. I wanted to leave, but then I heard you talking with a maid. I wanted to know why you were there at that hour with a maid," he said.

"But you heard everything," Mistress Yee said.

"I did," he said.

"So what is it? What are you trying to say?" Her voice broke and her face turned miserable and furious.

"I don't suspect you. But when your maid was being beaten in the yard, tied up to a bench on her belly, water poured on her buttocks so that the clothing wouldn't protect against the sting of the cane, she said nothing," Mr. O pointed out.

"You think she is innocent? Is that what you are trying to say?" Mistress Yee cackled.

"The normal reaction from a maid would be to protest that she is not guilty or to beg and plead for forgiveness. She did nothing. She only glared at you without crying. Her eyes cursed you, which I found beyond insolent. An evil maid who took an attitude while being punished! But if she had been guilty, would she have acted the way she did?" Mr. O asked, realizing that he wasn't saying much. He knew his wife. The price he would have to pay for speaking his mind out loud might be much more than he was willing to pay. And what was the point of his talking anyway? He believed Mirae's version of the story just because she was divinely beautiful. Mr. O was a little ashamed when he thought about the ring he had given away on an impulse. It had belonged to his late father who had received it from the governor of the province for having been the largest donor for some project. Mr. O couldn't remember which project it was now.

It would take a barrel of grease to make her husband's head spin properly, Mistress Yee thought. She laughed and said, "My dear husband, you heard a little while ago how I valued Mirae as a maid. She was my right arm, and it was detrimental to lose her. I knew her absence would inconvenience *me*. But I had to let her go to set an example for the other maids and servants. Besides, if she had done me wrong, I would have let it pass, but it was Mistress Kim who suffered because of her. Not that I am trying to say I adored Mistress Kim, mind you, the woman was unkind to me. But I had to show that what Mirae did was evil and unforgivable. It pained me to see her go. She was part of my dowry. Her aunt had put her in my father's house. She became my handmaid at an early age. We were friends." Mistress Yee's eyes glistened and turned red.

Mr. O felt bad. His wife was fastidious and fussy, maybe, but did not possess an evil bone in her body. She was an honest soul.

"Don't let the food get cold. Let's eat," Mr. O suggested.

"I've lost my appetite," she muttered.

"Oh no. Mistress Yee, please, open your mouth," he asked, picking up a slice of pressed pork with his chopsticks. "Ah," he said, leaning closer to her.

She took the food and said, "You hurt my feelings."

"Forgive me, Mistress Yee. I am a foolish old man," he said, smiling pathetically.

When Nani heard her master and mistress laugh, she left and went to the kitchen and found Soonyi dozing in front of the stove. Nani pulled her hair from behind and said, "Where is Quince?"

"She left, Big Sister," Soonyi said.

"Left already? She is supposed to stay until we are done with the dinner dishes!" Nani shrieked.

"She said she would come back real soon," Soonyi said.

"So what's calling her this time?" Soonyi asked.

"Her husband was whistling from over the wall behind the well. Quince talked to him through a crack in the rocks in the wall. Then she just darted out, giggling. She said she was going to come back real soon," Soonyi said.

"Did you pour water into the rice pot?" Nani asked, lifting the lid of the cast iron pot on the stove.

"I-I am not sure," Soonyi stammered.

"This is too much water. It will take forever to boil," Nani complained, using a long wooden spoon to remove the rice stuck to the bottom of the cast iron pot.

"Get the table ready for us," Nani said, stirring the rice in the water. The aroma of browned rice was nutty and flavorful.

While Nani and Soonyi readied their low table, Quince showed up again. Her appearance was comically messy, with her hair flying in all directions and her shirt ribbon loose, but her cheeks were rosy and her lips cherry red. There were also a few strands of straw in her hair.

"What did you do?" Soonyi asked curiously.

Nani snorted, disgusted.

"What?" Quince asked, smirking.

"Go home," Nani said.

"I am hired to work here," Quince said.

"Then why did you leave in the middle of work?" Nani asked, sitting down by the low table.

"I was waiting for you to return so you could tell us what to do," said Quince sarcastically in her high-pitched voice which didn't seem to suit the size of her body.

"By the way, I tell you what to do because I am supposed to," Nani shrilled, remembering her nickname.

"I know. I know," Quince drawled grudgingly.

"Go to Mistress Yee's quarters and wait until she tells you to remove the table," Nani said.

"And what about you?" Quince asked.

"I am going to have dinner," she said.

"I need to have dinner too," Quince said.

"Strictly speaking, you are not supposed to eat here. You are not part of the family. You are a part-time employee," Nani said.

Quince sat her huge bottom by the table and picked up a pickled cucumber with her fingers. "Mmm, that's too sour," she said, puckering her lips.

Soonyi offered her a pair of chopsticks, surveying Nani's face.

"Thank you, child," Quince said, grinning. "Give me a bowl of rice. I am so hungry."

Her eyes cast down, Nani snickered.

"Don't sulk, Nani. My husband was delayed coming home from the west coast. He just arrived and hadn't seen me for more than a day. You will understand when you get married. Sometimes men get antsy when they don't see their women-folk for a while," Quince blabbered.

With a look of contemptuous horror, Nani got up and left. She was headed for Mistress Yee's quarters.

"It's all her mother's fault," Quince said, stuffing her mouth with a large amount of rice and the marinated sweet potato stems.

"What do you mean?" Soonyi asked.

"Her mother taught her to believe that she deserved a better life than the one of a maid. With that in her head, she thinks she can boss us around. But a maid is a maid," Quince said, grinning at Soonyi, who looked puzzled.

At that moment, Chunshim came in and said that Buwon had just fallen asleep. She was hungry. Indeed, as she spoke, her stomach growled.

Quince said, "Sit down."

Ignoring Quince, Chunshim asked Soonyi to bring a tray of food to her room.

Quince rolled her eyes as Chunshim left the kitchen and said, "She doesn't see me, huh?"

Soonyi arranged the tray with rice and a few dishes. As she was about to take it out, Quince snatched the dish of fried squash patties and put it on her low table.

"Please, Aunt Quince, put it back. She doesn't have much here," Soonyi said.

"She is *another* one who is bossing you around," Quince pointed out. "You need to make sure you don't become the maid for a pack of maids."

Soonyi left, feeling bad. "A maid for a pack of maids," she whispered to herself.

Nani was walking back and said, "What are you mumbling about?"

"Nothing."

In the kitchen, Quince burped loudly. Nani frowned and said, "You may go now. Master and Mistress have blown their candles out."

Quince grinned and said, narrowing her eyes, "Just as I said. Men get antsy."

Nani frowned and went out to wash herself. She was tired. Catching Soonyi coming from Chunshim's room, she said, "You need to finish tidying up the kitchen. I am going to bed now. I think I am coming down with something."

"Do you want ginger tea?" Soonyi asked.

"What I might have isn't what ginger tea can soothe," she replied.

In her room, without lighting the candle, Nani undressed and lay on the floor. She reviewed what Mistress Yee and Mr. O were talking about at their dinner table. With her eyes closed, she conjured up the image of Mirae again, drenched, tied down on a bench. A large, smooth tree branch swung down to hit Mirae on her bottom, and it bounced up slowly, only to go down again. The hired beater counted loudly: *twenty, twenty-one, twenty-two.* That was when Nani had come in the yard. All the maids and servants were supposed to witness the beating for a lesson in what would happen to wicked servants, but Nani had not finished cooking dinner in time. So she arrived later. Mirae was glaring at Mistress Yee.

"Big Sister, are you sleeping?" Soonyi said as she came in.

Nani didn't answer. She wasn't in the mood to talk. She now thought about Min. He had changed a lot. He looked older, with a thinner body. How filthy he was! His hair was unkempt, and his skin was red and leathery from the sun. She thought about the shore where she had sat with Min. It was the second time she had visited the west coast. The first time there had been with Mistress Kim when she freed fish because she wished to be pregnant. That was almost a decade ago now. Her mother had sent her to the shore to play with shells while she escorted Mistress Kim to the boat. She still remembered her mother looking back again and again with a warning eye, silently telling her not to go near the water.

Soonyi lay down on her cotton mat and immediately fell asleep. Nani could hear her breathe evenly.

Nani yawned and looked over to the other side, where Mirae had once slept, away from them. She yawned again and fell asleep.

In her dream, she was back on the west coast with Min. They were on the beach, chasing each other, barefoot, laughing like kids. In her dreams Min was always able to laugh and talk. Water splashed on her. Suddenly, a wave engulfed Min. Nani's heart sank, but when the wave pulled back to the ocean, he still stood there. Nani rushed to him, and they hugged. They ran again by the shore. Sometime later, Min made a bonfire. Nani sat there, warming up her cold body. Min kept throwing on more branches to keep the fire going. Nani was feeling warm and cozy. The world burned bright orange, and the bonfire crackled louder and louder, and that was when she woke up.

NANI WOKE UP FROM HER DREAM. IT WAS THE MIDDLE
of the night, but the brightness outside was like the early
afternoon.

"Min!" she cried in a whisper. Like a dream, he was standing on the threshold, and the bright light was coming from the
kitchen. It was on fire. Nani got up, and Min left quickly. "Oh no!"
Nani ran out and saw what was happening to the house. The fire
was not just in the kitchen, but here and there, and she could
see the storage room afire too. She was about to run to check
on Mr. O's quarters, but then she remembered that her master
was at Mistress Yee's quarters. Suddenly, she turned and ran back
to her room and shook Soonyi violently. The room was getting
warm, and the crackling sound was getting alarmingly loud.

Soonyi woke up and cried like a baby. Nani couldn't take
care of her. She ran out, and Soonyi followed her, begging Nani
not to leave her alone. Something collapsed in the kitchen.

She ran to Mistress Yee's quarters. She turned back and told
Soonyi to go and tell Chunshim to get out with Buwon and
her own son. Soonyi didn't want to. She cried, trembling.

"Soonyi, go and get Buwon!" Nani shrieked. Soonyi jerked
but still didn't move. Nani clouted her on the head and
repeated, "Go and get Buwon!" Nani ran toward Mistress
Yee's quarters without looking back. Soonyi reluctantly trotted to the building behind the guests' quarters.

Mistress Yee's quarters hadn't caught fire. Nani stood in the
yard, ready to shout, but then she suddenly remembered that
Min had emerged from nowhere in the middle of the night
in her room. Why in the world had he showed up? Had she

dreamed it all? He had stood on her threshold as if he had come to rescue her. But how could he have known that the house was on fire?

"Mistress Yee, Nani is here," she said. No reply. "Mistress Yee, please wake up!" she shouted. "Fire!" she finally cried.

Mr. O came out. And then he rushed back to get his wife. They both came out. Mr. O looked about from the raised entrance, waving his hand in the air helplessly. Bright orange light everywhere felt like a sizzling summer day. He stepped down on the ground, and a sound emerged from his mouth, but it was incomprehensible. He looked lost. He ran to his quarters, which were completely engulfed. Then he ran, passing the guests' quarters, toward the building where Buwon was supposedly asleep. At that moment, Chunshim escaped the building with a baby in her arms. Soonyi stood in the yard, crying. Bok ran to the yard. Nani arrived, panting.

"Is that Buwon?" Nani asked.

Chunshim realized that she had left Buwon behind. Shrieking, she handed her baby to Soonyi and hastened back to the building. Buwon was shrilling from inside. Nani ran after Chunshim. Bok ran after Nani. Dubak and a few other peasants who had seen the bright light coming from Mr. O's mansion came hurriedly. Mr. O arrived and heard his son cry from inside the burning building. He attempted to go in, but the three men grabbed him by his arms. Another man went in instead. A few moments later, he came out carrying Chunshim. Nani followed out carrying Buwon. Bok came out coughing hysterically.

Mr. O stood there, holding his son, and he wept, even though the servants were urging him to leave the place at once. Finally, they had to pull his son away from him so that he would follow them. Outside the house Mistress Yee, watched the house burn, standing among the peasants who had come to lend a hand. Servants went into the mansion to pour buckets of water on the flames, but their efforts were in vain. By dawn, every

building had burned down, except Mistress Yee's quarters and
the guests' quarters.

Mr. O stood motionless in front of the main entrance for
a long time. Then he left to find Mistress Yee and his son at
the guesthouse by the village hall that was meant to accommodate government officers. His servants remained to salvage
whatever was left, but all was charred or partially damaged.
There was nothing much even to steal. Local government officers came in the morning to examine the site and come up
with a possible scenario, but they just stood for a while, awed,
for the house had marked one of the most impressive sights in
the village for many generations.

One of the officers found a torch that must have been used
as a lighter. There was only one torch, so the officers concluded
that the fire was set by one person, possibly one who knew the
place quite well. But almost everyone in the village knew the
house quite well. Even children drew pictures of it with chalk
without consulting a grownup. The officers interrogated the
village women to determine if their husbands had stayed out
the night of the fire, but they all said their husbands had gone
to bed early with them. When the officers asked if anyone had
seen a suspicious person that evening around Mr. O's mansion, everyone shook their heads, looking blank. And that was
the end of the investigation. One officer wrote a report on the
case and submitted it to the local government office.

Mistress Yee was ill from the shock of the fire. She whined
because she was disgusted by her temporary living quarters.

"I am going to build the same house on the same spot,"
Mr. O consoled her.

"It will take forever to build a house like that," Mistress Yee
said, frowning.

"No, it will take one season," he said. He said it confidently
to convince his invisible father in the atmosphere. He could
feel how angry his father must be to see that he had ruined the

house, four generations old. He could almost hear his father's stern voice: "I wish I had another son." That was what he had said sometimes when he was drinking with his guests. He didn't seem to want two sons. He seemed to want to replace his only son with another. At his deathbed, his father asked, "Will you be able to carry on my name?" Before Mr. O could muster up the courage to say that he would, his father had passed away. After the funeral, alone at his father's grave, he had cried like a child, telling him that he was not the coward his father had always assumed him to be. He wanted to have twelve sons, but as of now he only had Buwon, hardly a son.

"It will take only one season," he emphasized again, realizing that it would take more because the rice-farming season had begun and there weren't many free hands left.

"I can't live here more than a season," Mistress Yee said determinedly.

"I think we can do it in a season," Mr. O said.

"Well, we will see," Mistress Yee said skeptically.

"We will build the house in a season!" Mr. O shouted.

"Are you mad at me? Did I set the house on fire?" Mistress Yee asked, furrowing her forehead. Tears brimmed in her eyes.

"Of course not. Why should I be mad at you?" Mr. O asked regretfully.

"I don't know. You've changed. Just yesterday you suggested that Mirae had been mistreated and wrongly accused. I don't know what is going on in your mind anymore." Mistress Yee broke down and sobbed. She was tired and frustrated. The breakfast was not up to her standard. Besides, it was spring. She had planned to host an elaborate party at her house. That, of course, would have to be canceled. Also, she wanted to go and enjoy cherry blossoms by the Snake River, but that wasn't going to happen either. She had hired a seamstress to make a new dress for the occasion.

Mr. O took his wife's hand and said, "I will take care of everything."

Mr. O was not used to taking care of everything. His father, even after his marriage, hadn't entrusted him with the important matters in the house. After his death, Mistress Kim took charge of them with the excellent assistance of her maid Hosoon, Nani's mother, and so he never had to pay attention to the details of the housekeeping. All he needed to do was enjoy his life and not complain too much. Only today, when he was forced to relocate, had he realized that a couple of young girls had been running his household, and where were the menservants besides Bok? What was he thinking? There was no one who would have rescued him or his wife had they stayed in his quarters the night before. What was he really thinking? When he was little, more than a dozen servants and maids had served his family. Where had they all gone? He realized that morning he had only four, and two were bloody children. His forehead was throbbing. He didn't enjoy self-criticism. He got up. He wanted to go see the local government officers to ask about the latest findings on the fire, and he also wanted to find out how much land he would have to sell to build a new house.

Nani and Chunshim were taking care of Buwon in the rear room at the guesthouse. Luckily, he had escaped the fire unscathed except for singed hair. The hair would grow again.

"You were lucky," Nani said to Chunshim.

"I know!" Chunshim said. She still couldn't believe that she had forgotten Buwon when she ran from her burning room in the middle of the night.

"How is your baby?" Nani asked, taking Chunshim's hand.

"He is fine," Chunshim said, her eyes brimming with tears. The stress had been too great for her. She had almost let Buwon die. The thought still chilled her to the bone.

"No one's hurt," Nani said.

"That's true," Chunshim said. "Thank you for not telling Mistress Yee about what happened," she whispered, to make sure that Nani wouldn't tell their mistress.

"Not in a million years," Nani replied stoutly.

"Do you know where your Min is?" Chunshim asked.

Nani didn't reply.

"I want you to know that I never had anything to do with him," Chunshim emphasized.

Nani nodded.

"I haven't told you this, but I was never married," Chunshim said abruptly.

"Like I didn't know?" Nani said, grinning.

"I was a concubine to a wealthy man," Chunshim began. She hadn't intended to tell her story to anyone, but here she was, blurting it out. "He used to beat me!" Chunshim cried suddenly.

Nani shook her head sympathetically and squeezed the other woman's hand. "It's all right. You are not with him now."

"I ran away from that house one night. I didn't know I was pregnant. When my son was born, I didn't want him. I thought he would remind me of that man for the rest of my life. But he doesn't. He is just a darling," Chunshim said.

Nani wanted to hear more about Min, but Chunshim could talk only about her son. His sweet face so like her younger brother's. His chubby knees. His precociousness.

"I need to go and see if Quince is ever coming back with the groceries," said Nani, getting up.

"I should help you," Chunshim said.

"No, that's not your job," Nani said.

As Nani walked away, she realized that Chunshim didn't bother her anymore. For a long time, Chunshim's status had confused Nani. She wasn't a maid and she wasn't an aristocrat. She was a pain in the neck. She seemed to have it easy, just taking care of the baby. But now Nani felt sorry. What she did was not easy. When she pictured Chunshim running out with her own baby in her arms and forgetting Buwon, Nani was strangely moved. Her mother would have done exactly the opposite. She would have carried out the baby of her master, not Nani, even though she loved Nani more. For some reason, Nani was convinced about that. So she walked to the kitchen, admiring Chunshim.

Quince was waiting for Nani in the kitchen. When Nani entered the room, Quince whispered loudly, "Who set the house on fire?"

"No idea," Nani said, studying Quince's face carefully while she pretended to be checking the cabbage in the basket.

"Are you sure you don't know?"

"I am sure, Sister," said Nani, taking out the rest of the groceries clumsily. She was thinking of Min again. "He'll be damned if he has done something bad," she said. She had spoken aloud without meaning to.

"What did you say?" Quince asked, grabbing a cucumber from the grocery basket. She took an enormous bite out of it, screwing up her freckled face.

"Nothing," Nani said, snatching the cucumber back from Quince.

Quince chewed loudly, showing her crooked teeth and laughing. She now eyed the carrots in the basket.

"Go get water!" Nani said and slapped Quince's thigh, chasing her out of the kitchen as if shooing away a fly.

"All right, Mother-in-law," Quince said and ran out, giggling.

Nani sat by the stove thinking about Min again. She tried to convince herself that she had dreamed that Min was standing on her threshold. In fact, she *had* dreamed of him. She remembered it now. She and Min were on the shore. He made a bonfire. And she woke up when she heard the crackling sound of the wood in the fire.

MIRAE WAS DRESSED UP IN A BEAUTIFUL JADE-AND-RED outfit. She was having a cup of tea with Dimple, whom she called Big Sister, even though she could have easily been her mother. Dimple was flattered, and Mirae knew that.

"SO WHAT DID YOU THINK OF MR. O?" ASKED DIMPLE.

Mirae lowered her eyelids and smiled coquettishly.

"Well, the man is gold," Dimple said, smiling shrewdly and taking a sip of tea.

"Lord Ahn couldn't keep his eyes off of you, Big Sister," Mirae lied.

"He was my first," Dimple confessed. "When I joined the society, he had just returned from China, where he had studied. When he saw me, he said, 'You make my return worthwhile.' He was such a handsome man," Dimple reminisced.

"You must have been the most beautiful girl here. Of course, you still are. A real knockout," Mirae said, picking up a pumpkin-date rice cake with a bamboo pick. "Please, Big Sister, taste it. It is still warm." Mirae handed it over to Dimple, who was pleased to be so intimately treated. It made her feel young again. Most of the new kisengs froze when they saw Dimple and treated her like a lioness. She had enjoyed that role for a long time, but when she saw Lord Ahn showing a great interest in Mirae, she found herself boiling with jealousy. She no longer wanted to play the role of an old lioness, she wanted to be vulnerable again. Mirae wasn't the first girl that Lord Ahn had showed an interest in, but Dimple had never worried about it for she was sure she didn't have to. But Mirae was a different story. She reminded Dimple of herself.

"I thank you, Big Sister, for helping me with Mr. O. I was so clumsy with him," Mirae said, smiling and blushing.

"You handled him superbly," Dimple said, amused. "You haven't told me what you think of him. Tell me," Dimple urged.

"Shall I tell you the truth?" Mirae asked, smiling mysteriously, a little sadly.

"Always."

"Well, then," she began. "He is the most charming man I've ever laid eyes on."

Dimple let out a laugh of relief. Her left cheek still dimpled beautifully.

"Ah, Big Sister, look at you. You should live in a room made of mirrors so that you could look at yourself at all times. It's a pity you can't see your dimple every time it puckers. It's simply divine," Mirae said.

"You flatter me, Cherry Blossom," Dimple said.

"I am just telling the truth," Mirae replied, straight-faced.

"So what do I get if I arrange a rendezvous between you and Mr. O?" Dimple asked.

"My unwavering loyalty," Mirae answered, smiling playfully.

"You are the cleverest girl I know. I said exactly that to my boss, whom we called Fox, when she introduced me to Lord Ahn. You are my replica," Dimple said, pleased.

"You are much too kind."

"First of all, you should read romantic poetry. Mr. O loves poetry," Dimple said.

Mirae almost laughed. She didn't need to work on him any further.

"He loves the Chinese poet named Li Po. Get a book of his poetry," Dimple suggested.

"Tomorrow I will go to the marketplace and do some research," Mirae said, pouring more tea for Dimple.

"The first time Lord Ahn sat with me, he asked if I could recite a poem. I thought quickly and recited a poem from

China. 'Sharp sword too close will wound a hand/Woman's beauty too close will wound a life.'" Dimple said it with her eyes closed, as if she could see herself again in her heyday. "I warned him. But he jumped into the fire," Dimple said. And both women burst out laughing.

"But you must remember one thing. Mr. O loves his wife. He has never spent a night away from home. When he was with his previous wife, it was different. She was unable to produce an heir, and Mr. O spent a lot more time outside, but he always went home before the evening got too late. The current wife did produce an heir, but rumor has it that he is deformed. The baby is never outside the house, and Mr. O doesn't talk about him. Poor man. He is a good man, though. Everyone owes him a favor. Anyway, he is depressed. He doesn't come out of his house often enough," Dimple said.

Mirae listened with a broad smile. She was bored.

"But what attracts you to him?" Dimple asked.

Mirae knew what Dimple was thinking. Mirae was the prettiest, and she could get anyone she wanted, but why Mr. O? He wasn't the handsomest, he wasn't the youngest, and he wasn't the richest in the province.

"I've got a history with him," Mirae confessed, blushing, looking just a little gloomy.

"Oh!" Dimple clasped her hands together with the fingers interlaced.

Mirae's eyes reddened. "I am in love with him," Mirae said. "I would give my life if I could be with him," she added boldly.

Now Dimple's eyes reddened, and she extended her hand to Mirae's.

Dimple said, "You poor thing. Trust me. I will do what I can. We may not have husbands, but we sure deserve love now and then."

Mirae said nothing.

"There will be a gathering at General Hong's house at the end of this month. I will have a talk with Mr. O. I don't think it will have to be a long one, considering the way he looked at you. He was trembling! Did you see his hand?" Dimple laughed.

Tears welled up in Mirae's eyes.

"I thank you so much, Big Sister," Mirae said.

"Well, well, I think you and I make a fine team, don't we?" Dimple asked.

"Indeed, we do," Mirae said. "May I give you a little massage?"

"What an offer! I won't say no to that," Dimple said.

"If I could do half as well as you have, I would be satisfied," Mirae mumbled, anticipating a headache in between her eyebrows. She frowned. She could really use a nap.

"Oh, you will do well," Dimple said sleepily.

"Thank you for inviting me to tea."

"My pleasure," Dimple said, and clapped to summon her waiting maid.

A girl came in and removed the tea table. Mirae bowed and left. She strolled outside, thinking how awful it was to age as a kiseng. What would Dimple be like in ten years? Still talking about her good old days and how Lord Ahn had seduced her. Well, it wasn't her concern. She wasn't going to rot like that. She looked at the mountain, behind which Mr. O's mansion lay. She clenched her teeth and was about to cry. But then she burst out laughing, thinking about Mr. O's trembling hand. The passers-by turned around to look at the unusual sight of a woman laughing out loud on a street in public. But Mirae kept laughing uncontrollably. Later, in her room, she broke down and cried bitterly for a long time.

39

MANSONG CRIED AT NIGHT WHEN SHE FIRST ARRIVED at Mrs. Wang's house. She woke up twelve times at night and slept the whole day. Mrs. Wang wondered why anyone would want to have kids. Obviously, she had made a mistake by declaring in public that she would take care of the child. What had possessed her to come up with such an idea?

For several days, Mrs. Wang woke up every time Mansong cried. And she felt she was going to turn into a ghost if she went on like that. Her head felt light and her bones were sore. Finally, even when Mansong wasn't crying, Mrs. Wang could hear a cry in her head. She realized that childrearing was not her fate. In any case, she needed some help. She couldn't go on like that. But it was against her principles to hire a maid. Besides, she wasn't used to living with another person. Mansong was already one too many in the house.

One afternoon while Mansong slept, snoring, Mrs. Wang sat in her room and closed her eyes, breathing in and out slowly. The first thing she was going to do was somehow put an end to Mansong's nighttime crying. She had tried various herbal teas, but none of them worked. So she hired a shaman to perform Kut to soothe the sad spirit. Actually, Mrs. Wang despised the spirits that lingered between life and death. They were pathetic, she thought. And petty. She was getting ready to scold the spirit that possessed Mansong.

Lacking the funds, Mrs. Wang hired only one shaman and she arrived with no props, colorful outfits, or instruments.

She was a different type of shaman, the woman pointed out in a man's voice. All she needed was a bowl of uncooked rice and a spoon on a low table and a straw mat. And she wanted Mansong to sit on the mat too.

Mrs. Wang prepared everything for the shaman in a few moments.

The shaman knelt in front of the table and mumbled something for a while. The spoon that was standing in the rice bowl began to move. She talked louder. The spoon moved a little faster, dancing. She grabbed the spoon tightly, strangling it. As perspiration dripped down her nose, she mumbled again.

The whole time, Mansong watched the shaman expressionlessly, but toward the end, she cried fearfully.

Indignant and impatient, Mrs. Wang thundered while the shaman still mumbled something unintelligible. "Get out of that child! What business do you have to possess an innocent child? You damned pathetic spirit! Go where you belong, and let the living go on with their lives without you interfering. If I could see you, I would strike you! How petty can you be to linger among the living and pester people you have a grudge against! Move on!"

"Mrs. Wang, it's Mansong's mother. She wants to be heard," the shaman said.

Mrs. Wang rolled her eyes. She was fed up.

"She wants her daughter to be acknowledged as Mr. O's. She wants her to be at her father's house," the shaman interpreted.

"You see how ignorant the spirits are? The house burned down yesterday. If Mansong hadn't been here with me, she would have turned into ash."

Addressing the spirit, she shouted, "Is that what you would have liked?" She continued, "*I* don't know what it's like to be dead, but *you* know what it's like to be alive. Sometimes the living don't know what will happen the next day. What seems to be good may turn out to be bad. You want your daughter to be in Mr. O's household because she is his daughter. But that's how we think because we can't predict the future. I thought the dead knew better! But apparently you don't. So leave life up to us, and go find your way to sink into the world of the dead," Mrs. Wang scoffed, her spittle flying.

"She will go," the shaman said. "She wants to have your word that you will watch over Mansong."

"I've promised that already. Now go! Leave the child alone!" Mrs. Wang shouted menacingly.

Mansong stopped crying. She played with the rice in the bowl.

Mrs. Wang snatched the bowl away and pulled out the spoon and said, "Let her go."

So that was the end of that Kut. Mrs. Wang served the shaman lunch. They sat at the table and the shaman said, "Mrs. Wang, you can't mess with the spirits. Sometimes they enter your body and drag you around by the hair. A woman in another village used to cut herself with a knife because she had ridiculed a spirit."

Mrs. Wang guffawed and said, "It's all in your mind. If you let the spirit bully you, it will."

"Do you think it left?" the shaman asked, looking about as if she could see the spirit.

"There is no room for it here at my house," Mrs. Wang assured her loudly, as if to make sure the spirit heard her.

"So what are you going to do with the child?" the shaman asked, taking a large spoonful of fluffy rice.

"I will see. The woman was a good sort. She can't leave because she loves her child so. But all I am saying is that she is mistaken. The child would *not* be better off with her family. And I am not better off with the child. If I were clever, I would drop her off at her father's house and make the spirit and me happy while the rest, including the child, are miserable. Maybe I should leave the matter with the gods and forget about it," Mrs. Wang said, drinking water from a large bowl.

"Oh, by the way, did you hear? The criminal has been captured," the shaman informed Mrs. Wang.

Mrs. Wang raised her eyebrows apprehensively.

"It's the dumb boy," the shaman said.

"Really?" Mrs. Wang said nonchalantly.

"He pleaded guilty before the beating," the shaman said.

"That's smart. Why go through the beating if he was going to confess anyway?" Mrs. Wang said.

"All that's needed to get him hanged now is an official letter from Mr. O, relinquishing his contract with the servant. While he belongs to Mr. O, maybe the local government can't go ahead and punish him," the shaman said. "Well, on that note, Mrs. Wang, I need to go." The shaman got up.

Mrs. Wang got up at the same time and said, "Wait a moment. Let me pay you."

"Oh, please, Mrs. Wang. Don't pay me. You expelled the spirit," the shaman said sheepishly.

"I am going to pay you, so if the spirit comes back I can complain about my expense," Mrs. Wang chuckled.

"Ah, Mrs. Wang. You should," the shaman said.

Mrs. Wang entered her room to fetch the money. As soon as she was alone, her heart sank, picturing Min hanged in public. She went out and gave a generous amount to the shaman.

Her eyes bulging, the shaman hesitated to take the money, feeling awkwardly glad.

"Oh, take it. It was worth it," Mrs. Wang said.

"The spirit was stubborn, Mrs. Wang," the shaman said.

Mansong was putting her finger into the chicken cage. Mrs. Wang went over and told Mansong that the chickens would peck on her fingers. "No, no, no," Mrs. Wang emphasized.

"Well, then, Mrs. Wang, I will see you at the spring festival," the shaman said.

"Will there *be* a spring festival?" Mrs. Wang inquired doubtfully.

"Why not?" The shaman turned around.

"Who would fund the festival if Mr. O didn't? Surely he is not in the mood for a spring festival."

"Well, he is already recruiting builders and contractors," the shaman said. "In fact, today, the master of geomancy visited Mr. O's burned house and advised him to make a slight change to the new building. The earth breathes right onto the house, and its qi has been too strong, he said. Guess what, Mrs. Wang? He also predicted that Mr. O would have a blessing of a healthy son if he made that change," the shaman rattled on.

After the shaman had left, Mrs. Wang realized that she had always found the mountain behind Mr. O's house to be oppressively overwhelming. The house was situated at the mouth of the mountain, ready to be devoured.

AFTER DINNER, MANSONG FELL ASLEEP. IT WAS A MIR-
acle. Mrs. Wang placed a bowl of clear water on her altar, outside by the bamboo garden, and thanked all the gods of the
universe, known and unknown, for taking care of the matter.
She said, "I knew it would be fine, sooner or later. But I must
thank you for helping it happen so quickly."

The moon was waning, but it still brightened her yard
enough for her to sit out on the wooden bench and enjoy her
new life with a sleeping child.

At that moment, her dog, Tiger, barked, wagging his tail.
Instinctively, Mrs. Wang turned around toward her tired-
looking gate; it really was coming to the end of its life. She
silenced Tiger and listened.

"Mrs. Wang, it's me, Nani."

Mrs. Wang got up and went to unlatch the gate to let the
unexpected visitor in.

"What is it?" Mrs. Wang asked, turning around to go back
to her bench.

Nani bit her lip.

"Take a seat," Mrs. Wang said.

As she sat, she immediately burst out crying, her small
torso shaking.

"The crying demon must have entered you," Mrs. Wang
muttered. But Nani didn't hear, for she was crying too loudly.

Nani had begun to cry the moment she heard about Min's
arrest. Her eyes were puffy, her nose was red, and her head
was now splitting with the ache of too many thoughts and the
loss of too many tears.

"Life is never fair," Mrs. Wang said, grinning. She had just gotten rid of the crying spirit, but here came another one. Perhaps she shouldn't try to go against the flow, she thought. So she sat silently, enduring Nani's ceaseless crying. She looked up at the moon and then at Nani. Sometime later, she said, "When you are done crying, let me know. I've had a long day." Mrs. Wang got up and walked toward her room.

"Mrs. Wang, please don't leave me alone," Nani squalled.

Mrs. Wang stopped and said, "Well, then, I am going to get some water. Would you like something too?"

"Yes, well, may I have some rice wine?"

Surprised, Mrs. Wang raised her eyebrows. After a moment, she went to her kitchen and brought out a jug of rice wine with two bowls. Mrs. Wang set the bowls on the bench and poured a little into one bowl for Nani and filled the other one for herself.

"Drink it," Mrs. Wang said, and she drank hers in one gulp. "Ah, that cleanses my chest—my whole soul, actually."

Nani took a sip as if drinking hot tea.

"Mrs. Wang, I am the most unfortunate girl in the whole world," Nani said. She was no longer crying.

Girls normally felt like either the most fortunate or the most unfortunate. Nothing in between. Mrs. Wang found this bizarre.

"Min has been arrested, Mrs. Wang, for having set Mr. O's house on fire. He deserves to be hanged, but I must tell you what led him to do that." Nani told her how she had met him on the west coast, and in what condition she had found him there, and how he had wanted to marry her, and that she had rejected him. Her conclusion was that she was guilty, too. If only she had agreed to marry him, he wouldn't have gone out of his mind and acted so foolishly.

Mrs. Wang listened patiently.

"Mrs. Wang, he is going to be hanged tomorrow," Nani said, trembling. She no longer cried, only because there was no more crying left in her heart. She could only fear now.

"What is your crime?" Mrs. Wang asked quietly.

Nani thought for a moment. She sighed like an old mountain, completely resigned. There was nothing she could do now. "Heartlessness toward a desperate soul. Jealousy. Arrogance," Nani replied. She wanted to do something with her life. She wasn't willing to be Min's wife and live happily ever after now. Was it because he was dumb and deaf? No. That had never bothered her. There was nothing that she meant to say that he didn't understand; there was nothing that he wanted to say that she couldn't hear. Was it because of Mirae? No.

"Nothing wrong to reject a person you don't love. Love is not charity. Love and charity flow from two different spouts. One gushes out from your heart, the other comes from your head. And your head cannot stop what your heart is doing, if you know what I mean." Mrs. Wang paused. She realized that she had skipped her dinner. Unbelievable! How had this happened? She had been too preoccupied with the shaman and so stunned by the way Mansong had fallen asleep and was still sleeping. "If you would excuse me, I need to eat something. I am going to collapse if I don't." Mrs. Wang got up and went to the kitchen.

"Mrs. Wang, can I come with you?" Nani asked, getting up.

"What for? Are you hungry too?"

"Well, I am a little scared. Your house is not near anything. I mean, it's in the forest, and there are sounds," Nani said uncomfortably.

"See, you are not in love. If you were, you wouldn't be afraid of a twelve-headed demon. So wake up from your own misunderstanding. There is no need to feel it's all your fault that Min is in jail and will be hanged tomorrow," Mrs. Wang said.

The word "hanged" pierced Nani's heart, making it difficult for her to breathe. She sighed. Tears welled up again, but she swallowed them.

In the open stove, an amber fire was still going strong. Mrs. Wang put water on the stove and waited. They both sat on wooden stools and watched the fire. It was the only thing that was moving.

"When you rejected him at whatever beach you mentioned, it might very well have set his mind on fire and put him out of his mind. Nevertheless, he is the only one responsible for his action. The officers are not going to hear about what could have or would have happened had the circumstances been otherwise. So no need to go on improvising variations on the same theme. Now, are you hungry?" Mrs. Wang asked.

"Yes, Mrs. Wang. I have eaten nothing the whole day," Nani confessed.

Mrs. Wang poured boiling water into a large bowl with left-over rice. The water loosened and warmed up the petrified rice. She divided the rice between two bowls and gave one bowl to Nani. They ate the rice with kimchi. "Ah, hunger is the best meal! Even the emperor of China doesn't know the appetite hunger brings. How could he? He is never hungry," Mrs. Wang said, satisfied.

Nani ate little. Every grain of rice settled in her chest like a stone. The world was collapsing in front of her eyes, and there was nothing she could do.

"I love him!" Nani shouted abruptly and broke down with a pitiful cry. "I love him, Mrs. Wang. I can't bear knowing that he will die tomorrow. I can't live with him dead," Nani cried. "Oh, Mother, help me!" She clasped her hands.

Mrs. Wang kept eating, ignoring Nani. When she had finished her bowl of rice, she asked, "Aren't you going to finish yours?"

"Is this a dream? Are we in a dream? I think I am dreaming," Nani babbled.

Mrs. Wang clucked her tongue.

"Why don't you go to bed?" Mrs. Wang suggested. "Or do the dishes."

Nani took the dishes and went out to the water tub in the yard. Mrs. Wang followed. She sat on the bench and helped herself to some more rice wine. Mrs. Wang thought for a minute, looking up at the moon.

"Come and sit here," Mrs. Wang said gently. She poured a bowl of rice wine and gave it to Nani.

Nani was not able to thank Mrs. Wang: she had lost her voice.

"Drink it and go to bed. The room is warm. It will melt your bones. Sleeping is a short death," Mrs. Wang said, wondering what she was trying to say. "Min will be hanged tomorrow," she said, enunciating every syllable, as if to see how the idea sounded if she said it slowly.

Nani covered her ears and screwed up her face.

"He will be hanged ... unless," Mrs. Wang paused. "Unless," she said and stopped again. "Unless Mr. O says he doesn't mind that his servant burned his house and all his possessions. In other words, if Mr. O says he absolves his servant who meant to kill him and his family."

"He never meant to kill anyone. He wouldn't kill a fly, Mrs. Wang," Nani wheezed.

"Don't speak. Your voice is gone," Mrs. Wang advised her.

A little while later, Nani bowed to Mrs. Wang and tried to leave. Mrs. Wang said, "Stay in my house. It's too late to walk about. All the spirits who got lost on their way to the next life inhabit this mountain. You don't want to encounter them at this hour."

Nani went in reluctantly and fell asleep next to Mansong as soon as she laid her head down.

Mrs. Wang lit another candle and looked into her chest of drawers. She pulled out her journals and examined them. She picked one out, leafed through it, and put her finger on the page where a woman named Hong by the Snake River gave birth to a son. She loosened the binding of the book to remove the page. She read the page and sat there, thinking hard. She took her brush and began to compose a letter addressed to

Mr. O. It took a while to finish the letter. When she was done, she put the page from the journal and her letter in an envelope and sealed it. Then she slept next to Nani.

At daybreak, Mrs. Wang woke up and thundered to Nani, "Wake up, child! This is the day your boy will be hanged if you don't take this letter, as soon as your legs can carry you, to Mr. O."

Nani woke with a start. She looked awful, all puffed up and her hair flying in all directions. Nani took the letter from Mrs. Wang and stared at her blankly.

"I don't have time to say more. But if Mr. O reads that letter before he goes to the government office this morning, it might help. I hope it will," Mrs. Wang said, looking at Mansong in her deep slumber. "Go, now!" Mrs. Wang waved her hand, motioning Nani to hurry.

Nani ran down the mountain as fast as she could, constantly whispering, "Mother, Mother, don't let him be hanged!"

Automatically, her feet carried her to the old house. It was a horrid sight. The workers were piling up the debris in what had been Mr. O's courtyard. Just looking at the damage, she couldn't imagine how Min could ever be forgiven. Then she ran again to the guesthouse, crying because the sun was coming up. She didn't know whether Mr. O had already left for the government office.

When she arrived, she went directly to Mr. O's room. Standing outside, she caught her breath. She exhaled to steady herself.

"Big Sister, where have you been?" Soonyi asked. She was carrying a tray of food. "Quince burned the rice," she said, lowering her voice. "I had to put in some charcoal pieces to get the burned smell out of the rice."

"Why only one bowl of rice?" Nani questioned her.

"It's for the master. The mistress is not feeling well," Soonyi said.

"Give it to me," Nani said. "I will take it to him," she said as she snatched the tray.

"Look at you, Big Sister. Your hair is not tidy," Soonyi pointed out.

"Don't bring the other tray. I will come and fetch it," Nani instructed her.

Clearing her voice, Nani announced her arrival and opened the door impatiently. Mr. O was converting his land into currency at his study table. Nani bowed and transferred the dishes from the tray onto the low table. Her hands trembled. Clearing her throat once again, she said, "Master, here is a letter for you."

Concentrating on his addition, Mr. O didn't reply. When he was done, the muscle between his eyebrows relaxed, and he said, "Put it in the basket with the other letters."

Nani's heart sank. She knew nothing about the contents of the letter, but she trusted Mrs. Wang. Nani bowed and left the room to fetch the other tray with side dishes.

In the kitchen, Quince was helping herself freely to candied chestnuts. Nani couldn't speak. She picked up the tray and left the kitchen again.

"Poor thing," Quince said to Soonyi, taking another chestnut. "But the boy deserves the punishment. What an awful way of paying back his master who's been taking care of him practically since his birth."

Soonyi snatched the lacquer box with candied chestnuts and said, "You are eating all the chestnuts."

"Well, the mistress is not well, and she doesn't want to eat anything. So I offer my mouth to eat a little of what she would have eaten were she well," Quince grumbled with her mouth full.

Nani steadied herself again before she entered Mr. O's room with the tray. She bowed and glanced at the basket full of letters. She arranged the table for Mr. O and opened the lid of the rice and soup. Steam rose to her face.

"Master, there is an urgent letter Mrs. Wang sent. She says it has something to do with," she stopped. She didn't know what to say.

Mr. O raised his eyebrows, waiting for her to finish her sentence.

"Forgive me, Master. Mrs. Wang said it was urgent. That's all she said. Do you want me to bring it to you?"

Mr. O sat in front of his table and thought briefly before he picked up his spoon. "Bring it to me," he ordered her.

Nani picked out Mrs. Wang's letter from the basket and presented it to Mr. O. She lingered there, hoping Mr. O would open it. But he tasted his soup. He put his spoon down and said, "This is too salty."

"It might have been overboiled, Master. I will go and fix the problem." Nani got up and took the soup bowl.

"I don't feel like eating anything except some soup this morning. Bring it as soon as you can. I need to go out," Mr. O said. "In the meantime, I guess I will be reading this letter."

Nani ran out and went to the kitchen. She stood there, holding the soup bowl.

"What's gotten into you, Nani? Comb your hair. You look bizarre," Quince said, frowning.

"Big Sister, why did you bring the soup back?" Soonyi asked.

"Oh, shut up, Soonyi," Nani said, sitting down, still holding the soup bowl.

"Is there something wrong with the soup?" Soonyi asked.

Quince, chewing on something, protested, "What could be wrong with the soup? I made it."

Nani went out. She couldn't hear another word from the other maids. Her mind raced to Mr. O before her legs took her there. She didn't hesitate before she entered Mr. O's room again with the same soup bowl. Mr. O was no longer at the table; he was standing by the window, looking out, holding the letter in his hand. He didn't seem to notice Nani's presence. She bowed and placed the soup on the table and left the room. Again she whispered, "Mother, Mother, don't let him be hanged!"

As she stepped down into the yard, she heard the door behind her open. Mr. O was leaving. He passed her as if she were invisible.

She went back to his room in order to remove the food. She looked about, but the letter was nowhere to be found. Something about the way Mr. O had suddenly left told her that Min wouldn't be hanged. But she couldn't trust her intuition.

In the late afternoon, she heard that Min had been let out of jail because Mr. O had confessed to arson. This news traveled faster than the wind. By the end of the day, even the Chinese were laughing about the lunatic who set his own house on fire and lost everything.

FOR HALF A DAY MR. O WALKED ALONE LIKE A VAGA-
bond. He wasn't sure where he was going, but he could not
stop his legs from dragging him wherever they wanted. He
feared he would collapse and not be able to get up again if
he stopped. He ascended a mountain and descended to the
valley on the other side. He passed a lake with willow trees.
He crossed a creek full of trout. When the mountains swallowed the orange sun, he realized that he had walked all
day. But he was neither tired nor hungry. With the sun on its
nightly retreat, his shadow was no longer following him. So
he stopped, feeling strangely less shameful in the dark. He
heard himself breathe heavily and felt the weight of his life on
his chest. All day long, he had avoided thinking about himself,
but now he could no longer push his thoughts aside. The letter
that Mrs. Wang had written was like a death sentence whispered into his ear. He hated his own father for having treated
him like an inferior, but Min had been his servant for practically all of Min's short life. Did he know that he was the son of
the master he was serving? Judging from the way the dumb
servant had looked at him as he was discharged that morning
from the local jail, he did know the secret.

At the peak of his youth, when Mr. O had hated his father's
guts, he had partied hard and gotten into a lot of trouble.
Hong had been one of his many conquests. He hardly remembered her, actually, and he wouldn't have recalled her at all
had there been no mention of the Snake River in the page that
Mrs. Wang had attached to her letter. He hadn't known that
she'd had his baby. And he couldn't remember now exactly

how and when Min had come into his family. There had been
many babies in front of his gate. How many of them were *his*
babies? How was he supposed to have known that Min was his
son? No one had told him. A crime committed without evil
intentions isn't a crime.

He walked on for a while and heard music leaking out from
a large house. It was a pub. There were red lamps hanging outside to attract customers. He went inside. He was thirsty.

"Ah, Mr. O, what brings you here?" a woman greeted him
from behind.

Mr. O whirled around and recognized Dimple, standing at
the entrance with a group of women. Everyone had heard about
the fire at Mr. O's house. Seeing him, the women whispered
among themselves, estimating the value of his loss in currency.

"I happened to pass by. I am just thirsty," Mr. O, taken by
surprise, said uneasily.

"I brought my girls here tonight because today is the day
when my wretched mother gave me birth," Dimple said. "So,
Mr. O, will you buy me a drink?"

Mr. O said nothing. He was not in the mood for a conversation. He was tired now.

"I'm teasing, Mr. O," Dimple said. "I wish you a good evening," she said and bowed low.

Mr. O was guided by a maid through a maze of hallways to
a private room.

Dimple entered a room and six women followed her in.
Mirae was the last in line. Dimple stopped Mirae and smiled,
narrowing her eyes. And she motioned with her chin, telling
Mirae to go and see Mr. O. Mirae pouted at the suggestion,
theatrically, to express her regret that she couldn't then celebrate Dimple's birthday. Dimple pushed Mirae gently out of
the room.

Mr. O ordered a bottle of plum wine and told the maid not
to disturb him for the rest of the evening.

Mirae was looking for the maid in the hallway. Pressing her ear to each latticed door, she tried to eavesdrop. But she couldn't tell which was Mr. O's room.

Soon enough, the maid appeared with a tray of wine. Mirae inserted a silver coin in her sleeve and snatched the tray, saying, "Show me the room."

☽ ○ ☾

Mr. O took off his hat and set it on the low table. The small size of the room comforted him. There was a folding screen against one of the walls. He observed the embroidery. Two young women were on swings that were tied to the branches of a pine tree. One was high up in the air, the other close to the ground. Several young women were standing around the tree, chatting. A few men sat in a pavilion, looking out at the women.

Mr. O opened the closet door. Inside were several red silk cushions. He stared at them mindlessly. He sat by the low table and waited for the maid to bring in his wine. He tried very hard not to think about Mrs. Wang's letter, but it kept coming back to his mind. He frowned, feeling frustrated because he couldn't control his mind.

The door slid open quietly. Mr. O was really thirsty. He didn't look up, but sat up straight, readying himself to gulp down the wine.

A girl brought in a tray and poured the wine into a bowl.

"I'll do it myself," he said. He didn't want to be waited on. But he saw the ring on the finger of the hand that poured the wine; the piece of jewelry glittered under the candlelight.

"May I stay?" Mirae asked. Her voice sounded like an echo of a dream from the past.

Mr. O didn't reply; he was surprised to realize that he had forgotten all about Mirae.

For the first time, he saw himself in perspective. He lacked the willpower to say no to himself, he admitted reluctantly. He ate whatever looked good on his plate. He didn't even consider whether it might be poisoned or bad for him. He trusted the world and, until now, there had been no reason not to.

Here, another one of those attractions was being openly presented to him. To be fair, he didn't seek attractions out: they walked into his life.

Of course, he could tell Mirae to leave him alone. But why would he do that? She wanted to be seduced so badly. Who would say no to that? Maybe he could save himself some trouble later on. But what trouble could being with this pretty girl for an evening possibly bring to him? A baby at the gate. No, he was determined not to have that happen again. His new house was going to face west, which meant that his gate would be more exposed to the passers-by. Anyone trying to drop a baby and run would be noticed.

He was thirsty. He drank three bowls of wine without a break. And it felt good.

"Pour me another one," he said.

Mirae shot a glance at Mr. O as she poured the wine.

"How is your life?" Mr. O asked, looking at his ring on her finger.

"When I left Master's house, I thought becoming a kiseng would be the only way I could have a chance to see you again. So at the moment, I am ecstatic. But tomorrow, when you leave, I might feel differently," Mirae said.

He hadn't planned to stay overnight. Mr. O drank his wine and leaned against the side cushion. "Move the candle nearer to you."

Mirae moved the candle from his side to her side.

"You are exquisitely made."

Mirae closed her eyes briefly, her eyelashes fluttering, and then opened them to stare at Mr. O.

"What do you want from me?" he asked.

"I have it already," Mirae said boldly.

Mr. O laughed, pleased. "You are clever," he said. "Is it money you want?"

Smiling divinely, she said, "I would like a little wine."

Mr. O sat up and poured wine for her. Mirae drank it at once, like a thirsty man.

"Would you like another one?" he asked.

She stared at his lips intently. He poured another bowl of wine for her.

"I would like to taste it from your mouth," she said, looking directly into his eyes.

He didn't quite understand what she meant, but it sounded good. He smiled mischievously.

"Please, you drink it," Mirae suggested.

He drank the wine at once and crawled on his knees like a dog to Mirae. As soon as her lips met his, he forgot all about his burned house and Mrs. Wang's shocking letter. He forgot all about his wife, who might have a seizure if she found out about his clandestine meeting with her former maid. And he forgot all about his father's nasty, invisible eyes, which had seemed to watch him all day.

Life was sweet and short, after all. And it was a waste of time to worry about things that hadn't happened yet.

Life was fair. After the torture of the day, the most beautiful girl in the universe was rewarding him with the sweetest, bone-melting caresses. She was it: she personified happiness.

MISTRESS YEE'S JAW DROPPED. SHE COULDN'T SPEAK
anymore. She couldn't believe what she was hearing. Min
had been released. Her husband had confessed to burning the
house down. And now he was missing. The ground under her
feet was crumbling, but there was no one around to blame or
to abuse.

Mistress Yee was now lying on her silk mat with a bandanna
around her head to prevent it from exploding. Nani brought
in an herb drink that Dr. Choi had recommended for calming
Mistress Yee's nerves, but Mistress Yee waved it away.

Knowing that at that moment nothing would help, Nani
closed the door and left her mistress alone. Walking back to
the kitchen, she felt strange. What had Mrs. Wang said in the
letter that made Mr. O lie about the fire?

Nani sat in the kitchen and sipped the drink meant for Mistress Yee. Her own nerves definitely needed calming.

"Big Sister, what are you drinking?" Soonyi asked, panicked.

"You have some too," Nani suggested.

"That's for the mistress," Soonyi said in a hushed voice.

"She doesn't want any."

"Do I have something on my face?" Nani asked.

"No, but what's happened to you, Big Sister?"

Nani sighed. Only the night before, she had wailed about
Min. She had acted like a wild beast in front of Mrs. Wang.
Min survived, as Nani had hoped. But an innocent person, her
master, was now regarded as a lunatic. And her mistress was
unable to throw one of her infamous fits because the shock
was too great.

"I am hungry, Big Sister," Soonyi said.

"You eat with Chunshim. Take the porridge for Buwon. I need to go see Mrs. Wang. I will be back soon," Nani said, getting up.

"Big Sister, you disappeared last night too. It was real hard to fib about you being here when you weren't," Soonyi said.

"If anyone looks for me, tell the truth. I will be with Mrs. Wang. But it's not going to take long," Nani said.

"Do you think she knows where Mr. O is?" Soonyi asked. But Nani ran out of the kitchen without answering.

She ran up the hill and passed the old pine tree. By the time she reached Mrs. Wang's house, her throat was dry and she was coughing. Tiger barked from inside. Nani impatiently unlatched the door.

"Mrs. Wang, Nani is here. Mrs. Wang, are you here?"

The midwife came out of her room and said, "Is this your new job? Showing up here uninvited every night?"

"I am sorry. I came here because I didn't know where to go," Nani said.

"If you don't know where to go, don't come here. Stay where you belong until you know where you want to go," Mrs. Wang said, annoyed. She had just put Mansong to sleep. And she was ready to enjoy her time alone.

"Did you hear the news?" Nani asked.

"The birds chirped all day long," Mrs. Wang replied.

Nani knelt in front of Mrs. Wang. "Thank you, Mrs. Wang. Min has been released from jail."

"I live on the mountain because I don't want to hear every bit of news there is," Mrs. Wang said.

"But Mr. O is missing. And Mistress Yee has fallen ill." Nani said despondently.

"And you think it's all your fault, or is it mine this time?" Mrs. Wang said.

"I don't know. Min is responsible for the fire. But Mr. O is being punished now."

"Ah, you wish to go back to yesterday and do nothing about Min so that he would be hanged by now, and Mr. O would be at home, and Mistress Yee would be as healthy as a horse?" Mrs. Wang asked.

"No!" Nani shouted involuntarily. "I don't know," she whispered.

"Then let your tongue rest. Mr. O will be home soon. It would be unnatural if Mistress Yee didn't fall ill when her house had burned down and her husband was missing," Mrs. Wang said.

Nani was silent, wondering how Mrs. Wang knew all she knew.

"Mrs. Wang, I am starving," Nani said.

"Make yourself at home and eat whatever you find in my kitchen, child. I am tired," Mrs. Wang replied.

Nani bowed and went to the kitchen. Water was boiling on the stove. She took the water and poured it into the pot that held rice from breakfast.

Mrs. Wang came in and said, "There is cucumber kimchi Jaya brought today. You can have that, too, with your rice."

"Mrs. Wang, I have a wish," Nani said.

"Don't you like cucumber?"

"No. Yes, I do," Nani said. She got up and took Mrs. Wang's hand.

"What is it?" Mrs. Wang asked.

Nani knelt down, still holding Mrs. Wang's hand. "Mrs. Wang, I would like to be a midwife."

"When did this idea come to you?"

"I can't remember," Nani answered hesitantly.

"Why do you want to be a midwife?" Mrs. Wang asked.

Nani thought for a moment. She knew Mrs. Wang well. She didn't want to say anything unconvincing. Finally, she said,

"I don't want to waste my life being a maid. I want to do something more interesting."

Mrs. Wang weighed Nani's reply in her mind for a moment and asked, "Wasn't it yesterday that you professed your love for Min? Aren't you going to marry him, now that he is free?"

"No, Mrs. Wang. It turns out that I am more in love with my life than with him. I didn't want him to be hanged because he didn't deserve hanging. I cannot put the reason behind this into plain words, but if he set his master's house on fire there must be a reason for it that I don't know. And no life was harmed in the fire, so I thought he should live too. But to answer your question, I don't intend to marry him," Nani explained clearly.

"You can't have a family and have this profession too," Mrs. Wang said.

"I know, Mrs. Wang. You can't deliver your own baby," Nani said.

"That's not my point," Mrs. Wang said. "You can't have two lovers."

Nani blushed at the word.

"What I mean is that you have to choose only one. Or else you will fail in both jobs," Mrs. Wang said.

"I know," Nani said, vaguely understanding what Mrs. Wang was saying.

"You know how to read and write?" Mrs. Wang asked.

"Yes, I do. I read better than I write. But I will practice," Nani answered quickly.

"You really need to know how to write. You will be recording all you do every time you deliver a baby," Mrs. Wang said. "The first thing you do is get to know the women in the village. On a good day, I go around and visit with every pregnant woman to check the position of the fetus and the complexion of the expecting mother and so on. But all this you will learn in time. When you come next time, you will go with me to pick medicinal plants in the wild. I will teach you all I know. But again, you will have to write down the things I say."

"I will practice writing before I come," Nani said.

"Well, now, eat your dinner. And do the dishes before you go. I hate doing the dishes," Mrs. Wang said. And she went to her room to sleep.

Nani was feeling wonderful. She looked up at the velvety night sky and felt her mother was watching her. But she couldn't leave the house, for she feared the spirits in the mountain. She stealthily entered Mrs. Wang's room and lay down next to her. Mrs. Wang was snoring. Nani pulled the pillow away from Mrs. Wang, which made Mrs. Wang stop snoring immediately.

MIN WAITED OUTSIDE THE PUB THE WHOLE NIGHT. IT was getting chilly toward dawn, and he huddled under a tile awning and fell asleep briefly. He woke up worrying that Mr. O might have left the pub. He stood at the end of the alley and kept vigil.

When Mr. O finally came out, Min automatically hid himself. But when Mr. O came close, Min stepped into his path.

Surprised, Mr. O fell back onto the ground. Min groaned and helped him up.

"What brings you here?" Mr. O asked and craned his neck to see if anyone else was around. He actually felt repelled to be facing Min.

Min stood there, looking at his own feet, a servant's feet in a pair of straw shoes, and then he eyed Mr. O's cowhide shoes. Was this his father? He didn't know why he had waited all night long.

"I don't know what to say," Mr. O managed and tugged on his chin. He had no feelings toward the young man. The enormity of the newly discovered fact that his servant was his son hadn't congealed in his mind yet. Besides, his mind had traversed a different world for the night.

Mirae slipped out of the pub. She was dressed in white and iris purple. She wore a silver head covering. She spotted Mr. O next to a ragged young man in the alley. She stopped for a moment, and then she walked toward them confidently. There was nothing to be ashamed of. Mr. O was her husband. As she passed, she acknowledged Mr. O openly by bowing her head briefly. Then she noticed that the other person was Min.

Several paces away from the two men, she turned around slightly, but then changed her mind because she remembered something which made her laugh. She kept going. The only two men she had ever slept with were standing next to each other, one in rags and the other in silk. Mirae laughed aloud in the wide street, not minding the few other pedestrians.

Min didn't know what he should do. He had wanted to bow to thank Mr. O for having saved his life. But he could tell that his father was neither proud nor happy about what he had done to save him. Actually, he seemed a little uncomfortable to be standing there with him.

Min bowed quickly and then walked away.

"Come and see me another time," Mr. O said to his back. He had forgotten that Min was also deaf.

Min kept walking. From a distance he spotted a lake surrounded by tall grass. Now he moved faster with his legs stiff as if in need of emptying his bladder. He sighed in front of the lake. All of a sudden he undressed himself and plunged into the lake, shocking a duck that was sitting on the water. He swam, splashing wildly until he perspired. Then he waded the waist-deep water, crawled into the grassy area and lay on his back. His heart raced. His mind wandered off to the moment when Mr. O found him in front of the pub earlier that morning. Now it became clear that Mr. O felt nothing for him. Mr. O had not saved him out of love. Mrs. Wang had importuned Mr. O to spare his life.

But this was the way his master was. Mr. O did things on the spur of the moment, or because someone else urged him to. But Min knew that he himself was the villain of the story. He had burned down his father's house, jeopardizing many lives. He had gotten away unpunished because his father had taken the blame.

After seeing Nani on the west coast, he had followed Mistress Yee's carriage. He had wanted to talk to Nani once again, but there was no chance. He had lingered outside Mr. O's house all evening, hoping that Nani would come out and see him. As the night deepened, he was simply going mad with one idea: he wanted to set the house on fire and take Nani away. Only when the fire had become uncontrollable did he realize that he had done something very foolish.

He walked a while and arrived on top of the mountain. He would have liked to shout at the top of his lungs. But he only groaned pitifully. He looked down at Mr. O's house. From a distance, the house looked haunted, thanks to Min.

Smoke was coming out of the chimneys of the farmhouses in the valley. It was breakfast time. He descended to the valley. The gate of the burned house looked the same as before, but everything else on Mr. O's property was either burned down or blackened. When he stepped into the first courtyard, he heard something. He walked toward the noise. To his surprise, Nani was there, going through the debris. She was picking out objects and throwing them back on the pile of things, grumbling and sighing.

Nani shrieked when he came into view. She stood there on guard, ready to claw at him. She was boiling.

"Look at this! Is this how you repay your benefactor? Mr. O has fed you, clothed you, sheltered you ever since you were an infant?" Nani said, her spittle flying.

Min dropped his head, ashamed.

"You are an idiot!" she shrilled.

A little while later, Min and Nani sat on a rock behind the tool shed, where Min had once sat to sharpen the blades of sickles and mend other tools. He pulled his sleeve down to his palm and cleaned Nani's smudged face.

"You'd better disappear before the villagers stone you. No one believes Mr. O. Why on earth would he have burned down his own house? I know you did it. You should have been hanged," Nani said, tears trickling out of her eyes. She wiped her tears and her face was smudged black again.

"What are you going to do now?" Nani asked.

Min groaned and used his hands to tell Nani. She was the only one who understood his sign language.

"What are you going to do on the west coast? It's a rough place," Nani said.

Min groaned again, waving his hands in the air and jerking this way and that.

"On a ship? Where are you going to go?" Nani asked disapprovingly.

Min didn't know the name of the place where his friend Blane had gone. He pulled out the compass that Blane had given him before Blane had boarded the Chinese ship.

"What is it?" Nani asked, taking it in her hand. "It moves!" she exclaimed. She played with it for a while.

Min explained that a compass shows which way you should take.

"How does it know which way I should go?" Nani questioned. The small, round device seemed a little too superstitious. She handed it back to him. "I don't take random trips and go wherever something other than my mind tells me to go."

Min had felt exactly the same when Blane explained to him how to use it, but now he had become dependent on the little device. Even if he knew which way to go, he had to look at it to make sure he wasn't making a mistake.

"And then what?" Nani asked.

Min didn't know what he was going to do once he got where Blane lived, but he couldn't forget the tears of joy Blane had shed when he was about to board the ship. He had scribbled something on a piece of paper and given it to Min. If he ever wanted to go and visit, that was the paper he needed, perhaps. In any case, Min had carefully tucked it away in his sack. And just yesterday, he had wanted to get away from his country and go far away. He wanted to start his life all over again.

"Let me pack you some food before you go," Nani said. Soonyi and Quince would be cooking breakfast, but Mistress

Yee was always capable of mustering enormous energy, even when she was ill, to attack her maids with her sharp tongue.

"Stay here, will you? I will pack the food soon," Nani said, and ran off.

Min went over to the place where he had found Nani a little while earlier. What had she been trying to pick out? He stood there, inhaling the smell of destruction.

At the guesthouse, Quince was sitting in the kitchen, chewing on a large carrot. When she saw Nani, she got up and asked, "Where have you been?"

"Did you make breakfast for Mistress Yee?" Nani asked, panting.

"Dr. Choi is with her. Apparently her tongue isn't moving," Quince said, her cheek bulging with food.

"What do you mean?" Nani asked.

Soonyi popped in then and said, "Oh, Big Sister, something terrible has happened! Mistress Yee cannot speak! I just went and fetched Dr. Choi."

"Calm down. She is probably still overcome with shock from yesterday," Nani said.

Soonyi reported excitedly, "A little while ago, I took a breakfast tray to Mistress Yee. All I heard from inside was hissing. So I opened the door. Her room was a mess. Random articles were strewn all over the room. I asked Mistress Yee if she would like breakfast. She couldn't speak! She threw her fan at me. I was so frightened. I asked if she would like me to fetch a doctor. She threw her writing brush box at me. So I ran to fetch Dr. Choi."

Quince stopped chewing her carrot and cried theatrically, spitting bits of carrot, "Oh my gods!"

"She is probably still very angry with the master," Nani said dismissively.

"You heard what she just said. She must have had a stroke in the middle of the night, and her maid wasn't available for help," Quince said excitedly, showing the food in her mouth.

"Has Mr. O returned?" Nani asked Soonyi, ignoring Quince.

"No," Soonyi replied.

"The gods have set their minds against this household! Mr. O should have another Kut to really get rid of Mistress Kim's spirit," Quince said, clucking her tongue.

"Don't you breathe a word about this household to anyone outside! Now you can go, Quince," Nani said firmly.

"You can't 'go' and 'don't go' me as you please. I am an employee at this house," Quince said, looking sour. She got up and drank a large bowl of water, swishing it in her mouth to clean between her teeth.

"I said you go now or else you won't be coming back here after today," Nani said, clenching her teeth.

Quince looked at Soonyi, hoping for support, but she was looking at her feet. "Should I come back this afternoon, Missy?" Quince asked impertinently.

"I'll send Soonyi over to get you should the need arise," Nani said coldly.

"All right, then," Quince said and left.

Nani waited until Quince was gone. Then she said, "Let's go and clean up Mistress Yee's room and see what Dr. Choi might want us to do. I should have come back last night," Nani said, regretfully, leading the way to Mistress Yee's room.

Indeed, the room was in chaos. In the midst of all the articles that Mistress Yee had thrown, she was lying on her silk mat with her eyes closed, dozens of acupuncture needles stuck in her forehead.

"I put her out for a while so I could treat her," Dr. Choi said. "Where is Mr. O?"

"He is not home at the moment," Nani replied. "May we tidy up the room?"

Dr. Choi considered it for a moment and said, "I guess that would be all right. But when your mistress wakes up, it is absolutely crucial that she stay calm." He took Mistress Yee's wrist and felt her pulse with his eyes closed. He sighed when he put her hand back on her silk mat.

Nani and Soonyi were on their tiptoes, picking up and putting things away. When they were about to leave, Mr. O appeared in the yard, looking tired.

"Master, Dr. Choi is in Mistress Yee's room," Nani informed him.

"Bring me something to drink," he said as he took off his shoes and ascended to the anteroom.

In the kitchen, Nani prepared a tray of ginseng tea for three. And then she took away one cup, thinking that Mistress Yee wouldn't be drinking any. Suddenly, she realized that she had forgotten all about Min at the old house.

"Soonyi, I need to slip out for a few moments," she said desperately.

"No, Big Sister. You can't leave me alone here," Soonyi said, furrowing her forehead.

"All right. I guess I need to prepare lunch. You take the tea to Mr. O and then stay in the hallway to see if Dr. Choi wants anything more," Nani said.

After Soonyi had left, Nani began to grind the soaked soybeans in the millstone, adding a spoonful of water every now and then. The coarse yellow meal oozed out between the two stone plates. Nani was hoping that Min was long gone. Someday, maybe, she would see him again. She was not worried.

She put the ground soybeans in a linen pouch and squeezed the juice out. It would be the base of a noodle soup for lunch. She poured the juice into a pot and set it on the stove. While the soybean juice simmered, Nani began to practice writing, tracing characters with her wet finger on the side of the millstone.

IT TOOK MUCH LONGER TO BUILD MR. O'S HOUSE THAN he had anticipated. Twenty-five men worked on the site, even on rainy days, and five women cooked, cleaned, and finally pasted wallpaper.

On the final day when the women workers were sweeping the courtyards, Mr. O came and wept in his new quarters. He had done nothing quite so stressful in his whole life. "Well, I did it," he said out loud. He felt that his deceased father had not thought him capable of the task. But now he had proved him wrong.

He came out and looked about the place once again. Dubak appeared and congratulated him. Then Dubak accompanied Mr. O everywhere, telling him how everything was looking grand. Gradually, the villagers gathered and then the shamans arrived to perform a housewarming Kut. White rice cakes were served for good luck.

Nani, Soonyi, and Quince arranged the offering table in front of the main gate. The shamans put on their colorful robes and began slowly dancing. Some of the villagers were dancing too. All the spirits from the mountain behind them rushed down to find out what the brouhaha was about. Mrs. Wang was also coming down the mountain with Mansong. "Mansong, wait for me!" Mrs. Wang cried as she followed the little girl.

Turning around covering her ears, Mansong mumbled, "Loud."

"Listen carefully," Mrs. Wang said.

"Gongs and drums." Mansong frowned

"Listen to the voice."

Mansong stopped and listened. "Someone's shouting," she said.

"Yes, that too," Mrs. Wang said. "She is calling the spirits to come forth to hear what the people have to say."

"What do they say?"

"Who knows? People always have so much to say. Your father wants blessings on his new house," Mrs. Wang explained.

A crowd stood in front of the gate of Mr. O's magnificent new house. Mrs. Wang looked about. Mansong wanted to be lifted up over the crowd to have a look at the shamans.

Nani spotted Mrs. Wang and rushed to her.

"Ah, Nani, can you lift her up? She wants to see all the fuss," Mrs. Wang said.

"Come, my little lady," Nani said, hoisting Mansong.

"Where is Mr. O?" Mrs. Wang asked.

"Inside the house."

"You stay here with Mansong. I need to go see him."

Away from the crowd, Mrs. Wang slipped into the house. A few male workers were cleaning the rooftop, and several others were pretending to be busy doing a last-minute check-up before the move-in the next day.

A man greeted Mrs. Wang from the rooftop. He had recently become a father.

"Where is the master of the house?" Mrs. Wang asked.

"At the well behind the kitchen," he shouted.

Mrs. Wang walked to the well where Mr. O was pouring in a bowl of clear rice liquor to wish for a ceaseless stream of water to the well from the mountain. When he saw Mrs. Wang, he poured a bowl of the same wine from a jug and encouraged her to drink.

Mrs. Wang could not say no. She drank it at once and said, "I was just thinking on the way down here, looking at your beautiful house, that we are the only creatures who need a roof."

Mr. O smiled and nodded.

"Mr. O, how is Mistress Yee?"

"Ah, she is about the same. She improves slowly. She is able to sit up now and eat on her own."

"That's better," Mrs. Wang said.

"Thank you for coming to our house. Please have some food," Mr. O encouraged her. He was ready to leave the well. He was remembering the tone of the letter she had written to him about Min. It was the voice of a stern mother.

"I need to have a talk with you, Mr. O. It won't take long," Mrs. Wang said.

"Sure," he said, looking about. He led Mrs. Wang to the garden.

"Yes, Mrs. Wang," he said, politely offering her his attention.

"I brought your daughter today. I am so attached to her, and I would really like to keep her with me longer, but Mistress Kim, your deceased wife, would disagree with me. Mansong belongs here after all," Mrs. Wang said.

Mr. O thought for a moment. He was surprised. Of course, he knew that he had a daughter. But he had thought she was with another caregiver, Dubak's wife or sister, whatever her name was. His wife had said that she was in good care.

"I don't believe that is her name?" Mr. O suddenly pointed out.

"Ach, Mr. O, that is the nickname I gave her myself instead of Beautiful Flower. I hope you forgive me. I just thought she needed a name that's less susceptible to the elements, if you understand what I mean. Again, my apologies for having taken the liberty to name your daughter Ten Thousand Pine Trees. But so poetic is Beautiful Flower."

"Mrs. Wang, I thank you for all your efforts. I have been so preoccupied with building the house and with Mistress Yee that I have neglected my duty as a father," he apologized. "I should have had Mistress Yee take care of the matter," he said, and then he realized that she was in no condition to take care of any matter. So he blushed.

"There is nothing to worry about. I am here to ask you for a big favor, seeing as I have done you a favor by taking care of Mansong."

That simplified everything for Mr. O. He liked it when people expressed what they wanted because often he didn't even know what he wanted.

"Yes?" he said, eyeing Mrs. Wang blankly.

"I am getting old. I would like to have a maid, but I cannot afford one. But if I could borrow one of your maids once in a while to take care of some things at my house, I would be most grateful," Mrs. Wang said.

"Ah, Mrs. Wang," he said, relieved to hear her minor request, "let me arrange it for you. Let me go now and tell the first one I see to go with you. You may even keep one of my maids. Why borrow?" he said. "In fact, we are hiring more in a few days," he said, blushing again. Mrs. Wang made him nervous.

"No need for you to speak to anyone. I have picked one out already. Nani, she is called. I will ask her to come to my house after the move."

"Fine."

"But I would like you to come with me to welcome Mansong. She has been most eager to see you." Mrs. Wang walked out to the gate with Mr. O following her. The shamans were shouting shrilly to pacify the old spirits who had suffered in the fire. People were drinking and eating and gossiping about Mistress Yee's misfortune. And when they saw Mr. O, the crowd grew silent out of respect.

"Here she is," Mrs. Wang said. "My little Mansong, here is your father."

Mansong bowed deeply, and then said, "I have watched my house being built every day from the mountain. I am glad that it is finally finished. Please show me my room."

"Well, well. I am g-glad you are here," Mr. O stuttered. And he looked about. Everyone was staring at him and Mansong, even the shamans, stopping their routine temporarily. "Why don't you show Mansong her room?" he asked Nani. She hesitated because she didn't know which room was reserved for Mansong.

"No. I want you, Father," said Mansong.

The villagers clapped their hands and commented that she was the brightest girl in the whole village. One said that she was going to be the ruler of the province.

Mr. O disappeared into the house with Mansong. And the shamans resumed their dance. Mrs. Wang took Nani aside and said, "After the move, when things settle down, pack your things and come to me. Your master gave me permission to take you as my maid."

"Oh, thank you. Thank you. I have practiced writing every day, Mrs. Wang," said Nani, trying to hold her flooding emotion inside.

Mrs. Wang left the crowd to go and see a woman who was due to have a baby soon. In spite of her aching legs, Mrs. Wang felt good that she had fulfilled Mistress Kim's wish.

"When I become old and frail, remember me," Mrs. Wang said, looking back at the mountain, which loomed up beyond the crowd in front of Mr. O's gate. The mountain was beautifully dressed in its gorgeous fall colors once again.

Nani stood by the gate and watched Mrs. Wang walk away. Soon—very soon—she would go around with Mrs. Wang and learn everything there was to learn to be a midwife. She picked up a stone and wrote on the ground, "I will be a midwife." She got up and felt as though she would fly if she didn't make sure that her feet were planted firmly on the ground.

THE MOVE TOOK A WHOLE MONTH. WHENEVER THERE
was a new delivery, the villagers gathered near Mr. O's gate to
have a look at the impressive pieces of furniture. They were
built by a famous carpenter named Gong by the Snake River.
Gong would let his logs float in the river for three months and
then let them dry for another three months so that they were
seasoned before they were cut.

The first night, Mr. O slept in his quarters to let his ancestors know that he owned it so that they could feel free to come
and go. The maids and servants were in and out to clean and
to plant trees.

Some days later, Mistress Yee was carried to the new house in
a closed carriage so that no one would see her. Nani followed the
carriage with the servants. When the carriage arrived at the new
house, the servants carried Mistress Yee in on a Chinese chair.
Mistress Yee looked about and realized that the new house was
not exactly the same as the previous one. She shrieked, dissatisfied. The chair was carried to the rear of the house. Mistress Yee
trembled and turned purple when she saw where she was going
to reside. The servants carried her to her room. Nani and Soonyi
helped her sit on the mat in the room. Mistress Yee howled and
hissed.

"Big Sister, Mistress Yee is thirsty," Soonyi pointed out to
Nani. Soonyi turned to Mistress Yee to confirm this. "Am I
right, Mistress Yee? You made the same sound yesterday when
you wanted tea."

Mistress Yee raised her left hand to strike Soonyi. But Nani
pulled Soonyi away in time. Mr. O had warned the maids to
remove themselves when Mistress Yee got into one of her foul

moods and became violent. According to Dr. Choi, it was advisable not to speak to Mistress Yee at such a time.

Nani pulled Soonyi out the door.

"Don't make comments about Mistress Yee in front of her. There is nothing wrong with her hearing. She just can't say things properly right now. Dr. Choi says she will be able to speak again sometime soon, but it will take time," Nani said as she led the way to the new kitchen.

The kitchen was much more spacious, due to the high ceiling. The light came in directly through openings designed for ventilation.

"Look, Soonyi, up there!" Nani pointed her finger to one of the openings. Remarkably, there was a bird nest with baby birds.

"Oh, Big Sister, look at them!" Soonyi cooed.

"Ah, sweet!" Nani exclaimed, looking up. "Birds are a good sign," she said. Nani had broken the news the night before that she would move to Mrs. Wang's sometime soon. Soonyi had bawled like a cranky toddler. And she had said that she was going to go with Nani.

"Birds are a good sign?" Soonyi asked, looking up.

"My mother said so," Nani said.

"Maybe you will stay," Soonyi said.

There was a silence, and then Nani said, "Soonyi, I am going to Mrs. Wang's. I have moved some of my things already. But you can always come and see me. And I am sure that you and I will run into each other often."

They organized the kitchen in silence, avoiding eye contact. Only when there was a ruckus outside did they look at each other. Then they ran outside together.

Bok ran to Nani and said, "Here comes the new mistress!"

Nani looked at Soonyi meaningfully and Soonyi grimaced. They had dreaded this moment.

Mirae was coming in her carriage. She was six months pregnant and dressed exquisitely in yellow and light green. She smiled divinely, looking down at the villagers as if she were the queen of China. They had heard about Mirae's extreme good fortune, but seeing her arrive as the mistress of the house dumbfounded them. Everyone was waiting for the others to comment on the event.

"She sure is pretty," one voice finally said.

"Oh, she always has been," said another.

"As far as her beauty is concerned, the queen of China would envy her," a man said.

"Not just her beauty. Look at the life ahead of her!" his wife said and snorted.

"Great fortune has struck her," a voice said.

"'Struck' is not quite the word," a woman said. But she did not offer another word.

Mirae disappeared into the gate. She went to the mistress's quarters.

"How nice to see you again, Nani." Mirae smiled pleasantly. "Here is my maid, Kumi. I would like you to teach her. I've always thought that you were born an ideal maid."

Nani bowed slightly and found herself unable to answer. She swallowed her saliva and hoped to be dismissed.

"I have forgotten your voice. You need to speak so that I know you are the maid I remember," Mirae said sarcastically.

"Yes, Mistress," Nani said.

"There you go," Mirae said, composed like an arrogant peacock. "I would like some refreshments and tea. And then I would like you to take my maid on a tour of the house."

"Yes, Mistress." Nani led the way to the kitchen and showed the new maid how to make tea. She put the tea set on a tray and peeled a pear. Slicing it on a cutting board, Nani remembered how Mirae used to salivate over juicy winter pears. She had often picked out leftover winter pears, which bruised and browned so easily, from Mistress Yee's snack tray and devoured them in the corner of the old kitchen.

Nani asked Soonyi to take the tray to Mirae, and she took the new maid to show her around.

Mr. O was with Mirae when Soonyi brought in the tea tray with pear slices.

"Bring me another tea tray with refreshments," Mirae ordered her.

Soonyi's eyebrows shot up in surprise, but she said she would, immediately, and she left promptly.

"Why would you like another one?" Mr. O asked.

"I would like to take it to Mistress Yee," Mirae said. "She was my mistress. I am going to take care of her as long as I live."

Mr. O was moved. He took Mirae's hand and said, "You are pure gold."

"Oh, please," Mirae said, and she blushed becomingly. "I feel guilty absorbing your undivided attention," she confessed.

"Whom I give my attention to is my decision," Mr. O said, smiling.

"But would you hear my wish?" Mirae asked.

"Of course. Whatever you say."

"Will you spend time with Big Mistress?"

"I will if you wish. But she can't stand me," Mr. O grumbled.

Soonyi arrived with another tea tray.

"Shall we?" Mirae asked.

"All right. I guess I can't dissuade you from wanting to take care of her," Mr. O said, getting up. Mirae asked Soonyi to follow them with the tray. They walked by the recently planted persimmon trees.

"Ah, this is the perfect location for Big Mistress. Away from the noise of everyday life, and set back so that she is well protected and we can keep an eye on her health," Mirae said, standing in front of the small quarters behind the back corner of the house.

"Well, it was your wisdom that she is here," Mr. O said.

"Soonyi, announce Master's arrival and give me the tray. And then you may go," Mirae said.

"Master has arrived, Mistress," Soonyi announced. And she opened the door without hearing the answer from inside.

Soonyi withdrew, and Mr. O stepped in. Mirae followed him in with the tray.

Mistress Yee was drooling from the right side of her mouth. And when she saw Mirae, she groaned harshly. She waved her hand in the air to say something to Mr. O, stretching her left leg out tensely.

"Mistress Yee, calm down," Mr. O said, sitting down a few feet away from her.

Mirae kowtowed. "Mistress, your sister greets you," Mirae said as she lowered herself. She got up and sat down next to Mr. O and buried her face in his bosom. She sobbed and said, "Please tell me this is a dream. How can such misfortune have befallen my sister?"

Mistress Yee groaned wildly.

Mirae turned her face to Mistress Yee. "My sister, I am going to take good care of you. I am indebted to you deeply. I am going to pay you back for your many kindnesses. Oh, my heart breaks. Who would now know you were once the most beautiful bride in the whole province!" She turned back to Mr. O and said, "I must thank you, my husband, for bringing me here. Not only will I be serving you, but I will also be serving my sister. She used to say that I was her soul mate, because she and I think alike. She doesn't need to speak. I understand exactly what she thinks and wants."

"Thank you for your wisdom and grace. You are making everything so easy for me," Mr. O complimented her.

At that moment, from outside the door, Soonyi said, "Master, Soonyi is here. May I speak?"

"What is it?" Mr. O asked.

"I have a message from Lady Mansong. She would like the new mistress to come and introduce herself."

Mr. O guffawed, and Mirae turned pale.

"She is her mother's child," Mr. O commented, amused. "Tell her we will be there shortly."

Mirae sat there silently.

"Why don't we go and see the child?" Mr. O said, getting up. Mirae followed him out, calculating how to handle the situation.

In the courtyard, Mirae said feebly, "I am tired. I should lie down for a while. Not for me, but for your baby."

"Of course. You have had a long day," Mr. O said. He turned to Soonyi to tell her to escort Mirae to her quarters, but he hadn't thought about how Mirae should be addressed by everyone in the house.

"Take me, Soonyi," muttered Mirae, annoyed.

"Yes—" Soonyi said, breaking off her thought and silently wondering what to call Mirae.

Mirae walked slowly with Soonyi back to her new quarters. Mirae said to Soonyi, "Call me Mistress Mirae from now on because I am the mistress of this house. And do not walk next to me. Walk a few steps behind me at all times." Mirae's last name was Ma, one of the seven names that belonged to her class. She didn't want to use a working-class surname here in her new home.

"Yes, uh, Mistress Mirae."

On the other side of the house, Mr. O stood in front of Mansong's room and asked, "Who comes here?"

"The master of the house," she replied from inside.

"How did you know?" he said, opening the door and smiling.

"Because no one should come to me uninvited, unless it's my father," Mansong said.

Mr. O sat and took his daughter onto his lap. For some reason, he had fallen in love with this clever child.

"I was just with the new mistress, introducing her to Mistress Yee. You mustn't summon a grown up. That is not polite," Mr. O explained.

"But you told me to summon the maids as I pleased," Mansong said.

"Yes, you ought to, but not the mistress of the house," Mr. O said.

"But Quince told me that she had once been a maid at my house," Mansong said innocently.

Mr. O thought for a moment. He wasn't prepared to have this conversation with his daughter. "She is no longer a maid," Mr. O said.

"I see," Mansong said, confused.

"She is carrying your sibling," Mr. O said.

Mansong nodded.

"Will you give me a reading lesson today?" she asked. Her favorite pastime was studying with her father. And she had already advanced to the level he had attained at the age of ten.

"Ah, thank you for reminding me. Your father forgot because the new mistress arrived today, and he was busy with her," Mr. O said apologetically. Mansong took the book out from her drawer, opened it on the table, and they began their lesson.

Mirae sat in her room, breathing rapidly and shallowly. She was irritated because her husband hadn't returned yet. An hour later, her rage had turned to sorrow. She had been the center of attention and the envy of everyone when she became the third wife of Mr. O. But why had no one jumped to be her friend? Why didn't everyone love her when she was willing to give so much? All her relationships had resulted in betrayal.

Her baby kicked. This always scared her. She had never imagined life with a baby who resembled her. But now it was on its way. Sometimes she wanted to run back to the past, when she had been a little girl. She was pregnant by the richest man in the village, but she didn't feel happy.

At least she wasn't a maid anymore. She flashed on the worst night of her life, which she had spent in the storage room tied up, bruised, and with her mouth stuffed with a large pebble after eighty lashes of the whip. Recalling that scene always made boiling hot tears flow down her cheeks. She clenched her teeth hard and ground them in frustration.

When Soonyi announced that dinner was ready, Mirae realized that she had been sitting in the dark. She asked Soonyi to come in and light the candles.

"Where is the master?" Mirae asked.

"He will have dinner with Lady Mansong," Soonyi reported.

Mirae swallowed her saliva. Her baby kicked again. She realized that her baby must be born, whether she liked it or not. She told Soonyi to bring the dinner in. "I must eat," Mirae whispered between gritted teeth. She had to stay healthy and be strong to match up to the challenges of her life.

Soonyi came in with a large tray of food which she transferred to the low table.

"Where is my maid, Kumi?" Mirae asked.

"Oh, earlier she was helping Nani carry the dinner tray to Lady Mansong's quarters, and now I think she is feeding Mistress Yee."

"Listen carefully, Soonyi!" Mirae screeched. "From now on, serve my dinner first, before you serve the sick woman. And I want my dinner to be served by Nani. Do you understand?"

"Yes, Mistress," Soonyi said and left the room.

After Mr. O retired, Nani went into Mansong's room and asked, "Did my lady have a good day?"

"I did. I like this house. Are you ready to learn?" Mansong asked.

"Of course," Nani said, pulling out her book.

"Ah, I thought you might forget about the lesson because you were busy with the new mistress's arrival. But you are a good pupil," Mansong said and laughed pleasantly.

Nani recited a poem by Gosan that Mansong had taught her during the preceding lesson:

Mountains dressed in white
Chestnuts on amber
Summer days gone
Amber turns to ashes
Our hearts shiver in oblivion.

THE ROAD UP THE MOUNTAIN WAS FROSTY IN THE EARLY
morning. Spring was just around the corner—you could almost
smell it—but it was still chilly before the sun came out. Nani
climbed swiftly, carrying the sack of her things on her head.
She saw steam come out of her mouth and heard the swish
of her starched skirt as she moved. At the old pine tree, she
slowed down, as everyone else who climbed the mountain did.
Then she bowed to the tree, wishing for health and the wisdom
to be a good midwife like Mrs. Wang. She resumed her climb.
She looked down on the valley and began to sing feebly, but as
she climbed her voice got louder and louder. At the end of her
song, she was shouting at the top of her lungs. She ran the rest
of the way. At Mrs. Wang's gate, she was out of breath.

She stood there for a moment, expecting Mrs. Wang's dog,
Tiger, to bark, but he didn't. Through the crack in the old gate,
she saw Mrs. Wang sitting by the well, washing something in a
bowl. The dog was wagging his tail.

"Mrs. Wang, Nani is here!" she shouted. When she caught
her breath, she shouted again in her high-pitched voice, "Here
I come, Mrs. Wang!" and threw her arm over the gate to unlatch
it. She entered and dropped her sack on the wooden bench.

Mrs. Wang stopped cleaning the rice, turned around, and
said, "What an awful mistake I made to accept you as my
apprentice!"

Nani smiled, squatting next to Mrs. Wang.

"Mrs. Wang, I will try not to be so loud."

"That's the first thing you have to learn: to control what
you feel. When something goes wrong, stay calm. When

you deliver a deformed baby, don't gasp. When you deliver a healthy baby, don't compliment. Don't intrude on the emotional life of innocent and sometimes ignorant people," Mrs. Wang said.

"I understand, Mrs. Wang," Nani said humbly.

"It will take several seasons for you to understand that, but you are young and I am not dead yet," Mrs. Wang said, grinning. "Finish washing the rice. I am making red-bean rice and kelp soup to celebrate your commencement as my apprentice."

Nani's chest knotted. The tone of Mrs. Wang's voice reminded her of the voice of her late mother. On her birthdays, her mother had never failed to make red-bean rice and kelp soup, saying, "This is the day you came to this world to do something greater than your mother could ever do."

Nani swirled the rice in the water with her fingers and bit her lip, trying not to show her emotions. Suddenly, she got up and went to the bench. She pulled out a cloth from the sack. She ran to the kitchen and said excitedly, "Mrs. Wang, I have something for you."

"Speak in an even tone," Mrs. Wang said, and she frowned, not because of Nani, but because smoke had escaped from the stove and wafted toward her face.

"Mrs. Wang, let me handle that, please," Nani said confidently. She took the fan from Mrs. Wang's hand and skillfully tamed the fire. "I have done this most of my life, Mrs. Wang," she added proudly.

"I am glad you are good for something," Mrs. Wang said, getting up to go out to wash her hands.

After Nani fixed the fire, she went out and said, "Mrs. Wang, I have something for you."

Mrs. Wang was letting the chickens out of the cage. She turned around to see what Nani had brought. Nani unfolded a cloth she had embroidered for Mrs. Wang. It was a mountain in fall colors on a piece of coarse hemp cloth.

"I looked at the mountain this past fall, hoping I would come up here soon. And I began to embroider this, thinking that when I was done with this, I would come here to be with you," Nani said.

"Ah, Nani. Such a beautiful thing you've made!" Mrs. Wang said excitedly.

Nani was pleased to see how happy her teacher was.

"I will frame this on a wooden board and keep it on my wall as long as I live," Mrs. Wang declared.

They cooked together. The red beans bled and colored the rice purple. Kelp soup bubbled in the pot. Nani set the low table.

"How is my little Mansong?" Mrs. Wang asked.

"Ah, Mrs. Wang, she is the cleverest child I've ever seen. She amuses Mr. O so much that he says that he is getting younger every day."

"She belongs there after all," Mrs. Wang said.

After breakfast, Mrs. Wang pulled a book out of a drawer and showed it to Nani.

"What is this, Mrs. Wang?"

"It's my journal. I write in it every time I see a patient and every time I deliver a baby. It has taught me a lot. And I would like you to take over from now on. I want you to record all our visits with pregnant women."

Nani's confusion was written plainly all over her face.

Mrs. Wang explained, "First, you write the date, and then the name of the woman. Ah, never forget to record the name of the man who is involved. I mean, the father of the baby. And then you record what happens, what you see, and how you feel."

Nani was silent; she was still very confused. Mrs. Wang suggested, "Why don't you read one of my journal entries? In fact, you can read the one I wrote after Mansong was born."

"Oh yes," Nani said, still looking at the cover of the book.

"Let me find the page for you. Hand it to me," Mrs. Wang said. She took the book and flipped the pages. "I think it is in the previous book. Let me see." Mrs. Wang went to her drawer and pulled out another one.

"So many!" Nani exclaimed as she glimpsed the drawer full of journals.

"I started writing in my journals when I became a midwife. I was younger then than you are now. My grandmother told me to do so. And it is a very important part of the job. It sometimes saves lives," Mrs. Wang said, thinking of Min. But thinking of him, she remembered something. "By the way, Min stopped by some time ago. Now, where is that?" Mrs. Wang got up and opened the door to a small storage room, where she kept her money jar. She dipped her hand in and said, "Here it is!" She pulled out a knotted handkerchief.

Nani took it silently. Something was inside. She opened it and found the jade necklace she had lost in the fire. Min must have found it in the pile of debris while he waited for her to come and see him one last time. She remembered sitting in the kitchen, hoping he would leave and not wait. Before going to bed, she had gone back over to the house but had found him nowhere.

The handkerchief was smudged black from the charred necklace. She put it in her sleeve and thought of Min for a long moment. He might show up someday if she kept the necklace. Wherever he was now, she hoped that he would do something worthy with his life.

Mrs. Wang was still flipping through the pages, distracted by some of her own writings. She stopped and put her finger between two pages and handed the book to Nani.

"I believe Min was my son in a past life. He keeps returning to my mind," Mrs. Wang said.

Nani gasped. "Oh! What a coincidence! I feel exactly the same."

Mrs. Wang rolled her eyes comically and said, "You can read that page and see if it makes any sense." Then she lay down to take a nap.

Nani read what Mrs. Wang had to say about Mansong's birth:

Life is absurd. I can only sigh, feeling utterly ashamed of myself. Mistress Kim died. Even before I arrived! But she left a healthy baby girl behind. Somehow I feel responsible for this baby. I put her under the care of Jaya, who has just given birth to a boy. She has too much milk, she complains. The living have as many complaints as the dead.

Mistress Kim's house was ominously hushed. No one was present to receive the news of the death or the birth. Only two young maids, one of them practically a child herself. Earlier, a servant from that house had delivered a letter consisting of one sentence: "The mistress is in excruciating pain." I laughed. All the aristocrats are in "excruciating pain," and the peasants are about to die when the contractions begin. I told the mute servant I would come, by and by. He groaned and turned around to walk back down the mountain.

A little later, Dubak came up and said his wife would die if I didn't come immediately. I said I would come soon. He said he would carry me on his back. I snorted and scolded him, but he insisted that he wouldn't take one step from my house unless I came with him. So I walked down with him. His mother had prepared dinner for me. The newborn was enormous, so it took longer than anticipated. The happy grandmother so badly wanted me to stay to celebrate. So I had a few drinks.

Mistress Kim's house was in the dark; even the torch light at the entrance was out. As soon as I opened her door, I smelled death. I checked the woman's pulse. Too late. From now on, I shall spring up and go promptly when summoned, no matter who comes to fetch me, even if it means I will idle away half a day. Had I an assistant, it would be more efficient. Perhaps someday.

Tears welled up in Nani's eyes. She was feeling overwhelmed. She was entering a new world she knew nothing about. She was moved by what went on behind the scenes. Nani remembered very well how scared she had been when Mistress Kim had stuffed her own mouth with a cloth. Mistress Kim lay on her side and gripped whatever she could get hold of. She and Soonyi sat, feeling hopelessly worried, watching their mistress writhe in agony, groaning hideously. Mistress Kim grabbed her hand and Soonyi's in the end and wouldn't let go of them. When the baby came out with a great flop into a pool of blood on the mat, Soonyi and she looked at each other, but neither could go check to see what it was that had emerged into the world. Soonyi sobbed annoyingly. And then, Nani heard that Mrs. Wang had arrived. She went out with a lantern, trying to control her trembling hands. She wanted to say something to Mrs. Wang, but her tongue wouldn't move. She had been clenching her teeth so hard that her jaw ached. She couldn't even cry.

Mrs. Wang was sleeping. Nani decided to peruse some more of the journal. It was amazing reading. She pored over it until dusk. Mrs. Wang got up and said, "Light the candle. You are going to ruin your eyesight if you read in the dark."

"Should I start making dinner?" Nani asked. At Mr. O's house, she had to start thinking about dinner as soon as lunch was over.

"I always eat what's left from breakfast," Mrs. Wang said.

"Then I will warm up the kelp soup," Nani said, getting up. She went to the kitchen and took the jade necklace from her sleeve to wash it. It turned deep green in the water. She put it on and felt the coolness on her chest.

As she started a fire in the stove, there was a big thud from outside. Nani sprang up and went out of the kitchen. The old gate had finally given its last breath and lay collapsed on the ground.

"Big Sister!" Soonyi shouted. Bok picked up the gate and tried in vain to put it back.

"What brings you here?" Nani asked.

"Mirae—the little mistress—is in extreme pain. Her baby is on the way," Soonyi said with a broad smile, happy to see Nani.

Mrs. Wang came out to see what was going on. She thundered, "Who broke my gate?"

"It fell all by itself," Soonyi said. Bok was trying to fix it.

"There is a tool box behind the chicken cage. You can fix it. And I need to eat before I come," Mrs. Wang said. She went to the kitchen where leftover kelp soup was boiling on the stove.

Nani followed her in and said, "Mrs. Wang, I think we should go now."

"How am I going to walk all the way down to Mr. O's on an empty stomach?"

"But in your journal you regretted that you hadn't left promptly to see Mistress Kim," Nani reminded her cautiously.

Mrs. Wang clucked her tongue and said, "What an awful mistake I made to take you as my apprentice!"

Mrs. Wang went into her room and dressed herself warmly. She told Bok to finish fixing her gate, and she headed down to the valley with Nani. When they passed the old pine tree, Mrs. Wang said, "Bury me just beyond that tree when I am dead."

"Why there, Mrs. Wang?"

"So I can keep an eye on you. As you pass by, I will tell you if you are doing the right thing."

The moon rose. The two women walked by the barren rice field, talking about how the winter was almost over. Mrs. Wang said that she was going to plant cabbages and cucumbers in her backyard. Nani thought of reading all of Mrs. Wang's journals.

At the gate of Mr. O's house, Kumi came out with a lantern, looking like a frightened squirrel. Trembling, she guided the midwives to her mistress. Nani could already hear Mirae's shrieking voice. She noticed that Mrs. Wang kept a steady pace, even though Mirae's piercing cry was hard to ignore.

Mr. O was not available at the moment. He was reading a poem titled "Wheel of Fortune" with Mansong, which had been written by the country's only known female poet from the previous century. He was explaining the title to his daughter. He stopped abruptly. Life repeats itself.

"Father, what are you thinking about?" Mansong asked, looking up at him.

Mr. O came to his senses and asked, "What did you say?" His daughter's sparkling eyes stared at him intently, and he saw his reflection in her eyes. A long time before, when he was a little boy, he had stepped up to look inside a well. He saw a figure on the surface of the water. Behind it was a patch of cloud. The figure moved. He gasped, which immediately echoed in the well, sounding as if the well had gasped. A frantic maid pulled him back. He was dizzy. He told her that there was someone in the well. The maid looked in. She said, laughing, that it was his own reflection.

He had forgotten about this.

"My little one, I see myself in your eyes," Mr. O said to his daughter.

"I see myself in your eyes, too, Father."

He paused for a moment. Suddenly, the meaning of the conversation he had with the head monk some time before dawned on him. *He is you. He is I.* Mr. O pressed the middle of his eyebrows with his two fingers as if to expel a headache. But in truth he was trying to remember what else the head monk had tried to communicate with him.

Mansong yawned. She needed to be put to bed.

"Where is Soonyi?" Mr. O wondered.

"She went to fetch Mrs. Wang," she replied dreamily, leaning on his arm. She fell asleep within a moment. He put her down on the mat and covered her with a blanket. Observing her small, peaceful face, he lingered before he blew out the candle. She resembled her mother, definitely, but from a certain angle, she also looked a little like his father too.

Mr. O slipped out of his daughter's room. The moon filled the yard. Each time he walked about in his house, he was pleased that it was almost exactly the way the original was. In the dark, he knew it could fool even the spirit of his father.

A sharp cry issued from Mirae's quarters, tearing him out of his thoughts. He was about to enter the gate that led to his quarters. It took a moment for him to realize where the cry had come from. He stood in front of the stone step. Mirae must have given birth. He was going to sit in his room and wait for a maid to deliver the message.

He went in his room, lit candles, and sat in the middle of the room meditatively. He felt the weight of his life. He was an old man. And his wife, young and exceptionally beautiful, had just given birth to a baby. "Ah!" he exclaimed, remembering his haunting dream a few years before, in which he was an ancient man and his first wife was so young and beautiful. Now he knew that even dreams are made of life.

He heard footsteps rapidly approaching his quarters. It was not a maid, but a servant running fast to him, perhaps to tell him that the baby was born. Or that his wife had died while giving birth. Or that the baby was deformed. All was possible. Whatever it might be, the sun would rise again the next morning.

About the Author

AT THE AGE OF TWENTY, H. S. KIM MOVED TO THE U.S. After graduating from Teacher's College at Columbia University, she taught Creative Writing and English as a Second Language to a wide range of students, including teenagers in Harlem, prison inmates in upstate New York, businessmen in Austria, Laotian refugees in Oakland, and foreign scholars at various universities. A born storyteller, H. S. Kim began to write fiction after settling down in Berkeley, California with her husband and two children. *Waxing Moon* is her first novel. Her second novel, currently under construction, will be a depiction of the 1970s in a divided Korea through the eyes of a child.

Acknowledgements

I WOULD LIKE TO THANK THE FOLLOWING INDIVIDuals: Mary Bradford, Laura Gorjance, Cathy Hale, and Linda Wulf for proofreading and Amy McCracken, my editor at WiDō, for her excellent work and suggestions.